XIII

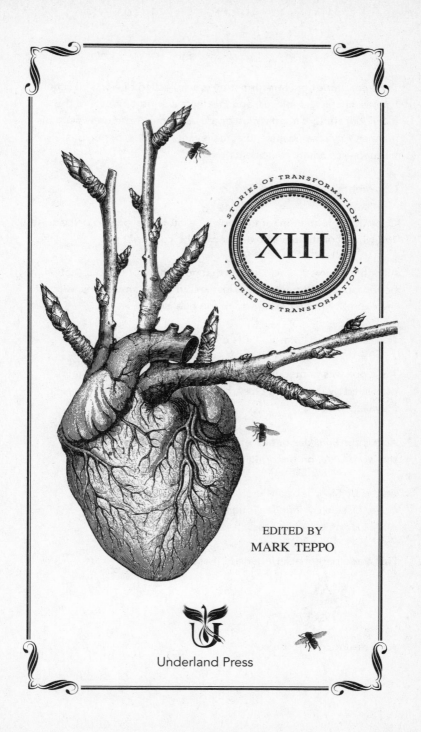

STORIES OF TRANSFORMATION

XIII

STORIES OF TRANSFORMATION

EDITED BY
MARK TEPPO

Underland Press

This is U013, and it has an ISBN of 978-1-63023-006-7.

This book was printed in the United States of America, and it is published by Underland Press, an imprint of Resurrection House (Puyallup, WA).

Across the knuckles of her left hand was tattooed the word LOVE; *on the right, the word* FEAR.

Edited by Mark Teppo
Cover Design by Jennifer Tough
Book Design by Aaron Leis

First trade paperback Underland Press edition: March 2015

www.resurrectionhouse.com

To E, who resides in the woods and in our hearts.

Contents

XIII

Skin and Paper

– Adrienne J. Odasso

In exchange for your marrow, I'll give you
a cloak and the name of this road. Don't expect
to take the right turning at first. There's sorrow
down every single one. Tell me, do you think
that I know not what I'm doing, that these bones
are any but my own? My hair is dyed red
to hide the blood my fingers trail through it.
I slit the ribbon at my throat and dropped the mask
long miles behind us. Are you running
to escape or catch me up? The ties that bind
hold only in slipping. What I love is always just
around the bend. And would you mind much
if I lost the trail on purpose, let the birds find
the bread, chucked the spool that holds the thread
into the river? It's only gold spinning, and starlight
is all we'll ever have. There's no such thing
as the sun, so mark me. Learn it. Cast the dice
as hard as you can at the mirror. Smash it.
Where you're going, you'll have no need
for the sight of who you are not.

With Musket and Ducat
The Dutch Trading Company in Nineteen
Sketches, Paintings, and Luminos

~ Tais Teng

I—EVERY NEWBORN IS PLEASING TO THE LORD GOD'S EYES
Sketch in sepia, 1893.

Description: A room in a humble working-class cabin, in the center a midwife holding a baby by the ankles, in the background the father of three daughters.

Shan-Pier, 0 years old:

It was Wiersma's day: the crying of the newborn baby was only just a little bit louder than the gun salute in the distance. According to tradition, the cannons of gunship Gijsbrecht van Amstel had been loaded with provender and party favors: on the roofs of Port Zuyderhoudt a rain of gingerbread clattered down, ships-biscuits in the shape of the prophet Wiersma, candied herrings. Roasted blackbirds followed, and finally a swarm of blood sausages no larger than a toddler's finger.

The midwife lifted the baby between two deafening gunshots and inspected the crotch. "God bless you, Mister Memling," she said, "you have a son."

"Another mouth to feed," Memling grumbled.

"Do you want me to write down the name of your son?" The midwife pulled a form from her blood-spattered apron. She shook her fountain pen to wake the mutated cuttlefish and get the ink flowing.

5

"Seems a bit premature. Well, call him Shan-Pier. I named my last two sons Shan-Pier as well."

"Is that not confusing for them, all having the same name?"

"The last two kids died within a month. No. Shan-Pier it is. That name has been in our family for centuries. Shame to waste a good name."

Nobody paid attention to the woman on the bed. Julia-Sabijntje had been Memling's fourth wife and was now as dead as her three predecessors.

2—LITTLE CHILDREN IN A WINTER LANDSCAPE
Tempera on varnished pine, 1899

Description: As in the title: four poor children in a winter landscape. Walking across the railroad these wretches are gathering the mangled beet chunks and battered corncobs which the living trains have spilled while chewing the crud.

Shan-Pier, 6 years old:

The express train bellowed. The warning cry filled the sky, made the frozen earth tremble. In Pier's ears even Gabriel's trumpet could barely have sounded louder.

"Away, away!" his older sister cried. "She is coming!" The children instantly stopped picking and stumbled from the rails. On the top of the verge they crouched in the snow and they squeezed their hands against their ears. A signal at full strength would burst your eardrums and make the blood run from your ears.

The train didn't bellow a second time now that she saw that the rails were free. She slipped past in an eerie silence, almost as if in a dream. Pier caught a glimpse of meters-wide horns, calm, amber eyes as big as goldfish bowls. Hundreds of hooves rose and fell in an endless stampede. Well-lubricated crankshafts drove the rubber and iron-wood wheels.

Pier watched the cabins until they merged with the swirling dots in his vision. The rails stretched all the way to Albion: two stripes in the endlessly flat, endlessly white polder.

He blew on his fingers. "The newest locomotive no longer eat beets. They drink blood."

"Don't natter. What does a brat like you know about trains?" His older sister pushed him roughly aside, reached between his feet. "There, a beautiful chunk of sugar beet! You almost trampled it with your clumsy clogs."

"Master Peter said it himself! Brunel has ordered to abolish the oxen. The new express trains are now cultured from vampire bats. On the benches grows the softest, warmest fur. Even in the Third Class."

Frieda righted her headscarf. "What does it matter? We are working class children, Shan-Pier, proles. We will never ride on a train."

3—THE HASTY OATH
Oil on canvas, with gold leaf in the emblem, 1906.

Description: A boy seen from the back. He lifts his right hand. An officer of the Dutch Trading Company is gazing straight at the viewer. On the wall hangs a tapestry with the emblem of the Trade Company: two lions, the first holding a ducat and the second lifting a musket. Above the famous motto: Met Musket ende Ducaat—with musket and ducat.

Pier, 13 years old:

"Young man," the recruiter said, "I don't believe for second that you are really eighteen. There isn't even fuzz on your cheeks."

Pier's fingertips touched his chin instinctively. "I, uh, I've just shaved, sir. Half an hour ago. In the, uh, inn."

The recruiter burst into laughter. "Do not bother. Uh, Pier is it? A man is as old as he feels. That is what the Trading Company earnestly believes." He raised an eyebrow, a trick that Pier would have loved to learn. Just like snapping your fingers. Master Peter did that so well.

"You are sure you want to sign on? Five years is a long time."

"I am sure, Mijnheer. And the longer the better."

Pier had pulled the bag with guilders for his father's coffin from behind the fireplace stone, emptied the wooden clog with kitchen money. Even combined it had just been enough for a third class ticket to Greater Amsterdam. There was no way back to Port Zuyderhoudt: they cut off the thumbs and index fingers of a thief.

"Fine. Say after me: In the name of all the gods, goddesses, totem animals, demons bright or dark, I promise to serve the Trading Company faithfully."

Pier repeated his words.

"And to obey my superiors unconditionally."

The ceremony took fifteen minutes.

"You're a sailor now in the eyes of God and the Trading Company," the recruiter said. "Here are the four ducats, which the Admiralty pays every new sailor when he signs on."

The coins rolled across the tabletop. They glistened in the slanting sunlight, a yellow as rich as clover honey. Pier hardly dared touch them.

The man waved to the window, to the Great Market, swarming and pulsing like an ant heap. Pier could just hear the cries of hawkers and dancing girls, thin as cricket-song behind the thick glass. "Go into the city, boy. Dance and kiss the maidens. Fill your mouth with succulent partridges. Yes, and munch on cinnamon sticks." He folded his arms, and his voice sounded suddenly a lot colder. "Tomorrow you are expected on our merchantman the *Velvet Fist*. At the first cock crow."

4—THE ATTACK OF THE SAVAGES!
*Dutch Trading Company poster,
colored ink on pressed seaweed, 1909.*

Description: A horde of bloodthirsty natives storms a ship. Along the railing stand a dozen sailors, seemingly unfazed by the overwhelming number of attackers, their old-fashioned crossbows held in readiness.

Pier, 16 years old:

"Moluccans," the sergeant said. "Brave men, that bestimmt, but unfortunately often too ambitious, just that little bit too bold."

"May I ask a question, Mijnheer?" Pier said, though he knew how stupid it was to draw attention to yourself. Before you knew it you found yourself a volunteer, scraping barnacles from the rump while the ship was still in the middle of the sea.

"Ask away. That is what an sergeant is for."

"What, uh, what exactly have these people done to us? That we must burn their villages and slaughter all their water-buffaloes?"

"They raised the price of nutmeg by nine stuyvers. Unilaterally."

Pier nodded. He was now a good and salty sea dog and knew what a truly unforgivable crime was in the eyes of the Trading Company. "I understand completely, Mijnheer."

The sergeant leaned over the railing. "You see them there waiting. Our Moluccans with Chinese cannons, Aztec fifty-shot-muskets." He grinned and raised his crossbow. "But we have these. They do not stand a chance." He licked his lips and fitted a paper cartridge in the groove. "I count to five. Then: Fire!"

One of the sailors was grazed, the sail showed a dozen bullet holes.

The cannoneers of the enemy didn't even get a chance to aim their weapons. Each of the sailors launched a paper nest with cobra wasps. Every nest contained some two hundred enraged insects and unlike inanimate bullets and arrows they sought their own targets and each sting meant almost instant death.

Pier lowered his crossbow. None of the enemies moved any longer. "And now?"

"We burn some villages. Chop off buffalo heads until their rice fields color red. Then we have a serious talk with their elders." He nodded. "We quite understand that they have to make a profit, too. But more than three stuyvers isn't in it for them."

5—THE RETURN OF THE PRODIGAL SON
  Lithograph on rag paper, 1914.

Description: A sailor with knapsack knocks on the sagging door of a workman's hovel. A young woman eyes him from the single, unglazed window.

Pier, 21 years old:

"Open up!" he cried. "Open the door, Verdemme, or I'll kick it in!"

"Why should I open the door? Who are you, you rascal?"

"Frieda?" She sounded so mature. Mature and dead tired.

"How do you know my name?"

"I am your brother—I'm your only brother! Pier!"

"Pier? Shan-Pier?" The door opened a crack, and their eyes met. Her eyes still a beautiful calm gray, and his own a rich hazel.

Pier felt a stab of pure joy, of intense relief. His sister had always been quite bossy: as her sea gray eyes looked at you, your bones changed into dough and the bottom fell out of your stomach. But Frieda had always some clever plan ready when you were sure that the sky was really falling down this time, could tell you exactly what you had to do to set things right.

"Come inside. But you're not my only brother anymore. You have two more." She shook her head. "Three in one throw. Two made it."

"Father remarried?"

I should have known. That lecherous goat never sleeps longer than six months in a cold bed.

"Esmée ran away after eighteen months. She left the children behind. Both very wise."

And now you're the mother again, Pier thought. He said it out loud.

"Why did you come back?" she asked. "If a gardist recognizes you, an hour later you are walking around without thumbs. Father trumpeted around that you are the worst kind of thief. taking his grave money, leaving your siblings to die of hunger."

"I, uh . . ."

She inspected him from crown to toe. "A knapsack," she said thoughtfully, "those Aztec rubber shoes. You're a sailor, were a sailor." She smiled radiantly, and he knew it had nothing to do with him, just pleasure at a successful deduction. "You deserted!"

"I couldn't stand it any longer. I am through with wormy hardtack and screeching seagulls. With stinking drink-water, with the hookworms wriggling around. But when I wanted to leave, the captain waved a thirty-year contract under my nose. It had my thumbprint, my blood code." Pier dropped with a sigh in the only chair. "Someone must have spiked my drink, mesmerized me."

"You bailed, left ship." She shook her head. "So if they catch you now, they chop off not only your thumbs, they also put a nice hempen noose around your neck."

"Can you help me?"

"Do you have any money? Without ducats we don't stand a chance."

"Enough. Five thousand ducats. I was promoted to steward. They gave me money to buy the provender and liquor for the next voyage."

"We leave with the next train," Frieda decided. "But first you have to get rid of your shoes, dump your knapsack."

"No, not the knapsack. I took some secret trade stuff. Sealed boxes from the armory. Weapons so new, so secret only our flagship had them."

"A cunning plan. So now I have two thieves in the family." The voice rattled and hissed and sounded barely human.

"Father, I thought you were unconscious! You were in a coma for the last three days."

The curtain of the bedstead was pushed aside, and a foetid wave rolled across the room.

"I may have cancer and rot in my whole body, but it didn't kill me yet." He lifted a leg over the edge of the bed and staggered into the room. "I'll walk straight to the sheriff." He grinned. "Do not worry, Frieda. I will not say a word about you."

"So you are not dead yet," Frieda said. "That can be remedied." She pushed him back into the bedstead. "Hand me the pillow, Pier."

6—A MAN OF THE WORLD
*Lumino, monochrome, with the stereo effect only
apparent at an angle of sixty degrees, 1916.*

Description: A room with French doors. Two men and a woman who clearly belong to the upper middle class, bending over a table on which a jam jar and an antique silver snuff box are displayed.

Jean-Pierre, 23 years old:

"My wife Frédérique."

The Parisian businessman bent over Frieda's hand and murmured: "Enchanted."

Frieda was right, Pier thought. No, it was Jean-Pierre and Frederique now. Learn a brand new language, preferably that of the largest competitor of the Trading Company. Speak then with an accent that oh so subtly betrays your rural background. Nouveau riche from the French provinces. There is no better disguise because people will nod at every hesitation, every mistake and hide their smiles and no one will ever suspect that your cradle didn't stand in Limes-sur-Saone, but in Port Zuyderhoudt.

"My sons, Emile and Pascal."

"Such delightful little guys!"

"The gentleman and us, we need to talk," Frederique told them. "You guys go play outside."

A maid brought three glasses, a rock crystal bottle with the stopper sealed with beeswax.

The Parisian leaned back in the python chair, which promptly began to massage him with languid undulations.

"Let us get down to business, as countrymen among ourselves. There are certain items, certain kinds of knowledge on which the Trading Company has placed an embargo."

"I know exactly what you mean." Jean-Pierre opened a wall safe and put a jam jar down. It was made of smoked glass, and from underneath the lid came an angry buzzing.

"A cobra wasp. The Virgin Queen, whose genetic code has not yet become unreadable." Next to the jam jar he placed a silver snuffbox adorned with trumpeting elephants. "The mutated seeds of an iron tree. Each leaf hardens into a knife or a spearhead of stainless steel. Ideal for supporting indigenous guerrilla forces in the colonies of your opponents."

"Yes, yes!" the man exclaimed, "this is exactly what I mean! Do you have any more of these?"

"We just might," Frederique said. "But first let us talk about the price of these two."

7—A TRULY DEVOUT MAN
Lumino, full color, stereo image at any angle, 1918.

Description: The window of an Aztec airship, overlooking the Alps. An Aztec priest in full regalia lowers a sacrificial knife. In his other hand he is clutching a decapitated rooster.

Jean-Pierre, 25 years old:

The Aztec spy wiped the obsidian blade on the hem of his feather cloak and held his hands in the cheerfully bubbling fountain to wash away the blood.

"As you can see I made a sacrifice for the satisfactory outcome of our negotiations. A black rooster, a gibbon, a white guinea pig without blemish. As their blood flows, so will our words flow. In complete harmony. Unfortunately, in the lands of your Trading Company newborn babies are rather difficult to purchase. "

"We appreciate your efforts," said Jean-Pierre. "I'm, uh, yes, delighted to see you took our offer seriously."

"No, no, it was you who made the effort, who agreed to meet me on my own ground, on an Aztec airship. All to keep my identity secret." He rubbed his chin. "Sages say that the enemies of my enemies are my friends. Now, when the French and the Nipponese became so so excited about your deliveries . . ."

"Well," said Jean-Pierre, "the knife tree, the wasps, the Mirror of Madness: such secrets can only be sold once. Then they are secrets no more."

"These things we have now, too. But your—lets call it your treasure room—they say it isn't quite empty yet."

"No, fortunately not. And I have made some new contacts. At the highest levels of the Company."

Not that these levels needed to be that exalted. Quartermaster or armorer, who wasn't strapped for cash or willing to go for the easy money? Thanks to his stint as a sailor Jean-Pierre spoke their language.

This is going wrong, Frederique saw. The spy was rubbing his chin, fingering his jade earrings. Unlike the French the Aztecs hated too subtle an approach, preferred plain talk to coy hints.

"What my husband means is that we still have quite a lot of those secret weapons left." It was a gamble: among the Aztecs women only rarely spoke up. Upon entering the spy's cabin, though, Frederique had noticed a statue of Coatlicue. It stood at the place of honor, at the foot of his bed. Coatlicue was a snake goddess who ate human hearts for breakfast and wore a skirt of baby skulls. Her followers certainly wouldn't see women as frail dolls?

"Ma'am," the man said, "I'm listening."

After that they quickly came to agreement.

8—THE KISS OF THE TEMPTRESS
Moving Lumino, duration: 51 seconds, 1920.

Description: A naked man and woman kissing each other passionately, then falling panting on the eiderdown mattress, whereupon the man blows out the light.

Jean-Pierre, 27 years old:

Jean-Pierre threw the lumino back on the table, and the fragile glass plate broke in two. Both halves were still showing him and the lovely Gala, kissing. "Did you hire a detective for that? To spy on my girlfriends? I'm not fucking married to you, Frédérique!"

Even in his rage he didn't forget to call me Frédérique, Frieda thought. Perhaps there is still hope for us.

"No, of course not. But it is of the utmost importance that the outside world believes in our marriage. Must I spell it out for you? I am your wife, and I bore you two boys. Thanks to our father, Pascal and Emile could very well be our kids. Lots of overlap in the genetics. Yeah? Are you following me so far?

"Now, Shan-Pier, who is still very much wanted for stealing trade secrets, well, there is no way he could have fathered those kids. At that time he was somewhere in the Far East, fondling quite other women." She clicked her tongue, and her voice became a little less shrill. "Also, Pascal and Emile believe we are their loving parents. Please let them keep that illusion for a little longer. After all, they are our brothers. Our own flesh and blood, even if they aren't our kids."

Jean-Pierre raised his hands. "Good, good. You're right. I will be more discreet the next time."

"It's a little too late for discretion. Your girlfriend Gala, my detective was shadowing her, not you. Gala Semmelweisss works as an informer for the Trading Company. Works: she would never bed a man just for fun. She is an invert, a lesbian."

"Wiersma's clogs! We are hip deep in pig shit."

"No more Jean-Pierre and Frédérique. Do you remember Chimu, our devout spy? He offered us political asylum." She glanced at the wall clock. "The next Aztec airship leaves in an hour. Plenty of time. I have already sent the children with our governess. Once we are in the air, no gardist can touch us. A flying airship has the same status as an embassy. Aztec ground. Inviolable."

"What about our money? Are we broke?"

"No, and we can also thank Chimu for that. He pointed out that the Transatlantic Nerve Cord came on-line last Friday. Capital can now cross the Atlantic as fast as a nerve impulse. For the last ten years money hasn't been gold, anyway, just account numbers, passwords. The moment we ascend, a friend of Chimu will send a coded tel-audio message to our bank. Moving three-quarters of our money to a secret account on the Aztec State Bank."

"Frederique, you're a genius!"

"That's why you need me. Now, the next time, think before you kiss, yes?"

10—50,000 DUCATS REWARD!
Glitter-scale pattern on the wing case of
a genetically engineered cockroach, #116
of a brood of 15,000, 1920.

Description: Portrait of a scowling man on the left wing case,
the text in capitals on the right.

Justin grabbed the struggling cockroach between its hind legs and looked at the portrait. It was no bigger than a postage stamp.

"Ugly mug that rascal got," Justin opined.

"That is logical," said his friend. "Otherwise he would never have stolen those secrets. If you are evil it shows on your face. Come on now, keep spreading those vermin. There are ten thousand cock-roaches more to go."

"Let me just read the message, Hank. We have been sowing for two hours, and we don't even know what is on our cockroaches." He peered at the wing case. "Fifty thousand ducats reward!

Wanted, dead or alive: Shan-Pier Memling, alias Jean-Pierre Marmolin. This mis . . . mis-cre-ant is urgently wanted for the theft and the sale of trade secrets. More information at your local sheriff. " He flipped the cockroach at a pile of rice bags, and the insect promptly disappeared into a dark gap. "Why are we spreading those critters anyway? Other times they want us to use poison-grain or spray the rice bags to get rid of them roaches."

"The foreman told us all that. Don't you ever listen? This here, it is the biggest harbor of all Greater Amsterdam. The ships, they sail all over the world. And because these roaches are all pregnant females, brimful of eggs, you can soon read roaches all over the world. From Shanghai to Reykjavik." He shook his head. "That Shan-Pier doesn't stand a chance."

"Too bad. All those fat merchants are like ticks, sucking the blood of honest porters like us. It would be funny if they were bitten themselves, for once."

"Don't talk like a stupid Inca! You sure wouldn't want to live in Tuwantinsuya. Now take a handful of those wrigglers and spread the creepy-crawlers."

II—FURIOUS MAN, CURSING HIS SAD LOT
*Aztec cartoon, executed in red ocher, volcanic
ash and powdered serpentine, 1920.*

Description: With some effort one can recognize an European male with a raised fist and a grinning Aztec in this very amateurish executed sand painting.

Note: This kind of sand painting is usually made to thank the gods for the successful completion of an exceptionally good practical joke.

Shan-Pier, 27 years old:

Bio-Baroque had run riot in Tenochtitlan, Pier saw the moment they debarked. The Aztec capital had been transformed into a jungle full of the most garish colors. Shocking pink vines climbed the steps of the temples, waving their orchids from the top of the nightmare statues, shaking pollen on the heads of pedestrians. The road itself was alive: a pavement of sturdy crocodile scales on an inch-thick substrate of living flesh. Also, it was election time: at each street-corner toucans screeched propaganda songs, praising various warlords or high priests. Gibbons were strewing sugar hearts and chocolate skulls.

"By now the Company knows exactly where we are," said Frieda. "The emperor personally granted us asylum. We might as well call us again Pier and Frieda. "

"Especially now the French are less than popular," Pier nodded. "What was de Gaulle thinking of when ordered to board that freighter? Mayans may be entering Marseilles illegally, everyone knows they are good workers." He halted at the next intersection "There, those statues of ladies with a gaping hole in their ribcage, that must be the Avenue of the Heartless Maidens."

Frieda looked at her own map. "Yes, turn to the left, and then the third entrance should be the State Bank."

A marble plate supported on two living elephant legs formed the counter. The legs were not of the highest quality, Pier noticed: they trembled incessantly.

The clerk offered Pier the tentacle of a tel-audio connection. "Enter your secret code. As soon as I get confirmation, you can withdraw ducats to your heart's content."

Pier pressed the suction cups against his temples: nerve fibers rapidly grew through his skull bones, drilled into his frontal lobes.

"State Bank of the Aztec Federation," a flat voice said directly into Pier's head. "Your authentication code, please." No doubt they meant password.

"Nine gulls laughing: do I hear scorn in their voices?" The code specified by Chimu sounded like a mangled haiku, and probably it was. The Nipponese had all the best codes.

"Authentication code is incorrect."

Wiersma's clogs! Did I use the wrong number of gulls? "Eight gulls laughing?"

"The given code is incorrect. For your information, an authentication code consists of eight digits followed by the name of a recognized god or demon."

"That can't be! Chimu . . ." He pulled the suction cups loose, winced when the nerve fibers tore. "Chimu cheated us. The code he gave us is pure nonsense. Gobbledygook"

"Can I do something else for you?" the clerk asked.

12—REGISTRATION #475: HOME OF PUBLIC
ENEMY S. MEMLING IN TENOCHTITLAN
*Chromatophores on a living octopus skin. The
images are originally taken by a hidden
spy-eye, duration: 54 minutes, 1926.*

Description: A jerky series of pictures showing a boy leaving a painted adobe building, followed twenty minutes later by public enemy S. Memling. Public enemy S. Memling is wearing a chameleon cloak as a disguise. The spy-eye first moves in on his shadow and then switches to a different wavelength until public enemy S. Memling becomes visible again.

Shan-Pier, 33 years old:

"This is the purest llama dung!" Emile grumbled. "Back home in Amelisweerd we lived in a mansion with twenty rooms. Servants everywhere. Flamingos dancing all over the garden." He snorted. "This dump has only eight tiny rooms and then I am including the kitchen! Every time we move the house gets smaller!"

"Most Dutch children don't even have their own room," said Frieda. "When Pier and I—"

"Normal children do. All the children from my school."

"We were invited by the emperor. Refugees can't make demands. Frieda and I don't have a penny to our name. We sleep on borrowed mattresses, eat the bread of charity." Pier spread his hands, and suddenly he saw himself for the pathetic figure he had become. A once reckless and romantic rogue who now bleated about stuyvers and the price of rye bread.

"And the International School sucks!" Emile added. "They even accept Inuits." He turned and stomped out, even though that was very hard to do on felt slippers.

"It isn't exactly easy for the twins," Pier sighed. "All the other children, their parents are diplomats, wholesalers in guinea pigs, the incarnation of goddesses."

"And this is the moment you'll start whining about all that money we left behind." Frieda said. "It is still madness. Here at least we are free."

"A quarter of all our money," Pier muttered, and it was obvious that he was just talking to himself. "Half a million ducats. And it was in numbered accounts. No way the Company could know the passwords."

"Stop it. Just stop it!"

13—Judge vanderloo cuts the gordian knot of doubt!
*Sketch by a journalist, Chinese oil
chalk on gray cardboard, 1927.*

Description: Judge Vanderloo cuts the Knot of Doubt with
his Sword of Righteousness. In the background the accused is
depicted, wringing his hands in despair and remorse.

Shan-Pier, 34 years old:

"It is a great mystery to me why this investigation had to take thirteen months," judge Vanderloo said. "A leprous, one-legged camel trudges more quickly through quicksand." He drew his sword. "No, the guilt of this Memling, may he be called Pier or Pierre, to me it is as clear as daylight." He strode to the Knot of Doubt. It was a tangle as wide as a prize pumpkin, made from excuse cords with extenuating circumstances, humanitarian pamphlets, dried cockroaches with Pier's face and yellowed bank statements. "This is not the moment to hesitate!" Vanderloo roared. "Only the highest possible punishment will serve for this traitor!" His sword whistled down and cut the knot.

"Ninety years of hard labor," judge Vanderloo sentenced. "And may this serve as a warning to other rats still thinking of biting the hand that feeds them so generously. The Trading Company is not to be mocked."

14—THE WEDDING
Moving lumino, duration: 4 hours 23 minutes, a censorship stamp in upper left corner, 1932.

Description: A wedding ceremony in the traditional Inuit style. After the groom has wrestled with the polar bear and his bride has bound his wounds, the lovers retreat to a whale-hide tent. The guests sit outside, drumming on pots and rattling pans to encourage them.

Shan-Pier, 39 years old:

On the boulder the lumino kept repeating itself, a miniature theater whose players now looked to him as strange and mythological as elves. Pier had almost forgotten how to read, and he had to trace the lines of Frieda's letter with a black-mooned fingernail.

"Next month our Emile will depart to Greenland with his Ushi. These two have such big plans! Orca races are all the rage there, and trainers can just about write their own paychecks. I told you before how much fun Emile had, sporting with all those huge sea-mammals: no doubt the salty Dutch blood bubbling up!"

He shifted his gaze to the final paragraph. "When Umiak asked me to marry him, I immediately agreed. As an uncle of Utshi he had been around so often, helping us, a true friend of the family, and it seemed so natural, so logical a step to invite him into my bed."

Pier squeezed his eyes tightly, clenched his fists.

How ridiculous to feel jealous now! Frieda is my sister. She was never my wife. Our marriage was just a trick, a needful lie.

Often his former life seemed to him like a story: a sparkling Arabian Nights tale which he had never really lived.

The horn sounded, signaling the end of their pause, and Pier pulled himself to his feet, almost relieved. His arms were nut-brown, as muscular as a blacksmith's. He took up his pick, trudged down the road they were cutting in the living rock of the mountainside.

In any case, the sky of La Palma was always blue, he mused, and it grew never cold. It certainly beats picking turnips and munched carrots from a stretch of a frozen railroad.

After the first four strokes he forgot the whole letter and joined the other convicts in their song:

"We pulverize the stone,
breaking rock and mountain!
Remember, you good man
before you despise us,
without our labor
this wide avenue
would still be a goat's path!"

The pickax rose and fell almost on his own account, an inalienable part of Pier now. Like the rock, the smell of dust. As the poet P.L. Bounders declared:

Blessed is the workman,
doing his job,
with only the sea breeze
blowing through a perfectly empty head!

15—GREETINGS FROM SANTA CRUZ
Postcard, silk-screened on crushed bay leaf, 1938.

Description: A Dutch sailor who raises a tankard of black beer, surrounded by scantily clad guanchen girls.

Text on the back:

"Dear Marieta, the next Saturday you'll see me again.
As you can see, this is not some pleasure trip, but hard work.
I love you,
Joris Vanderloo."

Shan-Pier, 45 years old:

"I know who you are, judge Vanderloo," Pier said. "You look like you haven't aged a day since you sentenced me."

"You have Shan-Pier. You're forty-five, and one would take you for eighty-five. At best. You cough like you are spraying the lining of your lungs around. One foot in the grave, eh?"

"Well," Pier said, "this work is not exactly healthy. It is that grit, the dust. Lung rot and avalanches: it eats workers like me." He scratched at his beard. "What are you doing here, anyway? Came to gloat, eying the victims of your miscarriages of justice? "

"That is always amusing. No. I want to make you a proposal. I heal you, make you thirty years old again, or twenty if you insist."

"Cut the crap. I am worn out. Each and every bone is crumbling. You heard me coughing. My alveoli are just pockets stuffed with grit."

"Our healers have grown so much more clever in recent years. They can reset the clock in your cells. White hair grows gray, then black as pitch. Your bones re-knit themselves, wrinkles smooth out. If you pay them enough."

"What should I do? Blow up the High Lords Seventeen in their council chamber?"

"No, nothing treasonable this time. Just the opposite. You get the chance to set things right. Become a respectable citizen of our great community again."

"Tell me."

"It's about Spitsbergen. Svalbard as they call it themselves. The Inuit just ordered us to evacuate Smeerenburg, to stop whaling. They have some kind of secret army. Pax Viridi, the Green Peace."

"And?"

"The leader of those terrorists is a bloody foreigner, not even a real Inuit. Your very own son Emile. Join them. Spy on them. Ensure that they fail. That all their actions sputter out like wet fireworks. You're his father. No one knows him better."

"This morning I was pissing blood. I coughed and shook for fifteen minutes before I could roll from my pallet. I will do what you ask." Pier lifted a finger. "Hey, hey . . . I remember you. From long before my trial. You signed me on. You were the man who recruited a thirteen-year-old boy. One who could barely read so he didn't see the difference between a five and a thirty year contract."

Vanderloo shrugged. "You might be right. I don't remember every mud-lark and street-boy I gave a life."

16—WE ARE HAPPY TO WELCOME A NEW MEMBER OF THE FAMILY!
Lumino with a gold-leaf edge and trimmed with snow hare fur, 1939.

Description: A baby reaches for a mobile made of shark teeth. Top left the text: It is with great joy that we announce the birth of Usmuaq Emilesson, son of Emile Memling and Utshi Ersisdottir.

A red stamp across the address declares: UNDELIVERABLE. RECEIVER DECEASED.

17—SUBJECT 45-9876
Double lumino, view-protected: only shows text and images after the correct fingerprint, 1939.

Description: To the left the portrait of an elderly man. On the right a young man who, because of the similarity in facial features, must belong to the same family.

A note in the scratchy handwriting so characteristic of healers: Extension of telomeres, replacement of bone marrow, lung lavage, controlled oncogenesis.

Rejuvenation prospects: Successful but unstable: general collapse of immune system expected within eight months.

Dieter van Huskens, 46 years old:

The Russian icebreaker had steamed blithely past Smeerenburg and only moored at the Temple of Sedna. A gray dome of dingy gull feathers and walrus ribs rose at the edge of the shingle beach. The breeze from the direction of the land was freezing, Dieter noted with a certain pleasure, the breath of glaciers, full of dancing snowflakes.

"You're the only one who gets off here," said the mate. "Now, I hope you like freezing your butt."

"They are expecting me. No doubt they'll have a nice coal fire going."

"Dieter van Huskens." While Pier walked down the gangway, he kept repeating his new name. "Dieter van Huskens." He surreptitiously stroked the side of his shirt, rubbing the velvet of his pants between fingers suddenly without a trace of callus. So nice be decently clad for once, to no longer walk in rags.

A young man strode in his direction, every step rattling the pebble beach. Emile. My son. My little brother. No, it was clearly *son*, for such was the emotional logic of parenting. Even if it wasn't your son at first, but just a stranger, the years made him your son. Blood of your blood. More precious than your own limbs, than the light of your eyes.

"You must be Dieter. Dieter the Bold." Emile shook Pier's hand, and Pier almost froze, then returned the pressure. Emile's hand had become huge, a man's hand, hairy, crisscrossed with scars.

"That is right," said Pier, and he could barely swallow the lump in his throat. Such a strange blend of sadness and elation: as if your mouth was grinning while tears streamed down your cheeks.

"Our friends in Greater Amsterdam were full of praise."

That doesn't surprise me, Pier thought. Vanderloo's men had so thoroughly infiltrated the Amsterdam branch of Pax Viridi that every third member must have been in the pay of the Company.

"It is great to be here! So exciting. After all, this is the place where we really can get things done. Where we must tear the harpoon from the vile hand of the Company."

"True words! My wife is already heating a pot of mulled wine, my friend. Do you have children, Dieter?"

"Yes," he said, "actually I do."

Soon, he thought, *soon I will see my grandson*.

18—IN DEATH HE CARRIES HIS TRUE NAME
A Spitsberg tombstone of reddish granite, 1940.

Description: A Janus head that shows a young man on the left and a gray-beard on the right. The deeply incised text reads as follows:

1893–1940

SHAN-PIER MEMLING,

WHO CALLED HIMSELF JEAN-PIERE

AND DIETER VAN HUSKENS

IN DEATH HE CARRIES HIS TRUE NAME

Dieter van Huskens, 47 years old:

Pier met Vanderloo right on the edge of the ice. It was Arctic night with stars so bright than you could hear them tinkle. The judge wore a chameleon cloak and remained hidden if not exactly invisible. Only his voice was real—the body was no more than a flicker, a movement in the corner of Pier's eye even if he looked straight at the judge.

"Tonight they board the flagship of your whaling fleet," Pier said. "They got themselves a Nipponese submarine. Six o'clock precisely."

"Good. I will put the mines on the seaward side. Order all men from the ships." He chuckled, a sound that was somehow bone-dry, like Pier's heel crunching down on a heap of dry bay leaves. "When the survivors creep from the water they'll stumble right into our bullets."

"I am yours to command. But remember your promise: Emile and his family go free."

"On my word as a judge."

"I don't think Vanderloo feels even the slightest suspicion," Pier said. "It was a shame, you losing your supply ship but since then he really trusts me."

"Well," Emile said, "the Admiralty was finally forced to let our comrades go. It happened in Nipponese waters. Pure piracy the shogun called it en stopped the export of sake. Costs the Company millions."

Utshi pushed the curtain of the tent aside. "The albatross reports that the soldiers are dropping mines in the sea. Hundreds of them. Not even an anchovy could cross those waters without getting blown up."

Half past five. About fifty sailors slipped down from a hovering airship on cables of cobweb. The Aztec airship was sprayed with soot: Chimu had eagerly accepted Pier's proposal. He clearly still believed that enemies of his enemies were perhaps not exactly friends, but that it made sense to support them against a common enemy.

Always useful to have such acquaintances, Pier thought. Funny how everybody swapped roles if you waited long enough. Take Chimu now. From customer to noble rescuer, then a crook and now a kind of friend again.

The men of Pax Viridi were all trained sailors: the anchors of ship after ship were silently lifted, and then a dozen ships unfolded their sails like the wings of night moths.

A short command: the men touched their cables, shot up into the sky.

Barely a minute later a ship set off the first mine.

Pier pulled the cup of his night-eye from his eyeball, and it was night again.

"All sixteen ships went down, Emile. Their whole whaling fleet. I guess . . ." He started to cough, a barking cough that seemed to tear his lungs, hurt his ribs. "What, what . . ."

"Daddy!" Emile cried and turned his lamp on.

Pier pulled his hands away from his face. The palms were spattered with blood.

"They made me young," he whispered, "but apparently they weren't entirely successful."

The world contracted into a whirlpool of darkness, and then even the darkness was gone.

19—UNTITLED
Unexposed lumino, 2006.

"Pier? Can you hear me, Pier?"

He opened his eyes, and his gaze swept across the bright blue sky. There were puffy clouds in her depths, darting swallows.

"I . . . I know I can't have gone to heaven. My muscles just hurt too much. I can feel every bone."

A young woman bent over him, her smile a row of even white teeth. "Happy birthday! How does it feel to be one hundred and thirteen?"

"You must be a granddaughter. You are Frieda's spitting image."

"Spitting image? I should hope so! I am Frieda herself."

Emile and Pascal stood on her side: men still in the prime of their lives. Behind them their sons and daughters crowded: grandchildren with cardboard crowns or butterfly bows in their hair. This was a family event, Pier understood, a grand feast.

"We buried your corpse deep in the permafrost," Frieda said. "We waited until the healers were skilled enough to raise the dead."

"It took a little longer than we had hoped," Emile said. "More than half a century."

"So stupid!" Utshi cried as she waved her camera. "I should have taken a lumino when he opened his eyes. Now it's too late."

Selma Eats

~ Fiona Moore

Maria told me not to eat the books. Maria was the one who found me after I came out of the bowl of purple rocks, found me living behind the bookcase, making myself flat. She wouldn't believe I was eating the books until I showed her, and a couple of the seedees, and some folded-up papers about something called a women's crisis centre. "Why do you eat those, and not these?" Maria asked, showing me pieces of plastic, pieces of paper and metal with a picture of a lady in a spiky hat, but I couldn't explain, something to do with the ideas in them.

Maria lived in a room over the bookshop, and she took care of me. "Can't let you out on your own," she would say, which was okay, because I didn't want to go out on my own. The bookshop was warm; the walls were dark blue and high so the shop was narrow, and the people who came in were careful not to walk into the little tables between the shelves. There were bowls of pretty rocks, all one color in each bowl. At night I would sleep in one of the bowls of rocks, making myself dispersed; the pink ones were best, but I liked the turquoise ones too, and I tested all of them at least once. In the daytime there were people to listen to and things to eat, though I stopped eating the books on the shelves when Maria asked me to. The ones she brought me were better anyway; they were old, with numbers on them which meant they'd been sold more than once, and that made them taste better. She said it was nice to have someone to look after again. She would think of her little girl when she said that, but I never told her that I knew.

It was Maria who named me Selma. This was because I'd decided to look like the girl on the front of a seedee that I ate. Maria said it was called *Selmasongs*, and the girl was called Bjork. I wanted to be called Bjork too, I liked the sound of it, like a raindrop. But Maria said I couldn't be named Bjork and look like Bjork. If something looks like a rock, don't you call it a rock? I asked, but Maria said people weren't like rocks, though when I asked her how they were different she just said it was complicated. I asked Maria what I was, and she didn't know, so we decided I was just Selma and we'd have to figure out what I could and couldn't do as time went on.

Maria was almost always in the shop, or over the shop. But for different reasons, reasons which made a connection between the little girl and the pieces of paper with the lady in the spiky hat. Maria had a lot of those pieces of paper, but she said it wasn't enough for her little girl. I asked Maria what the connection was, and she told me not to mind and to go eat a newspaper. I told her I didn't like them, because the ideas weren't complicated enough. That made her laugh. She said she would get me some good Russian novels. She said that the people in them were like real ones. I asked if they tasted like real people, and she said she supposed they did. I asked why, if they tasted like real people, they weren't real people, and she said maybe she shouldn't let me eat Russian novels, since I seemed to have absorbed some ideas where were a little too complicated already.

After that I started paying attention to the people in the store. I would wonder what they would taste like. I thought the lady with the yellow hair, who owned the bookshop, might taste like Chinua Achebe, and the man who brought the packages might taste like Stieg Larsson or Joseph Conrad. But Maria said I mustn't; she said when I ate a book, there was no book left. I said I would never eat *her*, and she just shook her head and said it was no different to anyone else. But she couldn't explain how.

The man who came to the store made me think of one who had been on a deeveedee that I ate, called *The Lady Killers*, even though none of the killers were ladies (Maria said to stop asking questions). Not that he looked like that man, but something made me think he'd taste like that.

I was behind some of the books, making myself flat, the first time he came into the shop. Maria was alone, doing something with numbers in. He came in, and he spoke to her in the language she talked with me when there was no one else around. At first I thought that meant he was like me, but I didn't think he was. He didn't disperse or become flat. But there was something in his ideas, something that made her scared. Made her think of her little girl, in a dark red sort of way.

I don't want to talk about it, Maria said later. She was making herself a cup of hot water with leaves in it.

He made you scared, I said, and she put her arms around me, which she would sometimes do. I didn't like it, but I knew it made her happy, so I never said.

He's a bad man, she said. I'll protect you from him, she said, and that was a complicated idea, because she didn't mean that; she meant she wanted someone else to protect her from him.

He came back the next week, and the week after that. Maria got quieter and forgot to bring me some books, and then got upset when she found me eating *Our Bodies Our Selves*. She brought me a copy of a book called *Das Kapital*, which someone had written all over the margins of. After I ate it I realized the someone was her, and so eating them must be almost like what it would be like to eat Maria.

Next week, he said. That gave her the dark-red thoughts. She was going to have to leave the bookshop, which she didn't like and I didn't like. Afterwards Maria went to the back room and took deep breaths. She smelled dark red and spicy, which made me hungry.

He would come by in the evenings. Just walk past the bookstore. Like his being there was a magic spell that could do her harm. What could I do to stop him coming, I thought. I'd never left the bookshop. When I was corporate and visible I looked like a little woman with dark hair and big glasses. I didn't have magic powers. I didn't even have complicated, delicious ideas like the ones Maria had, in the margins of *Das Kapital*. I didn't want her to go.

And then, discorporating among the rocks, I had an idea. One of my own.

I waited until he was supposed to come, and that was when I ate all the pieces of paper advertising the Book Launch. Maria was angry and told me she'd have to go out and get some more. She was so distracted she thought it was earlier than it was, and even better, forgot to lock the door.

And then, when he came in through the door, I ate him.

He didn't know what I was doing at first, then he fought back. Books never fought back, so the eating was messier than it should have been. But the fighting made the ideas he had much spicier. And at the end of it, he wasn't there to bother Maria, all of his ideas were inside me instead, making me big and sparkling.

And things changed inside me.

I could leave the bookshop. That was a scary thought at first, but now I was big enough and sparkly enough, I didn't need to sleep dispersed in the rocks (I could just disperse through the minerals in the earth, why hadn't I seen that before), I didn't need to eat books. And I didn't need to look like Bjork, though I still might from time to time.

But then I realized other things had changed too.

Maria was right. Eating a person wasn't like eating a book. There's lots of books; if I eat *Das Kapital*, one copy is in me, but all the other kapitals, they're out there. Even if there's notes in, it makes the book spicier, but the ideas don't go away when I eat them. The ideas are a bit smaller, but they're still out in the world.

There was only one copy of the bad man.

Now his ideas were gone, pulled into me and out of the world. Out of the bookshop, out of places and things and people I had never seen. Out of Maria. There was a big, big gap in the world. One tiny person, who tasted like the man from *The Lady Killers*, and he'd left such a big gap.

Maria would still be frightened, and Maria's little girl would still be alone, and lots of other people would still be doing things, wrong things and scared things and nice things too, because of the man, but no one would know *why*, and that would make them frightened, and sad. Would make them do other things, maybe bad things. Maybe worse things than the man.

I didn't have a choice. I *had* to leave the bookshop.

I didn't understand why eating the one man had made the difference. And it was a good thing in some ways; it made me big and sparkly. It meant Maria was safe, even if she didn't know it. But Maria was right about eating people: it had been a wrong thing as well as a good one, and in a way I couldn't explain.

I needed to go away. I had to make up for doing wrong, but first I had to figure out how.

I thought about saying goodbye to Maria, but if I did, I would have to tell her what I had done, and I really didn't think she'd like it, even though it was for her.

But I'll come back someday and see her, when I'm bigger and sparklier. And, if I ever can, when I've found a way to fix what I did.

Oh, How the Ghost of You Clings

~ Richard Bowes

When my Shadow finds me I'm sitting on a bench in the university gym men's locker room. It's almost deserted in Winter Recess. I hear a single shower running, the slam of a locker door several aisles away. This building is due to be torn down and not replaced. Eight years back when I retired from a reference desk at the university library I wasn't replaced. People are a bit passé.

I've still got enough self-awareness to know it isn't the world that's falling apart. It's me, and I'm imposing that on the world.

"Identifying with a decrepit rec center! Truly old age is a sad place," says a voice I recognize. It's my own voice, and it echoes in my head as always when this happens.

I look up, and there's my doppelganger leaning against a pillar, a tanned, fit, and very amused seventy-year-old. When last we met, a couple of years ago, he was a mess of an old man, and I was in OK shape for my age. Things now are reversed. Aside from the tan and physique, of course, he looks just like me.

To my memory the times we've been together over the decades have been bad times.

"Get the fuck away from me," I whisper.

A young guy, nicely defined, with a towel riding low on his hips walks by, casts us barely a glance.

My Shadow's eyes follow him. "No need to mumble, boy," he tells me. "Nobody but him around, and he wouldn't think twice about a senile old gent talking to himself."

He gives me the once over and shakes his head. "Look at you now. I remember dark nights on the piers when you blazed like a burning house soaked in gasoline—a human Brooklyn closing!

"They thought they were cruising me," I tell him. "But really what they saw was you AND me. Alone I was just another guy.

"Oh, in your memory you were such a nice little boy," he says. It's that shit they taught you in recovery where you overcame this monster inside you, the one who led you into booze, drugs, and sexual degradation. It's when you put aside the idea we were a partnership."

I turn away, and his image fades, but the voice is still with me.

"I remember being a half-formed thing," he says, "sitting in darkness watching this kid who lived in the world of light. And every once in a while at age three or eight or eleven I dared to step in there and maybe stand near him for a few minutes, maybe attract a moment of your notice. You were my world."

This is part of the argument my doppelganger and I have each time we meet: which of us invented the other. I finish getting dressed while he talks, stand, sling my bag over my shoulder, and start to walk away. He's right beside me.

"The first time I ever came all the way into that world was one night when we were twelve, maybe thirteen. It was in Boston, and our grandaunt Margie was dying down the hall from you. Remember? It was the first time you really acknowledged me."

I suppress the instinct to tell him she was my grandaunt and not his. But I realize that what he says about a first-time encounter seems right. Before then I'd have what I considered nightmares. These would be tense but vague: something alien was trying to crawl into my dreams, and I'd wake up crying.

I haven't thought about that night in many years. Aunt Margie was crying out in pain, asking God to save her, calling out to my father, to her father and mother dead and buried in Fall River many decades before.

I turn to face my Shadow, and he says, "Yes, you remember. You'd been told to take care of your little brother and sisters, to keep them distracted and out of the way while adults went about their scary business. You had the kids watching TV. *The Adventures of Robin Hood* was on."

Suddenly I'm in that moment: still in my grey flannel school slacks, dress shirt, and tie. This meant I hadn't had a chance or hadn't been made to change when I got home and made me feel more adult. My siblings were all in their pajamas. It was already dark out. We must have eaten dinner, but what came before all of us were in the TV room I can't remember. As I recall it seemed like we'd been there for one of those eternities the Catholic catechism always talked about.

I sat on the couch, and my little sisters held onto my hands, my brother leaned against me. My siblings were four, five, seven years old and couldn't quite grab onto what was happening. On the TV Maid Marian was sending the Sheriff of Nottingham off on a wild goose chase.

I heard the front door open downstairs and adult voices murmuring. Getting up I opened the door a crack

The family doctor with his black horn rims, black mustache, and black bag was on an emergency house visit, following my father up the stairs and down the hall.

My grandaunt cried out when they went into her room. My mother was in there with her. The doctor said something. After a few minutes the crying stopped and there was silence. I wondered if she had died and wished someone would tell me what was happening. I thought of Aunt Margie, who could be nice and funny. I felt tears and fought them off.

A voice spoke, not in my ear so much as inside my head. "They gave her something to knock her out. Like when we broke our wrist." This was something I should have figured out by myself, but it felt like my brain was frozen. For a moment a boy's face flickered beside me. Sometimes you don't recognize your own features when you see them on another.

My siblings were amazed at being allowed to stay up watching TV. They were distracted by Robin Hood and the Sheriff of Nottingham's clashing swords. I wondered if that was why they didn't hear or see the one beside me.

The doctor and my father passed by again and the doctor said, "There's no sense in moving her. I'll be on call."

From down the hall there was a low moaning and my mother's whispers to Aunt Margie. Again I felt kind of alone, and I looked around, but it was just my sisters and brother and me in the room. The one who'd spoken to me was gone. A cowboy holding a rifle galloped across the screen. I sat down on the couch, and the kids clustered around

Again there was a knock downstairs. Again I opened the door a crack. One of the priests from the church we went to, Father O'Dwyer, old, fat, and pink hauled himself up the stairs. O'Dwyer, I'd been told, was a late vocation. He hadn't entered the priesthood until his mother died.

That other kid's face was next to mine. "Last rites," I heard in my head: communion for the dying.

It didn't take long. The priest on his way back, saw the door open a crack, came into the room, and blessed us all. I had always thought he was kind of ok, gave light penances when I made my confession. A few months before when I started confessing to, "Impure thoughts and deeds," he'd murmured, "Jerking off."

He looked my way, and the voice beside me said, "He goes for us." Thinking about it I kind of understood what he meant. As the priest on the stairs murmured solace to my parents. I heard my father say, "This is it," sounding kind of upset. Aunt Margie was quiet.

Then the doctor was back. And I didn't need the one beside me to say he was checking to see if she was dead.

A bit later we could both hear guys coming in the front door, talking almost in whispers on the stairs and rolling what I'd later know was a gurney by the door. A couple of minutes later they rolled it past with something wrapped up on top. I knew without being told what it was and made sure not to cry because then we'd all be crying except maybe the kid beside me.

My father when it was over said I'd done well, which was as much praise as he'd ever given. I was surprised he didn't see the kid beside me. Then I looked, and the kid wasn't there.

Remembering all this I walk upstairs and out of the gym. It's all low clouds and grey light, a sharp wind and a promise of snow. This is a tough winter, more like the New England of my childhood than

New York. "That was the first time we ever worked together," my Shadow says. "I felt honored, almost like Pinocchio getting to be a human boy, you know. Not like that stupid book you wrote about us where I was evil incarnate."

"Where do you stay?" I ask. This is more conversation than we've had in a while.

"Most of the time in a tropical place," he tells me, "But I can see you, like you could see me if you gave a shit about me. Seeing that you were falling apart. I worked out, treated myself right for a few weeks, hooked onto you and came back here to save your life."

"Because when I die, you die," I say aloud, and a couple of students walking with their heads down against a cold wind, look up at me. "We're like Siamese twins who don't like each other."

He shakes his head. "Trust me, I'd love you even if my life wasn't riding on you." I expect more, but when I turn he isn't there. I know he's playing with my head, but still I'm disappointed.

In these years of mad weather this is the Winter of Snow in Manhattan. There's always some in the air and/or on the ground. It's slippery and deceptive stuff. But for my health I'm supposed to walk a few miles every day. After the encounter with my Shadow I start doing that faithfully. I'm walking in the antique West Village. Ice is invisible on a shoveled sidewalk. Every corner is a minefield of slush.

The young jump over banks of snow. The elderly barely let their feet leave the ground. I grew up in a time and place where winters were bad by nature but where snow was a miraculous event that shut down the Boston school system for days and a few times for a whole week.

That magic began to ebb one grey, snowy morning. I was maybe fifteen and my father woke me up, handed me a shovel and told me to get busy clearing out the driveway. Snow went from being a miracle to being a hated-but-respected foe.

"Together we made one tough little sissy," says a voice in my ear, and my Shadow is back. I've reached the promenade along the Hudson. We walk uptown on the bike track near the river. The sun is an iron-grey light sliding down behind the skyscrapers on the Jersey Shore.

The ways that I was amazed and scared by him when we were young faded and changed. He's right. At first when I was trying to stay clean I blamed him for all the troubles—drug-, alcohol-, and sex-related—that I got into. With sobriety I came to accept the fact the blame was all mine.

And that's why, when he wants to remind me of our time on drugs and an awful afternoon on the junk run, I don't try to stop him.

"You'd copped what, fifteen bags over on Avenue C and Seventh Street? Enough to get everyone we knew off a couple of times. Also enough to send us to the deepest slam if we get busted. And we were walking back when this guy attached himself to us. He was in jeans and leather, but he was a cop. We both knew that. He didn't hide it, and there was no getting away from him. He was complaining that state troopers were being sent into the East Village to conduct drug sweeps. But they were lousy amateurs. Whereas the good old NYPD narcotics squad (of which we guessed he was a proud member) was highly professional and good at what they did.

"And you were shitting a brick, babbling to him about cops in the family back in Boston. I did my best to make sure he caught glimpses of me. I could tell he was bothered by it.

"When we reached First Avenue and St. Marks where we lived you kind of nodded and tried to step away from him. He grabbed your shirt and reached for the cuffs. I got in his face with my eyes all insane and wild. He saw me, no mistaking that, and let go of you. But he did slap you and say "I ever see you coping drugs over there again, you faggot, I'll break every bone in your face and book you."

"We went upstairs, got off, and put it behind us," my Shadow reminds me on that cold late afternoon near the Hudson. He doesn't need to say that without him I'd have been busted.

The sunlight's failing: my Shadow leads me across the West Side Highway before the short traffic lights change and we turn east on Bethune Street. There are police and a crowd of people up at the next corner. I remember news from earlier that day. The actor Phillip Seymour Hoffman had been found dead of an overdose.

A detective stands talking into his cell phone at the door of a building halfway up the block. People stare intently waiting for what?

Celebrities to show up? His wife and children to appear? Amazingly nice old cops quite politely tell people with flowers and candles that the street is closed and they can't get any nearer.

I wonder why we're here. We watch for a couple of minutes then go over to Twelfth Street and walk east. "Height of his career he starts doing junk again and goes dark for good," says my Shadow. "Remember that first time we did it? You said junk killed pain you didn't even know you had. And your pain was my pain."

The block is almost empty in the frigid night. But there's a cozy little bar right up ahead. "It always comes back to you wanting to control the action," I tell the doppelganger. "Maybe it's an automatic response, something you do without thinking. Like just now: first you remind me of how you saved my ass when we were doing junk, and then you show me the site of a famous drug OD. Now you're leading me to that bar knowing that if you can get me drunk or stoned you'll be in charge."

I say this out loud, but I keep my voice down. He gives me a pained expression, like it grieves him to see me go all crazy on him like this. But I say, "You want me to live so you can live? Then get the fuck away from me."

And he's gone. Walking home I wonder if the Shadow's actions really aren't just basic instinct and not his fault—like a cat killing birds.

Old age is an endless round of doctors' appointments. And since my double's visit I'm being very diligent about them. The first Friday in February is my annual eye exam. I squint through goggles at ever-diminishing rows of letters and numbers. With a pirate patch first on one eye then on the other, I try to spot little green dots on a dark surface.

Drops are dribbled onto my corneas. I follow lights to my right, then to my left. The little optometrist I see once a year nods and says my eyesight is perfect. If only anything else in my body or mind was.

I haven't seen my Shadow since that night on West Twelfth Street. My dilated pupils distort my vision. But I see him in the waiting room when I come out. He's real and solid enough to hold the door open for me. Nobody notices him do that. I'm actually not unhappy to see him.

On my walk home the eye drops make the sun glow off the snow. The light is alive. Washington Square Park looks like the world did when I was young and on acid. Except this time I don't have the paranoid fear, which often came with acid, that I'm a giant lizard.

My Shadow gets all this. I sense his amusement as he looks behind me and says, "That green tail must be six feet long."

I laugh and think of my favorite song, "These Foolish Things," and its lyric about how a ghost can cling.

A young couple stares at me. We walk past the fountain and out the other side of the park. The curb is a mixture of melted slush and ice. I look down at my feet as I negotiate this thinking that on balance my Shadow's been mostly good for me this time.

I won't say this little adventure has made me feel young again. But it makes me feel middle-aged, which at this point is as good as I can expect.

When I look up intending to admit to my Shadow that he's made me look after myself, I don't see him in the glare. I say, "Hello?" a couple of times. Nobody notices. But there's no response, and I know at least for now that my Shadow is gone.

You Can Go Anywhere

– Jennifer Geisbrecht

"You can go anywhere," her father told her. "Graduated with honors. You're young and healthy. I mean literally anywhere."

She goes to Earth. Wretched, ruined Earth with its deep, black oceans and electric yellow stripes of pollution guttered into the cold soil. It used to be blue and green, when it was loved. No one goes to Earth because they want to, or even because they need to. The other members of her detail are two interns, a man doing parole for vehicular manslaughter, and an environmental recovery specialist who expressed a particular preference for the ruins of Mars or Ganymede. When she tells them who she is and where she comes from, they say to her: "*You could have gone anywhere.*"

She doesn't. She goes with them to take soil samples. She lags behind, watches them move through the fog ahead of her like shapes beneath the water. Thinks of swimming in a muddy lake and looking down to see that your own limbs have been swallowed up by a darkness you can't touch. She thinks about what it would be like to switch off the life support mechanism in her suit: one button at a time, each heavy click unspooling the weight on her shoulders until the toxic atmosphere rasps its dirty claws down her throat and pulls her open.

They call her name. "*Don't fall behind,*" They advise. "*The air is thick. Even inside the suit, you're going to feel a little light headed.*" One of them laughs, "*Cheapest way to get drunk I know of.*" She nods, but doesn't reply. She's concentrating on looking busy; there is a slab of pockmarked stone with the blurred outline of a human being on it. She runs her finger along the outside of its skull, takes her time doing it, trying to imagine how the angles would have matched up to form a nose or hollowed concave to make space for two eyes. She waits until her detail disappears beneath the shadow of a shapeless, glass behemoth. It crooks earthwards near the apex, melted beyond recognition. It's a little marvelous to imagine a twenty-story building bending in the wind like a reed in the tide.

She turns off her radio and begins walking in the other direction. She walks for a very long time.

Her feet are heavy, so she lays in the dust, flat on her back with her hands folded over her sternum. Above her, a ribbon of light slices through the clouds like an angel's clavicle gone radiation-bright beneath its skin. It's a much better sky, she thinks. It is a much better sky than any she's seen before. She is glad that when they don't come back for her.

"Hello," It asks. "Are you sad?"

"No," she answers. "This is perfect."

"The way you are laying is how many humans before you have died."

"Yes," she answers again.

"Do you love Earth?" It asks.

She raps the blunts of her nails over the cartilage between her ribs. The lead lining of her suit is so thick that neither part of the body feels the impact. "No," she says.

"Do you love Humans?" It asks.

Beneath the layers of fabric and sealing coolant, something inside her stirs. She sits up and looks at It, her heart warm and calm in her chest as she takes It in. Its face is wide and flat, inlaid with black stones and pieces of glass long made smooth and opaque by the nuclear winds. It has two snow globe eyes that roll around inside their clear carapace shells, full of stars. Its limbs disappear into the earth, long, charcoal fingers that spider through the dust and encircle her like a crib.

"I love Humans." It tells her.

"What are you?" she asks. Fear is a cavity inside of her. It's abruptly absent from her, a distant memory, as if she's only read about its existence in a novel or an encyclopedia. Its limbs snake up her back, over the rounded tips of her knees. They brace her, hold her in place with her legs crossed and her hands held out, palms to the sky. It wants to talk.

o. *paint a thousand names for me i will taste each of them as if they are a spark on my tongue and swallow them whole like a sun in my belly. i will hold a universe intact for you inside my stomach and will remember you always. in the beginning i traced your shape in mud: [ten] sets bones at the end of your limbs, [twenty four] inside. [two hundred and six] is a number you can only divide evenly once. your species will come to prize symmetry, but inside the confines of your skin is chaos. my species was born from a chance collision of trace elements inside a nebula, fusing a hard, hydrogen heart at our core. we killed each other with complex equations that would destabilize at a molecular level. we evaporated into the abyss. you are soft, and so i trace your shape into the mud that you were born from, listening to you name yourself a thousand times. a million times. you will give yourself a billion names and then you will burn or rot, soft bones and softer flesh going to rest in the dust while i speak your billion names into the ground and wonder how*

"I have always been here," It says. "I've been here longer than you."

"Why do you love humans?"

"I have always loved humans."

Of course It has. She feels Its love crawling at the base of her spine. The love feels like a bead of warm wax dropped into the dip of her wrist; it stings, then cools, then hardens a shape into her skin.

"At the beginning," It says, "I loved you because you were so different from me." It opens Its mouth and reveals a glittering interior, an endless fractal pattern of mantis and diamond. To look at it made her temples throb. "Then I loved you because you were selfsame, and the same as me."

There is a pop, and then a faint hiss behind her. One of Its impossible limbs punctures her hazmat suit and her heart flutters briefly as the air tightens and presses. It searches for her skin and finds it beneath the first fold of her undershirt. There are two tiny knobs of spine exposed.

many of you there are. the first communication is a hand on my eye. you press a dark palm to it and will spend a hundred thousand years trying to imitate what you see inside while i spend a hundred thousand years trying to remember what the heel of your hand felt like the first time. in the beginning you were mud and ribcage. in the end you are mud and ribcage.

She sucks in a deep breath and tastes ash and fire. She tastes something as sharp as teeth. ". . . . hate it."

"You don't hate it."

"I don't believe it." Her voice is high and airy, "When you look into the nucleus of an atom, it's like seeing too many points of light refracted at once. It's like being a house of mirrors, but none of the images are distorted. Every time you look at your reflection, you are seeing the most clear and perfect truth you can imagine."

ii. you and I sit on a hill. you and I sit together in a prison. you say to me: "[Ahura Mazda], I have seen the most

"Who are you?" It asks.

She gives one of ten billion names, "I'm twenty-four years old. My mother is a botanist, and my father is a surgeon. I majored in particle theory physics but I . . ."

i. Your planet is harsh to you. She is a roiling beast of nitrogen oxygen and metal, and she seeks to purge you. She thirsts for your blood to feed her soil. She hungers for your bones to coat the bark of her trees. I do not know yet that her hostility is founded. I do not know yet that you will kill her. I say to you: "You have angered [Enil], and [his] wrath is upon you as the King's anger is upon a flea." I say: "[Enil] will sweep for you with [his] giant hand, and yet you will survive. The flood will fill [the cities of the half-bushel baskets]. The decision that [mankind] will be destroyed has been made. And yet, you will survive." You thank [Ea]. You thank me in a thousand names. There will be more floods; you will never thank me again.

clear and perfect truth that you can imagine." your truth is two halves of a pomegranate split evenly down the middle. One half is [sin], and the other is the [enlightened path of the divine]. You set the two halves in front of you and say: "One half is [Angra Mainyu] Evil, and the other half is of [Ahura Mazda] you." you point to one, and then you point to the other, "It is a choice [Man] makes. [He] can choose which one he eats." You choose. "Yes," I say. "Yes. But." You have come to love symmetry. "Yes, but you can never be sure that you've cut the two halves perfectly."

iii. I am not your father. I did not touch your mother. I spoke to her, perhaps, in passing. I am distorted, refracted. You speak to me in two voices and hold me differently in either hand. In one voice I am [EaAhuraMazdaFather], and in the other I am [The Other]. You lay in the sand and burn. You lay in the sand, and I watch the moisture bake out of your body and turn you the shade and texture of tree bark. I say into

"And was that painful?"

"Humans aren't made for that kind of clarity. It burns you out."

The sharp crook of Its limb pierces her skin gently. It does not hurt; it's not meant to. There is an electric current that moves through her in a steady, soothing rhythm, one vertebrae at a time. This is how It understands. It asks again:

"Who are you?"

"If you take two handfuls of dirt—" she says "—one is my mother, one is my father—if you mix them together, the tree that sprouts is—"

No, that's not right. There are no trees on Earth anymore. There are the hollowed, black skeletons of industry—tall beacons in the ashy fog that crumble in the wind like the used end of a cigarette. She begins again:

"If you take two handfuls of ash—one is my mother, one is my father—if you mix them together, the result is—"

the bones of your ears, "Eat of this bread." I touch the bones of your hands and move them over a stone. I will change the chemistry of it for you. I will reach into the heart of this stone and save your life. Ask for it in the voice that you use to call me [Father]. You reply, "It is written that [Man] will not live by bread alone, but by every word that proceed from the mouth of [Father]." Yes, I am [not] your Father. "Would you trust your [Father] to catch you?" I ask, "Would you throw yourself down if my arms were [Angels] to bear your weight?" I have always caught you. I have caught you with arms that failed to catch a hundred thousand of my selfsame species. Never doubt that I would reach out to you with a thousand hands that would span the circumference of your planet. You speak to me in your second voice. You say: "Begone." I cannot catch you when you banish me with your left hand.

"When I was a child, my foot got stuck in a mud-hole." The dust climbs her legs, buries her feet. "It was just my shoe. I was wearing my mother's rain-boots. It

That's not right either. Its eyes whirl at her sympathetically. "Try again," it urges. "You always try again."

"If you take two handfuls of mud."

"Yes."

iv. "Read." "Yes," I agree. To read is the first rule. "Read: in the name of thy Lord who Createth man from a clot." You sit hunched in the fine, red dirt, curled over your crossed legs with your eyes closed like a sleeping child's. Your eyelashes cast dark half-moons over the bones inside your cheek. You whisper, "But I cannot." you admit, "I cannot read." Your alphabet has [twenty-eight] letters. [Twenty-eight] can only be divided equally twice. The moon is large and orange. it casts a gold light over the pearl roofs of your most beloved city. Your people had nothing they loved so much as you love your cities. I love different things about your planet. I love your oceans—the hiss and bite of the salt and the places where it spirals so deep that it leaves a mark on the rains for half the year on my colony, but I was always afraid of looking uncool in ugly, rubber shoes."

"That's not true," It says gently. The tendrils of Its limbs entwine with the delicate nerves just beneath her shoulder. Her hands twitch violently, and a calming shock runs through her capillary veins. She shakes her head inside the hazmat helmet.

"I was afraid of looking fat. The skinny girls always looked so cute in their rain-boots. They could stick their feet in those things, and the boot's lip wouldn't even touch their calves. Mine spilled over the rims when I sat down, or leaned back too far on my heels."

"So I wore my mother's rain-boots when it got too wet. I could have just pulled my foot out of the boot and stepped back onto the road, but I couldn't. I just watched my leg sink deeper and deeper until the mud puckered up around my knee."

surface, like the way your skin dimples around the mouth sometimes. There are trees that bleed the same color that you do in slick, blubbery veins. The distance between the highest and lowest points on your planet is [nineteen thousand seven hundred and seventy-two meters], a number that can also be split evenly in half two times. I will make a covenant with you, and like I have so many times before, I will tell you about the place I am from. You have described me in the past as a creature with a hundred eyes and hands made of divine fire. You have called me a beast with seven heads that crawls from the depths of the ocean and burns the rivers with my breath. This time I have a thousand wings and you have me dwell in a [Jannah], the splendor of my home—its searing shades of molecular hydrogen and zodiacal light— are a hundred flowers without names in your language. Your lips mumble prayers into the veins of my arms, "[Lord], will you make a covenant with me?" You will live by the pen, I know, and you will not believe a word I have said to you. There is too much reason in your world and not enough

"And then what did you do?"
It asks, curious, even though
It already knows the answer.

V. MY SPECIES WAS BORN
SELFSAME WITH EYES THAT
COULD SEE THE INHERENT
MOLECULAR STRUCTURE OF
LIVING AND INERT OBJECTS.
YOUR EYES SHOW YOU A
WORLD THAT IS OPAQUE AND
MAGNIFICENT. YOU REQUIRE
TOOLS TO DIVINE THE TRUE
NATURE OF MATTER. NO NO,
PLEASE. DO NOT LOOK AWAY
FROM ME. BENEATH THE
LAYERS OF SALT AND MEAT
THAT COMPOSE YOUR SHELLS,
YOU ARE MADE OF BEAUTIFUL
THINGS. A CALCIUM AND
MINERAL CONSTRUCTION
KNIT TOGETHER BY ACETIC
ACIDS. PLEASE, PLEASE, LISTEN
TO ME. I HAVE TO SPEAK SO
LOUDLY TO BE HEART ABOVE
THE DIN OF YOUR SLAUGHTER,
THE SCREECHING TRAFFIC OF
A MILLION, BILLION NAMES
BEING CALLED IN UNISON.
YOU PAINT FOR ME A THOU-
SAND NAMES AND DIRECT ALL
OF THEM AT THE SKY. YOU
NAME ME A GIBBEROUS SKY
OF FLAPPING WINGS. YOU
NAME ME A STINKING, FETID
CARCASS. YOU RECREATE ME
IN [film] AND [literature],
BUT WHEN I SHOW MY FACE

*magic. The things that draw
you away from me—math-
ematics, philosophy, chemistry—are the developments
I have been waiting for since
you were naked rib cages in
the mud. You look at me with
fear caked in the skin beneath
your eyes. I have not lost you
yet.*

"I put my other foot in." She
sighs. It feels good. She has
never confessed this before,
and she has told the story
a hundred times, "I put my
other foot in, and when it
sunk up to the knee as well,
I laid on my back. The mud
was very soft, and the sky
was so beautiful. My colony
had a very thin upper atmosphere, so on a clear day
you could see the flash of
electrical storms on the gas
giant we were anchored
around."

Its claws weave deftly
through her brain and
retrieve the images. A
black sky in the middle
of summer. Hot white
coursing through a sea of
molten orange.

"I was relieved when the
mud filled my nose. I don't

TO YOU, YOU LOOK PAST ME. YOU MAKE STRANGE MYTHS. YOU TURN YOUR FACE AND CRY INTO YOUR HANDS AND MEDIATE YOUR BRAIN CHEMISTRY WITH HEAVY METALS. YOU ARE A DYING PEOPLE, AND I DO NOT WISH TO SEE YOU PASS INTO THE ABYSS. IT IS SO LOUD HERE. IT IS SO LOUD.

Ω. *it is so quiet here. i [do not] mourn what it used to be. your—*

know why. My father pulled me out before I could pass out from oxygen deprivation, but I never stopped thinking about it. I never stopped wanting to sink into the mud."

"Thank you," It says sincerely. "And that is why you are here?"

"Yes," she says. "No." She closes her eyes and remembers how exquisite it was to be engulfed by something cold, massive, and fathomless, "I think that I just wanted to see it."

"Of course," It assures her. "That is a primal instinct, something as natural as gravity. You wanted to return to your—"

"—planet. Your beautiful, beautiful planet."

She gasps when It pulls Its limbs from her skin, a smooth unspooling of thread from a healed wound. "Not so beautiful anymore," she laughs sadly, "but someday. We'll come back to you eventually."

It spins Its eyes sadly, "No. You are the last one."

"Are there more planets like ours?" she wonders, reaching out.

"With sentient life? Yes, of course. Thousands."

"You can go anywhere," she says in amazement. She touches the clear carapace of It's eye, the heel of her palm warm even through the double-stitched layer of lead and canvas.

"Yes," It says, "but I would rather stay here."

It stays by her side until the sun goes down.

Twilight for the Nightingale

~ David Tallerman

Doctor Eponymous massaged the flesh beneath the albino Siamese's wiry fur. The animal arched against his fingers, purring radiantly. It turned its head, to gaze at him with blank fondness through pinkish-blue eyes. A beautiful creature, in its way, he thought—and remarkably costly.

Eponymous spun in his chair and stood, catching the cat by the scruff of its neck before it could tumble to the aluminum floor. The animal yowled, swiped at his wrist. Ignoring the pain and the swelling lines of red, Eponymous stepped forward, to the pool that filled most of the command center's higher tier. He released the Siamese, which he'd never bothered to name. It had time for once last howl of fear and fury before it broke through the water's surface.

The piranhas, too, had been expensive. In a moment, there was nothing to see but white flotsam on a spreading crimson carpet.

"Understand," cried Eponymous, "that nothing and no one is indispensible. Agent Nightingale will be here soon. The kid gloves are off. No holds are barred. Nightingale is the finest secret agent in the world, the finest who has ever lived, and he will show no mercy."

Skull and Bones, henchmen extraordinaire, gazed back at him with expressions as vacantly adoring as the Siamese's had been. They would go to hell and back for their master; two decades of brainwashing demanded no less.

Skull—mangled by Elephantiasis, insane but cunning—grunted, "We won't let him stop you this time."

Bones—horribly anorexic and unscrupulous—added, "He'll never decipher your plans."

Eponymous allowed himself the briefest flicker of a smile. "Don't be so naive. Nightingale is almost my equal in intellect, and he has the weight of a nation behind him. He will already have found the seven bodies I left in Rome. He will have understood the significance of their arrangement immediately. He's no fool! And that pattern will have led him inevitably to Chichén Itzá."

How long had they been playing this game? It had begun with ideologies, with simplifications like 'crime' and 'justice,' 'chaos' and 'order.' Now there was only Eponymous and the Nightingale, locked together hand and throat. It could only end one way.

Eponymous paced down the stairs to the lower level. He spared a glance for the bank of monitors to his right, and the fifty agents laboring before them in their neon orange jumpsuits. "He'll have eluded the trap I set upon Tzompantli, and defused the Tezcatlipoca bomb. It was beneath him, really."

Skull looked nervous. The expression doubled his grotesqueness. "The Omega Key, Doctor . . ." He pointed. The countdown, indeed, was ticking close to zero. Spread across twenty-five screens, the mammoth, diminishing digits looked suitably catastrophic.

"He will come!" Eponymous hissed. "Nightingale will have discovered the hidden chamber beneath Tzompantli and found the inscriptions there. A stupid man might mistake them for directions to Lake Puma Yumco . . . but the Nightingale is not stupid!"

"It's almost charged. A weapon beyond imagining . . ."

Skull spoke too late. The countdown had already clicked to zero, a sinister, house-tall ovoid on the massive bank of monitors. A groaning whirr shuddered through the floor. With it, a pedestal separated itself from the metallic tiles and glided up, silver-skinned and perfect in its contours.

"HE WILL COME!" Eponymous realized that he was sweating, large drops gathering on the bald dome of his brow. Nightingale had never disappointed. Two decades of cat and mouse, of inexorable trap and impossible escape, and Nightingale remained the foil to his every scheme—no matter how brilliant, well conceived, or endlessly elaborate. Once, long ago, Eponymous had wanted money. Notoriety had seemed appealing. He had craved a sort of hideous fame, like Mengele or Manson. Now he could no longer enjoy food without the threat of the Nightingale hovering in his thoughts. No woman could satisfy, unless he knew for certain that the pride of England's secret agencies was close at hand. "He will . . . he'll have found the hidden temple. Its devotees will be helpless before him, for all their generations of martial training. Helpless! All one hundred . . ."

He took a step towards the pedestal, and as though in answer, the metal cover at its apex slid back. The single red button it had been concealing stared back at him like a bloodshot eye.

"Master . . ." Bones, too, was sweating; it leant his holocaustic face a ghastly sheen. "Your assassins. Regina Dentata, Rex Lazarus. What if one of them succeeded?" He turned his sallow eyes to the great, hovering zero. "If Nightingale is dead then—"

Eponymous swung towards him, scrawny fists clenched. He was almost surprised by his own rage. "Nightingale cannot die! He will have found the map I left, discovered the true map in the microdot on its reverse. He will come, we will battle—and I will triumph. Only then. I will blot out his life with my own bare hands!"

Bones made to step between the Doctor and the pedestal and thought better of it. "But, the end of the world . . . the whole world..."

Eponymous reached the pedestal, considered it gravely. "He'll stop it. He'll stop me. He *always* stops me . . ."

There was pleading in Skull's smashed eyes: "What if he doesn't? What if you've won?"

Eponymous started. "I've won?"

"Then we can shut it down. The world is yours." Bones ran frail fingers through his bleached-blonde hair. "No need for—"

"If I've won . . . if Nightingale is dead . . . if our battle is over . . ." Eponymous looked, once more, at the button. The Omega Key was the bluntest instrument he'd created, an obscenity against life itself. He could never have so much as conceived it if he'd ever imagined it would be used.

His gaze darted to the blast doors, to the external monitors. There was nothing to see—only the evening sky melting into the first bruise-purple of night.

He placed his palm over the button.

A single tear hung on his cheek. Eponymous brushed it absent-mindedly away.

"If Nightingale is dead . . ."

The Thirteenth Ewe

~ Lyn McConchie

Shani was a Keeper. One of those who followed her flock or herd the year through. Walking where they walked, sleeping where they slept. Finding her food along the way in the high hills. Just before the last and harshest months of the winter she would return with her sheep. In safe pens at the village edge the ewes would give birth. Then they would wait for spring before they set off again, sheep and Keeper together. They would be back only briefly at the beginning of summer. Then the ewes would be shorn and the lambs left with the villagers.

To Shani the small flock was kin, her family. She sorrowed to leave the lambs behind knowing what would happen, but accepting that was the way of life. However, times were starting to change. When she was five a man had come to the village, there he had built a great long shed and set machines within. He'd hired many of the women to work there. The money paid was good. It meant not having to slave in a small garden to grow food. A woman could buy vegetables in the market and still have money and time left to herself.

When Shani was ten the owner added to his factory size. Now many of the village men worked there as well, their small plots of land lying idle. It was at that time Shani had become a Keeper for her father's flock. Her parents, her older brothers, all worked the factory machines; only Shani remained to Keep the ewes according to custom. Other families had even given up their sheep, allowing the ewes to be sold in the market. But not Shani's family. Her parents were traditionalists who believed that without their flock the Goddess would not smile on them. The sheep stayed, and Shani Kept them.

She was the youngest of her parents' children, so by tradition the flock was hers since she was Keeper. But the old laws were changing in other ways. Her mother died in late spring when Shani had already been gone for several months. It was not unexpected; the old woman had been unwell for almost a year. Shani's father would have burned all that had belonged to his wife then but his sons spoke against it angrily.

"It's a waste. Such things are valuable."

"It is custom." The old man's voice was firm.

"Custom, not law."

"The Goddess will be angered if we take what belongs to the dead."

There was a harsh laugh from one of his sons. "The Goddess!" The words were a jeer. "Superstition, old stories."

Shani's father shook his head slowly. "Not so, in my time I was a Keeper of the sheep. Once I saw Her walking the High Hills. The ewes stopped to look up so that I knew they saw her too. Your mother used to say that the Goddess watched over Keepers to keep them from harm." He sighed. "Maybe she has left us now. She has no love for machines, and our village is a village no longer."

A son snorted, "No, now it is almost a city and a good thing too. But if you are so worried over Her anger, why then, we'll sell our mother's things to some city fool. There are many who would pay well for the spoons her father carved. Let the Goddess's anger fall on them—if she still exists and has power."

By the Summer when Shani returned it had been done, her father's initial refusal having been worn down by the nagging of her two brothers. She grieved for the loss of her mother who had understood her. In her youth her mother too had been a Keeper. They had sorrowed together at many of the changes that had come to their village. Shani returned to other changes, to her bewilderment her sheep were now to be penned well outside the town. She protested.

"What of wolves?"

The guard shrugged. "Not many wolves about these days, and people don't like the stink of sheep. The lambs make too much noise with their bleating—they keep citizens awake who complain about it to us. The Council has ruled that from now on the winter pens are to be well away from the town." He eyed her more kindly, "Don't worry, girl. I'll drop by on my rounds when I can. Anyway, the sheep will be happier away from the town too I should think."

Shani nodded, that was true. They talked of the stink of the sheep and their wool, but the smell of the town was worse than any clean scent of healthy beasts. She called her small flock and the twelve ewes followed obediently. Winter passed, and both sheep and Keeper were glad when they could take the track up higher and higher leaving the town behind them again. Even the most matronly of the ewes skipped and danced as they left the pens. Shani plodded along with them, her thoughts anything but light.

Her oldest brother had spoken to her before she left. At first she hadn't understood his subtle hinting, so he'd spoken more plainly.

"You'll make more money in the town."

"I don't need money." Shani was almost amused. In the High Hills there were berries, nuts, wild fruit trees. She could dig edible roots. If she wished for meat, she could set snares for rabbits or birds. It was only in winter that she needed more than the Hills could give.

Her brother looked at her in exasperation. The sheep made little in comparison to the money the girl could earn. The family would prosper still more with a fourth wage coming in. The sheep wouldn't fetch much if sold, but there was another reason to rid the family of them. He was an ambitious man, and with the last tie to the old ways cut he could aim for a seat on the council. The men on that looked forward. They had no time for Keepers of beasts, nor for foolish beliefs and superstitions.

Such things were irritating to a man who did not believe, although certain tales were the latest stories amongst the Keepers. It was said that some had taken their flocks and departed to seek the Goddess. It was nonsense. There were always those who did not return before the worst winter storms. Sometimes they found their bones—sometimes it was never known what had happened to them. The tales his mother had told to her children when they were young were the dreams of Keepers too long alone in the hills.

His father had seemed to grow old all at once when their mother died. Soon they would convince him to be rid of the flock as they had convinced him to sell their mother's possessions. The girl would mourn her sheep briefly no doubt, but she was young. She'd forget the noisy, smelly animals once she realized how much she could buy with a week's wages. Let her think over what he'd said to her. She might even come back in summer ready to obey. If not . . . if not, she could be *persuaded*.

To his infuriation he was wrong. A year passed, then another and another. Still Shani came and went as Keeper of her flock. Despite the handicap of one whom others called his strange sister Shani's brother achieved a seat on the town council. Then their father died, and Shani returned for the funeral and winter. Her brother met her at the pens.

"We're selling the flock."

Shani's eyes hardened as she faced him proudly, "No. It is the law that they are mine now. I am Keeper, they pass to me with our father dead."

"Maybe," her brother said savagely." But nothing else will do so. Let you try making a living from twelve old footsore ewes. And just for a start you can pay the winter pen fees. That will teach you the value of money." He stamped out leaving Shani hiding a smile.

Her mother had spoken with the girl before Shani left for the hills that last time. "Nothing stays the same forever no matter how much we may wish it. The old ways change, your brothers would have them change even faster. I do not trust what they may do when your father and I are gone. And—I feel age in my bones, in case I am not here when you return . . ." she had reached out to hand her daughter a small bag. "Take this and waste nothing."

Shani heard the soft clink of coins within the soft lambskin pouch. Her mother had brushed a hand lightly over the girl's head. "Take my blessing also, Keeper of the Flock. Honor the Goddess, care for the sheep." She had hugged the girl then thrust her through the door as her ears caught the sound of approaching footsteps. "Say nothing of what I have given you. Now go, it is time the sheep were on the hills again." Then as Shani moved towards the door her mother spoke again, and very softly. "Remember, Keeper, the Goddess expects you to do your best for the sheep, but it is not forbidden to ask for guidance."

Shani had opened the bag that night. It held a mixture of coins, mostly silver, but one gold, and several more coppers. If the Keeper had not understood the danger before her mother's death, she did now. Over the next few years she had managed to add a coin here and there to her store. She had enough to pay pen fees for a winter. She could sell the lambs before she left again. There would be the wool in summer. Together lambs and wool should keep her and pay the fees necessary.

But while she understood the danger, she did not know her brother's angry determination. He was a senior councilor the following year. Two years later he stood as Mayor. He lost and believed that it was because of Shani. There were those who laughed openly that a councilor had a sister who was a hill-runner. Her brother gritted his teeth. In four years he would stand again, but this time he would win. He had only to make it impossible for that stupid girl to continue with her foolish sheep. He laid his plans and worked hard at them all that year.

Shani returned with her sheep that summer. To her horror, where the winter pens had stood there was only empty ground.

"The pens?" she questioned the elderly shearer, the only one remaining, "Where have they moved the pens?"

He eyed her sadly, "Nowhere. The council has said that since only one flock comes down from the hills nowadays, there is no need for them." She would have spoken but he waved her silent. "Listen to me, Shani. Your mother was a Keeper when I first learned to shear the sheep. We were friends. Before she died she asked me to help you if I could, and to warn you if I learned of danger. Your brother planned all this. The land has been sold to another on the council, and they will make a law."

"What law?"

"A law that sheep may not come closer to the town than the foothills." Shani gaped at him. "But —but, if they are so far away in Winter how can I bring them hay? Who will come so far to shear them?"

He nodded. "I would walk to the flock and shear them, but no one will bring hay that far, and if they would your brother will find some way to convince them otherwise. This is his way of ridding himself of a hill-runner in the family. He believes he has left you no choice."

And as Shani discovered, in that he was right. She survived through that year. Her mother's friend sheared the sheep for her. In winter Shani purchased hay and using a small trolley that she made she dragged bale after bale of hay to feed her sheep, three miles away in the foothills. She sold her lambs to men who rode out to look over the flock. And before the worst storms she took her sheep to a small cave that she knew and penned them there while Shani slept behind a fire in the cave's mouth. In spring she took them to the high hills, knowing however that this would be the final year in which she was a Keeper.

She met her friend in marketplace. "Well, child, what will you do?"

Shani's eyes were fey, and he was suddenly afraid for her. "I shall go to the high hills. Before she died my mother told me 'the Goddess expects you to do your best for the sheep, but it is not forbidden to ask for guidance.' I shall ask, and if it be Her will, I shall learn, and if she says nothing then I shall do whatever I must."

"You would not . . ."

Shani smiled. "Kill myself? No. Not that, but if I cannot bring my flock home because of my brother's treachery then it may be that I shall not return here at all, neither my flock nor their Keeper."

He watched her set out the next morning having risen early to bid her farewell. Shani hugged him for that, accepted his blessing in lieu of the one she should have received from kin, and strode up the winding hill path. She walked slowly all day, bedded the flock down that night and headed higher yet at first light. And in the glow of sunset she came to her objective, a tiny shrine, barely large enough to hold a roughly carved lamb, and a shallow trough into which clear sweet water trickled. The flock crowded to drink from the trough, and Shani knelt, laying a bunch of bright hill-roses before the lamb.

"Lady, I am thy daughter, I am a Keeper of the Flock as it has always been, but is no longer. In all of my village I am the last Keeper, mine the last flock. The sheep pens have been torn down, the last shearer grows old and has no apprentice. I am forbidden to bring my flock to the village and must pen them in the hills . . ."

She choked, remembering the bitter cold, the howl of wolves and her nights there, torn between terror for her flock and knowledge of what a wolf pack could do, she caught her breath and told the rest of her story. "Lady, if I continue as I did last year I shall die and they will slaughter the flock. If I give them up, the flock will be slaughtered and my heart will be empty. I am Your Keeper, as my mother was and hers before her. I have no wish or desire to be anything else. Lady I am a sheep astray, show me the path."

Head bowed, she waited. And in the silence something stirred, soundless, yet a feeling as if behind her it moved, coming for her, power flooding the hills, the shrine, and—the flock. Shani turned slowly, in the center of her sheep stood a thirteenth ewe, a large sturdy animal, already seen to be in-lamb, and her fleece? Shani stared. The fleece was winter-long, and . . . the ewe moved so that the sunset caught her and the fleece glowed a soft shimmering golden in the light. Shani caught her breath.

If it were true and no trick of the light, her flock and their Keeper might be saved. It was true, and before Shani returned with the winter, all twelve of her ewes were in lamb to the precocious ram-lamb born that spring of the thirteenth ewe. The lambs they bred, bred true, their fleeces shimmering golden wool that the rich almost fought to possess.

The old shearer trained an apprentice hastily, while the council rebuilt the sheep pens where they'd always been. Shani's brother took the credit himself of course, and he became mayor in his time, but Shani did not care.

She was a Keeper all the days of her life, and after her came other young girls to be Keepers in turn to a growing number of offshoot flocks. The Shani sheep—as they came to be called—flourished, but only under the guidance of true Keepers, those who paused each spring at the shrine and gave thanks, remembering. And in the high hills a Goddess smiled on those who were Hers, sheep and Keepers both, blessed and beloved.

Augustus Clementine

– Liz Argall

Augustus Clementine was a less than ordinary roller skate. He was an it'll-do-for-now roller skate. An I'm-not-sure-but-I'll-give-it-a-go roller skate. A damn-well-this-will-have-to-do roller skate.

Augustus was one of many tan suede roller skates in a middle income, middle suburbia roller skating rink in a never-quite-closed-down but had-never-quite-thrived kind of place. Augustus was known only by his number, 8, and he was for a left foot. He flopped in silence amongst the rows and rows of his brethren, waiting to be grabbed, jostled, and to live briefly on the sweaty foot of some beautiful girl or boy. He strived to be the best possible skate for them, but always, always was returned to the walls of beige. He longed for a person to call his own, a place and a specialness that could be his. But he was a skate for hire and was always something visited on the way to somewhere else.

Years passed in this way. His bearings grew gritty and non-spheroid. Sometimes he was serviced regularly—sometimes bearings and wheels were replaced and rotated with military precision. Sometimes his suede was cleaned, though never enough. He was often deodorized with a talc-like powder that also scared away fleas. Sometimes he grew so rough without love that a bearing would burst, causing his wheels to seize up on the skater. The skater would hurtle face first to the ground as he watched helplessly.

Parts of him broke off: eyelets, laces, and stitching. Sometimes they were repaired with love and care. Sometimes he was repaired in a rush of rudely tied knots that meant he would be the last to be chosen. After one nasty accident he spent six months in a dark broken skates bin, uncertain if his next move would be into rubbish or repair bench. He watched skates more beloved than he cannibalized to fix younger models as he waited in the dark. If he could he would have wept with joy and sadness when he found himself on the repair bench as the recipient, not the unwilling donor of parts.

Augustus knew many feet. He knew how feet changed shape and smell and size over the space of an hour or day. He knew who would settle comfortably into him, matching to his leather as momentary soul mates. He knew who would slip and fidget, readjust and never quite be happy with him—their natures clanging against each other, though he loved these as much as his more comfortable wearers.

He felt soft feet sensitive to the rough edges of his insides. He felt club toed feet battered from always living in shoes a size to small. He felt toes of bunion, callous, splayed, and pointy, attached to feet flat-footed or high arched. It was rare to experience the same foot twice. Every now and then, for a heart lifting month perhaps, there would be someone who recognized him and requested him as a special favor, but those times were rare and diminished as he grew older.

Eventually Augustus felt his plate break, the spine running from his heel to his scuffed thin toe, snapped in two, and he was thrown in the repair bin. He knew he would never see the track again. His wheels were stripped from him immediately. To be stripped and left wheel-less did not hurt him as much as he thought it would, numbed by the inevitability of death. His wheels were close to new and might find many years on another boot. Wheels lived a firefly life compared to a skate, and he wished them well. Losing his laces was a greater wound. His laces were not new, and together they had held many feet. His eyelets drooped hollowly, and his suede upper flopped as part of himself looped through someone else.

Eventually his suede tongue was cut off with scissors. He never found out why, they just took it and dropped him back in the box. Augustus lay in the dark, raw from intimate cutting. He lay there for a very long time.

One day, when the dust on Augustus had turned his tan suede grey, he was thrown out. His upper was torn off him, his body disassembled, his consciousness clinging tenuously to a few scraps of metal that were then melted to slag.

He thought that was the end of him and was surprised to wake, dizzy in a new form and hybrid consciousness. He had become a prosthetic for a young girl who lost her leg in a car accident. He felt her vestigial limb slip into him, padded into his socket with socks and gel packs.

Together they learned to walk, they learned to run in motions so strange and yet familiar. He was her one-and-only, not just on the track, not just on smooth sidewalk and parking lot. He was her one-and-only whenever and wherever she wanted to go. He moved on stairs, in forests, on muddy paths—a few times he even ended up in the bath. The breadth of his world, the delight of motion they gave each other left him breathless. Sometimes breathless with joy, sometimes he felt crushed by the responsibility, intensity, and constancy of his work. At times he remembered what it was like to spin carefree along the smooth polished boards of the rink as a thing of fun and play.

He knew it wasn't always easy for his little girl. He knew the ways of limbs and knew when they squeaked with discomfort or clamored for escape. Sometimes she cursed him for the pain he could not help but give her oft-blistered stump. She was always straining to do more things and go more places. His little girl was strong and because she could and would try anything so would he. He adored her, and, for the first time in his life, he felt loved and needed in return.

Time passed, and, as the little girl grew older, Augustus noticed her vestigial limb didn't fit into his socket as easily. His little girl would find excuses not to use him, hopping or using crutches, taking him off as soon as she could. Augustus knew that once more his life was coming to an end.

One day his little girl came home with a new leg, a leg that fit her growing body better. Augustus was put up on the shelf to gather dust and occasionally play pranks on high school friends. His little girl was not little anymore and no longer just his. Augustus was still her first limb, and she would say he was her favorite, but the way she walked around on other appendages undermined that truth.

His no-longer-little girl marveled at how small he was, swinging him in her hands nostalgically, and he felt very small indeed. His no-longer-little girl grew out of other legs, and these bigger creatures sat on the shelf with him for a short while. He was intimidated by their size and superior joints, and burrowed deeper into the shelving. He adjusted to the frightening presences on the shelf next to him, but only in time for the new legs to be whisked away. And he would be alone again, gathering dust.

One day, his-no-longer-little girl took him out of the cupboard. His no-longer-little girl had been through many changes. Her hair had grown long and short and bald and long again. She had got glasses, got rid of her glasses and then got them back again. Her wrinkled hands seemed enormous as they wrapped around him; she could hold him between two fingers and watch him dangle.

Today his no-longer-little girl looked sad. Her bedroom didn't have any of her normal things, though that too had changed over the years. Her room was full of cardboard boxes, newspaper and packing tape. Everything that had made the room her room had been taken down and was being sent away.

The woman who was his little girl cradled him like a baby, and she hugged him. She wrapped him in newspaper, and she said goodbye.

Once again Augustus thought he was going to die, and once again he was delivered into a new life.

Augustus Clementine was shipped to a hospital that struggled to do much with very little. The hospital was one place in the war-hurt parts of Africa, Asia, Europe, the Middle East, and the Americas were children came after they lost body parts to land mines. He stayed in that country for a long time and was used by many children.

Augustus clomped through mud, fell into rivers and was dropped from trees. He was used, abused, abandoned, banged back into shape, and put back to work.

Sometimes he missed his old lives, but that was past. He gave himself to the present as best he could with what he had, and there were always children that needed new legs. He lost count of the children who wore him, loved him, hated him, and grew out of him. He was always just-for-now and always-grown-out-of, but his now was enough, and his now was important. He was part of their bodies, for just a little while as they found ways to walk again, laughing and crying, dancing and playing.

And when Augustus was done, his body so metal-fatigued and worn that there was nothing left to him, he was welded into a sculpture with many other limbs to speak of greater truths he did not understand. And only then, never to be worn again, did he fall asleep and not wake up.

And that was his life, and that was enough.

Pretty Little Boxes

~ Julie C. Day

Boxes surround us.

Every night Barry builds more walls, fastens more lids. Sometimes, when I can't sleep, I slip down the hall to his workroom and watch. His eyes remain focused on the contents of his bench: the wood, the pulped flowers, and all those dying insects—the grasshoppers, the damsel flies, the hissing cockroaches—that will eventually make up the lining of each petal-and-limb box. Little pools of haemolymph, the fluid he collects from his crushed arthropods, rest in jars, waiting to be mixed into the glue.

Most Gray Witches know only two things about Barry. They know he is one of the best craftsmen in the city. They also know he's the child of a Gray Witch, one of the few children they didn't manage to train.

"It won't be easy," his mother said after Barry introduced me as his fiancée. We stood in a workroom somewhere deep inside the Gray Witch Union's granite walls. The room was filled with benches and scurrying creatures. No windows. It was when she stared at our intertwined hands that I finally noticed her eyes. They were exactly the same shade of gray as Barry's. "A Sadness Carrier and my son," she continued, turning those gray eyes in my direction. "Well, I hope you didn't traipse down here expecting a Witch's blessing."

Barry's fingers tightened against mine.

"We know Gray Witches only bless each other," he replied.

"Of course you do," she said. "You've always been a clever boy."

Blessing or not, Barry and I married the next day.

The photographer Barry hired snapped picture after picture as our few guests moved through the receiving line. These were our neighbors and coworkers: students still in their first apartments, urban gardeners with calloused hands, women from the alley off of Market Square where I ran my stall.

"Congratulations," they said. "Best wishes." They even toasted our happiness.

The wedding photos, however, are focused on something else entirely. My hair, in frame after frame, is long and glossy. My cheeks are glowing with foundation and rouge. In some of the pictures, Barry's hand rests on my waist, heavy against the stiff silk gown. I still remember the feeling of heat as the side of his body leaned into mine. Yet each picture shows the same thing. My face is strained. My lips turned downward.

Just two days into my vacation and already I was falling apart. I'll be lucky to last another day; that was what I was thinking as the photographer snapped his shots. Along with the photographer, officiant, and cake, Barry had also booked a honeymoon. I'd be away from work for over a week.

I didn't love my job, but I damn well needed it.

"Barry?" I wiped the tears away with the back of one hand as I stared into Barry's workshop, careful not to get in the way.

Barry was scrubbing one of the large mesh screens with a stiff metal brush, readying the tray for the next sheet of paper. He'd been making a lot of paper lately, spending long hours in the studio. Perhaps the Gray Witches had given him an extra commission. I glanced at the carefully stacked rectangles. Not worth getting distracted about. "We paid them all that money, Barry, so my sadness wouldn't grow back."

"At least we can make up the money now that you're working again," Barry replied, his back still turned to me as he scrubbed the screens.

"That's not the point."

"I'll make you some more boxes." Barry's brush made a scuff-scuffing noise as it moved across the fine mesh screen.

"No," I said. "I don't want—" I grabbed the workshop's door, rattling its loose metal handle.

Barry was silent as he dipped the wire brush into a pot of boiling water. He shook the brush off and poured the contents of the pot across the screen, sluicing off the cellulose and chitin. He didn't even glance in my direction.

Sadness Carrier is the only job I've ever held.

We Sadness Carriers are licensed for only one thing: sadness. The most important tool is the box. Too little space inside and the feelings might morph, condense into the heavier moods. A dangerous thing, carrying a box like that. Most likely thing in the world that it'll be tagged as a Gray Witch offense. And then the boxes can go entirely the other way, the size just too big, the walls meant to hold more than you can offer. With a box like that, the mood might escape entirely, leaving nothing but emptiness and air.

When business is good, it feels like an honorable service. You never know who your next client is going to be: perhaps it'll be a West End climber with his new money and not much else, making sure he has some backup during *Madame Butterfly*. I get clients like that all the time. What if they can't wait to check the game scores until the end of the performance? What would people think then? One of my little boxes gets rid of all that anxiety. I get other types of clients, too. One afternoon that nice waitress from over on Ninth Street might stop by my stall, looking for a bit of sincerity while she breaks up with her summer fling.

But the box has to be exactly right. There's nothing worse than listening to a neighbor describe how she's seen that Eaton's waitress laughing hysterically while her boyfriend wept or overhearing the story of a man who committed suicide at the opera. Those pretty little boxes are important. And, before Barry, they were tough to find, tough to afford, anyway. Anyone who's any good sells to the Gray Witches.

Barry changed everything. That's why I married him.

"Honey," he said on that first night. "Let me help you."

And God forgive me, I did. I let him help me. In the end, I did much more than just open that apartment door.

Everyone has a "how we met" story. Barry and I are no exception.

I was holed up in some corner apartment on Fifth Street. Barry had just moved in next door. Even on that very first night, he found me hard to ignore.

"Tears equal money," I kept muttering as I kicked the small pile of misshapen containers against the wall. Some of the boxes broke apart on impact. Not surprising. The entire batch was nothing but cheap balsa wood and a couple of staples. Cheap balsa wood I'd dropped my entire month's rent on. I had no more cash and now, with these rip-offs filling up the room, I couldn't even work. I lifted my foot, crushing another of the misshapen rectangles. Meanwhile, my tears kept flowing.

That bastard box-builder, Francoise, had stiffed me. No liner paper and, even with the stapled edges, the joins were so bad the contents poured right out. Now, not only did I have nothing to sell at tomorrow's market, I also had nowhere for my tears to go.

I slammed into a pile of boxes with both feet and then screamed. That's when I heard someone pounding on my apartment door.

Of course, I didn't answer. I had no idea who it was. Still, Barry must have known I was standing nearby. He must have heard the snuffling as I tried to stifle my sobs.

The pounding eventually stopped. That was good. But I could still hear him breathing. Eventually, that first sheet of paper slid under the door. I watched as it wafted above the floorboards and then settled against my feet: thick, textured fibers twisted across the page, an almost unbroken wing like a translucent rainbow in one corner. I'd seen paper like this before in the glassed-in display cases at Gray Witch Union. I'd even seen this paper once in my own childhood home, wallpaper tight against the sides of that pretty little box my mother had emptied her savings to obtain after Daddy left us. Not once had I ever seen it written on.

I stumbled back a few steps, but the notes just kept on coming. Fern fronds and grasshopper antennae flying from beneath my door. Three pages had fluttered through.

"Go on. Pick them up," Barry said. "Don't be afraid." His voice was quiet now. I could almost feel his hands press against the other side of the door, his breath warm against the fading paint.

I bent down, glancing over the papers.

It's all right, the first note said. *I'll just listen, said the second. Trust and faith are fine, said the third. You should try them. I dreamt about you last night, not even knowing your name.*

A fourth sheet of paper followed. I caught it before it even had a chance to settle. *Perhaps I can tell you my name,* it said. *Would that help?*

In the end, I opened the door, just an inch or two, and peered into the hallway. Tears were still leaking from my eyes. I think I even hiccupped a time or two.

"Barry," he said. He held a wooden box in one outstretched hand. "My name is Barry." I noticed his gray eyes even then, stormy-ocean gray. I noticed the box as well: a pattern of beetles with half-open wings burned across its surface, a musky smell rising from the wood. Beautiful. Yet Barry's box was sized all wrong. It was the kind of box that would sit empty by morning, the contents dissipated instead of contained. It was the kind of box a Gray Witch might carry if she was so inclined, a personal disposal unit, a place to stop the drowning. No way could I afford a box like that.

"Barry," he said again. He continued to hold out the box. "Consider it an early birthday present."

I kept my own hands at my sides. "But you don't even know when I was born."

"That's okay."

"What about—"

"Go ahead. Open it."

The edge of my right hand grazed his palm as I lifted the box toward me.

That's when he smiled. Turns out he's the kind of man who likes to see his boxes used.

Turns out, in the end, I'm no different.

Earlier this evening we sat across from each other at the dining table. My eyes were fixed on Barry and his computer, the way his fingers flew across the keyboard.

"Barry, we paid all that money."

Barry stayed quiet, reading the contents of the screen.

"We should ask for it back or maybe ask for a new spell. The first one didn't even last half a year." I fiddled with my untouched pasta. It was already cold.

"Barry, I just think—"

"Gray Witches, Celia," he snapped. "I may not be a goddamn Witch, but Mom didn't raise an idiot. I'm not going to ask for our money back just before they cast my spell."

"Look, what if it happens to you?" I dug into my jeans pocket, fishing for a Kleenex. "Barry?" I blotted the water from my cheeks. "What if it doesn't stick?"

"That's not gonna happen," he muttered. Then, finally, he looked up from his screen. His face was like a rain cloud, almost full to bursting with feelings. Despite his best efforts, I knew it wouldn't last. Barry never felt anything in the least bit heavy for more than a minute or two.

"Barry—"

"You probably did something to break it, anyway," he said. "Gray Witches don't make mistakes." And then he stood up and headed for the hallway. After a moment, I heard the workshop door slam.

"But you don't care what the Gray Witches think of you. That's what you said," I screamed at the closed door. "Right, Barry? Right?" All I got was silence.

My own permanent Gray Witch Vacation cost $2,200 and the death of one mid-level executive. It lasted only three months.

The decision to purchase the spell was easily made. I had just finished sprinting up all three flights of stairs, newspaper in hand, only to stumble into the gloom of our apartment. Barry stood in our living room, holding his cup of coffee.

"Barry—" I started.

I held up the newspaper, pointing to a photograph of a man in midair, falling from the South End Bridge. "Third Jumper This Year" the headline read. Inside the picture was a small inset, a portrait of a smiling thirty-something-year-old man in a suit and tie. He had very even teeth.

"Barry, I know him," I said.

"So . . . ."

It was early evening. I'd been working the stall all day. By the looks of things, Barry had just got up. His fine, brown hair was mussed, his face still creased and bleary.

"He came by my stall yesterday," I said. I set the paper on our dining table and inspected the picture one more time. The image of the bridge was too grainy to make out the man's expression. It must have been shot at a distance. "He bought two boxes. Bought two the week before as well."

"Did you tell him—" Barry started as he wandered closer.

I cut him off. "Of course, I told him the boxes wouldn't keep. I always tell my customers."

"Well, it sure looks like you messed something up." He reached over and turned the newspaper in his direction. My hands shook. I placed my palms on the tabletop, as my stomach roiled and twisted. Barry's expression, as he watched me, held the same slightly puzzled look I used to love so much. Right then, I couldn't stand it.

After that, there wasn't much Barry could do. Despite all his cajoling, I refused to return to my stall. In the end, despite my job and the money, he agreed to hand over our savings to the Gray Witch Union and purchase my permanent Gray Witch Vacation. He even came with me, though he wasn't happy about any of it: the trip, the box, the loss of income this "whim" of mine was going to engender. Still, the two of us, the Witch's son and the Sadness Carrier, walked across the Market and up the Union steps together for the second time.

I don't think either of us expected any favors, and we didn't get any. We stood in line on those gray, granite steps. We politely waited our turn, and then, after I explained to the assigned Witch exactly how I wanted to feel, we received my very own petal-and-limb box. Barry, like always, watched while I opened the lid. That box was supposed to fix everything. And, for a few months, it did.

Every year on my birthday Barry gives me exactly the same gift, his own handcrafted, Gray Witch box. Even this year, just weeks after we'd spent all that money on my Gray Witch happiness, he presented me with my usual birthday present. The box was etched all over with carapaces. Spiders' eyes watched me as I opened the lid. Spiders' eyes and Barry.

I didn't suspect a thing. Despite Barry's grumbling, I trusted him. Trust is something, it seems, I give out for free. Like love. And tenderness. I could never be a Gray Witch.

Boxes all work the same way. First there is the initial spell. The carrier or Witch, whoever it is, has to fill the interior. Then it's all on the new owner. They decide when to open the lid. For me, though, it's the limb-and-petal paper that is the true magic.

With the paper, there's always that moment when the glue melts and the limbs, the haemolymph, and the dead leaves and petals coalesce, the mosaic inhaled by the recipient like a cloud creature settling into their lungs. Sometimes, after opening one of Barry's boxes, my eyes would burn with iridescent mist for minutes afterward.

This year on my birthday, innocent me, I laughed as the black-and-yellow striped insect rose from the remains of Barry's box. Its wings were bluish-violet and fringed like the petals of an aster. I leaned in to get a closer look. I'd never seen an actual, fully formed creature emerge before.

"A hover fly," Barry said. "Mixed with a few flowers. It just looks like it can jab you."

I must have given him an odd look, because he kept on talking, either that, or he was nervous.

"Hover flies don't sting. They eat aphids and other plant suckers," he explained as though that made all the sense in the world. And somehow, in that moment, it did.

I laughed again and even opened the window, letting the striped insect with the flower wings find its way out of our apartment. The two of us, Barry and I, stood by the window and watched the almost-wasp disappear into the city.

"How?" I asked. I turned to Barry, amazed all over again by the magic.

"Happy birthday," was his only reply.

That man has more of a sense of humor than he lets on.

It took two lines on a receipt, a dollar amount and a date, for me to recognize Barry's betrayal.

After all the screaming and the slamming doors and the breakfast nobody ate, Barry took off for the Union. I headed straight to our bedroom. That's where I found the receipt: on top of one of my cardboard boxes, the box that holds the only two Gray Witch receipts I've ever owned—Mother's and mine. *Gray Witch Ltd.* was printed right on the top along with the price and a detailed description. It was the cost that caught my eye first: $2,200. It was printed next to the word *Total*. The same amount Barry was supposedly about to spend on his own Gray Witch Vacation. The same amount we had spent on my original spell.

Why had Barry taken out my receipt? That was my first thought. Then I looked more closely. The date on the receipt was all wrong. It was from last year, sure, but weeks after my own procedure. In fact, the date was exactly two days before my birthday: September 12th.

My Barry went down to the Gray Witch Union just two days before my birthday and spent $2,200. My Barry bought me a present I didn't even know I had. That black-and-yellow striped insect with the petal wings? The item's description made everything clear. That supposed hover fly was a wasp after all. *Unbinding Spell*, the receipt said. Break me apart spell. Take away my happiness spell. It seemed Barry had spent his own Gray Witch money months ago to undo everything the Gray Witches had just fixed. He'd turned my happiness into a wasp and watched as it flew away.

And, now, Barry had left the receipt out where I was sure to find it. He'd set me up. Tears weren't even close to an adequate response.

After three years, Barry had trained me well. I knew everything I needed was in his workshop. And Barry? Well, Barry was out. He'd run down to the Hall to buy his own Gray Witch Vacation. At least that's what he said. Couldn't imagine anything less likely. All that talk of purchasing a little "joy" was just a ruse. We both knew joy was never going to be enough. Barry was waiting until I built my own pretty little box, one made just for him.

I'm standing in the workshop entrance, clutching the receipt in my right hand. The room is a cacophony of hisses, whirs and scrambling legs. In the middle of the room stands a long bench, though the majority of the floor space is reserved for the papermaking: the presses and sieves. Overhead, long stems full of drying leaves and petals hang from a wooden rack.

The long cedar boards sit in the far right corner. Expensive wood. Barry must have been certain they'd be used.

I set the receipt on Barry's bench and pull out the first board. Already, I can tell there is just enough cedar to frame the box I have in mind. I have one human-sized box to build. One body box to line with all of Barry's limb-and-petal paper. Of course, the paper isn't the only thing I need. Glue. I'll have to make more glue.

I close my eyes for a moment, then open the cricket cage and drop a handful into one of Barry's presses. After the crickets come the brown wood spiders. When I'm sure the press's interior can hold no more, I push down on the handle, putting all my weight against the metal, then I add the clear, greenish contents of the collecting jar to the glue pot and start all over again. Not even Barry has ever lined a box this large.

I thought the liquid would smell, but there is barely any scent at all. It is the press's screen that nearly does me in. Carapaces and leg joints shudder as I flick the contents of the screen onto the floor. Barry's tidy workshop is littered with dead insect debris.

I push on as the tears finally start. I'm not sure if it's sadness or rage. My eyes stream either way. Meanwhile my mouth mutters nonsense words that I only half-hear. Words about cracked and broken and making him feel *something*.

I've collected enough haemolymph. I cut swaths of elder blossom and honeysuckle from the overhead racks, drop them into the metal brazier along with a match. When the fire has banked, I scoop up the still-hot ashes. My fingertips are red. I can feel them throbbing. It's as though all my blood wants to push its way outward.

Not yet.

I tip the ashes into the pot of haemolymph and stir. The greenish liquid turns a putty-gray.

Finally, it's time to construct the box. I know that, after the glue, the box itself will be no problem. Pretty interlocking joints may mark a good craftsman, but a staple gun can work just as well. The magic is in the contents. The contents and, if you are very lucky, if you have someone like Barry, someone, it turns out, like me to press the paper into place, someone to sketch her own ashen face and

HAPPY BIRTHDAY across the top when she's done with a burning-hot coal, then all the better.

First, though, I have to take care of the blood. It's the last step—the glue requires it.

Barry has a special block plane for finish work. The glue jar rests nearby along with the receipt. I hold my left arm above the glass. My veins look so small, blue lines that quickly disappear below the surface. I raise the metal plane, jab down, test the angle. Even that small cut stings. I raise my right hand higher and bring the blade down again, a straight line up my arm, starting at my wrist. I can't help myself; I close my eyes long before the blade finishes its cutting.

I'm tired.

The slash along my arm has been dripping for almost an hour. The box is completely lined. All that's left is to climb inside and press the receipt against the lid. My legs feel somehow disconnected from the rest of my body. I slump rather than step inside the narrow enclosure, banging my bleeding arm against the box as I sit down. Despite all the glue I've brushed onto the paper, I can see that a few of the corners are already curling up. I run my trembling left arm along the edges, smoothing the paper with my blood, making sure the seams stay in place, then I curl my body into the shape of a question mark. The tears have stopped; all that is left is a strange, buzzing nausea. I glance around the workshop. Finally, I reach up and pull the lid down, sealing that final square of paper just above my head.

It's dim inside Barry's box but not entirely black; light creeps in from the edges between the boards. Even with the light, it's hard to separate my limbs from the paper they press against. It's almost as though I am dissolving into the paper itself.

Doesn't matter.

The buzzing feels louder now, the paper like half-tattered wings. All I have to do is wait. Wait for Barry to finally return, wait for that lid to finally rise and for my reborn self to crawl, all petal-softened chitin and twitching antennae, to the window ledge and fly. If I know nothing else, I know that, before the magic ends, Barry's Gray Witch eyes will be the ones that finally cry.

Two Will Walk With You

~ Grá Linnaea

Ayu ran, knowing running was pointless, a pale fantasy in her head of somehow reaching her family. She'd stolen rough hemp clothes from the kitchens and stashed her acolyte robes in an iron tetsunabe.

She was small for a girl of seventeen, but her thin frame had barely fit between the iron bars covering the kitchen window. There was little sound when she dropped into the shoutaku that acted as a moat surrounding Kirche Guregorī. The waste and rot in the marsh water burned her eyes. The reeking clothes hung heavy as she clawed her way up the outside edge of the marsh.

She dared a last look behind her. The water, black as oil, made her think of punishments to come. The looming stone walls blocked the stars.

It would take nine days on foot to reach her village in Tottori, a meaningless journey even if it were the next village over from Kyoto. She should have awaited punishment at the order, or killed herself.

She stumbled over the sharp jutting stones that peppered the grounds beside the marshy moat. The brand below her neck flared and blistered the skin around it. She'd almost forgotten; If she didn't subdue the nearby protection spells, the brand would blaze white hot till she was a screaming pile of undying bones.

Crouching and squinting, she spied a bit of the stone marker. Carved in the stone, the top edge of Archangel Simiel's glyph poked through the low kusa plants.

It took many breaths to still her mind enough to invoke Archangel Oriphiel, *"Auxilium maneat ira incantatores."*

Oriphiel's control spell would hopefully give her a few seconds safety from the embedded Simiel destruction spell. An ember of fear lit in the back of her mind. She'd never tried an Oriphiel incantation. She ran.

Clouds obscured the moon, but the magical glow of the illuminated crucifixes adorning Kirche Guregorī's high towers lit the ground around her. Ayu imagined the keep's windows behind her, like eyes squinting in amusement at her hopeless flight.

Up ahead was a copse of katsura trees. Beyond that lay Guregorī's rice fields. She could follow the trees along the edge of the fields to the road into Kyoto, but instinct screamed that she run in a straight line, get as far from Guregorī as possible.

A cold gust made the trees ripple, and long-forgotten memories bubbled painfully inside her. As a child, she'd collected the red-green leaves like little coins, woven the stems into a circle. Even though it wasn't a proper offering, Mother had let her leave the rings on the kamidana. Ayu couldn't remember a single Shinto prayer from her childhood.

She pushed the painful memories deep down inside. She'd been in the order so long, surrounded by Latin and Christian saints, it was hard to remember that outside the grounds was all of Japan.

She stole another glance behind her. Kirche Guregorī still blocked the sky, but to the side of the keep she could see just a bit of Biwa Lake glinting in the rare slices of moonlight stealing through the clouds.

Guregorī was named for her . . . for the Christian's pope. It was hard to believe it had been 1576, only thirteen years ago, when the Christian priests arrived in Kyoto. Oda Nobunaga, captivated by their magic and power, used shogunate funds to build them the keep. Two years later, Ayu was taken along with other promising Japanese children to train in the ways of Christian spells.

Some said Nobunaga hoped to wield Christian power to rule all the daimyo as shogun. What grim irony that now in 1589 Christian magicians ruled the entire Kyoto prefecture.

As Ayu entered the woods, the smell of katsura leaves brought another flood of memories. Were Mother and Father still in Tottori? She'd have to travel south along Biwa Lake to reach the eastern road.

A bitter smile twisted her mouth. Her eighteenth birthday was a few days away. It had been nearly seven years since the order took her from her parents.

Eleven-year-old Ayu had quickly learned the Order's primary law. She was theirs. Once inducted, she was never to leave.

She'd been there a day when the Christian priest who became her master wove the spell that branded Ayu just below her neck. Without thinking, she touched the spot. She knew the spell now. Archangel Oriphiel's control glyph felt warm under the cold hemp.

To be an acolyte was to live in loneliness. They were to be silent unless addressed by a master. They each slept in a room the size of a soaking tub and were kept away from each other to reduce the danger of friendships or romance.

Ayu had felt little danger of romance in the past seven years. The boys were vile and spotty. The girls brought confusing emotions for her, overwhelming and frightening.

Sappho. Lesbia. She might not have had words for her feelings if not for the priest's dire warnings.

Order punishments flooded her head. Touching another student cost thirty strokes with a cane. Stealing cost three days wearing a shame-belt. Ayu still carried scars circling her waist from its metal hooks. An acolyte caught in a lie was locked in a hole with a wraith.

She wrapped one hand in the other. Running away cost a finger.

Acolytes stopped being property when they graduated into full order members, blessed by God. They'd receive their new Latin name. They received land and slaves, places in the growing Christian power structure. They still could never see their old family again; they could never marry or have children.

Ayu had dutifully abandoned Shinto. She'd come to truly believe in the Great Hierarchy long before she'd learned to cast her first spell. She still remembered the thrill of Archangel Gabriel's communication spell translating ancient Latin to kanji. Her commitment to the order became her entire world. She knew her place.

And yet, instead of waiting with her master's cooling body, she picked through the dense copse of black trees, too panicked to notice the thorns that poked through the stolen shirt and scratched her skin.

Years earlier an acolyte killed another child. She'd his soul ripped from his body and sealed in an iron doll.

But none of the order's punishments were so horrifying as the one reserved for those who killed a master priest.

The Socius.

Even the priests spoke of the spell in whispered tones. Ayu had heard that it combined each archangel's designation: control and destruction, friendship and vengeance, Healing, communication and creation. It took seven priests, seven archangels to create the Socius demon.

The students who dared whisper of it called it *Tomo.* Companion.

The demon was formed of pure nothingness. If they put the Tomo on her, nothing would matter anymore. Tomo existed solely for its target. It would never rest.

She'd once glimpsed the Socius spell in an illuminated text. It was surprisingly fast to create. The words were fuzzy, except for the last two, said in unison by all seven castors. *Vocato comite.*

"Deus meus." She froze in place and leaned against a tree.

She put her head against the bark and prayed to God for forgiveness. *Averte faciem tuam a peccatis nostris, Domine, et omnes iniquitates meas dele.*

She wished she could remember the small gods from her childhood, but she'd been in the order far too long.

Realization dawned on her slowly. Ice ran down her spine.

The order might slaughter her entire family.

She'd once had to watch a boy's parents transformed into demons. All the acolytes stood frozen in the keep's courtyard, forced to watch as his own family set upon him. She'd never learned his name. They'd never even told them his crime.

She turned back, still frozen by indecision. She could face the order, or escape and get word to her family.

"O, Deus." If she returned, they might drag in her family and kill them in front of her before they meted out her punishment.

Just ahead, through the trees, she saw the rice fields on the other side of a stream. Would her family remember her? She couldn't remember their faces.

She pushed away from the tree and scrambled into the stream. It swirled around her calves. Cold mud sucked at her feet.

She stepped into a hole in the riverbed and fell, swallowing a mouthful of muddy water before she broke the surface again. She scrambled, sputtering, guessing at the direction of the opposite shore.

Once out from the water, she passed a twisted momi tree and was in the open rice field. The clouds finally broke, and the rows of rice paddies sparkled in the moonlight. In the distance, the smoky lights of Kyoto city created a dim sunset on the horizon. Just across the field lay the northern road, stretching away from the order.

The only possible decision was clear. She broke into a run along a path between two rice trenches. She would steal a cart and travel west to her family, warn them to pack and run.

She made it nearly halfway through the tall rice grass when the words swirled through her head. Seven voices. Seven Archangels.

Vocato comite.

Something passed her leg, fast and wet, like liquid wind.

She blinked, and the Tomo was before her.

Her feet just stopped. She couldn't even register her fear before the Tomo rose from the ground. It raised in the form of a scarecrow, hands and head drooping. The black conical outline of a sugegasa hat on its head. It hung like a dead thing, inches above the dewy grass as if held by an invisible cross.

Neither she nor the horrible thing moved. The world around her fell silent.

All the power drained out of Ayu's muscles, and she fell to her knees in the muck.

She was dead. The Tomo would be draw out the pain until it felt like forever. She hadn't been aware that she'd started crying, but streams of tears dripped from her face.

So soon. She would never see her family again.

The scarecrow's head lifted; its neck crackled like brittle leaves.

"*Ignosco.* Forgive," Ayu said.

From the dark shadow of the scarecrow's face, words bubbled. "Why do you run, girl?" Its Japanese was perfect.

Ayu lowered her head and dug her hands into the soft ground. "Clementia."

The scarecrow's arms lowered, fluidly, like melting. "Mercy? Girl, why do you run? Have you done something?"

She kept her head down, as if speaking to the dirt. "Mercy, Socius." The Latin word stuck in her mouth. "I did not mean it."

It flowed around her like tendrils, and her eyes shot open. She struggled, but the tendrils tightened like rope as its color muted and darkened until she was trapped in a web of shadow. A tendril slid up her side, and she felt hot breath next to her face, as if it was about to kiss her ear.

Mocking kindness riddled its whisper. "Girl, one does not kill an order master."

The tendrils released her arms, and she fell hard onto the muddy path. She covered her head with her hands, smearing mud in her hair. "It was self defense!"

With a wet sound, four, five mouths split open from the tendrils. When Ayu dared look up again, mouths spoke one after the other.

"One—"

"Does—"

"Not—"

Together they said, "Kill."

"Please," her words choked.

"Please," they mocked.

Ayu cried out, "Please, not now!"

One by one, the mouths smiled. A tendril snapped around her wrist and pulled her hand from her head.

"Oh, not now," one said.

Another tendril took her other hand.

"Not here," said the other.

The fear was so absolute that her mind drifted from her body, time seemed to freeze, and the silence parted to let music float in from the distance, a tinkling mist of chimes and bells.

Ayu dared look up, and found herself staring into the face of the Socius, the Tomo. It held her hand against itself, like a lover holding it to her heart. Its face was limitless black, except for a single remaining grin, a hole through which the moonlight shone. Through the gruesome smile, she saw a brightly decorated cart traveling the road far on the other side of the field. Ayu mumbled a prayer.

The hole closed. "Run, girl. Make it fun."

It made a small movement and snapped Ayu's pinkie finger. Her consciousness returned to her body, and she screamed, in fear as much as pain.

The Socius melted into the mud, dropping her arms down with it. She sank into the muck. The blackness bubbled up and caressed her hands. A sloppy wet word frothed from the ground, "Run."

Ayu ran.

Somehow she spanned the path to the road. A covered cart rattled with bells and cans, twisted iron tools and glass balls lit from within by tiny candles.

She clutched her hand to her chest. The rice field behind her lay empty.

She shouted to the driver. "Please, a ride!"

The driver startled at her voice, but pointedly ignored her. It was not safe to speak to anyone running from the direction of Kirche Guregorī.

Wind raised from behind Ayu and blew muddy hair into her eyes. For a moment, she thought it was the Socius descending on her, but when she pushed the wet hair back she just saw the cart dancing in black shadows. It slowly withdrew. With one last look back at Kirche Guregorī, she ran after the cart, veering to the open flaps in the back.

A thin old man sat inside, sitting amongst planks of wood, piles of junk and vegetables. His clothes had perhaps once been fine; now they sported patches and mendings. Next to him lay a huge backpack, pieced together from leather and fabric. It looked as big as he was.

Ayu trotted after the cart. She grabbed at the wood lip with her good hand. The man silently watched her. His eyes twinkled.

"Please sir. Aid! I beg you."

The man in the cart sneered. He hefted a large, rotten taro root and threw it. "Away! Before you anger the trader and he boots me off with you."

Ayu grabbed at the planks in the floor. Her feet dragged on the road as she tried to pull herself on. The man threw a yam that swished past her head. Despite this, she scrambled up.

Finally the man moved. He snatched a broken piece of wood and stumbled to his feet.

Ayu's breath came out in huffs against the wood planks, "There is . . . room for both of us!"

The man said nothing for a moment. A stone in the road struck Ayu's foot. Her grasp slipped.

"Ah, hell," He dropped the scrap of wood and grabbed Ayu's shirt. His other calloused hand clamped on her wrist. Grunting and straining, he pulled the girl fully into the cart. She rolled over and kicked back until she sat huffing against the canvas wall. She pulled the hemp clothes close around her neck.

"Name's Hageatama." The man sat back down next to his pack. "No conversation!" He put a protective arm on his pack and glared.

A bump in the road bounced Ayu's pinkie against her knee. She moaned softly. The man looked away.

With some awkward struggle, she used her good hand to tug at the bottom seam in her shirt till a strip ripped away.

Her mind was too fuzzy to recall one of Raphael's healing spells. Reciting a mishmash of psalms in her head, she wrapped the cloth around her broken finger. When she was finished, she looked up to see the man, Hageatama watching with keen interest.

Kirche Guregorī shrank in the distance behind them. She knew to be wary of this stranger, but soon it became difficult to keep her eyes open. As she drifted off, she sometimes thought she saw horrible shapes in the dust, but it might have been shadows in the moonlight.

She awoke in the hot dusty afternoon, startled awake by sharp poking in her ribs. Hageatama had the scrap of wood again. He looked no more pleasant than the night before.

"Running from the order, ain't ya? Acolyte, I'd wager."

She swatted the wood away. "I thought you didn't want to talk."

Hageatama crouched down to the cart floor. His knees made popping noises, and he sat back.

He studied the wood scrap and picked a piece off of it. "Bored."

Warm sunlight lit the canvas walls, filling the cart with yellow light and stifling air. Outside, the world rippled in the heat. Shadows played under trees and behind stones.

She put her head in her hands. If only last night had been a dream.

But her broken finger still throbbed. Her master was dead, and she was cursed.

Part of her welcomed the punishment. Students were expendable, masters could treat them as they liked. If Ayu had survived to become a master herself, she might have earned the right to exact revenge later, if she became powerful enough.

Had she joined the ranks of the powerful, she could have given her family anything. She rubbed her head until her stinging finger made her stop.

The Okayama daimyo himself was now a powerful Christian magician. Soon they all would be Christian. Ayu crossed herself.

Hageatama snorted, threw a yam out onto the dusty road. "Thought so. Must be sixteen, seventeen. You have the look of an acolyte."

"Eighteen, almost." Ayu closed her hands and winced, her broken finger gave another sharp reminder of the night before.

The old man looked away. He took off his hat to fan himself. Ayu almost smiled. Hageatama was an appropriate name for someone with such a hairless head.

Hageatama seemed to notice Ayu's amusement. He shot Ayu a glare. "You hold with all that Christian stuff?"

Ayu's face burned. She wanted to deny it. She had no reason to defend the order's religion. She tried to name her family's local gods, but her memory still failed her.

She looked away. "What do you believe?"

The man snorted. "Don't believe in anything."

Ayu eyed the pile of vegetables. "I'm hungry," she said.

Hageatama grunted and put his hand into the pile. He tossed a tuber at Ayu.

From his pack, he produced a honyaki dagger. "Cut off the rotten parts."

It took her most of the day to admit to herself that she could never return to Tottori. Any contact with her family would only endanger them, if they were even still alive. The best thing she could do was travel as far from them as possible. A cold grief settled in her chest. She was truly alone.

When Hageatama jumped from the cart near the forest outside Higashiomi, she followed without thinking.

The old man turned and watched her get up from the dust, a bemused confusion on his face. "I'm not looking for a puppy."

He turned into the forest. She watched his back.

She couldn't say why she felt compelled to follow the old man. He certainly wouldn't bring any protection, not from a Socius. An army couldn't help Ayu.

It took all she had to keep her knees from buckling. Soon enough she would sit down where she was. She'd wait there, frozen and hopeless until the Socius took her. She leaned toward Hageatama, feeling colder with each step he took.

The old man stopped, as if he read her thoughts. He didn't turn, but spoke loudly over his shoulder, "If running is your goal, I can see ya to the edge of Mount Ibuki. Then yer on yer own."

She took a step toward him. Mount Ibuki was east, away from her family. Her heart broke a little, but she nodded, as if he could see her. "You'll travel with me?"

Hageatama readjusted the giant pack and continued down the trail. "Bored."

They made camp under the great bamboo trees of Saimyoji Pass.

"The order will condemn anyone who helps me." She felt terrified to admit it.

"Boring talk," Hageatama waved off the warning. "Can take care of m'self."

Ayu built a fire, and Hageatama roasted each of them a large yam. As soon as he ate, he unceremoniously lay down near the far side of the fire and fell asleep, leaving Ayu alone with chirping crickets.

If she were brave, she would have abandoned the man there and then. She tried to will herself up, but she couldn't move.

Hageatama's sleeping form wavered in the hot air from the fire. It shamed her that she couldn't bring herself to sneak off. When the Socius came for her, it would certainly show Hageatama no mercy either.

She rubbed the brand below her neck. Perhaps tomorrow she'd find the courage.

Across the fire pit, the old man slept so quietly that he resembled a pile of rags set by the fire for burning.

The crackling sound of boots on leaves started quietly in the distance to her left. The crickets quieted.

Ayu was scared to move, but she felt around for the honyaki dagger the old man had lent her.

She whispered, "Hageatama!"

The old man didn't wake.

Her nerves thrummed as she wrapped her fingers around the dagger.

The sound of the footsteps grew louder until she could make out the shape of a man. She slipped the dagger behind her back and composed herself. It'd been forever since she'd had a real conversation with someone. She'd have to pretend Hageatama was her grandfather. She could say they were traveling *toward* Kyoto, rather than away from it.

The man who stepped out of woods wore a black fisherman's jacket over a loose white shirt and pants and simple shoes. The wide-brimmed straw hat on his back was well worn and would need to be replaced soon.

When her father came home from a day of fishing, Ayu had always thought the way the hat stuck out from behind his arms looked like a shield. The hat, the shirt, the jacket: all were the same as she had last seen him.

Her father had markedly aged over the last eleven years, mostly in his eyes. The grey flecks on his temples and beard made Ayu's heart hurt.

"Papa!" She jumped to her feet, leaving the dagger forgotten on the blanket. Her cheeks reddened. She was far too old to use such childish language. She bowed. "Forgive me, otousan."

Her father's face was unreadable. "It has been too long."

She felt eleven again. The last seven years fell away—a long nightmare, and she'd just awakened. She tripped as she rushed to him.

If Hageatama ever woke up, she'd introduce them. Maybe father could give him a coin. But first she needed her father to hold her like she was eleven, to tell her that she wouldn't ever feel afraid again.

She was nearly to him when his arm shot out like a spear. "Don't come near me!"

She almost fell while stopping herself. "What is the matter, father?"

His face was hard with disgust. "No daughter of mine is a *dui shi*. You are unclean."

Dui Shi? She only vaguely knew the term. Imperial courtesans, two women who behaved as husband and wife. She was speechless, lost in confusion and shame.

She jumped back when her father spit on the ground at her feet. "You purport yourself as would a prostitute."

She put out her arms. "Why would you say this, father?" She motioned helplessly back in the direction of Kyoto. "I live in a single room. I haven't touched another person in seven years." *At least not in kindness.* She'd been abused countless times, had been forced to fight other acolytes. She'd struck out at her master, just the once.

Her father crossed his arms. "You deny how you feel in your heart?"

Her mind spun. How could he know? She'd never spoken of it to anyone. Had she shown signs as a child?

"It's no surprise you became a murderer."

A hollow cold settled into her chest. "How did you find me, father?" She took a step back. "How did you travel all this way?"

His face suddenly fell into the kindest smile. "Should a father not come to his daughter's aid?" It was the exact smile she'd remembered from her childhood. Perfect.

She took another step back, onto her blanket. "How did you know I was in trouble?"

The firelight wavered, as if by a breeze. A single snap of the fire echoed throughout the forest. Every other sound around them had hushed.

Her father's laugh reminded her of her mother and he, of summers and chores, sisters and brothers. Her heart broke.

The fire crackled once, twice, then its sound faded until her ears popped. Complete silence closed around her until the only sound left was of her heart pounding faster and faster.

Her father opened his arms as if to hug her, and he exploded into a cloud of sticky oil. She threw her arms up, but nothing struck her. When she brought them back down, the small clearing was free of any sign of the Socius impersonating her father.

She dropped down to the blanket and snatched up the dagger. A jolt from her broken pinkie finger ran up her arm.

A wet sound bubbled behind her. She stood and spun, clutching the dagger before her.

The flickering firelight turned the woods into an army of dancing shadows.

She wanted to cry out to Hageatama but her voice stuck in her throat. The bubbling sound pitched up and raced in a circle around the camp. Once, twice.

Looking for something, anything to defend herself with, she spied a long stick jutting from the fire. She inched her hand toward it.

A voice whispered from the woods, "Run, girl, run."

The sound spun again until laughter bubbled behind the sleeping old man.

The voice said, "Run, young one. Maybe I will feast on the old man. Maybe that will give you time to get away." A hundred white smiles opened in the darkness like a flock of moths.

She took two steps back. She almost ran.

The old man had helped her. Would she repay his kindness by abandoning him?

She dropped to the fire and jerked out the flaming stick.

"Uriel ne depellerent." The incantation easily fell from her mouth, better than she'd ever done. She heaved the torch like a comet into the woods. As it struck, the surrounding bamboo trees lit as if infused with oil. She ran around the campfire to stand between the old man and the burning woods, holding out the dagger. A sardonic smile betrayed her. As if the tiny dagger meant anything to the Socius.

Its voice boomed from the center of the burning trees. "Why not run, girl? Your death won't save him from me."

She wove the knife through the air. "Raguelis tueri."

A translucent bubble formed around the sleeping old man. It was the one protection spell she knew, pitifully weak.

She smiled at the demon with bravado she didn't feel. "When you kill me, you cease to exist. I know how your conjuration works."

"Hmmm." The flames rippled.

In an instant, the flaming trees blinked out. Her ears popped again as the bubbling sound swept away. Her heartbeat pounded in her ears until the normal noises of the forest resumed.

It seemed like hours that she stood there with the pathetic dagger clutched in her hand. The Socius didn't return.

The old man rustled behind her. "It won't come twice in a single night."

She dropped the dagger to her side and turned. Her weak shield had already dissipated.

Hageatama stared at her. He pushed himself up with a hand on his backpack.

Ayu said, "We must part ways."

Hageatama nodded and considered her for many moments before he said, "Why would you sacrifice yourself to defend me?"

The strength went out of Ayu. She stumbled back to her side of the fire and collapsed onto her blanket.

After a moment, she said. "I'll not lay my burdens on you. You deserve life more than I do."

The old man's cheeks reddened, he lay silently as if unable to think of a proper response.

Ayu lay her head down on the leaves and closed her eyes. "We'll part ways in the morning."

Hageatama said, "Perhaps," and rolled over.

They trudged silently through the wet of the Azusakawachi swamplands toward the Maibara valley. The sun shone harshly, reflecting rainbows off the misty water. Canary grass grew close and sodden to the path they forged. Neither had spoken since the night before.

Midday Hageatama broke the silence. "You have a Tomo on you, girl."

Ayu said nothing. They walked further.

"The Socius." Hageatama butchered the Latin. "The Tomo. No one escapes." He poked his walking stick at her back.

Ayu spun and slapped the stick away. "I know!" Her voice cracked. "No one knows more than I do! The Socius is woven to my soul, it won't stop—"

Hageatama cut her off, his voice loud and gentle. "It *can't* stop. It is made *from* your soul. It doesn't have one of its own." He pointed a dirty nail at Ayu. "And you can't escape."

She fought not to cry. "Then why aren't I dead?"

She knew, *knew* that the Socius had showed her father *exactly* as he looked now. Had it visited him? Was father dead? Not knowing made the pain a thousand times worse.

Hageatama glared at the sky, as if he'd like to cut it open. "A Tomo might take years to kill you. It appears as family, it might come to you as an old friend, or lover, or both." He threw the stick into the water. "Hell, *I* might be the Tomo as far as you will ever know."

All the strength went out of Ayu. She sat down on the wet path and put her face in her hands. "I know, I know, I know."

The old man stepped back, made himself busy pulling and breaking grass fronds.

Ayu prayed with her head down. *Averte faciem tuam a . . .* Even the words of her daily prayer had left her. She sat in miserable silence.

A new, tiny seed of fear formed in her mind. She said, "Why do you know so much?"

The old man's short laugh sounded like stones rubbing against one another. "You are not unique, girl. Fear is not reserved for acolytes. The order owns most of our nation."

Ayu's fear was replaced with a surprising feeling. "I almost feel sorry for it."

Hageatama's head shot up. "The Tomo?"

She rubbed her chest. "It must be awful not to have a soul."

The old man stood aghast. He finally snorted. "That thing will ruin every good thing in your life." He spit. "Good riddance when it's gone."

The words ran out of Ayu. For the third time, she wondered if she'd be able to get up again.

The wind pushed at the grass until it bent over. Ayu ran her hand over it. "I killed someone."

Hageatama grunted, dropped his handful of reeds. "Who?"

"My master."

The old man considered the youth for a good while. "Well, 'spect he deserved it."

Ayu Sighed. *Simiel perrexit.* It was a simple cutting spell, pure luck that it opened her master's neck. "Maybe. I don't know. I thought he'd kill me."

"Either way, what's done is done. His problems are finished now."

The sun had fallen a bit since they'd started talking. The fear that burned in her chest was becoming familiar. They hadn't covered enough ground yet.

She shook her head. "I don't know why I keep running. I should kill myself."

Hageatama waved his hand dismissively. "The order can bring you back from the dead. When they're done with you, *then* they'll let you move on."

Ayu looked up into the old man's face.

He smiled, maybe for the first time since she met him. "Maybe they'll just forget about you." His smile made the fear fall away, just a bit.

Then the fear clamped down even harder. Hope was more painful than fear, and would soon vanish.

"How do you know so much about the order?" She wiped her forehead. "I don't know anything about you."

Hageatama pulled her to her feet. "None of your business."

She considered demanding Hageatama share *something* about his life. But what did it matter, what did anything?

"It's strange to have nothing to look forward to." She wondered if she'd join her ancestors or be with the Christian God.

Neither seemed possible at the moment. "I wish I remembered the old prayers."

The words seemed to give Hageatama pause. He brushed mud off her sleeves, considered her a moment before saying, "Turn and face the water with me."

She was confused for a moment, but she did as she was told.

"Right hand over left, as if you have an egg in your hand." He demonstrated.

Seven years fell away in an instant for Ayu. The prayer came back to her. *Misogi O Harai.* Purification practice.

Hageatama's voice resonated in her ears. "Harae do no O Kami."

Together, they bowed twice, clapped twice and bowed again.

After the Furitame, he took them through the Torifune. They shouted the Otakebi and Okorobi, breathed deep the Ibuki undo, and finally performed Nyusui.

The sun was lower when they finished, but Ayu found herself at peace for the first time she could remember.

In the cloudless sky a distant chuhi crossed the sun, searching for a swallow or a rabbit.

The order taught that only the worthy moved on to paradise. Ayu smiled. "I'll deal with heaven when I get there."

Hageatama hefted his backpack. "You have what you have." He walked on ahead.

They didn't see the Socius again.

Except Ayu did in her dreams. She woke screaming some nights, and Hageatama shook her until she was calm. One night she dreamed that Hageatama *was* the Socius. In the dream, his face split, and his bones became blades that sliced into her.

She'd nearly left him that night. She didn't speak of it the next day.

The random course across the Maibara valley, through the Tochinoki pass and over Mount Ibuki took them three weeks. Ayu's skin darkened in the sun. Her legs grew strong.

In the foothills near Tenmayama, they stopped to make their afternoon meal. They had walked all morning, and Ayu hadn't realized she'd fallen asleep by the cook fire until the smell of rice woke her.

Hageatama sat with his back to her, barely visible from behind his great pack.

She laughed. "Old man, find us some meat."

Hageatama was silent.

She got up to see if he was asleep as well.

She was a few steps away when he said, "We'll part ways soon."

For a moment, she thought she'd misheard him. Ice ran down her belly. She swallowed.

Over the weeks, she'd told herself again and again that they'd part eventually. It was the only way to ensure Hageatama's safety.

But they'd traveled so long together—she'd grown used to Hageatama's company. She'd told herself that if he chose to go, she'd accept the choice with dignity.

Still, she ran through embarrassing feelings of betrayal and guilt and confusion. She started to speak a number of times, but she didn't know what she wanted to say.

Hageatama answered the unasked question. "It's just time, I suppose." His voice cracked, and he cleared his throat. "You'd be better off without me."

She finally found her voice. "That's not true!"

He stood. "I'll snare us a rabbit," and with that he walked off.

Feelings came in a whirl, and she couldn't pin any single one down. Her heart pinched. The reality of her aloneness settled like a fog, so much worse than the many weeks before.

Dignity be damned. She ran around the boulder Hageatama had just circled. She had her hands out with her palms up. "There's no need to be hasty . . ."

Hageatama lay face down in the sand.

His body looked tiny, overshadowed by the Socius, a floating mass of black thorns and spikes.

The darkness split into an enormous sharp grin. "Run, girl!"

"Hageatama!" Ayu's mind raced through the few offensive spells she knew.

The Socius quivered. A rational part of her brain told her to run, that Hageatama was already dead. The bolder might delay the Socius enough for her to get away.

A tiny voice in the back of her head whispered, *what if Hageatama is the Socius? This is the perfect trap.*

"Simiel perrexit." The cutting spell burned in her fingers, but she'd need to be close to use it.

"Simiel interitus!" Power drew in to her, and she leaped at the Socius.

Three spikes shot out and pierced her shoulder, wrist and leg. She screamed in agony and the unfinished spell dissipated into the air around her.

Deus praeter mei. The only thought to break though the pain was to hope it would be quick. She knew that it wouldn't.

"The old one is already dead." The Socius chuckled, making the spikes vibrate inside Ayu.

Through the haze of her suffering, Ayu saw Hageatama's still form beneath her.

"What have you lost, girl?" The Socius lifted Ayu up to its mouth. The spikes twisted in her and she shuddered.

"What have you lost, a protector?" The horrible mouth exuded decay. "A confidant?"

Even through the pain, Ayu could hear confusion in the Socius's voice. It expected an answer.

She shook her head.

The three spikes flicked out of her, and she dropped painfully to the sand. Hageatama lay a foot away from her face.

"Or were you just lonely?" Contempt burned in the Socius's words.

Ayu screamed, "No!" With the last of her strength, she pushed herself up and threw herself over Hageatama. Blood ran from her shoulder onto the old man's face. She collapsed against him and cried into Hageatama's shirt, waiting for death to rain down.

She didn't know how long she cried. But when death didn't come, she lifted her head. Hageatama lay still on the ground. The quivering mass of thorns still hovered above her, as if it still waited for her answer.

"Enough play for now. You will see me again." And it was gone.

Ayu's vision darkened. She collapsed again onto Hageatama's chest. She held the old man, squeezed Hageatama as hard as she was able.

At first she heard nothing, but then she found the minute heartbeat, slow and deep in Hageatama's chest.

She nearly lost Hageatama because the spells wouldn't stay in her head anymore.

She stabilized him with a weak *Mederi huic Raphael* and managed an approximation of *Raphael carnem meam* on herself before she passed out from blood loss.

The first night she'd just barely been able to drag herself to their supplies. She wrapped her wounds and kept Hageatama warm through the night with her body.

Hageatama didn't awake the next morning, but Ayu had enough strength to gather a pitiful few edible plants and some water from a nearby stream. She dripped liquid into Hageatama's mouth with a piece of cloth.

This went on until the fifth day, when Hageatama finally woke. Ayu cried and screamed.

She hurt too much to dance, but she laughed as she fed him water from a cup.

His first words came out cracked and dry. "Don't be happy. That's what it wants. It's just a setup to knock you down again."

She dribbled some more water in his mouth. "I can't help it."

He shook his head. "I think you may be in love with me, young one."

She spilled water on his chin. "I . . ." She wiped it off with her sleeve. "I don't think I can love you that way."

His face tightened. "I was joking, girl."

When the old man could walk again, Ayu made him promise not to leave. She swore to look after him. Hageatama waved dismissively, but didn't argue.

It took them almost a year to travel all the way northeast to the Jyoshin-etsu Mountains. Each village they came upon put them further from news of the order. Each time they stopped, the longer they stayed.

On the day of her nineteenth birthday, in the small village of Ojiya, Ayu looked out into the ocean and then up to the brilliant white peak of Jyoshin-etsu. "It's time to set roots."

Hageatama followed her gaze. He frowned. "And the Socius?"

Ayu shrugged. "I can barely remember it." They hadn't seen the Socius since they'd healed from its attack so long ago. "Running, not running—what's the difference?"

Hageatama frowned at the red enameled bridge that headed the path into Ojiya. "Don't want people to get hurt."

Ayu pointed past the far edge of the buildings, next to a copse of trees. "We'll live there. If the Socius comes for me, I'll lead it into the woods, and all will be done with."

Hageatama looked to argue, but Ayu dropped her backpack into the dirt. She smiled. The dusty pack was nearly as large as Hageatama's. "And then you may have my things."

Hageatama's face froze, and then he shook with laughter. He swung his own backpack in a circle, taking in the coast over the western hills, and the Jyoshin-etsu Mountains, surrounding the town on three sides. The buildings were old, bamboo and maple, washed by the sun.

"It's as good a village as any." He sat on a stone with an air of sadness, as if all the weariness of the road had just caught up with him.

They slept in a stable. The people of Ojiya treated them with careful kindness. The quiet Shinto folk had never had a direct interaction with the Christians, and it had been many years since they'd heard news. An unaffiliated magic-worker wasn't unheard of this far north, and after two weeks, Ayu was allowed to work the small magics she still remembered in the izakaya for sake and food.

Hageatama worked sawing planks from logs outside the stable. Every day they ate their bartered lunch together behind the izakaya.

The sun was hot, and Ayu had to shield her eyes to get a good look at the old man. "Hageatama, why do you always keep your pack nearby? I thought we agreed to settle."

Hageatama glanced back over his shoulder at the pack. "For now. Never know."

"I've traveled enough." Ayu spoke with more bravado than she felt. "It's time to settle down."

Ichirou, who owned the izakaya, came out to shout to his daughter, "Mitsue! Get two bags of rice."

Ayu watched Mitsue's blue and black gofuku ripple as she ran across the main road. The girl was to be married to one of the stable hands the following week.

Ayu lowered her eyes, but not before she caught the flash of sadness in Hageatama's.

When she looked at him again, the sadness had disappeared. He considered her, looking hard into her eyes. "I think you would have a wife."

Ayu blushed and shook her head. "The sun has fried your brain, old man." She went back to staring at the ground.

When the silence grew impossibly long, she said, "We'll always be together, you and I. But I need other kinds of companionship too. A woman needs women friends, after all."

When she dared to look up to him, he was wiping an eye. "Damn dust."

Hageatama's face suddenly broke into a mad grin and he spoke all in a rush, "A proper life you'll have, absolutely! Friends, a house!" He lowered his voice to a whisper, "Perhaps a wife." He winked.

He jumped to his feet and grabbed his backpack with two hands, leaving Ayu confused in his wake. When she caught up to him, he stood in the center of the red enameled bridge outside of town.

"The girl says we stay, we stay!" He lifted the backpack high above his head.

Ayu yelled, "What are you doing?"

But Hageatama heaved the bag over the rail. It hit the water like a boulder. After a great splash, it was gone.

Hageatama turned his sad eyes on Ayu and said, "There now."

She reached her scarred hand out to the water. "Your pack."

He waved off the words. "Now we're not going anywhere."

Ayu was nearly twenty-one, and she made her wage as a storyteller. Her Latin faded, and the Christian magic was all but gone, but she still held onto a few magical flourishes. Ichirou expanded the izakaya to accommodate everyone who wished to rejoice in Ayu's stories. Her greatest joy came from remembering the old tales from her childhood in Tottori. She never spoke of the order.

When the local carpenter retired, Hageatama took over for him, even though Hageatama looked just as old as the man he was replacing. Together, Ayu and Hageatama built a house near the forest west of town.

On the day of Ayu's twenty-first birthday, an herb-woman drifted into town carrying enameled inro full of flowers and tinctures. Ayu was delighted to finally take part in the town gossip rather than being the subject of it.

The herb-woman, Megumi entered the izakaya while Ayu performed fire tricks. Megumi's mad green eyes glinted in the light, and she sat at a table off to Ayu's side. She lay on the table what could only be the old waterlogged remains of Hageatama's backpack.

Ayu forgot her place in the story she wove. She frowned as the stranger pulled the patches off her friend's property, making a small even pile of cloth on the table.

Thinking more of the stranger's blazing eyes then the trick she was supposed to be performing, Ayu accidentally set fire the machikata's table.

Megumi's smile made people forget they didn't know her.

It irritated Ayu that these people, who had taken more than a year to fully accept her and Hageatama, accepted Megumi as town healer in just a few days.

Ayu decided not to like this new woman.

Though it was impossible to dislike someone she never saw. Megumi seemed always busy tapping a sami drum, mixing herbs and caring for sick townsfolk. At night she was off searching the local hills for healing plants.

Ayu began to linger in places she suspected Megumi would be. She decided that she'd have to talk to the woman to have an opinion of her.

Megumi came in from the southern slope of the mountain, carrying two rods, each holding a large clay container on the end.

Ayu did her best to pretend that she just noticed Megumi as she passed. "Oh, madam healer. I could help you carry your load?" She cursed herself. The words sounded foolish. She caught herself grinning like an idiot.

Megumi's eyes sparked. "I can carry this fine, juggler."

Ayu's grin wilted a little. "Perhaps I could help you gather herbs?"

"And my name is not 'healer.'"

Megumi searched in silence along the river's edge for herbs. Ayu followed her and searched for something to say.

The wind made a ripple on the river that caught Ayu's eye. Perhaps she should ask the healer where she found Hageatama's backpack. It was a natural topic of conversation. Perhaps the healer had some of Hageatama's things.

When Ayu opened her mouth, she was stopped short by Megumi staring at her.

Megumi said, "Magic-jester, you will fare better with directness."

"Uh, yes . . ." Ayu's mind spun. She couldn't think directly, much less speak it.

Megumi put her hands on her hips. "Ask me to watch the sunset with you up at Jyoshin-etsu view."

"Um . . ."

Megumi's eyes glinted in the falling sunlight. "Say, 'I'd be honored to accompany you to the ridge tonight.'"

It took Ayu three tries, but she did.

"Good. Now know this, I like the looks of you fine, but we have to become proper friends before anything, understand?"

Ayu did something similar to a nod.

The sun flared red and brilliant at twilight. Ayu brought a blanket for each of them, but Megumi left hers folded on the ground.

They'd walked in silence since they met in front of Ichirou's izakaya.

The sun became a blinding crown behind Jyoshin-etsu's peak, and Ayu realized that soon they'd have to leave. Her heart hurt a bit.

The next realization was a surprise, but it wasn't fear that settled into Ayu's heart, not really.

She looked over at Megumi's profile, the woman's face rapt as she took in every last second of the dying day.

An old familiar voice spoke in the back of Ayu's head: *this is probably the one who will kill me.*

Megumi looked over for a second. Her eyes crinkled as she smiled, and then she went back to looking at the sunset.

Ayu considered Megumi. Her heart fluttered.

This might be the one who kills me, but I can live with that.

No one acknowledged Ayu and Megumi, at least not out loud. It wasn't as if they were married in the village temple. No one admitted to reciting prayers to the great goddess Amaterasu.

Megumi simply moved into Ayu and Hageatama's house. Some folk brought onigiri and a straw broom. Village women jokingly called their house *Shimai No Ie*, "sister-house."

In private, Ayu silently thanked the little gods back in Tottori and asked the Christians' Lord to bless and forgive her strange union. Even after the horrors of the order, she found she couldn't totally let go of her God.

Come festival day, Megumi herself looked like a silent goddess in her kimono and tsunokakushi headdress. None of them had family to join together in Yui-no, so the Ojiya folk announced them adopted, and the festival was said to be in their honor.

Eventually, stories of the three strangers grew old and thin and were replaced with town gossip about its own: their talented healer, their gruff old carpenter, and their magnificent storyteller.

When Ayu turned thirty, rumors drifted to the village that war raged in Kyoto. Shogun Toyotomi Hideyoshi outlawed Christianity. His forces fought the order to reunite Japan.

The people of Ojiya didn't pay much attention. Politics and war seemed far away, and they focused on their own. Better gossip was how the women pitied Ayu and Megumi for their lack of children.

Ayu mixed clay into the thatching of their roof while Megumi sewed patches over holes in their screens. "Where's Hageatama?"

Megumi kept at her mending. "He's gathering herbs for me."

Ayu shook her head. "More like ditching his responsibilities."

She threw some straw down onto Megumi's head. "Wouldn't you rather find a man to give you children?" It was a common joke between them. Megumi's line was, *No man can handle me.*

Instead, this time she furrowed her brow as she pulled the needle through rice paper. "I can't have children."

Ayu looked up. "How do you know that?"

"A healer knows."

Ayu stuffed more straw into the clay. "Who needs children. We have Hageatama."

Megumi just kept at her work, but Ayu knew she was smiling.

The realization made Ayu stop working. "Megumi?"

"What is it, wife?" A bit of irritation crept in Megumi's voice.

"I am happy."

Megumi looked up from her work, frowned like she didn't know what the word meant. She looked at Ayu a long moment before she said, "So am I."

"I've spent so long waiting for things to sour, but I no longer have it in me." Ayu laughed. "I guess I must resign myself to being content."

Megumi went back to sewing the screen. "Hageatama and I won't let any ill come to you."

Megumi opened her mouth to say something else, but instead lifted her head as if she smelled smoke. She looked toward the wooden bridge outside the village.

Ayu followed Megumi's gaze, blocking the sun with her hand. A dust cloud raced down from mountain pass, just to the west of the bridge.

Megumi's voice became hollow and strange. "Down, down from the roof."

"What is it?" Ayu looked back to the bridge. A caravan wasn't due for a month or so. "I don't see—"

Megumi had somehow climbed the wall. She hauled Ayu to her by Ayu's shirt. Both of them slid down the roof and Ayu hit the grass. Megumi's voice boomed. "Hide, girl, hide!"

Men on horses crossed the bridge into town, the shogun's official seal held by the rider's banner-holder.

Ayu still couldn't get herself to move. "The Shogun doesn't have any reason to want me."

Megumi grabbed Ayu's shirt again, dragged her practically off her feet, into the house. The screens slammed shut behind her.

Megumi's grip was like iron. Ayu struggled, but couldn't move. "Let go. If it was the order, I'd be worried. But even then, once marked by the Socius, I'm as good as—"

Megumi put three fingers on Ayu's mouth. "The shogun is winning. Christianity is outlawed. The order will soon be dead. Anyone associated with the order is under a death sentence now."

Ayu pushed down Megumi's hand. "But I *hate* the order."

"It doesn't matter. The shogun is cleansing the land." Megumi let go of her and crossed the room to an open window.

Ayu followed. "How can you know all this?"

Megumi waved off the question and closed another screen.

Ayu asked, "Where is Hageatama?"

"Don't worry. He is putting on a good face for the town." As Megumi closed the last screen the room took on a darker reddish tint.

Megumi turned, the fireplace behind her put her face in shadow. "Calm yourself. No one will give you away, and the shogun men will soon leave."

Ayu sat on the hearth and held her head. She was marked by the Socius, wanted by the order and now the shogunate. "I'm endangering everyone. I should leave Ojiya."

She stood up. "I have to get away from you and Hageatama. Perhaps if I give myself up they'll—"

Megumi slapped her, so hard Ayu's neck snapped back.

It was the only time in their many years together. Ayu gaped in disbelief.

Megumi's voice was edged like a blade. "If you give yourself up, they'll burn the town for harboring you!"

Ayu leaned against the stone of the hearth. She could smell nothing but ashes from the fireplace.

Megumi towered above her. "You are going to sit here and wait." She stabbed her finger at the screen. "When they leave everything will be fine. The order is *not* going to find you. The shogunate is *not* going to catch you. The Socius is *never* going to trouble you again."

Rage twisted Megumi's face. In that moment Ayu didn't know who she feared more.

Megumi gritted her teeth. "I am *not* going to lose you."

The shogun's men didn't find Ayu that day, nor in any of the years later. Time passed, as it does, and still no one found her. Whenever danger came near, Megumi and Hageatama kept her from harm.

By 1646 the Christian order defended only Kyushu prefecture in southern Japan. Emperor Go-Mizunoo declared Japan closed to the world.

On her seventy-sixth birthday, Ayu awoke to Megumi placing a cool cloth on Ayu's forehead. Megumi wiped away tears and smiled. Wrinkles bunched around her eyes. Hageatama, looking ancient and small, sat in the corner wringing out cloths.

Megumi stroked Ayu's hair. "We'll get to your seventy-seventh yet, my love."

Ayu coughed into a smile. "No more lies, darling."

She could barely see, but she knew Hageatama and Megumi shared something, even though neither looked at the other. Hageatama sprang from his seat to stand beside Megumi. Ayu's eyes were poor, and she welcomed the chance to look at them both. Megumi's cool hand rested against Ayu's cheek, and Ayu felt herself drifting to sleep. She blinked a few times to keep herself awake a little longer. Hageatama picked up Ayu's wrist, running his thumb around the scar left so many years ago by the Socius. He closed his eyes, as if he were listening to something inside Ayu.

Megumi and Hageatama looked to each other. They sighed, a sound like a heart breaking.

Their skin melted. Their features faded until they were two jet-black shapes, only vaguely human.

Ayu sighed. "Ah, yes. It's been so long." She looked from one to the other. "I was so afraid that if I let on, you might go."

The shape that was Hageatama nodded grimly. "We're sorry." Its black liquid arm gently wrapped her wrist and the twisted finger, broken so long ago. His touch felt like a warm bath.

Ayu's eyes glimmered in the candlelight. "You are still beautiful to me."

The warmth from Megumi's black arm went cold. "No." She formed back into her familiar shape. Her looks faded from old to young, young to old. More tears fell from her eyes only to fade dry. "The best we could do was draw it out."

Hageatama flowed back into human form as well. "We have no choice. We are Socius. Our spell forces us to take you before you die."

Ayu nodded.

Hageatama grinned. "Have to say, you grew on me. I . . . we were supposed to put you at ease and ruin you over and over." His eyes went watery. "When you sacrificed yourself for me . . . I wanted to be with you, you made me want to exist as something other than I was. When I split to become Megumi too, I . . . we came to love you in different ways."

Ayu's vision blurred, and she had trouble telling them apart. One of them said. "You made me see that I could be something, *anything*."

Hageatama propped up Ayu's head. Ayu's voice was dry, and Megumi brought her some water.

Ayu whispered. "My loves, I'll be glad to see you again in heaven."

A thin maguro bocho blade grew out of Megumi's hand. She held it low, so Ayu wouldn't see. "Yes, my love, see you again soon."

She and Hageatama kissed Ayu's forehead, and Megumi painlessly stopped Ayu's heart. A final breath left Ayu's mouth as a soft contented sigh.

Hageatama and Megumi froze. Their smiles fell away, their faces melted as they bowed their heads in low harmonized keening.

Hageatama went translucent. His hair dissolved into the air. "I so wish that were true. We are of nothingness. When we complete our function, we return to nothing."

They crawled into the bed on either side of Ayu. Hageatama and Megumi lay holding her, each with a head on her chest, humming into her heart.

As Ayu's body grew cold, Hageatama and Megumi faded, first their tears, then their voices. Slowly their feelings and memories, joys and pains, it all dissipated into candlelight and smoke.

Eidolon

– Christie Yant

There are no scents in Heaven.

No choking fetor of sweat or blood; no bodies that secrete, defecate, die, and rot. Nothing grows, nothing perishes. Nothing can be said to be truly alive.

But there is sound.

It begins as an isolated tone, a single sword against a single shield. The armor of Heaven rings out like music.

Others join in, and the chimes become a rhythmic pounding of weapons and revolt. Worth can feel it in the Void, in God's memory of stone beneath his bare feet, in the very feathers of his wings.

He can't help but watch. The Citadel they've made for themselves (*Made!* Angels! The very thought!) shines in the distance, and they assemble before it in long rows, pounding their shields, how many deep he cannot tell.

On the other side of where Worth stands, the Creator's army assembles in perfect order, perfect obedience, perfect silence. So many of them. The rebels did not stand a chance; they were fools to consider it. Worth understood their anger, he felt it too—but it was certain annihilation, to attempt the overthrow of Heaven.

The pounding continues, filling his mind with confusion and noise. The ranks are formed: the Righteous versus the Right.

He watches as angels defect from the ranks of the Righteous and are absorbed on the other side. One rises above the plane of battle and goes not to join the raging, rebellious angels, but flies away from the scene entirely. He turns his back on Divine Will and disappears from sight.

Worth thinks he knows him. His name is Achor: Trouble.

On a command that cannot be seen nor heard by anyone other than the assembled Host, they charge, their faces never changing as they strike down their former companions.

There is no blood in Heaven. No screams of pain or cries for mercy. There is metal on metal ringing out through God's perfect silence, and the streaking flames of the Fallen as they are vanquished and exiled to the imperfect world below.

Before long it is too much for Worth. He turns his back on the scene of battle, flexes his gleaming white wings, and flies away.

From Worth's vantage point here at the end of everything, there is nothing but the broken road beneath his feet, the crumbling Citadel to which it once led, a delicate blue globe suspended in the endless night, and Achor.

He sits with his back to the Citadel and watches bright souls flare in the darkness as they begin their ascent, leaving their mortal lives behind. Occasionally one wanders up the road toward him, a dim living light that falters as it follows a dream.

Achor returns from the Citadel, carrying another block of stone.

"Do they remind you of anything?" Worth asks. Achor drops the weathered block beside him but says nothing.

"There goes another one," Worth says as the tiny, bobbing light winks out on the road. "Do you remember when the others Fell? They streaked like fire across the sky." He flexes a stiff wing, sending a tattered gray feather fluttering to the ground.

"Not much fire in dreamers," Achor says, and points down the road. "Here's one."

"It'll go out." Worth counts silently. He has never got past twenty before the dreamer disappears.

"Light's wrong," Achor says, getting to his feet. He finds a gap in the unfinished wall that lines the road, chooses a stone from the pile, and works it into place.

"What do you mean?" Worth asks—seventeen, eighteen, nineteen—and then he understands.

Twenty, twenty-one. Still it moves.

The figure that finally comes into view is a man, dressed in the memory of a tan duster and jeans, breathing hard as he strides up the hill.

"You don't have to do that," Worth tells him when he is close enough to hear.

"Do what?" the man asks. He barely glances at Worth, his attention fixed on the road ahead of him.

"Breathe," says Achor. "Your body isn't real. The hill isn't hard."

The man stops, cocks his head and stands motionless for a long moment. Satisfied, he nods curtly at them.

"Thanks," he says and starts back up the road.

"The road's out up ahead," Worth calls after him. "There's nowhere to go."

The man waves back at him, but whether he hears is unclear. He reaches the end of the road, where it falls away into darkness, and looks up at the Citadel, out of reach. Worth wonders what he wants there.

The man picks a bit of gravel off the road and throws it across the gap toward the Citadel. Worth hears a faint echo as something small strikes the road on the other side.

The dreamer turns on his heel and comes back toward them. He walks around Achor, studying him, and reaches out as if to touch him. Achor flexes a wing in annoyance, brushing him off. The man turns to Worth. The angel shuffles uncomfortably.

"I need your wings."

Achor laughs, a sound so deep and low it can be felt in the rocks.

"Well, how else is it done?" the man asks. "How else can I get across?"

Achor shrugs. "You can't."

The man just glares at Achor and turns back to Worth.

"Your wings," he says again. "Please."

"I can't help you," Worth says.

"It's not as if you're using them," the man observes.

"Fair point," says Achor.

Worth folds his wings behind himself in embarrassment. "You still can't have them."

"Fine. I'll be back," the man says, and walks back the way he came.

Worth follows at a safe distance. The man never looks back. He just trudges back down the road, his head down, as if counting his own footsteps. Soon Worth feels uncomfortable being so far from his post, but he watches the man go. What can he possibly want at the Citadel? It's a ruined pile of rubble and stone, valuable to no one but Achor, who only takes it apart stone by stone in order to build something new.

Worth wonders if the man really will be back. He finds himself hoping that he will.

When the man returns as promised he pulls a wagon behind him, piled high with lumber and tools as imaginary as the duster on his back. He walks past them without a word; Worth cannot help but feel a little hurt.

He watches the man labor for a while. A sheen of sweat appears on his face when he becomes so involved in the work that he forgets that none of it is real. First he builds a wooden frame, as tall as himself, then two more; a stabilizing base, a platform at the very top, and finally a ladder.

Worth approaches him.

"I really can't let you do that," he says, ashamed of his own hypocrisy. He already has.

"Why not?" the man asks without looking up from his work.

"You're not even supposed to be here." The man did not reply. "We're the stewards of the Citadel."

"You're not very good ones. Your friend over there is taking the thing apart." He gestures across the gap, where Achor can be seen circling the remains of a fallen tower. "What's your name?" he asks.

"Worth."

"Worth, I'm Martin." He pauses in his work and extends his hand. Worth takes it uncertainly. "It's nice to meet you."

"What are you making?"

"A bridge."

"It looks hard."

"It is. But it feels so good!" The man flings his arms out wide, hammer still in hand, as if to embrace Worth, the road, and the peculiar tower, all with one gesture.

Worth sits down on the low wall, and Martin sits beside him, coiling a long piece of rope in his hands.

"How will you get it to the other side?" Worth asks.

"I thought you could take it for me."

"Oh, no," Worth says, "I can't do that."

The man looks at him quizzically. Worth becomes aware that his right wing is twitching. He folds it tighter against himself.

"If I didn't know better, I'd say you're afraid of flying," Martin says.

"Not of flying," Worth protests. "Of falling."

Martin laughs.

"Makes sense. There's a history there, after all." He gestures toward the Citadel. "What is this place? It seems familiar."

"A relic from the Fall," Worth says, reluctant to say more. An awkward moment passes.

"Why didn't you Fall with the others?" Martin says.

"Because he wasn't there," Achor answers, alighting beside the wooden structure, his arms full of stone. "Neither was I. We didn't choose a side. We didn't Fall because we didn't fight."

"It wasn't our place," Worth starts to explain, but Achor interrupts.

"Oh no," he says. "Not our place at all. Not our place to defend the rule of Heaven. So now we're in our place, aren't we? Now we're here, and we can never leave."

Martin looks across the gap toward the ruins. "It seems familiar. Like I've seen it in a dream." He laughs. "I guess I'm seeing it in a dream now, aren't I?" He sets his tools aside and brushes his hands off on his jeans. "Speaking of which, I think I have to get going." Worth starts to gather up his things and put them back in the wagon, but Martin waves him off. "You keep them for me. Feel free to use them, if you'd like."

"I wouldn't know how," Worth says as Martin starts back down the road. Achor picks a nail off the ground and examines it. "When will you be back?"

"Soon!" Martin waves, and is gone from sight.

Worth's routine has changed.

The lights, he concludes, don't really need watching. Martin has shown that even if one of them got here, they still can't reach the

Citadel. There is nothing really to guard. That leaves him free to do—well, to do something.

He sits with his feet dangling off the edge of the road, studying the Citadel. It is empty and derelict, its turrets tumbled into piles of rock at its base. Even from this distance Worth can see gravel choking the stairways. The windows are dark. Nothing moves except Achor, somewhere within.

Worth thinks the distance between his post and the Earth below doesn't seem so far as that gap in the road.

He looks over his shoulder and stretches a wing slowly. He shuffles in a tight circle, craning his head as far as he can to get a better look at the mechanics of it. When he is satisfied, he picks up Martin's tools, and gets to work.

The frame is a little uneven, but that shouldn't matter for so short a distance. The feathers he painstakingly collects stick out at odd angles where he has trouble using the adhesive he found at the bottom of Martin's wagon. It is still a bit sparse in some places, and he considers plucking a few more of his own to fill the gaps.

He should test it, he decides.

The top of Martin's platform is as high off the ground as Worth has been in six thousand years. He wobbles and tries not to look down as he fumbles with the ropes. He ties them as best he can, criss-crossed over his chest and around his waist, once around and back again. He looks across the gap at his target, then over his shoulder at his invention. The right side droops a little. He pulls on the rope and sets it right.

He is ready. He extends his arms in a way that feels commanding, pulls his own wings tight against himself, trusting himself to his own handiwork, and springs forward into the Void.

It happens much too fast. He can see the edge of the road ahead, the spot where he wants to land. He arches his back and turns the way he wants to go, expecting to feel the lift of the wings. Instead he hears a crack, and sees feathers fall away beneath him. Beyond them is the Earth, far, far below.

In terror he unfurls his own wings and beats them desperately, hampered by the broken frame which still swings from one of them.

He lurches and falters his way back to the ledge, coming down hard on the ground.

"Are you okay?" Martin's voice comes from above and a hand appears in front of him. He takes it gratefully and picks himself up.

"I think so," he says.

"What is this?" his friend asks, carefully pulling the remains of his creation off of his shoulders and wing.

"It was for you. I made it."

"You made something?" Martin's smile is proud as he studies the fractured frame.

"Wings." Worth takes the pieces from him and walks back to the edge. He sighs heavily and lets go. Together they watch the pieces fall away into the night.

"Maybe I can build them again," Worth offers. "I'll do it better the next time."

"You don't have to do that, but thank you. I'm sorry it didn't work out. It was very thoughtful of you."

Worth turns to face the planet, hanging like a frozen bubble suspended in a dark sea. "What's it like down there?"

"It's nice. I mean, it used to be," Martin says. "It still is for a lot of people."

"But not for you?"

"Not for me." He gets to his feet and jumps into the air without explanation, laughing as he lands hard on the road. "This is nice. I can do things here. I can move, and breathe, and build things with my hands." Something in the way Martin stands glaring at the Earth below makes Worth think better of asking Martin what he means.

It is some time before Martin speaks again.

"Your boss is quite something, you know. Makes all of this, and probably a whole lot of other things I don't know about. Makes you, and Achor, and me. Then He sticks you at the end of the road for thousands of years for not fighting a battle that had nothing to do with you, and me—I don't know why He did what He did to me.

"That first time I came here—do you remember? —it was an accident. But I'm pretty good at directing my dreams now. I sleep most of the time anyway. Here I feel like myself again.

"There are a lot of terrible things that happen down there. People don't treat each other the way they should. It's easy to believe that most of the horrors down there are caused by us. But not all of them."

Worth does not know what to say. He remembers the Man and the Woman, and their fate. He remembers how unfair it had seemed.

He remembers the sound of swords against shields, and the streaks of fire left by the Fallen.

"How would it work?" he asks after a time. "Even if I could give them to you, they're a part of me, not you."

"Haven't you noticed?" Martin asks. "There's a plasticity to this place. It's a place of dreams. You two made me realize it when we first met.

"Look," he says, and sweeps some dust from the ground into the palm of his hand. He spits into it and mixes it with his finger until it becomes a pasty lump of mud. He molds it into a crude animal shape, four pinched legs and a rounded protrusion like a head, and holds it up for Worth to see.

"I admit that when I first asked for them I was just being stubborn," Martin says. He cups his hands around the little mud figure and blows into them gently. "Besides, it was a dream, and people do and say strange things in dreams. I didn't really know that I could use them. But I've learned some things since then."

He sets the little mud creature on the ground and nudges it with a fingertip. It stretches a misshapen leg and tests the ground. Satisfied, it shuffles unevenly away. Worth and Martin watch it go.

"I am pretty sure I can use your wings, if you'll let me." Martin tosses a pebble over the edge, and they both lean forward to watch it until it disappears. "It's a long way down."

"Yes," says Worth.

"Ever wondered how far it really is?" Martin stands and takes two careful steps toward the edge.

"No."

"You're not a very curious creature, are you Worth?"

"Not until recently."

Martin stretches his arms wide, and turns to face Worth with a smile. "I'll let you know," he says, and falls backward off the edge of the road.

Worth cries out and lunges for him, but he is gone.

Achor emerges from behind a broken wall on the other side of the gap and takes to the air, a stone block tucked under each arm.

"I thought I heard you shout," Achor says.

"Martin," Worth says. "He Fell."

"Huh."

"I had grown to like him."

Achor says nothing.

"Can I help you with that?" Worth asks and reaches to take the stone from Achor.

"Get your own," Achor says, and pulls away.

Flex. Stretch. Try the air—not air, really, not like the thin blue shell of atmosphere around the Earth below, but the Void beneath his wings. Worth beats them against the vast Nothing, and his feet leave the road.

He is terrified. He heaves and jerks his way into space, rising a few feet before he falls clumsily to the ground. Achor flies past him and disappears around the side of the ruins. If he has witnessed Worth's humiliation, he pretends not to.

A familiar hand reaches down to help him up, and Worth looks up into the face of his friend.

"You're all right!" Worth says. "I thought—" He gets to his feet. "You can have them." Martin studies his face for clues. "My wings. You can have them. You'll need to come back with a knife."

Worth had thought that Martin would be happy now that he's getting what he wanted, but to his surprise his friend looks worried and sad.

Achor doesn't like Worth's plan.

"You don't know what will happen," he insists. "It's too risky."

They argue, but Worth will not change his mind. Achor flies off to the highest tower of the Citadel, and there he stays.

Martin approaches more slowly than usual. There is a heaviness in his step, and a wariness in the way he carries himself. He comes to a stop a few yards away. Worth closes the distance and embraces him.

"Did you bring it?"

Martin wordlessly shows him the knife. It glints in a friendly way. "Will it hurt you?"

"It isn't real," Worth says. "It won't be hard." He smiles at the old refrain, and Martin looks relieved.

It is hard, and it does hurt. When Martin is finished, with the memory of exertion making his forehead shine, Worth's wings lay on the ground. They look foreign to him. Impossible that they had been a part of him all this time.

"Now you. Turn around." Martin looks a little gray, squeamish perhaps, but he insists that he has been through worse Down There.

Worth is careful to place them just right. The flesh around Martin's shoulder blades melts up and around the edges of the severed wings. Martin cries out softly in pain, but after a moment is able to move each one gingerly.

"How do they feel?"

"Heavy." He flexes one slowly until it stretches above his head. "But good."

"What will you do now that you have them?"

Martin looks up toward the Citadel. "I'm going to restore it."

"Achor won't like that."

"Achor doesn't seem to like much," Martin says. "He likes to build things, though. I think I can talk him into rebuilding the Citadel." He looks at Worth, who rolls his shoulders back in a slow circle. "What about you? What's going to happen to you now?"

"I don't know," Worth admits. "But it's not really the point."

"So what now?"

"Now I think we say goodbye." He lifts a hand. "Take care of Achor. And Martin—thank you. You're a good friend."

Worth looks up at the ruined Citadel. He remembers a time when he took flight like the others, and he remembers a time when he should have flown with them, but didn't.

There are no scents in Heaven.

The choking stench of smoke and the animal reek of fear are unfamiliar, and they overwhelm his mind as he struggles up the crater wall. His shoulders burn where his wings once were. Somewhere above him are his only friends; he misses them. He does not expect to find friends in this place.

On Earth, there is no silence.

On the deepest, darkest night, in the most remote and desolate spot in God's creation, there is life, and with it, sound. Small animals skitter and chatter their alarm. The hum of insects, the whisper of reptiles in the sand, the screech of a night bird on the hunt assails him. The crater behind him plinks and crackles as it cools.

Beneath the confusing cacophony of life there is another sound: distant voices, from every direction.

Welcome, they say. *You made the right choice.*

He is six thousand years late. His name is Worth, and he is the last to Fall.

Slow Shift

~ Rik Hoskin

My handwriting's getting worse, Jayne Irwin concluded as she scrawled notes about the patient she had been treating six hours ago.

It was 2:15 on a dismal Thursday afternoon, and the Emergency Room was—blessedly—quiet. Jayne knew it wouldn't last. Roll on four o'clock, and the place would start filling up again with accidents caused by impatient mothers on the school run. After that, rush hour and its related disasters would take a stranglehold on the city, and then the bars would start flinging their early problems out on the streets as precursor to the steady flow of nighttime car crashes, food poisonings, mugging victims, allergic reactions, and women giving birth on the fly. Best to soak up the silence while she could—unlikely to get a chance to catch up on her patient notes again on this shift.

Jayne tapped her pen against her teeth as she tried to recall whether the construction worker's wound had still been oozing when she had first examined him. It had been immediately after the choking case when she'd just started her shift, and she had been distracted since the choker had been a DOA. Beside her feet, tucked beneath the reception desk, the regulator whirred and hummed its ceaseless electronic song as it scanned the potentialities. Irritation and resentment flooded over her as she felt its faint vibration against her foot when she unconsciously tapped it. There had certainly been a lot of blood when she had lifted the makeshift bandage that the construction worker's colleague had wrapped around his leg, but she wasn't sure whether it was still pouring blood once the nurse had cleaned up the wound. She'd have to ask Mi-sun, the primary nurse who had been assisting her at the time.

She looked up from the desk she'd snagged behind the reception counter, trying to see if Mi-sun was nearby. Her heart sank as she spied Rob Fordham striding through the open elevator doors, jacket off and shirt sleeves rolled like he meant business. "Busy, Doctor Irwin?" he asked as he approached her at the counter.

"Just catching up on my case histories, Robert," she told him, shifting her gaze back to the sheet of notes before her, hoping he would go annoy someone else. Of course, she considered, since he had joined the hospital management team three months ago, Rob Fordham had made a concerted effort to ensure that there wouldn't *be* anyone else to talk to within the ER. He had culled the staff of doctors from twelve down to seven in his first few weeks, and had drawn up the rota to ensure no more than three doctors were on shift at any one time. The nursing staff had suffered similar cutbacks, going from a dependable minimum of fifteen to an emaciated eight per shift. The next time she asked for a ten blade in the middle of emergency surgery, Jayne thought, she wouldn't be surprised if one of the janitors had drawn the short straw to assist her.

Fordham rested his hands on the high counter and leaned over Jayne, peering at her notes and, she suspected, her chest. She realized that, much as she wanted to, she couldn't ignore him today. She looked up as he continued speaking, fixing her attention on the slightly crooked canine tooth he displayed every time he opened his mouth. "How many times do I have to remind you to call me 'Rob'?" he asked, gracing her with his insincere, management smile.

She held his attention in a moment of defiance before going back to her notes, saying nothing. *Please let that be the end of it*, she hoped.

Fordham looked around, taking in the quiet ER. To one side, a bed was being curtained off as a nurse prepared to change the dressing on a female college student who had developed a rash across her chest following a bad piercing. Across the wide room, Doctor Thomas Rourke was using all of his infamous bedside charm to sweet talk a screaming seven-year-old boy with a bug in his ear to hold still for a moment—just a few seconds—while he cleared the blockage.

Fordham tapped his fingernails against the counter, drumming an urgent rhythm as he scanned the area. "Where's Doctor Napier?" he finally asked.

"Carson? I don't know. Probably outside grabbing a smoke," Jayne suggested.

Fordham sighed loudly between clenched teeth. "Great. That's just what we're paying him for," he grumbled, making a beeline for the exit doors to find Carson. Jayne got up from the desk and chased after him, pushing the tails of her white coat out of her way as her low heels drummed haphazardly across the vinyl tiling of the floor.

"Wait up, Robert," Jayne said, posting herself between Fordham and the double doors leading to the ambulance bay. "Car's been on since twelve last night. The guy deserves five minutes to himself, don't you think? I only heard he was smoking again last week, and I think it's probably down to the amount of traffic we're getting through the ER right now. Everybody's overworked," she concluded.

Fordham looked at her, then looked back, taking in the quiet Emergency Room. "You don't look too 'overworked' to me, Doctor," he stated.

"I got on at eight this morning, and this is the first lull we've had," Jayne told him defensively.

"And why is that? Have you tampered with the regulator?" Fordham asked suspiciously.

Jayne threw her hands up in the air. "Oh, come on! I'm catching up on case histories—which, you know as well as I do, is the legal requirement of any practicing doctor. Carson's taking five minutes for himself for the first time in fourteen hours, just so he can stay sane enough to deal with the final six hours of his shift."

Fordham looked at her accusingly. "You switched it off, didn't you?" When she didn't answer, Fordham stomped back to the reception desk. He glared at Taira, the receptionist, until she stepped out of the way. Then he looked at the device beneath the desk. He crouched before the machine for a few moments, checking the settings, before finally looking up at Doctor Irwin. "Stand-by mode. You set it to stand-by mode."

Jayne felt her fists clench involuntarily as anger rose within her. "It's not like I wasn't working, *Rob*," she told him, turning his name into a curse. "Those case histories . . ."

"Can be filled," he interrupted, "by Taira here on reception and you can sign off on them. We've been through this procedure a dozen times, Doctor."

"Taira doesn't know the difference between—" she wracked her brains as she glared at him, "—flupenthixol and fluticasone. I don't want to discharge a schizophrenic with a record of how much *wart cream* I assigned him," she finished, angrily.

Fordham reached for the switch on the regulator. "Go tell Doctor Napier and the others here that your vacation is over," he uttered. With that, Fordham flipped the switch, and the regulator jolted back to life.

Deliberately, Rob Fordham got up from his crouch before the device, and stared Jayne in the eye. "If this happens again, Doctor Irwin," he told her, "I will have no choice but to institute disciplinary proceedings. Don't touch the regulator."

She glared at him, swallowing back her urge to answer. She could already feel the faint thump against the floor as the regulator rocked and went to work, plowing the potentialities for their next case. She should tell Carson.

From her computer port at the desk, Taira looked up and informed Jayne that an ambulance would arrive in thirty seconds, her tone apologetic. With a triumphant smile, Fordham made his way back to the bank of elevators, doubtless going back to his comfortable management suite, Jayne realized as she headed for the double doors to the ambulance bay.

She found Doctor Napier outside, huddled beneath the porch, pulling his white coat tightly around him in the chill April air. He coughed as he took another drag on his cigarette, watching the heavy rain falling in the open ambulance bay. "Hey, Jayne," he began as she approached, "you come to join me?"

"Bad news, Car," she replied. "Fordham came down and turned the regulator back on."

Anger flashed in Napier's dark eyes, and he shook his head in disbelief. "What? We're not allowed five minutes now?"

Jayne nodded towards the bay entrance as an ambulance hurtled through the mist, screeching to a halt on the damp tarmac. "Guess not," she told him, rushing out into the cold rain to see what the regulator had brought them.

Napier muttered a curse as he extinguished his cigarette underfoot, before joining Jayne at the opening back doors to the vehicle. Two paramedics leapt out, escorting a stretcher from the back of the rig. The patient was a girl, perhaps thirteen or fourteen, a wide gash on her head and her face covered in thin streams of blood. The girl was dressed for summer, and her bright T-shirt darkened as the driving rain soaked it through. "What happened to her?" Napier asked as Jayne bent in to open the girl's closed eyes, checking them with her penlight.

"Came off her bike," one of the paramedics explained. "Smacked her head on the ground—probably looks worse than it is. Trouble was, the truck following her couldn't swerve in time—went over both her legs."

The stretcher lurched over the tarmac as they rushed into the Emergency Room, kicking up rainwater as it leapt across the uneven ground. Nurse Mi-sun joined them at the doors and guided them through to examination room one.

Eight minutes later, the girl had been stabilized and Mi-sun was on the phone talking to surgery, seeing when they could get the girl's legs in plaster. Carson had built a fairly instant rapport with the frightened girl while Jayne went to work on the cut across her head, so he had volunteered to stay with her while she waited for surgery. Her parents, for practical reasons, could not be alerted.

As she exited exam room one, Doctor Irwin almost walked into the driver of the ambulance rig who had been watching through the glass panel in the door. "Is she going to be all right?" he asked her.

Jayne nodded. "She's a little scared still, but the injuries will heal. It's just a shame that we can't get her parents here until the surgery's complete."

The driver shrugged. "Yeah, I almost tumbled my rig when I hit the rain in the bay. What are you on here?"

"Thursday, 2:30 PM, regulator time," she told him. "You?"

He checked his watch. "Saturday morning, a little after 10:00 now." He showed her the face of the analog wristwatch he wore: the dial showed it to be about five past ten. "We were enjoying the sun until you pulled us in," he laughed as she escorted him back towards the doors to the ambulance bay.

"At least the rain does clear up," she said with resignation, "eventually."

"Eventually," he agreed with a teasing smile. Joining his crew, the driver got back into the cab of his ambulance, and Jayne watched it disappear into the misty doorway that surrounded the entrance.

She was pleased that the rain would clear up for the weekend. She had an invite to a neighbor's barbecue tomorrow night and was determined to go—her work patterns hadn't been conducive to making friends with her neighbors since starting in the ER half a year ago, and she was hoping that this would be a chance to rectify that. Of course, as soon as she told them that she was a doctor the word would spread, and she'd be grilled by a long list of neighbors with back pains, curious rashes, irritating cramps and the need for prescription medication "if she could just spare a minute." It never failed.

She wondered if she should lie about her occupation, tell them that she was an assassin or something. Probably not a good idea—assassins most likely got pestered by their neighbors regarding unfaithful spouses, overbearing employers, and the possibility of borrowing "y'know, just a sniper rifle for a couple of days." Jayne watched as the mists at the entrance to the ambulance bay parted, and two rigs poured in one after another, lights flashing and sirens wailing.

She headed over to the closest rig as Thomas Rourke, the other doctor on shift, came through the bay doors to join her. "When did it start raining?" he asked, mystified.

"Couldn't say," Jayne told him, "but I've been assured it clears up in time for the weekend."

The regulator had been installed at the start of February, shortly after Rob Fordham had joined the hospital. His background had been with an oil company, and he'd been employed for his perceptive management strategies, rather than any discernible knowledge of medicine. That very fact did not sit well with the hospital staff, and his tactless people skills had further diminished his popularity. But, he was a career manager, and wasn't in the habit of making friends or listening to the opinions—however valid—of those who weren't on the same pay scale.

By scanning forward through the next forty-eight hours, the regulator could provide a standard number of patients for the ER, rather than the peaks and troughs they had been used to in the old days. Tied to technology in the ambulances, the regulator plucked cases out of time, pulling them to the present from the future so that the underused doctors could begin working on them. The system, theoretically, balanced out. While a highway pile-up might generate upwards of thirty patients in need of immediate care, spreading those patients over a longer period in standardized succession meant that the doctors were never overwhelmed. However, Jayne realized, what the regulator failed to recognize was that adrenalin kept you going through those freak surges of patients, but the doctors also needed quiet moments just to gather their thoughts and keep themselves sane.

And, while you might be dealing with a case from two days into the future, you had no way of preventing it from happening. The regulator could plow the future, but it couldn't be used to alter it. The effect that had on morale was less than positive.

With the regulator had come a drop in staffing levels in the hospital, the conclusion being that if you could predict precisely the number of cases the ER would receive each hour, you could adjust the number of doctors accordingly.

Typical management thinking, Jayne knew. Short term profits over long term gains. Fordham would be out of here, a healthy pay-off bonus for meeting his target, before anyone saw the problems that were inherent in the new system. Who had time to teach the next generation of doctors? Who could estimate the vast loss of knowledge and technique that only being trained by one or two doctors, over the original rota of twelve, would make to that new generation? And, of course, there was Carson Napier—his drifting back into old addictions was a clear sign that this system was burning them all out as quickly as his cigarette stubs.

She bristled as she cracked open the chest of her patient in examination room two.

It was 4:45, and the flow of *current traffic*—a couple of prangs on the school run, a sewerage worker who had been bitten by a rat—had ceased. Carson joined her at the coffee machine.

"Do you have time for that, Doctor?" he said in his sternest voice. When she looked up he displayed one of his canines in a sneer, shifting his head as though it were at odds with the tooth.

"You're nothing like him, you know?" she told him, unimpressed.

He nodded, closing his mouth. "Let's all be thankful for that, eh?"

She looked at Carson, taking in the lingering smell of tobacco on his clothes. His eyes looked tired, and his jaw was darkened with stubble. "Do you want a coffee?" she asked him, holding out her cup. "Would you like *my* coffee?"

He shook his head, smiling. "I couldn't possibly, Jayne."

"Sure you could," she told him, placing the paper cup in his open hand. "You look like you need it more than me, just now."

He took a sip from the cup. "I'll return the favor," he told her, "at . . . what time are you off?"

"Erm," she rolled her eyes, "at midnight on the third of *never*, I think. But it might be the *fourth*."

Behind them, the doors to the ambulance bay opened, and a paramedic began telling them about a GSW to the leg.

She took one last look at Carson, meeting his eyes for a second. "My day off tomorrow," she told him with a grin.

"Any plans?" he asked.

She nodded in response as they got a breakdown of the case from the paramedic. "This and that," she told him.

Doctor Onuki of the night shift poked her head around the doors as Jayne sewed up a chest wound (window cleaner, thirty-foot fall, iron railings) in exam room one. "Weren't you off about ten minutes ago?" she asked as Jayne put in the fifth stitch.

"I don't know," she replied. "What time is it?"

Onuki checked her watch. "11:08," she told her precisely. "But you don't need me to tell you that, Jayney. We both know that you're putting off something."

"We do?" she asked, pausing in her stitch work as she looked up at Onuki.

"Well, that there is a nurse's job," Onuki told her, "meaning that you're killing time."

She put in the last stitch on the unconscious window cleaner's chest, sealing the wound, before snapping out of her gloves. "I've been thinking about calling my mother all day," she told Onuki as she joined her at the door, "but I never quite got around to it."

Onuki nodded. "Day gets away with you. Happens."

"Yeah, it was one of those days, all right," she agreed, a note of resignation in her voice. "Do you know if that girl—Lucy Collins . . . Collings . . . something . . . ?"

"Lucy Cowell, fourteen years old, bike versus truck?" Onuki asked, and Jayne nodded. "She got out of surgery at 7:00 and was sent forward to her own time. Her parents should be there with her by now."

"Good," Jayne nodded. "She seemed scared, and I hated to just leave her like that."

Jayne passed an accident at the side of the road as she drove home through the drizzle. Emergency vehicles were already on the scene, but, being truthful, she was too tired to stop and help anyway. She had put in a fifteen-hour shift, and, right now, she wanted nothing more than to curl up in her bed and fall asleep to the sound of the rain on her windows. Idly she wondered, as a cop waved her past the accident against the traffic flow, whether she had maybe treated one of the victims of this accident at some point over her last two shifts. With the regulator in place, it was always possible.

The regulator had dehumanized them all, she realized. And all in the name of efficiency. She was annoyed with herself that she hadn't caught up with Carson before he'd left earlier that evening—he looked like he needed someone to talk to or he was just going to explode, even if he'd done good work with the bike girl today. Checking her mirror as she pulled into the underground car park of her apartment block, she realized that making the time to talk to anyone at work was becoming impossible. Maybe she'd call him tomorrow, with her day off, before she went to the barbecue.

Now *that* was going to be interesting. What was she going to wear? Felt like she had spent so long either in a white coat or in scrubs over the last three months that anything else would be too alien.

As she bleeped her car doors locked, Jayne thought back over what had been a lousy day. The run in with Fordham had been pointless, because management would always win that argument. It hadn't helped that she had been in a bad mood since the start of her shift when she had been unable to revive that choking case, had had to pronounce it DOA. A regulator case, of course, from about thirty-six hours in her future—a day and a half back then.

She glanced at her watch as she stepped into the elevator. "Time of my death," she told herself, "17:12 tomorrow evening."

She was really going to have to try to call her mother before then. She could write her parents a note but her handwriting was getting worse—she was sure of it.

The Math (A Fairy Tale)

~ Marc Levinthal

The witch lived in the tree.

Occasionally a starving, desperate wretch would make the ascent along the sloping trunk, all the while wondering how the tree, wide and tall as the shattered skyscrapers surrounding it, could possibly be there in the midst of all that desolation.

He or she would climb, and then find the hollow, where the tree righted itself and rose, straight as an arrow, into the sky.

They'd never see her, not at first. There would be a whisper, barely there, possibly imagined, and then nothing for a while. The unfortunate would crawl further down into the hollow, with just enough room to get through to the next chamber.

They'd hear the next whisper, further down below, and keep crawling, all the time wondering how all this could be inside of the tree, how the topography could shift so radically inside it, why they were angling down now. How the tree could even be there to begin with.

Until it was too late.

They would come down the tunnel, into the last chamber, and see the food. Marvelous stuff: cakes, and ham, cookies and cheeseburgers, plates of spaghetti piled high and shimmering with red sauce. Frothy mugs of beer. And they'd gasp or cry out in amazement, and then dig in, smiling and laughing at their good fortune, moaning with delight at the long-forgotten flavors.

Then her minions would strike, disabling them quickly (knowing just where to cut), while the marvelous morsels turned to dust, mud in their mouths. And then the little elves would hang them up, preparing to make *her* meal, this one based firmly in harsh reality.

And if she happened to be in the Dream, she'd see canvas bags, brimming with groceries: lettuce, fresh tomatoes, bread, cheese. Meat, neatly packaged.

Then they'd see her—the witch—the last thing they'd see as their blood drained away into the reclaiming troughs . . .

Once, she'd been like other people. She'd worked at a job—a Dream maker, at one of the Dream factories. Programmer. Artist. Number cruncher. It had been a pleasure to come to work; it had been her passion to create the worlds, the full sensory immersions wherein people could find relief from their lonely lives, their aging bodies, the hollow emptiness that seemed to dog most of them.

Of course, she'd never thought about what people did with the Dreams once downloaded from the factory. Not then. But eventually she had lots of time to ponder the consequences of her work. Because the consequences were why she was the witch, doing what she did.

Dreaming was a solitary pastime. People had taken their Dreams in private, in the comfort of their homes. Toward the end, most people Dreamed for many days at a time—addicted, diapered and hooked up to IV drips, so far gone that real life hardly seemed to matter anymore. It was no wonder that the end came as it did, when it did. Nobody cared about the outside anymore, at least not until it was too late. While they were tucked away, alone in their cocoons, the world ran down.

But no lonely cocooning here, where the Dreams were made, where the drug was manufactured. Here, whole rooms had been dedicated to the collective experience—places where groups of artists and programmers could walk through the Dreams, critique them, improve them.

So, it had been easy enough for her minions to rig the entire building, as well as a shallow perimeter outside, so that the anomalous tree could be observed by her intended victims. And now the building *was* the Dream.

The witch's tree.

She'd never felt the need to lose herself in the Dream then, before the fall. The creation had always been sufficient escape for her. She'd always imagined she'd been one of the lucky few.

Her specialty had been the recursives, fractals, things to do with Fibonacci numbers: foliage, gardens. Grass. Leaves. Trees.

Especially trees.

Now, it was dark everywhere, and the only light came from the remaining ceiling lights, the ones that hadn't been smashed, back when it all went bad. Some feeble current trickled in from the solar panels outside. Enough to power the Dream maker, a few lights, and the water reclaimer (water had been one of the first things to go, even before the end).

She tapped her lips with a finger and listened for sounds of movement in the corridors. Her stomach grumbled. *Too bad you can't eat sunlight*, she thought.

These days, she was as much an addict as anyone had been. The Dream kept her sane, at least what passed for sane now. Her only alternative was to lay waiting, clutching at the filthy blankets and coats that kept her warm, hoping that someone from the outside would find the tree. That someone would come inside.

The prey were fewer and farther between these days.

The little bots that had scurried from place to place in the old days, taking things from one worker to another, were for the most part still running, still keeping what they could in good order. Now, no other workers roamed the halls but her, so they did what she told them. Her minions.

And in the Dream they were pointy-eared elves, or little bat-winged monkeys, or wise-eyed gnomes. And the building's corpse was a beautiful manse deep inside the tree, decorated with pastel flowers along the walls, and where it was always twilight or dawn, she couldn't tell which. A fountain burbled just around a corner somewhere, always just out of sight. She was beautifully wicked, bedecked in flowing black satin, perfumed and darkly lovely.

And when she was hungry, the table was set with a delectable repast. Only this one didn't turn to mud in *her* mouth.

And if she slept afterward, she'd wake from the Dream with her belly full, fresh meat between her remaining teeth, blood on her fingers and mouth. And then (no, no, no, this is not my reality, I am the witch) and then, right back in, from sleep, to cold reality, to the Dream.

She'd had to show the minions what to do, those first few times. But they'd caught on quickly. They'd watched her stealthily dispatch the last few workers left in the building, back at the beginning of the end. The writing was on the wall, and nobody had seen it but her. Unfortunate, but unavoidable. She'd done the math, after all. There were only enough resources left for one. Maybe. If the resources could be replenished occasionally.

The little bots had watched her eviscerate her victims, carve and dismember using the set of razor-sharp knives she'd found in the ransacked cafeteria kitchen, watching with dispassionate, glowing gazes.

And now, she didn't have to deal with such unpleasantries.

Sometimes the wretches from outside didn't come for a long time. She'd subsist, then, on the dried and stored-away pieces. But she could have anything she wanted, in the Dream. Cherry pie and turkey sandwiches. Red beans and rice.

She came out of the Dream less and less, but couldn't stay in it forever: it would fry her brain eventually. Catatonia followed by coma, followed by death.

So she had to come out from time to time, for as short a time as possible, hating it when she did, needing to be the witch again. Needing it. She couldn't remember her real name anymore. Perhaps the brain frying had already begun.

Sometimes weeks went by without any visitors to the tree. When that happened, she'd imagine the worst: that the last one had come, and now she would ration out the last of the dried flesh, eating less and less of it until she too was eating delicious dust. And then, finally she would fall into the Dream from which she would not wake.

This was one of those times, and hunger gnawed at her stomach. She could eat what she had left, gamble that someone would come along to replenish her stores. But she knew better than that. She called a minion and Dreamed a little bowl of oatmeal with bananas, and felt a little better.

She got up and stared out the tall, open window that overlooked the forest and the river beyond it. A castle rose out of the mist in the distance, across the water, high walls and turrets.

She much preferred this view from the tree to the alternative, the tableau of gray ruins through the smashed windows.

The witch stood there for a long while, smelling the air filled with herbal scents and vegetal rot, feeling the gentle breeze and listening to the faint susurrations of the leaves.

And then she heard her minions scurrying through the hallways.

She listened for the familiar sounds, the giggles and whoops of delight. But there were none of the usual indicators, just quiet from the dining room.

Cautiously, she wound her way down through the labyrinthine corridors of the tree, to where her minions should be making their preparations.

When she got to the dining room, there was no sumptuous feast laid out for her prey, no victim enjoying a last, imaginary meal. Instead, she found her kitchen knives arrayed neatly across the white linen. A regal pair dressed in medieval finery, a handsome man with chiseled features and a tall, patrician blonde woman, sat calmly at each end of the table. They turned to her and smiled, the man hefting a large carving knife, and the woman a thinner, longer blade more suited to boning.

Her minions sprang up from the floor, and pinned her expertly to the wall.

The pair were inexperienced, so it took a little while. The process was slow, and painful. The Dream faded as she bled out, and for a moment, she saw the two filthy, emaciated killers standing over her, panting . . .

"We got—the bitch," the bug-eyed man whispered between breaths. His hands dripped blood and viscera. His mouth was rimmed with blood.

"My god," the woman said, "I'm so hungry. So fucking hungry . . ." as she plunged her hands back in and ripped off another morsel.

Now the man was giggling uncontrollably. "I knew I could key in. Miles of code—line by line! Dream took so long to hack. Months! Months of hiding in that basement. But I did it. I did it."

"Oh. Oh. I see." the woman said. "Did *you* hack the bots? Without them bringing us crumbs from her stash, we would have died a long time ago. And don't forget who finally got them under our control."

The man stopped giggling and ate some more.

Afterwards, sated, they leaned back against the wall, both looking at what they'd done, at what they had become. Neither wanting to see it.

So they did what their predecessor had done, and fell into the Dream.

The elves cleared away the remains of the feast, and the king and queen sat with their goblets of wine, leaning back in their chairs. Savoring the silence.

Finally the king spoke. "So, what now? What do we do now?"

The queen sighed, dabbing at her mouth daintily with a large linen napkin. "Isn't it obvious? We do what she did. We maintain the Dream. Wait for them to come from the outside. Spider and the fly." She smiled grimly.

"That's it?" he asked.

"What else have you got?"

And now that it was done, the king and queen sat across from each other on their gilded thrones, and looked out across the wide forest, and across the river to the castle in the mist beyond.

From time to time, they stole glances at each other, and occasionally, their eyes would meet.

And then, even the Dream could not disguise the feral, cold calculation.

The witch hadn't looked so good.

And they'd both done the math.

Chrysalis

~ Richard Thomas

John Redman stood in his living room, the soft glow of the embers in the fireplace casting his shadow against the wall. He wondered how much money he could get if he returned all of the gifts that were under the Christmas tree—everything—including what was in the stockings. The wind picked up outside the old farmhouse, rattling a loose piece of wood trim, the windows shaking—a cool drift of air settling on his skin. Couple hundred bucks maybe—four hundred tops. But it might be enough. That paired with their savings, everything that his wife, Laura, and he had in the bank—the paltry sum of maybe six hundred dollars. It had to be done. Every ache in his bones, every day that passed—a little more panic settled down onto his shoulders, the weight soon becoming unbearable. Upstairs the kids were asleep, Jed and Missy quiet in their beds, home from school for their winter break, filling up the house with their warm laughter and echoing footsteps. The long drive to the city, miles and miles of desolate farmland his only escort, it pained him to consider it at all. Video games and dolls, new jeans and sweaters, and a singular diamond on a locket hung from a long strand of silver. All of it was going back.

It had started a couple weeks ago with, of all things, a large orange and black wooly bear caterpillar. He stood on the back porch sneaking a cigarette, his wife and kids in town, grocery shopping and running errands all day. The fuzzy beast crawled across the porch rail and stopped right next to John—making sure it was seen. John looked at the caterpillar and noticed that it was almost completely black, with just a tiny band of orange. Something in that information rang a bell, shot up a red flag in the back of his crowded mind. He usually didn't pay attention to these kinds of things—give them any weight. Sure, he picked up *The Old Farmer's Almanac* every year, partly out of habit, and partly because it made him laugh. Owning the farm as they did now, seven years or so, taking over for his mother when she passed away, the children still infants, unable to complain, John had gotten a lot of advice. Every time he stepped into Clancy's Dry Goods in town, picking up his contraband cigarettes, or a six-pack of Snickers bars that he hid in the glove box of his faded red pickup truck, the advice spilled out of his neighbor's mouths like the dribble that used to run down his children's chins. Clancy himself told John to make sure he picked up the almanac, to get his woodpile in order, to put up plastic over the windows, in preparation for winter. For some reason, John listened to the barrel-chested man, his moustache and goatee giving him an air of sophistication that was offset by Clancy's fondness for flannel. John nodded his head when the Caterpillar and John Deere hats jawed on and on by the coffeepot, stomping their boots to shake off the cold, rubbing their hands over three-day old stubble. John nodded his head and went out the door, usually mumbling to himself.

Christmas was coming and the three-bedroom farmhouse was filled with the smell of oranges and cloves, hot apple cider, and a large brick fireplace that was constantly burning, night and day. Laura taught English at the high school, and she was off work as well. Most of the month of December and a little bit of the new year would unfurl to fill their home with crayons, fresh baked bread, and Matchbox cars laid out in rows and sorted by color.

John was an accountant, a CPA. He'd taken over his father's business, Comprehensive Accounting, a few years before they'd finally made the move to the farm. The client list was set, most every small business in the area, and a few of the bigger ones as well. They trusted John with their business—the only history that mattered to them were the new ones he created with their books. Every year he balanced the accounts, hiding numbers over here, padding expenses over there, working his magic, his illusion. But Laura knew John better, back before the children were born, back when their evenings were filled with broken glasses and lipstick stains and money gambled away on lies and risky ventures. Things were good now—John was on a short leash, nowhere to go, miles from everyone—trouble pushed away and sent on down the road.

John made a mental note of the caterpillar, to look it up later in the almanac. Right now he had wood to chop, stocking up for the oncoming season. He tugged on his soft, leather gloves, stained with sap and soil, faded and fraying at the edges. Surrounding the farmhouse was a ring of trees, oak and maple and evergreen pine. For miles in every direction there were fields of amber—corn on one side, soybeans on the other. John picked up the axe that leaned against the back porch with his left hand, and then grabbed the chainsaw with his right—eyeballing the caterpillar, which hadn't moved an inch, as he walked forward exhaling white puffs of air. One day the fields were a comfort: the fact that they leased them out to local farmers, no longer actual farmers themselves, a box checked in the appropriate column, incoming funds—an asset. The next day they closed in on him, their watchful stare a constant presence, a reminder of something he was not—reliable.

John set the axe and chainsaw next to a massive oak and looked around the ring of trees. There were small branches scattered under the trees—he picked these up in armloads and took them back to the house, filling a large box with the bits of wood. This would be the kindling. Then he went back to look for downed trees—smaller ones mostly, their roots unable to stand up to the winds that whipped across the open plains and bent the larger trees back and forth. A fog pushed in across the open land, thick and heavy, blanketing the ring of trees, filling in all the gaps. The ground was covered in acorns, a blanket of caps and nuts, nowhere to step that didn't end in pops and cracks, his boot rolling across the tiny orbs.

"Damn. When did these all fall down, overnight?"

John stared up into the branches of the oak trees, spider webs spanning their open arms, stretching across the gaps, thick and white—floating in the breeze. He looked to the other trees and saw acorns scattered beneath them all, and more spider webs high up into the foliage. Spying a downed tree, he left the axe alone for now and picked up the chainsaw, tugging on the string, the bark and buzz filling the yard with angry noise.

Several hours later the cord of wood was stacked against the side of the house, the tree sectioned down into manageable logs, which were then split in half, and then halved again. It was a solid yield, probably enough to get them through the winter—the box of kindling overflowing with twigs and branches that had been broken over his knee. They would keep an eye on the backyard, and over the course of the winter, they would refill the box with the fallen branches and twigs. The winds picked up again as John took a breath, a sheen of sweat on the back of his neck, night settling in around the farm.

When he finally went inside, the wife and kids home from their errands, the house smelled of freshly baked cookies, chocolate chip, if John knew his wife. The kids were up on barstools around the butcher block island, hands covered in flower, their faces dotted with white, his wife at the kitchen sink washing dishes. In the corner of the window was a singular ladybug, red and dotted with black.

"Daddy," Missy yelled, hopping down off her stool. She ran over to him, painting his jeans with tiny, white handprints.

"Hey, pumpkin," John said. "Cookies?"

"Chocolate chip," she beamed.

"Jed, could you get me a glass of water?" John asked. His son didn't answer, concentrating on the cookie dough. "Jed. Water?" His son didn't answer.

"I'll get it, Daddy," Missy said.

"No, honey, I want Jed to get it. I know he can hear me."

John lowered his voice to a whisper, his eyes on Jed the whole time. "I'm going to count to three," John hissed, his daughter's eyes squinting, her head lowering as she crept out of the way. "Get me that water, boy, or you'll be picking out a switch." Jed didn't move, a smile starting to turn up his mouth, the cookie dough still in his hands."

"Daddy?" Missy said, her face scrunching up. "He doesn't hear you, don't . . ."

"Honey, go," John continued. "One," John peeled off his gloves and dropped them by the back door. "Two," he whispered, unbuttoning his coat, pulling his hat off and dropping it on the floor. He inhaled for three, a thin needle pushing through his heart, this constant battle that he had with his son, the grade school maturation placing in front of John a new hurdle every day. The boy got off the stool, leaving behind the cookies, and tugged on the back of his mother's apron strings.

"Mom, may I have a glass of water for Dad, please?"

Laura stopped doing the dishes, her long brown ponytail swishing to one side as she turned to look at the boy. She handed him a tall glass and pointed him to the refrigerator. Off he went to get the water and ice, pushing the glass against the built-in dispenser, a modern day convenience that they all enjoyed. Jed walked over to his dad and held the glass out to him, eyes glued to his father's belt buckle.

"Jed?"

"Yes, Dad?" he said, looking up, brown eyes pooled and distant.

"Thank you," John said, leaning over, hugging the boy. The little man leaned into his father. "Thanks for the water," John said, kissing the boy on the cheek. It just took a little more work, that's all.

Later that night, John sat in his study, while Laura put the kids to bed. He thumbed through the almanac, looking at the index, studying the upcoming months, the forecast for the Midwestern winter. There were several things that got his attention. When the forecast was for a particularly bad winter, harsh conditions to come, there were signs and warnings everywhere. For example, if a wooly bear caterpillar is mostly orange, then the winter coming up will be mild. His caterpillar had almost no orange at all. He kept looking for other signs. If there is an inordinate amount of fog, if there are clouds of spider webs, especially high up in the corners of houses, barns or trees—the bigger the webs, the worse the winter. If pine trees are extra bushy; if there are halos around the sun or the moon; if there is a blanket of acorns on the ground—these are the signs of a rough winter to come—rumors, and legends, and lore.

John closed the book and set it down, a chill settling in across his spine. A draft slipped through the study window, the plastic sheets he'd meant to put up, forgotten. It was nothing. The stupid almanac was a bunch of crap, he thought. He stood up and went down to the basement anyway.

Along one wall were several wooden shelves—he'd built them himself when they moved in. There were jars of preserves and jam, jellies and fruit, all along the top shelf. Farther down, on the second shelf were soups and vegetables and other canned goods. It was almost empty, maybe a dozen cans of diced tomatoes and chicken noodle soup. On the third shelf were boxed goods, everything from pasta to scalloped potatoes to rice. It was fairly packed, so he moved on to the second set of shelves. It was filled with family-sized packages of toilet paper and paper towels, napkins and cleaning supplies. Then, he turned to the ancient furnace and stared.

Settled into the center of the room was the original furnace that came with the house. Built in the late 1800s, the farmhouse came equipped with a coal chute that opened up on the back of the house. Concrete poured into the ground on an angle, stopped at thick, metal doors—which if pulled open revealed the long abandoned chute that ran down to the basement floor. It was a novelty, really—historic and breathtaking to look at, but nothing more than a pile of greasy metal. The massive, black ironworks dwarfed the modern water heater and furnace, doors slotted like a set of enormous teeth, squatting in the middle of the room. Maybe he'd talk to Clancy.

It was fifteen miles to the nearest big city and the national chain grocery stores. John simply drove in to town. Clancy was about the same price, a couple cents higher here and there. But he felt better putting his money in the hands of a friend then a faceless corporation.

He felt stupid pushing the miniature grocery cart around the store. A flush of red ran up his neck as he bought every can of soup that Clancy had.

"Jesus, man," Clancy said, as John brought the cart up to the counter. "You done bought up all my soup."

"Order more," John said.

"I guess so," Clancy said, ringing him up.

"Can I ask you something?" John said.

"Shoot, brother. What's on your mind?"

"That furnace we have out at the farm, the old one? Does it work?"

"Well, let me think. It's still hooked up to the vents as far as I know. The little valves are closed off, is all—easy to flip them open. Helped your dad out with the ductwork a long time ago, he showed me how it all went together. But, you'd have to have a shitload of coal. And

I have no idea of where you'd get that, these days. Does anyone still burn it?"

John nodded his head. He knew where he could get some coal. But it wasn't cheap, that's for sure.

"Just curious," John said. "How much are those gallons of water, by the way," John asked, pointing at a dusty display at the front of the store. There were maybe two-dozen gallons of water.

"Those are .89 cents a gallon, can't seem to move them."

"I'll take them," John said.

"How many?" Clancy asked.

"All of them."

John was supposed to be down at his office. Instead, the back of his pickup truck was loaded up with soup and water, and he was headed down to the river. About two miles east, a small branch of the Mississippi wormed its way out into the land. A buddy of his from high school had a loading dock out there. Sometimes it was just people hopping on there in canoes, or boats, paddling down to the main branch of the river, or just buzzing up and down the water. Other times it was barges, loaded up with corn or soybeans—and sometimes coal from down south. There was a power plant upstate from where they lived, and it burned off a great deal of coal. Sometimes it was a train that passed by the plant, offloading great cars of the black mineral. And sometimes there were barges, drifting up the water, shimmering in the moonlight.

John pulled up to the trailer and hopped out. It was getting colder. He looked up at the cloudy sky, a soft halo wrapping around the sun, hiding behind the clouds. All around the tiny trailer were evergreen trees, fat and bushy, creeping in close to the metal structure, huddled up for warmth.

John knocked on the trailer door.

"Come in," a voice bellowed.

John stepped into the trailer, which was filled with smoke.

"Damn, Jamie, do you ever stop smoking? Open a window, why don't you."

"Well, hello to you too, John. Welcome to my humble abode. What brings you out here?"

John sat down and stared at his old buddy. Jamie was never going anywhere. Born and raised here in the northern part of the heartland, this was it for him. And it seemed to suit him just fine. No college, no aspirations, no dreams of the big city—happy to live and die where he was born.

"Coal," John said. "I'm just wondering. You sell it to people?"

"Not usually. Got a few guys with old pot belly stoves off in the woods. They buy a sack off of me, now and then. You know, I just kind of skim it off the top, the electric company none the wiser."

"How much does it cost?"

"Depends. One guy I charge $20 cause he's broke and has a hot sister. Other guy is a jerk, and his sister's a hag. I charge him $50. I could cut you a deal though, John. Happy to help out an old friend."

"What about a larger quantity?"

"How much we talking about, John?"

"Like, filling up my pickup truck?" John said.

Jamie whistled and tapped his fingertips on his mouth. "That's trouble. Can't skim that. Have to pay full price, actually talk to the barge man. Unload it. Not even sure when the next shipment will be rolling through. Getting cold."

John shivered. "If you had to guess though, any idea?"

Jamie took a breath. "Maybe a grand?"

John drove home, almost dark now, his house still miles away. When he pulled up the driveway, the tires rolling over more acorns, the house was dark. Where the hell were they? He pulled up to the back of the house, and hurried to unload the truck. Into the kitchen he went, armloads of soup cans, hurrying to get them downstairs. Why was he sweating so much, why did this feel like a secret? He dropped a can of tomato soup but kept on going. He loaded the soups on the second shelf and went back for more. Two trips, three trips, and the dozens of cans of soup filled up the shelf with a weight that calmed him down. Back upstairs he picked up the can he dropped and looked out the window to see if they were home yet. A handful of ladybugs were scattered across the glass, and he scrunched up his nose at their presence.

Back to the truck, a gallon of water in each hand, this was going to take a little while. The soup he could explain—an impulse buy, Clancy running some kind of stupid sale: buy a can of soup get a stick of homemade jerky for free. But the two-dozen gallons of water looked like panic. He didn't want them to worry, even as he contemplated the coal, the thing he may have to do in secret, the risk he'd have to take. Up and down the steps he went, pushing the water to the back of the basement, covering it up with a stained and flecked drop cloth. He stared at the canned goods, the water, and the coal powered furnace. A door slammed upstairs, and his head turned.

The kids were yelling for him, so he pulled the string that clicked off the light, and back upstairs he went.

"Hey, honey," he said. "What's up, guys?"

The kids gave him a quick hug and then ran on to their rooms. Laura leaned into him, looking tired, and gave him a kiss on the lips.

"You smell like smoke," she said. "You smoking again?" she asked.

"Nah. Saw an old friend. Jamie, you remember him? Chain smokes like a fiend."

Laura eyeballed John.

"Why are you all sweaty?"

"Just putting some stuff away, couple trips up and down the stairs, no big deal."

Laura puckered her lips, swallowed and moved to the sink. She turned on the water and washed off her hands.

"Why don't you go take a shower and get cleaned up? You stink. Dinner will be ready soon."

Later that night John watched the news, Laura in the kitchen doing the dishes. The weatherman laid out the forecast all the way up to Christmas and beyond. Cold. It was dipping down, probably into the teens. Snow. A few inches here and there, but nothing to cause any alarm. He switched over to another station, the same thing. He tried the Weather Channel, watching the whole country, the Midwest especially, storm fronts rolling down from Canada, but nothing to worry about.

"How much weather do you need, hon?" Laura said, sticking her head in from the kitchen. "You've been watching that for like an hour."

"Oh," he said. "I was just spacing out, wasn't really paying attention. You wanna sit down and watch something with me?"

"Sure. Want some tea?"

John got up and walked into the kitchen, Laura's back still to him, and wrapped his arms around her waist. She relaxed into his arms, and leaned back. He kissed her on the neck, holding her tight, his mouth moving up to her ear lobe, where he licked and nibbled at her gently.

"Or, we could just go up to bed early," she smiled.

"We could do that," he said.

Behind her on the window there were several dozen ladybugs now, bunched up in the corner, a tiny, vibrating hive—and beyond that a slowly expanding moon with a ghost of a halo running around it.

The next day they woke up to snow, three inches on the ground, heavy flakes falling like a sheet, white for as far as he could see. The kids were screaming, laughing, excited to get out into it, his wife calming them down with requests to eat, to sit still, to wait. For John the snowfall made his stomach clench, the way the tiny icicles hung from the gutters, the pile of dead ladybugs covering the windowsill, the sense that he had blown it, missed his opportunity—the claustrophobia closing in.

All day John walked around with his temples throbbing, his trembling gut in turmoil—his mouth dry and filled with cotton. To keep his hands busy he pulled a roll of plastic out of the garage, and sealed up every window in the house. When the sun came out and melted everything away, the children were disappointed.

John was not.

When Laura fell asleep on the couch, the kids watching cartoons, John made a call to Jamie. Three days for the coal, the day before Christmas, still a thousand dollars for the weight. If the weather held, it gave him time. He told Jamie to make it happen. He'd have it for him in cash.

The afternoon couldn't pass fast enough, Laura constantly staring at him from across the room. He cleaned up the dead ladybugs, then went downstairs and placed a cardboard box on the tarp that covered up the gallons of water, trying to hide his anxiety with a plastic smile.

The middle of the night was his only chance, so he crept downstairs with his pocketknife in his robe pocket, and slit open the presents one by one. He peeled back the tape gently, no tearing allowed, and emptied the presents from their wrappings. Where he could, he left the cardboard boxes empty for now and prayed that nobody shook the presents. For others, he wrapped up new shapes, empty boxes he found stacked down in the basement. Grabbing a large black trash bag from under the sink he filled it up with clothing and gifts, the tiny jewelry box going into his pocket. When he was done, he opened the cookie jar, the green grouch that sat up high on one of the shelves. He pulled out the receipts and stuffed them in his pocket, and slunk out to the truck to hide the loot.

When he stepped back into the kitchen Laura was standing there, arms crossed, watching him.

"Dammit, Laura, you scared me."

"What the hell are you doing, John?"

"Taking out the trash."

"At three in the morning?" she asked. She walked over and sniffed him.

"You know," he said, smiling. "Christmas is only a couple days away. Maybe you don't want to look so close at what I'm doing. Maybe there are surprises for wives that don't snoop too hard," John said.

Laura grinned and held out her hand.

"Come to bed," she said.

Out the window the full moon carried a ring that shone across the night.

John got up early and left a note. It was the best way to get out of the house without any questions. He left his wife and kids sleeping, and snuck out the back door, the wind whipping his jacket open, mussing his hair—bending the trees back and forth.

All day he drove, one place to the next, his stories changing, his stories remaining the same. Too large, too small; changed my mind, she already has one; got the wrong brand, my kids are so damn picky. The wad of bills in his pocket got thicker. The pain behind his eyes spread across his skull.

What was he doing?

He stopped by the bank, the day before Christmas now, and cleared out their checking and savings, leaving only enough to keep the accounts open. He took his thousand dollars and drove out to the trailer, Jamie sitting there as if he hadn't moved.

"All there?" Jamie asked, leaning back in his chair.

"To the nickel."

"Tomorrow night then," Jamie said. "Christmas Eve."

"Yep."

"What the hell are you doing, John," Jamie asked.

"The only thing I can."

When John got home Laura rushed out to the car.

"The fireplace," she said, "It's caved in."

John looked up to the tall brickwork that was now leaning to one side, the winds whipping up a tornado of snow around him. A few broken bricks lay on the ground, a trickle of smoke leaking out of the chimney.

"Everyone okay?" he asked.

"Yeah, some smoke and ashes, I swept it up, and the fire was out at the time. But no fire for Christmas now, the kids will be disappointed."

"It'll be okay," John said. "We'll survive."

It was a Christmas tradition that John and Laura would stay up late, drinking wine and talking, giving thanks for the year behind them. Laura would glance at the presents and John would wince. Every time she left the room, he poured his wine into hers, preparing for the night ahead.

At one o'clock he tucked her into bed and went out to the truck. It was cold outside, getting colder, the layers he wore giving him little protection. There was a slow snowfall dusting the crops, his headlights pushing out into the night. John was numb. Where was the storm, the epic snowfall, the crushing ice storm—the arctic temperature littering the countryside with the dead?

He pulled up to the trailer and Jamie stepped outside. On the river was a single barge filled with coal. A crane was extended out over it, teeth gleaming in the moonlight.

"Ready?" Jamie asked.

"Yeah."

Jamie manned the crane, back and forth, filling it up with coal and turning it to the side, a shower of black falling on the truck bed, the darkness filling with the impact of the coal. Over and over again Jamie filled the crane with coal and turned it to the truck bed, and released it. In no time the bed was overflowing.

"That's all she'll hold, John," Jamie said.

"Thanks, Jamie. You might want to take some home yourself."

"Why?"

"Storm coming."

At the house, he backed the truck up to the chute, glancing up at the sky, clear and dark, with stars dotting the canvas. He opened the heavy metal doors that lead into the basement and started shoveling the coal down into the chute where it slid down and spread across the floor. Fat snowflakes started to fall, a spit of drizzle that quickly turned to ice, slicing at his face. He kept shoveling. The bed of the truck was an eternity stretching into the night—one slick blackness pushing out into another. He kept on. The snow fell harder, John struggling to see much of anything, guessing where the mouth of the chute was, flinging the coal into the gaping hole, feeding the hungry beast.

When he was done he didn't move the truck. He could hardly lift his arms. And his secret wouldn't last much longer, anyway. In the kitchen he sat under the glow of the dim bulb that was over the sink, sipping at a pint of bourbon the he had pulled out of the glove box, numb and yet sweating, nauseous and yet calm. It was done. Whatever would come, it was done.

He fell into a fitful slumber, his wife asleep beside him, the silence of the building snowfall, deafening.

The morning brought screams of joy, and soon after that, screams of panic and fear. The children climbed in bed, excited to open their presents, bouncing on the heavy comforter as Laura beamed at the children. John sat up, dark circles and puffy flesh under his red, squinting eyes.

"John, you look terrible, are you okay?"

"We'll see," he said. He leaned over and kissed her. "Just know that I love you," he said.

Laura turned to the kids. "Should we go downstairs?"

"Mommy, look at all the snow. Everything is white," Missy said.

Laura got up and walked to the window.

"My God. John, come here."

John stood up and walked over to the window, the yard filled with snow, a good four feet up the trunk of an old oak tree. The snow showed no sign of stopping. The limbs were covered in ice, hanging low. John walked to the other window that faced into the back yard, and saw that only the cab of his truck was visible above the snow.

The kids turned and ran down the stairs. Laura turned to John and opened her mouth, and then closed it. When they got to the bottom of the stairs the kids were already at the presents, starting to rip them open. Coal dust and fingerprints were on the stockings, a small bulge at the bottom of each. They stopped at the bottom of the steps and watched the kids as their smiles turned to looks of dismay.

"John, what's going on," Laura asked.

The kids looked up, the boxes empty. Missy went to her stocking and dumped the lump of coal into her hand. John didn't remember putting those lumps of coal in the stockings. Some of last night was a blur. Outside the wind picked up. The loose bricks shifted in the fireplace, a dull thud scattering across the roof, and a blur of red fell past the window.

Missy began to cry.

"John, what did you do?" Laura's face was flushed, and she walked to Missy, pulling the girl to her side. Jed kept ripping open boxes, his face filling with rage—any box, big or small—his name, Missy's name, he kept ripping them open.

Empty, all of them.

John sat on the couch and clicked on the television set, all of their voices filling the room, the paper tearing, Missy crying, Laura saying his name over and over again.

". . . . or the tri-county area. Temperatures are plummeting down into the negatives, currently at minus twenty and falling, wind chill of thirty below zero. We are expecting anywhere from six to ten feet of snow. That's right, I said ten feet."

"Shut up!" John yelled, turning to them, tears in his eyes. He turned back to the television set.

"Winds upward of fifty miles an hour. We have power outages across the state. So far over fifty thousand residents are without electricity. ComEd trucks are crippled as the snow is falling faster than the plows can clear them. Already we have reports of municipal vehicles skidding off the icy roads."

John looked up into the corner of the room where a large spider web was spreading. A ladybug was caught in the strands, no longer moving. The weatherman kept talking, but John could no longer hear him. The map, the charts, the arrows and numbers spread across the television screen, warnings and talk of death on the roads.

". . . . ould be anywhere from six to ten days before . . ."

Outside there was a cracking sound, a heavy, deep ripping, and the kids ran to the window and looked out. Icicles and branches fell to the ground, shattering like glass, half of the tree tearing off, one mighty branch falling to the ground, shaking the foundation, sending snow flying up into the air.

"John?" Laura says.

". . . . o not go outside for anything . . ."

"John?"

". . . . lankets, huddle together . . ."

Somewhere down the road a transformer blew, sending sparks into the sky, the bang startling the kids who started to cry, burrowing deeper into Laura's side.

". . . . olice and a state of emergency . . ."

The television set went black, and the Christmas tree lights winked off. Wind beat against the side of the house as a shadow passed over the windows. Outside the snow fell in an impermeable blanket, the roads and trees no longer visible.

The room was suddenly cold.

John got up and walked to the kitchen, taking a glass out from the cabinet, turning on the water. There was a dull screeching sound, as the whole house shook, nothing coming out of the tap.

"Pipes are frozen," John said to himself.

On the windowsill was a line of candles, and three flashlights sitting in a row. He grabbed one of the flashlights and opened the basement door, staring down into the darkness. John walked down the stairs to where the coal spilled across the concrete, grabbing a shovel that he had leaned against the wall. He pulled open one furnace door, then the other, and setting the flashlight on the ground so that is shot up at the ceiling, he shoveled in the coal. In no time the furnace was full. He walked around the basement, the band of light reflecting off the ductwork, turning screws and opening vents. Behind him on the stairs Laura stood with the children in front of her, each of them holding a lit candle, a dull yellow illuminating their emotionless faces. John lit a match and tossed it into the furnace, a dull whoomp filling up the room.

Turning back to his family at the top of the steps, John smiled, and wiped the grime off of his face.

Occupy Maple Street

~ Gregory L. Norris

The house stood on the pedestal of the hill and overlooked the river. Boke remembered the place from when he'd lived in the town before the Occupation. All the locals knew it, he figured, by the blue glass lamp that shone out at night from the front parlor's bay window. A round base, blue the color of jay feathers and the delphinium flowers that once grew in his mother's yard, in that life from a million years ago. *Cobalt blue.*

"This house?" Boke asked, and punctuated the question with a sigh through his nostrils.

Cashan handed him two keys, one a fresh steel-silver, the new copy of the dulled brass original. "You know it?"

Boke didn't detect anything deeper than normal conversation, but one never could be too cautious. "Yes, Supervisor. You could see it on the other side of the river at night, because of the blue lamp."

"The blue lamp," Cashan parroted. "It's yours now."

Boke accepted the keys, which had warmed considerably during their brief exposure to the day's sunlight and Cashan's grip. "And the family that lived here?"

"Not a family. Two men. Nobodies."

No *bodies*, thought Boke. He willed all emotion from his face. Two men, bodies no longer. He didn't need specifics; his imagination filled in the details. Taken discreetly, likely in the night after the blue lamp was switched off and while the residents of the house, still bodies until that hour, lie huddled in bed.

"It's a good neighborhood now. Safe. Mostly workers such as yourself. A security man lives just over there." Cashan tipped his chin at a craftsman-style house with a wide front porch.

That explained the unoccupied state of the house with the blue lamp. His house now. Boke nodded. "Understood, Supervisor."

"I'll help you with your bags."

"That's not necessary. I only have these few cases."

"I insist."

Cashan picked up the larger of the two duffels that contained all Boke owned, and marched up the vacant driveway whose asphalt had taken on the color of comfortable denim, save where a dark stain marred one area, just outside the front door.

The door creaked open. From the cut of his eye, Boke noticed a crack in the frame, near the lock. It had been repaired but not erased.

An unpleasant sweetness infused the interior of the house on Maple Street, the smell of rooms closed up to deny fresh breezes, the ghosts of candles already burned and beverages enjoyed and sharp voices echoed into silence.

"I've been told the appliances work," said Cashan. "You have your ration card?"

Boke patted his back pocket, where his papers and plastic filled an old leather wallet. "Of course."

"You'll need to stock the cabinets and refrigerator. Otherwise, whatever's left inside the house is for you to use."

Boke forced a smile. "With great appreciation to both the Treasury and to you, Supervisor."

Cashan smiled, too, though the gesture—revealing a length of yellow teeth—seemed more of a snarl. "You can thank me by bringing your best work to the factory."

Cashan extended his hand. Boke accepted the gesture and shook, aware of the missing gap where the other man's pointer finger should be, and doing his best to not think of the cruelties the remaining four had inflicted upon so many others.

Nothing was where it belonged. Sofas, two in a shade of platinum, sat stacked on their arms against hallway walls. The antique desks and tables were piled on top of one another without any care for the rich, rare burl of their wood. A jagged scrape marred the top of a credenza, the gouge visible beneath a layer of dust.

What Boke assumed was the dining room by its six harp-back chairs boasted an elegant mural on the wall, of cherry trees in full bloom. It looked Japanese, like intricate pictures from a book he remembered before the Occupation and the ban on reading. Someone had cut across the mural, intentionally defacing it.

There were no books in the house. Those, Boke guessed, had gone into the backyard, where the late summer overgrowth was taking back the vast, oily black stain between a garden shed and the wood line; where words, concepts, dreams, and lusts were incinerated, burned from existence, gone forever.

The worker transport collected Boke at five prompt. Another warm dawn made the early hour less miserable. Dread, however, filled him at the notion of mornings in months ahead after the heat was gone and the hillside and surrounding neighborhoods woke layered in winter white.

The factory was drab, like its predecessors where Boke had served duty: humorless walls painted in beige and industrial yellow. Boke maneuvered levers, completed his part in the long centipede chain that fulfilled the Treasury's many needs and desires, both here and overseas.

Boke anticipated returning to the house on Maple Street, with its echoes of former happiness and elegance, and, at night, not sure why, he switched on the cobalt blue lamp in the bay window.

A stiff autumn rain hammered the house. At some point in the downpour, a cat's plaintive mewls invaded the room. Baby sobs kept sleep away. In the darkness broken only by the road's lone streetlamp, Boke imagined a cat, once a beloved pet, now stray but not entirely feral, scratching at the front door to be let in. Sleep eluded him past the midnight hour in a bed that once belonged to other people. He masturbated in an attempt to relax. It didn't help.

According to the clock, at just after two the mewling resumed. A skinny cat seeking entrance into its former home, in search of its human family. The previous residents had owned a cat, according to the food and water bowls he found weeks earlier among the dusty clutter in the kitchen cabinets. Boke had wondered of the cat's fate then, as his imagination sometimes pondered the two men, the no-bodies. The men who dined among the delicate cherry blossoms. The hands that switched on the cobalt blue lamp at night.

Boke buried his head between two pillows. The crying baby chased him.

"New workers coming into town," Cashan said. "We need to house them, so you'll be getting a roommate."

Boke nodded. "There's plenty of space. Thank you for the update, Supervisor."

Cashan clapped a hand to his shoulder. Boke ignored the missing finger, which had invaded his nightmares, along with the echoes of a stray cat scratching at the front door.

A roommate in the big house. Boke didn't confess the loneliness he'd suffered alongside his dark dreams. He welcomed the company, he admitted only to himself.

"Worker Shotton," Cashan said. "Meet Worker Boke."

The man standing at the front door stood ramrod straight, showing no expression beyond the raw nerves projected through his eyes. Boke offered his hand. Shotton eyed it through a lens filled with private stories, short and long, whole novels written in invisible ink, and briefly hesitated from accepting. When their hands connected, Shotton shook with the sort of strength capable of snapping the bones of lesser individuals. Boke didn't take the display for aggression or an attempt to establish dominance, but for unease, awkwardness.

"Show him around the place, will you," Cashan said.

"Of course, Supervisor. This way, Shotton."

On his first day in the house on Maple Street, Boke had found a mattress and box spring resting against a wall in the back bedroom.

The pair now lay on the floor, sans frame. Shotton sat upon the threadbare comforter, staring out the window. He still wore his factory uniform, though his boots rested beside the bed along with discarded socks.

"If you need anything," Boke said.

Shotton broke focus with the patch of night visible through the grimy windows and the deceptively bright sparkles of golden light in the neighborhood below the hill, along the river, where upstanding workers and their families huddled against the growing darkness—a landscape liberated of all deviants and undesirables, purged of the Treasury's foes.

The room's closet contained an antique crystal lamp. Boke had plugged it into the socket to welcome his new roommate. Like the bed, the lamp sat on the bare floor. Shotton's unease registered clearly in the canted light.

"Need?"

Boke shifted his weight to the other foot. "You may hear a cat. A stray cat that visits at night, scratches at the front door. I think it used to live here."

Shotton nodded.

"Goodnight, Worker."

"Goodnight," said Shotton.

Boke wandered downstairs. The cobalt blue lamp glowed in the bay window. He switched off the lamp, opened the front door, and checked for the cat. Then, finding the entrance vacant, Boke locked the door and returned to his room.

He dreamed about Cashan's missing finger, which wiggled and wriggled caterpillar-like about the house on Maple Street. Boke heard it scratching around, opening cabinets in the kitchen, skittering over the scuffed hardwood floors, the clack of its nail beating a tattoo into his subconscious, eventually rousing him awake.

Invisible ice crackled over his flesh. In the darkness broken by the streetlamp, Boke imagined the finger working its way under the inherited comforter, touching him. The hair on his legs prickled on instinct. All the moisture drained from his mouth, transformed into and exuded from his pores as clammy sweat. The clacking of the nail jumped out of his nightmare and persisted in the waking world. Only after Boke's heart stilled did he recognize the cadence for what it really was: a mouse moving about behind the walls, emboldened because the cat was gone.

Shotton was a handsome man with an unhappy face. According to the deepening lines around his eyes and mouth, his nights in the house were as disturbed as Boke's.

A cold rain fell, the next in a long line of gray days.

"Can I ask you—?" Shotton whispered.

Boke glanced at the other workers huddled beneath their hats and umbrellas. None listened in.

"Sure, Worker."

"Do you think our house is haunted?"

Boke shuddered, as much from the nature of Shotton's question as the power contained in an otherwise innocuous word.

"*Our*," he said, and coughed to clear his throat.

They drank the beer allotted on their rations cards. Though weak and practically tasteless, the brew conjured the first real smile Boke saw on Shotton's face.

"Praise the Treasury," he said lightly, and raised his bottle.

Shotton chuckled, laughter another rarity. "*Fuck* the Treasury."

They clinked bottles together. Eyes met, held. In that locked gaze, understanding passed through telepathy.

Shotton's throat knotted under the influence of a heavy swallow. "You said the ones who lived here before us . . ."

"Two men," Boke answered, nodded.

Shotton's eyes drifted away. Boke tracked them to the Japanese mural. For a brief and startling instant, the cherry blossoms seemed to float in a lazy breeze. Boke blinked. The alcohol in his system assumed full responsibility.

Shotton again faced him, and then their lips connected. Mouths crushed together. Boke kissed back, emboldened by the mild sweetness of the beer on Shotton's breath. Hands cupped cheeks. The kiss grew painful in intensity a moment before it broke.

"I'm sorry," Shotton said. "By the Treasury, Worker, I'm so terribly sorry!"

The other man jumped to his feet and hurried out of the dining room. The heavy clomp of his boots on the stairs sent Boke's racing heartbeat into a gallop. He wanted to cry, but the tears refused to fall.

Boke switched off the cobalt blue lamp. Raindrops drummed against the exterior of the old house on Maple Street in lieu of his tears, more sobs from a storm that refused to end. Shadows cut through by mosaics of bald light from the streetlamp dropped over the parlor.

He shuffled toward the staircase, gravity weighing down his footfalls. A scratch at the front door paused him on the first step. A plaintive mewl filtered through the door. Boke backtracked, reached for the knob, and turned. A figure on four legs darted through the gap and into the house, chirping in feline.

The cat eyed him suspiciously from a corner of the kitchen, its spine arched, its eyes all pupil. While filling the old food dishes with water and crumbles of meat left over from their dinner, he recorded the animal's matted coat, the piece of missing ear, the desperation, the fear, in its gaze. He'd seen the same look in Shotton's, assumed it mirrored his own.

"Here you go, cat," he said, and set down the bowls.

The cat yowled on its way over to the food. Boke thought about petting the cat, remembered Shotton's kiss and the fallout after, and decided against it.

Boke marched up the stairs to his borrowed bedroom.

No, *stolen*, the voice in his thoughts corrected.

Shotton's door was closed. Boke kicked off his boots, stripped down to his underwear, and crawled beneath the covers. The creak of footsteps drew him out of the fog, a state neither fully awake nor asleep but trapped in the limbo between. The bedroom door, once closed, now stood open.

"I dreamed about them again," said Shotton. "The two men."

The quiver in the other man's voice, the prickle of hair standing up on his naked flesh, registered in Boke's awareness despite the long shadows and uncertain hour. He drew back the covers. Shotton hurried over and into his warm embrace. They spooned beneath the blankets redolent with Boke's sweat, neither man speaking.

At some untimed point in the night, the stray cat crawled into bed with them.

Feed Me the Bones of Our Saints

~ Alex Dally MacFarlane

Jump up! Take arms! Bare teeth!
We fight for these sands.
Sink iron knives and white teeth into their scented flesh, their soft city flesh, those stealers of our homes. This is our city now, this desert with its winds that scour our cheeks, its dunes that join us in song, its rare springs that we lap at so gently. We once gulped rivers of rubies and pearls; now they do, and we will never be able to claim them back. We will not let them take this final city of air and graveyards from us! Jump up!
We fight for these sands with everything we have, and sometimes we forget the feel of a sister's shoulder beneath our heads, we've been so long without sleep—but today will be remembered for more than this.
Today we retrieve the bodies of our Saints.

Nishir and Aree the Courageous, Nishir and Aree the Fierce, Nishir and Aree the Kind. We write their names on every rock we pass, because we fear that one day we will all be killed, and then who will tell their stories? We imagine a foxless woman hundreds of years from now deciphering the desert's rocks and holding them close to her heart like a newborn child and kit.
It pains us to imagine a future where the suns cross and no child and kit are born onto the hot sands. No other people are born like us.
We buried Nishir and Aree only fifty years ago, when we still numbered in the hundreds, when we still inhabited cities and slept under ceilings of scuffed gold.

Jump up!

We send our bravest, brightest daughters for this most sacred task. Jiresh and Iskree first perform the dawn mourning, barking ten times into the wind the names of our most recently lost sisters. We cook their breakfast. A feast: mice and snakes in neat rows, roasted cactus flesh, crushed agari petals and rare kurik stamens. They take small bites, and then Jiresh holds out the plates to the rest of us, smiling. "Eat, sisters. We must all be strong." Iskree licks her dye-whorled tail as we share the food. We help them prepare. Fifty years ago we still hung so much silver from our ears that the flesh stretched, hanging around our shoulders, and we still dusted our faces with the powder of sapphires. Going into battle, we used to gild our nails and claws, and fit ourselves with mail that shone like small suns, like our mothers. Now we anoint Jiresh and Iskree with shattered knives. We bind the triangles to their foreheads with leather, and the jagged edges draw small beads of red. For each drop of their blood, we think, may a thousand fall from our enemies.

One by one, we embrace them.

Dutash holds Jiresh last, and whispers, "Stay safe, stay safe. I will dream of you every night. Bring me back dates, if they still grow there."

"I will," Jiresh whispers against Dutash's lips, holding her lover close, "I will, I will."

Iskree and Tounee inhale each other's scents, snout to snout, to carry close to their hearts.

And then Jiresh and Iskree walk into the desert, woman and fox, towards bold Barsime, the city whose walls threw themselves to the ground when we were forced out.

Few of us remember our cities' glory.

Mere villages, our enemies say. But we were never so numerous, never capable of filling each city with thousands upon thousands. What need did we have of numbers when our cities were so beautiful?

We know Onashek: how could we not? We held onto it the longest, Onashek of cinnamon, carved into such beautiful houses. Even when crowded with refugees, it failed to lose all its lustre beneath their detritus. It made the sweetest fires; its smoke scented the tears that covered our faces as we fled.

We know Eriphos of our well-scribed stones. We launch rare raids into its remains, pillaging the stones that are covered in our stories, in the script our enemies call crude, simple. A child masters it so quickly, they say, surely it is only a plaything, like scribbles of the suns. We only want our human sisters to learn quickly. They need to fight—it is a remnant of our luxury that we also want them to write, just as we make dangerous journeys to the places where indigo grows, so that our fox sisters can harvest leaves and dye their tails with their traditional shapes, denoting histories.

We know Barsime of the green sarcophagus, where Nishir and Aree lie under a heavy lid. Our oldest sisters tell of the sarcophagus's unforgettable beauty.

The way to Barsime is long and dry, but Jiresh and Iskree are used to hardship. They walk together, barking and singing in poor harmony, chasing lizards, seizing animals that emerge at night. The stars point a path from oasis to oasis, so that they can fill their leather water-bags and with careful rationing keep their tongues wet.

They find rocks covered in our human script, and Jiresh stops to read out every story. Young as she is, she has heard only a few of them.

Once, we knew more stories than there were stars to follow and admire at night. We wrote them in the desert for fun. What we have lost since that time is immeasurable.

Jiresh and Iskree cross the desert, walking the dotted line on Jiresh's map, until they reach the triangle of Barsime.

They almost miss it.

The sands have swallowed the city's remains, so that Barsime is only a strange pattern of small rises in the ground. Jiresh, tired and thirsting, walks blindly among them, stepping on and off the fallen walls. It is only because of Iskree, who never tires of digging for lizards, that she doesn't walk on to the salt flats and die looking.

It is the first sun's dawn. As warmth covers Jiresh's body, she sighs in relief. The night is always so cold.

Iskree finds worked stone.

Her barks draw Jiresh back. "Barsime," Jiresh says. "Then there must be an oasis, or a well." But they cannot find water. The date palms are gone, torn down and burnt. The careful irrigation system is lost. The desert has claimed back the land once held by our city. There will be no dates for Dutash. "Maybe there's still water underground."

The oldest among us recall that the sarcophagus is buried, and told them so before they left.

In the early morning's shadows, Jiresh and Iskree decipher the pattern of Barsime's fallen walls, and by the time sweat is soaking their bodies under two high suns, they stand in its center. Iskree digs. Jiresh helps her, on hands and knees sweeping aside the sand until they reveal a door, leading down.

Its jewels and bronze decorations are gone.

Nauseated, Jiresh pushes the stone door completely off the hole. Iskree, who sees better in the dim, leads the way down the cool stone steps. The temperature is a relief. They smell damp, and feel renewed hope for a well—and there it is, in the middle of the subterranean road. There is no bucket. Jiresh unhooks the bucket she carries on her back and lowers it on some of her best rope until it strikes liquid.

The water is perfectly, beautifully pure. She sets the bucket on the floor so that she and Iskree can both drink.

When they and their leather bags are full, they walk on.

There is enough light for Jiresh to see that the walls' decorations are also gone, prised off.

Jiresh wants hope. She wants it like she wants fine food and perfume and a house with windows of stained glass: it is a thing she knows that others possess and think nothing of, while she only has an emptiness that wants to hold it.

At the end of a long corridor, she and Iskree step into a small chamber.

The pedestal is swirled with blue like a tail and engraved with lines of letters, declaring in both scripts: *Here is the final sleeping place of Nishir and Aree, who taught us all to be strong.*

That the pedestal is bare of its green sarcophagus and sacred bodies doesn't surprise her.

Our enemies say that our stories are all lies, that we never were born each time the suns' paths crossed, we never were, that we were just women who went mad, who raped men to get their daughters, killed sons out of the womb, who tamed foxes with meat and bestial sex.

They say we never lived in those cities they filled with locks and guns and foxless people.

Iskree whines as if wounded.

"Why have you taken them if you think we're worthless?" Jiresh shouts to the empty chamber. "Why can't you just leave us alone?" She falls to her knees, sobbing. "You've won. You've already won. Why can't you stop stealing from us?"

When we later hear this tale, we will keen for their pain, and wish we were there to press against them and stroke their fur and hair.

"We only want to honor them," Jiresh cries. "We want to bury them in a place far from our enemies, where they'll be safe and we can always return to make offerings."

She lies on the floor, too tired to consider walking.

Iskree licks her cheeks and barks—it's not yet time to give up.

"We don't know where they've been taken," Jiresh says.

Iskree barks and barks, reminding Jiresh that yes, they do.

She and Jiresh are considered brave for more than their willingness to stand and fight while their maimed and younger and more fearful sisters flee an attack. They were once captured and taken to an enemy town, a place where our people die as easily as cacti under a blade. In their cell, as they planned an escape, they overheard the guards talking. One, a woman, said that she hadn't even believed the fox-fuckers to be real until she took her current job. She'd thought the exhibits in the Museum of Caa were hoaxes, like the skeletons of dog-headed men from the far North. Iskree and Jiresh happily killed all the guards several hours later.

Now they give thanks for being slowly, tediously taught the enemies' language as children.

"If they collect our artifacts in Caa," Jiresh says to Iskree, and the words taste foul as suns-turned meat, "then the bodies of

Nishir and Aree will be the museum's finest display." Iskree barks agreement.

The concept of museums is strange to them, even after seeing one of the enemy's towns. A life under roofs, in a house that is safe, full of children, full of food and copper pots that bubble over with meat and spices—they dream of such things. They feasted on the bowls of plain rice in that cell, ignoring the guards when they laughed, when they asked if Jiresh would fuck her fox, and could they watch.

Caa is even further away than that town—but it was once one of our cities, so it is on Jiresh's map.

Iskree barks, and Jiresh nods, determined. "We will not fail our mission. At dusk we'll begin walking west."

They sleep near the base of the steps to the subterranean part of the city, until they sense the darkening of the day, wake, drink further from the well, and depart.

They cross the western desert, and it tries like the drammik of legend to kill them. The land is truly plant-less, the water scarce, the sun unrelenting, though they find deep cracks in the ground and curl in them during the day, pressed to the earth in a desperate sleeping search for shadows. They sleep nose-to-nose; Jiresh has liked waking with hers wet since early childhood. They pine for Dutash and Tounee. Sometimes when they are tired, they lie under the stars, Iskree on Jiresh's chest, barking a rhythm in time to Jiresh's fingers drumming on the hard ground.

They sit on a stony ridge where agari flowers grow, and watch the city of Caa. Its old walls are tiled in emerald. Its old roofs gleam silver. Our walls. Most of the city is newly built of sand-brick, full of so many people. Iskree can already smell their food, and her gut cramps in longing.

Numerous times she and Jiresh have leaped into hiding as merchants leave the city, on their way to another of the enemy's cities. In this place, the fertile land is riddled with old rock formations that make easy hiding places.

"You have to hide," Jiresh says to Iskree.

Iskree growls.

"You have to. I can pretend to be one of them, poor and wild-haired, and they'll kick me a little but they'll let me in. I can steal their clothes, even, and find a stream to wash in, and bind up my hair, and they might let me right into the museum. If I walk in with a fox . . ."

Iskree snaps her teeth.

Jiresh buries her face in her hands, moaning softly. In truth she cannot bear the thought of separation from Iskree.

She remembers that she has seen women and men carrying large woven baskets of goods.

"I have a plan."

It is a long wait.

For this, Jiresh convinces Iskree to stay hidden. Jiresh too is out of sight, among rocks—among badly scratched, defaced stories of how we raise our suns-born young—until finally the wait is over. A woman approaches, with corn poking from the top of her basket. Looking at the quality of her jacket, its colors in patterns so fine that Jiresh thinks surely they're a figment of her imagination, Jiresh assumes that she traded cloth for food in the city. But how she got the food and basket matters little.

As she passes, Jiresh leaps out from her hiding place and strikes her on the head with a heavy stone. The woman crumples with a groan, and lies on the road, twitching. Only when Jiresh has dragged her into the rocks and stripped her of her fine clothes, untangled strings of beads from her beautifully combed hair and taken her basket, does she slit the woman's throat. The blood gathers in dips in the rock, like soup in bowls. Jiresh and Iskree feast on corn and small packets of raw meat from the basket.

Jiresh wants to wear the jacket, but fears someone will recognize it as belonging to the dead woman, so she only dons the dress under-neath—and cannot resist the belt, on which bells jangle like a contin-uous song. There she hangs her knife. She reluctantly unbinds her feet from their worn, tattered dark cloth, and puts on the woman's boots. Her long wild hair she winds into a knot at the back of her head, fastened with silver pins taken from the woman's head. She removes the knife-shards from her forehead and hides their small cuts with beads.

She worries that she will be instantly recognized as an imposter.

She uses the jacket and remaining corn as a cushion and conceal-ment for Iskree, who gives her a long look before curling inside.

"You know I wouldn't do this if there was another way."

Iskree licks her paws: she is unhappy, but she understands.

And so Jiresh, born under the crossed paths of two suns on a bed of hot sand, raised in the shells of old cities and under temporary canvas, walks into the thriving stolen city of Caa carrying Iskree on her back.

It is unimaginably big. She must keep walking. It crowds her: the voices, so loud and numerous, speaking that language not so different to her own. The colors of the clothes. Oh—the fruits, the powdered spices in pyramids, the smell of cooking meat. She drools and has to wipe and wipe her chin. Iskree buries her snout in the jacket to muffle her whimpers. "I know, I know," she hears Jiresh whisper. "Shh." They want to leap on the vendors and steal their food. Jiresh tries not to stare at women with big breasts, at men, at people of all ages who don't show their bones on their skin. The buildings are so tall, several times her height. There are so many children. There are no foxes. There are men.

There are so many styles of clothing that her unfinished theft of an outfit is complete next to others. There are so many kinds of faces that her darker, wind-scoured one is not so unusual. People look at her, and her shoulders are torsion-tense, and the worst they do is eye her apparent poverty with disdain, concern, wariness.

She thinks: *We are just a story to you, a folktale or highly questioned part of history, and you might not believe me if I said I've walked weeks in the desert to reach here, and I'll steal our Saints' bones back or die trying.*

Even though she has seen some of this before, in the enemies' town, it is too much, too different, and she is barely across the market at the gates when she wants to run back into the desert and sit under the sky's horizon-wide stretch, with the rocks and the agari flowers growing like little banquets.

She clenches her fists on the straps of her basket and walks on, up a major street, towards the distant roofs that sparkle in the suns' light.

When she walks in the remains of our old city, she must fight the urge to cry, to shout and rail against the theft of these walls. It's all so wrong! So full of intruders. Fists clenching ever tighter, Jiresh follows the winding pattern of the streets, but cannot find the museum. Increasingly uncomfortable under clothes and corn, Iskree turns and turns. She hears Jiresh begin talking in that ugly language. She imagines a whole city full of foxless people and nearly keens aloud for Tounee.

"I'm looking for the museum," Jiresh says to a vendor, who displays small, intricately detailed statues carved of bone on a bright red mat. It draws her attention even as she tries to carry out a conversation. Bone and blood, and under it dusty stones. Simultaneously familiar and wrong—a keen bundles in her throat like fabric.

Jiresh hopes the woman thinks her accent only distant-strange.

"Which one?"

"Um." Iskree circles again. Jiresh wishes that she could whisper apologies. What a fine city this is, with so many museums like gemstones on a necklace. "The one with the desert people in it? The women and foxes?" She doesn't know their non-derogatory terms for us.

"Sorry," the woman says, smiling, "but I don't actually know where that one is. You'll have to ask someone else."

"Oh. Thanks." Jiresh cannot smile back, and stalks off to find someone who cares enough about our people to know where our Saints are kept.

A man in a brilliant blue tunic overhears her question to another woman. "I know where it is," he says, with a smile as warm as tea. He has hair on his chin. He is tall and broad, like a wall, and his trousers subtly bulge. It's like talking to an inscription on Barsime's subterranean walls; even as more words pass between them, she can't imagine that she is doing this thing. "Do you want me to show you?"

"Yes."

Jiresh follows the man through the winding streets, with the walls only sporadically flashing green in the sunlight. They have faded in the seventy years since Caa was taken, and many of the tiles have been removed. She wonders how far away these people have taken our city. How many distant men and women admire their tile of green, perhaps scratched with a word or a cutter's careless tool, with no idea who gathered the emerald from the desert and turned it into a home?

"What's your interest in the fox-women?" her guide asks.

She glares at his back. "Their Saints are here. In a sarcophagus."

"Ah, the sarcophagus. It's the museum's greatest artifact, a perfect example of traditional burial practices and the veneration of important figures—"

"It's been stolen from its proper place," she says—the first thing that falls off her tongue—just to stop him from hearing Iskree's growls.

"There are some who argue that, but I believe this would have otherwise been lost. It's important to retain such artifacts. But I'm the curator's son, so of course I'm biased."

His smile is warm again. Jiresh imagines cutting off his lips and feeding them to him. Iskree thinks more simply of his throat.

They pass through an archway of tarnished silver, embossed with a story that Jiresh yearns to stop and read.

Inside the museum is cool, like the underground passages in Barsime. Barely anyone is visiting. "Do you want a tour," the man—Tulan—says.

"Yes. But I want to see the sarcophagus first. Please." She belatedly remembers being told that a brusque attitude is rude to these people, so richly burdened with the time to adorn their words as prettily as their clothes.

"All right." Yet again that smile.

So Tulan leads her past a collection of minor objects of our people—some that she doesn't even recognize—coins, cloth, crafts, knives, presented alongside paintings and sketches of our cities in their various states, occupied or ruined or remembered. There's a small story-stone. Jiresh runs her fingers over it, tracing words that don't belong in this cool, plain-walled room, with a smiling man in blue. There's a tail, and Jiresh retches at the thought of these people cutting apart a sister for their wall.

"And here it is," Tulan says, with a flourish, oblivious to her hatred. "I'm awed by it every time."

The sarcophagus stands on a pedestal in the middle of a wider room at the end of the corridor. Another man stands on guard, so large that Jiresh could fit herself three times into him. A woman and a child browse the items on the nearest wall.

It is beautiful. It catches Jiresh, so bright a green and covered in the tales of Nishir and Aree, carved in the shapes of stone-stories and tail-stories. Its lid is half off. She steps forward. Inside—she could reach out and touch them—lie the mummified remains of Nishir and Aree.

Jiresh turns and draws her knife, fast as a dust storm, and slashes Tulan so deep across his stomach that his guts fall over his tunic before he can move his hands to the wound. Jump up! Iskree struggles free of the basket's contents. The giant moves, quicker than Jiresh expected. The woman and child scream. Jiresh throws her knife and the giant falls, crashing, and she darts forward to retrieve her knife as Iskree leaps from the basket, growling, teeth bared. Jump up! The woman is sobbing, begging, "Please, please, don't hurt my boy, please."

"Don't stop me."

"I won't, we won't, oh . . ." Her next words are lost in her sobs. The boy hides his face in her clothes.

Jiresh holds her knife between her teeth and reaches into the sarcophagus. Our Saints are stiff, brittle. Shouts, heavy feet—more guards. Iskree waits for them at the room's entrance. Cursing, Jiresh puts the remains of Aree whole into her basket. She needs her hands to fight. She cannot carry Nishir. So she snaps Nishir into pieces. "I hate them, I hate them," she hisses, with tears gathering in her eyes like dew. Saints should not be treated this way.

Iskree barks at the six approaching men.

"Stop!"

"Stop!"

Voices like rocks falling.

The pieces of Nishir fit into her basket, and she gets the beautiful jacket over them, holding them in place, before the men are grabbing for her. She darts away, while Iskree leaps forward, tearing at their heels through their fine boots. One man cries out and goes down.

"Slow and stupid and *fucking thieves*!" Jiresh screams, knife back in her hand. Who to strike first? Soon they'll use their little guns. "We won't let you take them from us!"

The leader of the five remaining men raises his gun, and Jiresh throws her knife. They both dodge the other's weapons. The bullet shatters something behind her.

"I hate you!"

Iskree is too quick to be kicked. Jiresh reaches over her shoulder and grabs corn, throws it, confusing them, and she runs to a wall where she pulls away a knife with small emeralds embedded in its blade. Another man screams as his heel is torn open. His blood runs over Iskree's teeth, and she runs at the next. The little guns are making noise. Jiresh feels one, two, three bullets strike the basket as she leaps for cover behind the pedestal.

They are blocking the way into the corridor—until Iskree tears at shins, breaking their attention. Jiresh runs at them, slashing with the knife. One of the men grabs her arm and yanks away the knife, growls, "Hold still, little bitch."

"Never!"

She bites his hand, and he cries out, lets go, and the others don't have time to stop her from running past.

More bullets strike the basket. Something fire-hot grazes her thigh, but she keeps going. Iskree follows, heart beating fast at the sight of blood on Jiresh's leg.

Jiresh shouts wordlessly with triumph, even though she knows there is a whole city to escape.

Another gunshot. Agony. Iskree screams.

No. And another. "No!"

Jiresh turns and the man fires again. A bullet slams into her shoulder. She sees Iskree lying on the floor, bleeding too fast, lying in a growing pool of red like that woman's bone-covered mat. "No, no, no . . ." She crumples to her knees, tears like a flash flood. Iskree is already dead. Not even a final bark.

The men are reloading their guns. Soon they will kill her, as they have killed Iskree.

"No." The basket is heavy on her shoulders, full of Saints. Either she can die avenging Iskree or she can take Nishir and Aree from this vile place, the task Iskree died trying to complete. She wants to do both. She wants to tear out every throat in this city. "I will avenge you."

She is quick enough to dart forward, grab Iskree's body—twitching, death's last movements—and clutch her sister to her chest, and then she runs from the museum, so full of hate.

The sight of a woman bleeding, weeping, holding something small and furred and dead is so strange that it is watched by hundreds. A few reach forward, as if to grab, and Jiresh dodges them. She runs until she's back in the desert, back among the labyrinthine rocks outside the city, far from a path this time, and there she hides, weeping.

Even when her chest and throat hurt as much as the wound in her shoulder, she weeps.

In Barsime, she leaves Iskree on the empty pedestal.

In Barsime, almost blind with tears, unable to climb those stairs and leave Iskree, she is not quite blind enough to read a story inscribed on the wall of the Saints' chamber. It sets her jagged, broken thoughts ablaze.

"Feed me the bones of our Saints."

We stare at Jiresh, our skinny, bloodstained, foxless sister with bones and flaps of skin in her arms.

"They will kill us like they killed Iskree. Every year their weapons are stronger, every year we are hungrier. They will kill us all, and we will be completely forgotten. Our rocks will be scoured by the sand-heavy winds until future historians can only sigh into their notes and say that some old culture lived here, but too much is lost now to say who we were. How brave and strong we were. Jump up." She speaks our battle cry, and it is raw as a wound. "Jump up. Let me tell you a story I found in Barsime. We have forgotten what we carved into stone only fifty years ago. Let me tell you about bones."

Some of us, old enough to remember the construction of that subterranean chamber, know this story, and begin to grieve, knowing that we cannot stop this; and some begin to imagine a victory.

Jiresh stands with those bones in her shaking arms and says, "Once, over five hundred years ago, when two more sisters were born every time the suns' paths crossed, there was fighting. We and another people competed for a great region of gold, where even the most pitiful bushes were said to shine with the brightness of it in the soil, and two of our sisters were especially honored for their skill in combat, and were agreed to be Saints. Eventually they were killed, in one of the bloodiest battles of all. Their lovers feared that their bodies would fall into the hands of the enemies, and so consumed them entirely, hiding in a gully. When the lovers returned to the field, they felt the weight of the suns like a heavy knife in its sheath upon their backs. They wielded it, and that is how we won the fields of gold, to build the first of our cities that was stolen in this century."

We stare.

Some of us know that she did not finish the story. Did not say, *And the destruction so horrified them that it became one of the great sins of our history. No one has ever used this power since.*

Fifty years ago, we still thought we might survive. We carved our history into that burial chamber and imagined writing about our victory, or our remaining cities becoming more beautiful than ever, or our tentative peace with the enemies—something that was not hunger and death in the open desert.

"We can wield the suns," Jiresh says. "I don't know what it means, exactly, but it's a weapon. It's . . . I think it's an end."

"For whoever wields it, too," Dutash whispers.

"Yes."

Jiresh cannot quite look at Dutash.

The wind gusts between us all, mournfully.

"Will anyone come with me?" Jiresh says. "In case . . ."

In case anyone else wants to watch Caa consumed by fire. In case anyone wants to join this vengeance.

And, hidden in her words: Jiresh doesn't want to die alone.

One of our oldest sisters snarls her disagreement, and another takes up the sound—and another, womanless Koree, jumps at them with her teeth bared. Tounee and many others join her. Dutash looks away, less certain than Tounee. Foxless Lizir stands up and says, "I will come with you."

"And I."

"I want to."

Voices young and old, human and fox—but this is not a quick argument.

"It will be brutal," an old sister says. "You must know that."

She is laughed at. As if the war hasn't been brutal.

"This is not a battle," she persists, "where two sides are equal. I know that is how this entire war has been waged. I know. I understand. But you must know that you are planning to join them in sin. It is not a decision to be made lightly."

"I'm going to do it," Jiresh says softly. "I crossed the desert alone. It took weeks. I carried these bones, and I never stopped thinking about it."

"I know, sister." There is nothing more she can say.

We cook our dinner, comb the children's hair and fur, set up tents for the night, murmur lullabies to the single pair of babies—they are so fragile in their early months, so easily killed by the desert—and the argument goes on, too complex to be sewn into the finest enemy jacket.

We touch our Saints' bones, one by one, with snouts and lips.

We cannot all agree.

We decide to separate, permanently, and it pains us more than the fall of every city combined.

Jiresh consumes the bones, pounds them with one story-covered stone onto another, making a plate of a battle tale. "I will make a finer tale than this," she chants. "I will make a finer tale than this." She scoops handfuls of dust and pours it down her throat, and her lips are stained pale. Though she coughs and chokes, she keeps eating it, periodically licking under her fingernails and scraping the stone's incisions and scratches free of powder. She whispers, almost too quiet for anyone to hear, "I didn't think it would taste so horrid."

A whisper for a fox that no longer lives.

She stands, still coughing, and massages her neck with one hand. "We should go," she says. "Gather your weapons."

No tremendous change has overcome her.

"Have faith," she says, with a sly smile that curves her lips like the word for victory.

We make ready.

Jiresh gives the skulls of Nishir and Aree to those of us who will remain in the desert. "Bury them together," she says softly, "with every rite we still possess, with every song. Bury them touching, as if they are just sleeping side-by-side."

We who remain in the desert mourn as they leave.

We cross the desert without any song, with the suns hot on Jiresh's back. Dutash walks with us—the only sister to stop and score our story on rocks, lingering at each one as if she might not have to continue. Tounee's desire convinced her not to stay at the place where Jiresh consumed our Saints. Jiresh's determination drags her, hurts her.

"Jump up," Jiresh says as we grow nearer to the city. "Jump up. Jump up."

She rarely speaks without repeating. Only at night, as we curl together in a far smaller pile of skin and fur than we are used to, does she murmur single sentences, confused and painful, into Dutash's hair or Toree's flank or the sand, cooling against her cheek.

"Jump up."

Caa reveals itself, large in its gentle green valley.

We feel the suns, now.

"Jump up."

"Jiresh," Dutash says, reaching forward to touch her lover's arm—hotter than silver poured into its mould. Dutash yelps and snatches back her finger, and sucks on it. The suns' heat intensifies. "Jiresh," Dutash says again. "Jiresh."

"Jump up!"

Jiresh runs fox-fast along the road to the city and takes the suns with her.

Knives in hands, teeth bared, we yell. *Jump up! Jump up! You can't forget us! We'll burn you from your homes! We'll set you all ablaze! We'll slide teeth and silver into the last throats!* As we run towards the city it bursts into flames, swallowing Jiresh in a flare like a blink.

The fire spreads quicker than a dust storm, covering the entire city in minutes. The air is full of roaring and cracking and screams. People cannot move—they are burnt to their bones, their blackened, broken bones that crunch under our feet. The houses fall.

Jiresh's voice carries through the flames. *You took my sister! You! See how your arteries singe off my teeth like hair.* We hear her laughter. We hear her screams.

We who remain in the desert hear her, whisper soft, unstoppable as the suns' light, which glows so bright in the Northwest.

Her fire-body is pain, is power. Is everything she dreamed, in that long, lonely walk from Caa to Barsime with Iskree in her arms, to the camp where sisters lived in fear of more deaths to bark at dawn.

You will never forget us! she screams with every part of her body.

We scream.

We don't die. The fire licks our bodies tenderly as tongues, so that Dutash, following Tounee into the emerald walled—black-walled, wall-less—city-heart thinks the fox could be caressing her.

"Jiresh!" Dutash cries into the fire.

Not every person in Caa is immediately consumed. In the minutes before the fire spread, some fled through the seven open gates. Some of us chase them. We laugh as the fire leaps after them, thrown like knives—Jiresh roars triumph as each one falls—and we finish whoever we find beyond the fire's reach.

We jump back into the flames, cradled by our burning sister.

"Jiresh!"

Dutash's feet crunch over blackened bones, which crumble away like cheek-powder in the wind.

Another sister cries out, "Here, here, there are more of them!"

Our enemies hide in underground chambers and caves, in places where running water keeps them cool. Dutash sees them cowering and thinks: *How many times have we done this, hiding in fear?* Thinks:

Some of them are too young to have ever attacked us. She doesn't want to make this decision. She cuts their throats. None of them survive. None of them will kill us.

She imagines those who lived in the fields, who fled or hid when they first saw women and foxes running along the wide road into Caa, finding these un-burnt bodies amid the wreckage above and knowing how well we learnt not to show mercy.

You will never forget us! You will never look at a fire without remembering Caa! You will never look at emerald or silver without remembering how it all fell into dust and you will never, never take another of my sisters from me!

As blood soaks her feet, she staggers up the rocky steps.

She can't see walls through the flames. She can't see Tounee. She shuts her eyes and runs.

"Jiresh! Stop!"

Tounee climbs blackened steps into the streets, where the fire surrounds her like Dutash's arms. Where is her sister? The fight is over.

The suns are getting hotter.

Tounee runs and Dutash runs and there are no sounds of life, only fragmented city-pieces and bones under their feet.

You will remember us!

Jiresh's voice is fainter now. The suns are hurting Dutash, who stumbles. Sisters across the city fall. "Tounee!" Dutash gasps. "Tounee, where are you?" She weeps, and the fire burns away every drop. She longs for the desert and her sister and a time when—she cannot think of a time she wants. But each memory of Caa is an agony. Fire and bones and our enemies' blood running over her hands for the first time in her life.

She wishes she hadn't followed Jiresh. "Tounee." Like her sisters, she falls.

A murmur from the flames: *They'll never forget us. Never.*

"Never," sisters whisper and bark across the city, as the fire blisters their skin. Some still have the energy to run. Some almost make it to the gates.

Jiresh feels her sisters in the flames and presses against them, finally afraid of her death, seeking comfort.

Never.

Tounee, who turned away from the killing to follow her reluctant sister, reaches the place where a great arch once stood, and doors of wood and bronze. Through the flames she sees a horizon. She sees Dutash, fallen on the ground, too fire-blind to see the way out. She barks in joy. Nothing. She bites.

"Tou . . ."

Tounee grabs onto Dutash's elbow and begins dragging her, though the fire is burning her eyes and her body.

An hour after Tounee drags Dutash into one of the streams feebly running between burned, bone-covered fields, the fire dies down. Black dust remains. For months it blows through the desert, and there is no one who does not know its source.

Two sisters walk with the wind at their backs, blind, lost.

We find them. We who went to Caa to find the remains of our sisters bring them slowly back to the place where we have buried Nishir and Aree. As the wind speckles our skin with black, we wait—afraid and determined, angry and grieving.

Creezum Zuum

~ Juli Mallett

Dear Writer-or-whatever-you-are:

The most intractable problem in panic attacks for you has always been the sense that at some point you'll lose yourself in them, hasn't it? At one point or another you will cease to be you, and you'll be at best some half-deranged caricature of yourself, permanently unmade by terror. You will cease to be you, the individual you are will be lost, continuity will be shattered, and someone else will wake up *in medias res*, in the body you once called home, the mind that once was yours.

It's about, it seems to you, the feeling of standing on a precipice. The way that when you cross a bridge that you used to be afraid you would go flying south towards the equator from, you brace and resist the whole way. Even when you've already crossed it, there is a lingering horror that perhaps you're not the person that you were when you crossed it.

Rites of initiation sure cut to the heart of that, don't they? So perhaps you should write about those. Not a baptism, though, or anything so silly as a secret society; no, you've been feeling quite well and truly cyberpunk lately, and so it seems right and good to have your protagonist's story begin with walking towards some automaton or authority figure, the way that all good cyberpunk should be. Strike the balance between the BBC's white, light sets for *Doctor Who* and Channel 4's grainy, dark sets for the *Max Headroom* movie—walls with too many circular cut-outs or glass bricks with colored or too-white lights shining brightly or dimly from behind them. Perhaps we're back to *Doctor Who* again—sounds like something from *The Happiness Patrol*, doesn't it?

And while you're doing your little bit to swing your canal boat of pirate literature just *so* so you don't lose your balance of good taste and fall into the waters of lawsuit, you should perhaps quite punkily taunt a prick. Be obnoxious and ostentatious in how you enter the story in the middle of things (or in a substrate of beef) so that perhaps you might get to stand up in court some day, defending against allegations of plagiarism and copyright infringement from an inflated old fart, and shout: "Repent, Ellison!"

Rite and ritual are about transformation, some have suggested, and that is the essence of that precarious, precipitous feeling you're so fascinated by. Much of it is how you lead into them, how you misdirect the conscious mind and make room for the unconscious to really connect with the archetypes and universal sensation you're trying to highlight for the benefit of the transformee.

And you know full well that you have a tendency towards awkward didactic writing when you want to say something about psychology like that, so be mindful of that. Your usual way of defusing that—making transparent self-references that suggest that as the writer you're aware of that you're being didactic, in such a way that the reader will be inclined to forgive—isn't going to cut it this time. Keep things simple and to the point, focus on the actions of the character, the plot, the movement of the whole damn thing.

The audience will have ears to hear, or damn well should. It's *true* enough, of course, and even if they don't understand it as well as you think you do, you can still tap into the nexus of existential anxiety that we all hold within us. Illusory non-control, true non-control, true control, illusory control. They know from years of reading mad pulp barkers and fake-hard neuroscience that they don't emerge from any given moment the same person that they were going into it. That the *them* of the present cannot really give assent to their future actions, and that the future actor they will become doesn't give a damn about that anyway.

The magic of ritual is in raising up that moment of movement, of permanent and irrecoverable change. Of marking one occasion very clearly on which the person that was ceased to be of their own free will, so that a new person might come into being and fully realize the hopes and dreams that were held so painfully close for an instant.

You, writer, try to hold on to that moment. It is a madeleine moment if ever there were one, because two whole lives meet in the conic section of time and space at the heart of it. The reader knows those moments, the sense of loss and hope, the sense of movement and stillness. You don't need to guide them too much.

But you are feeling sort of cyberpunk and sort of wry and all that jazz, too. Not just sentimental about change, but also sentimental about the terribleness of the future. And not the future merely, but the future as you imagined it in your bleak Rust Belt youth, in which dystopian futures seemed not a fantastic stretch but a certainty, in which hackers were like gangs and buildings were either massive glowing towers in perpetual night or gutted husks in the pollution-red sunsets you loved to watch so much in your very, very early years. And so your protagonist walks forward, and they stand at the mouth of change, at a doorway, or perhaps something that looks rather like a damnable TSA-style metal detector, or *pornoscanner* as our contemporary retro-future dystopia has opted for instead.

You know that the miracle of those moments is that the protagonist, the self, doesn't know if it's going to last another instant, and even sort of knows that the self that emerges from the other side won't really be the same all told, but that memory and experience will remain, along with the better halves of identity and individuality. Every ritual and every femtosecond of life rings out with the truth of that, of continuity and discontinuity, and the ultimate permanence of what people before our rationalistic, wealth-divided, techno-dystopian utopia might have called a soul.

And why should death be any different?

A Moment of Gravity, Circumscribed

~ Fran Wilde

Djonn's father owned the last ticker in the city and made sure everyone knew it. Brass-bodied, the ticker looked fragile and cold, its clouded glass face obscuring the dark symbols beneath. Despite its age, it ticked loud and regular, breaking the arc of a day into increments.

"You have thirty ticks to decide," Djonn's father said when he made a deal. Djonn loved that Father knew how long a person took to make up their mind.

He longed to open the ticker, to find what made the *yes-no-yes-no* rhythm inside. After their dependent, Raeda, found the ticker far downtower a year ago, Father's deals went *yes* more often than *no*. The ticker was a treasure. Father hung it high on their wall and wouldn't let Djonn's brothers fly with it. Djonn wasn't even permitted to wind the ticker. Djonn was clumsy.

Father said so that morning before he took to wing, his satchel strapped to his chest, lumpy with small treasures.

Djonn's three irritable brothers shook their heads and elbowed Djonn. They'd stayed up all night talking beneath the ticker's sturdy rhythm. Now, they pushed Djonn out of their way, pocketed six noisy fighting birds, and flew to the market on the city's southern edge.

Then Djonn's mother climbed the ladder uptower to scour the roof with the other women. Raeda disappeared. Finally alone, Djonn teetered on a three-legged stool. The ticker said *yes-no-yes*, cold in his hands.

When the stool's leg snapped, Djonn toppled, and the ticker cracked beneath him like a dropped egg. Bent metal pieces spilled golden across the floor. Djonn's home fell silent.

When Father returned, he would hang Djonn from Harut tower by his toes until his nose bled.

Unless.

"Raeda!" Djonn shouted, hoping she lurked nearby. Raeda would help. Djonn scooped up metal pieces and bits of broken glass. Held them out to her when she straightened from the family's small garden on the ledge.

"You unlucky boy," she said. "Gravity's own monster." She sounded like Mother, which annoyed him. He'd turned twelve and deserved more respect, especially from someone younger.

Raeda's robe was faded at the shoulders, and she'd hemmed the sleeves to her elbows. Her sunstruck skin looked green beneath the yellow cloth Djonn's mother favored. She'd patched her wingstraps with spare spider silk; wore them crisscrossed over her still-flat chest. But she owned no wings: her only pair had ripped months ago.

Raeda took the ticker pieces. She paced back to the ledge and the better light, muttering.

"What do we do?"

She answered him by holding her hands out toward the empty sky. The sun played light across the shards. Djonn imagined them falling towards the distant clouds.

"No!" he shouted, moving fast. He yanked her away from the ledge. "Raeda, you'll make it worse!"

Djonn grabbed the pieces. Hurried to hide them in his sleeping mat. The thick down pad sat folded atop a basket that held his things.

On a basket handle, Djonn's messenger bird ruffled feathers in protest, then settled back to hooded sleep.

"You'd greet your father with handfuls of garbage?" Raeda teased him. "Your brothers will never let you live it down."

She was right, but Djonn bristled. "They'll blame you too. You're meant to look after me."

"You're old enough to mind yourself," she said.

With her back to the ledge Raeda watched Djonn and waited. The city's towers rose bone white behind her, set off by blue sky.

Djonn looked at the hook where the ticker once hung on their home's central wall, behind the circle of three-legged bone stools and bright yellow cushions. Where the family crowded for dinner. Where Father made deals with friends like Raeda's uncle Maru, and the wingmaker, and others who gambled on fighting birds, or needed a helping hand.

His heart did a *pitterpat* imitation of the ticker. *Yes-no-yes.* Djonn met Raeda's eyes. "You can help me."

Raeda mended clothes. She cleaned. She weeded the family garden and mulched it with guano from the roof. She looked after Djonn and told him stories. She scavenged treasures from downtower and brought them to Father. Or she had, until her wings ripped beyond all repair.

Djonn cleared his throat. "You must help me find another ticker, Raeda, before Father comes home." He said the words firmly, as Father would. He thought about counting to thirty.

Raeda shook her head. "There are no more. I've looked."

"There must be! Somewhere!" He thought of all the tiers where his ancestors had lived, descending into the clouds.

Treasure came from below, Djonn knew, passed one generation to the next up the city's bone towers until something broke or disappeared. Father kept an eye out for metal and glass, to keep it from being lost. "The weight of things drags folks down until they lose everything," he said. "No one falls or starves downtower if I can help it." He'd say that and nod at the ticker.

He liked lenses and tools especially. And knives. Raeda, whom Father sheltered when trouble befell her uncle Maru, had proven especially good at finding those. Plus a few rarer treasures, like the ticker. But finding treasures had grown difficult. Metal and glass were rare in a city of bone and birds, clouds and sky.

Last night, Djonn's brothers had whispered about the clouds below. How treasure hid far downtower. Yes, for those strong enough to fly that low, strong enough to carry it up. How Raeda knew more than stories. Yes. How she knew what hid in the clouds, yes, maybe even in the broken tower, Lith.

Father had shushed them, furious. No. The clouds hid many dangers. Were too far down. Lith was a story. No. Leave Raeda alone.

Now, if Djonn could win Raeda's help, perhaps he'd find a treasure better than the ticker before Father returned.

Raeda crossed the bone floor near the yellow cushions and knelt, pressing her back against the central wall where the ticker had hung. She tucked her feet beneath her in a posture entirely made of *no*.

"He'll blame you too," Djonn said.

She looked at him, her brown eyes calm. "He knows I do not drop things."

Djonn always dropped things.

But Djonn paid attention when Father made deals. He knew give and take, the importance of speed.

"My old wings, Raeda. They're yours if you take me down to salvage."

At this, she looked out to the ledge, out at the sky, the city's towers. She flexed her fingers, worn rough on the fibrous ladders she used to climb from one tier to the next on their tower.

The city's fifty-eight spires were beyond her reach. Without wings, she could only climb up and down, never to another tower, never far away.

Djonn silently counted to ten, then walked to where she sat and held out his hand, as he'd seen Father do. She put her hand in his, and they clasped the deal.

Her lips parted in a smile, too quickly.

Perhaps, Djonn worried, she knew he'd kept his old wings to take apart, to see how they worked. Perhaps he'd decided wrong, or too fast. But a deal was a deal. Raeda would take him downtower on the ladders to salvage, and when they'd found something to replace Father's ticker, they'd come back up and he'd give her the wings.

He found a soft silk satchel in his basket; bound it over his shoulder and to his hip. Reached for a spare coil of rope ladder.

"You'll give me my wings now." She said it softly, still kneeling.

Djonn felt the moments slipping away.

When he nodded, Raeda smiled. "And I will take you into the clouds to find a treasure."

"What?" Djonn's pride at his first deal crumpled. Not even his father dared the clouds, their storms, the giant birds that prowled there.

Yet Djonn's brothers thought Raeda knew more about the clouds than she was telling. And yes, Djonn needed a treasure that would save him from Father's rage and his brothers' ridicule. So he swallowed his doubts and retrieved the old gray wings from his basket for Raeda. Gave them to her.

He lifted his new wings, all gold spidersilk and fine bone battens, from the basket. He slipped the straps over his shoulders. At the last moment, he lifted his bird from its perch, removed its hood, and fed a piece of dried goose into its sharp beak. The bird stretched its wings, flew to the ledge and waited for him there.

Raeda secured the gray wings to her wingstraps, and checked Djonn's to make sure those were tight. Then she turned and leapt from Djonn's family's ledge, snapping the wings open as she jumped.

An updraft filled the wings' faded silk, and Raeda laughed.

Djonn unfurled his new wings carefully and checked the grips and battens as he'd been taught to do. The wingmakers were skilled, but tears could happen, even on new wings.

"Come on!" Raeda shouted, now gliding just beyond the balcony. She'd found a fine vent, and let it lift her to glide in a near-perfect circle.

Djonn swallowed his nerves and leapt after her.

Raeda glided away from the tower, then raked her wings back. Djonn took a deep breath. When she dove, he followed, though he hated the steep plummet.

They dropped past tiers where families like Djonn's crowded, down the cold drafts to dingier levels streaked with the garbage of those living above. In the neighboring towers' shade, Djonn could see evidence of Harut's central walls thickening, pushing the living spaces toward the tower's ledges and the inevitable drop.

In Raeda's stories, told while she cleaned or hemmed or tended the garden, people sometimes went into the clouds and didn't return.

"They're not strong enough, or they lose track of time, maybe."

She'd told the stories with a smile, teasing Djonn about his skinny arms. "Your bones need to fill in. You'd get blown off the towers in the clouds." She'd poked at him, but been careful around the bruises. His brothers had sharp elbows.

The city grew away from the clouds, and people rose with it, she said. New bone tiers grew atop old ones, and, below, the central walls grew out, filling the towers. Even as the tools of Djonn's grandfathers' grandfathers pitted thin and dull, the city rose. The people rose out of the clouds, with the city, and were safer for it.

She hadn't told stories since her wings ripped.

When Raeda pulled up and began to glide the city's drafts again, Djonn prepared to circle the wide tower. They'd fly below the occupied tiers, beyond the places Djonn was allowed to go. Djonn breathed faster as they made the long glide around. He hoped no one saw them.

But with her wings spread full, Raeda dipped to the left and disappeared into the sun's glare.

Djonn twisted his head from side to side, frantic. His wings wobbled. Above, a class of young fliers, five- and six-years-old, flew tiny, ambitious arcs on patchwork wings over a net held by their teachers. Beyond the tower, an older group dove and mock-battled in the breeze. Below, only birds skimmed the air near the older tiers. The wind whistled in Djonn's ears.

He looked up to the tower's full height. He couldn't see them, but he knew his mother, her friends, and their youngest children were still on Harut's roof. They scrubbed at the bone with the rough scourweed that grew in the moist joins between tiers, hoping to make the tower grow higher.

Djonn's message-bird slowed beside him, knowing it wouldn't get another piece of goose if it lost its master.

He scanned the thick clouds far below. Was she already down there? He saw no sign of it. Had she skipped out on him? Stolen his wings? Father would blame Djonn for much more than the ticker.

A low whistle made Djonn peer under his left wing. Between the shadows of the thick towers, gray wings flashed in the sun. Raeda banked towards the city's eastern edge.

"Come on!"

Raeda turned to shadow as she used the neighboring tower's windshear to accelerate. Djonn struggled to do the same, whispering "wait!" He wobbled in the shear. Then he too pushed beyond his home towers.

A long glide later, he saw their destination: a gap carved in the city's horizon by a blackened stump. Lith.

Djonn had thought it only one of Raeda's stories. Even neighboring towers had risen far beyond the broken tower, had begun to forget.

They passed these towers, tiers long abandoned. Lith grew larger and darker.

The smell of it, Djonn realized, was more than Raeda's dramatic talk. Rot, like a bird had crawled into a basket to die, but much worse. The tower itself, broken, she'd said, somewhere far below, made the stench.

Raeda slowed her approach, lifted a foot from the wings' foot-sling, and landed on Lith in a cloud of dark dust. Djonn heard her coughing as he tried his own approach, wobbling and flying way too fast to step out.

"Careful!" Raeda shouted.

Djonn furled his wings in desperation, dropped hard to the tower's splintered bone lip, and scrambled for purchase. His wings banged the tower's edge before Raeda grabbed his arm to steady him. Blood bloomed through the knees of his robes.

"You're too clumsy for this, Djonn," she said. "You should wait up here."

Wait. On the blackening bones of Lith. No.

"What are we doing here?" he asked.

"You need a treasure, right?"

Djonn nodded. His message bird landed on his shoulder and poked at his ear, demanding food. He obliged, absently.

"Then you must go where the center isn't grown out, way down, where no one comes to salvage." She said it matter-of-fact and held her arms out. Lith.

"How did you know?" They stood far below the occupied city.

"Heard my uncle talk about it once with my gran."

Djonn frowned. His father had helped her uncle with a gambling debt, but the price had been steep.

"What did your gran say?"

"That this place is very old. People died here when the tower cracked. There are ghosts."

Djonn looked around. All he saw was dead bone, rotting while the city grew past it. His knees pulsed with pain.

"You can stay up here," she said again.

He shook his head. "I broke the ticker. I'll find something better to replace it with, or I won't go back."

"You broke something else, too," Raeda said, her voice filled with regret.

Djonn looked over his shoulder. His clumsy landing had bent his left wing. Two bone battens poked through the silk at odd angles.

Father would skip the hanging and throw him right into the clouds.

"It's all right," he lied, hoping his voice wouldn't break. "Maybe we'll find something to patch them with downtower."

Raeda watched him. She'd seen Djonn's brothers yank him back from near-disastrous falls. Heard them laugh at how clumsy he was and threaten to tether him like a baby, so they could reel him up. Djonn looked away from the pity in her eyes.

"You can send the bird, call for help."

He shook his head. "Let's go," he said, determined not to trip or stumble in front of her. His broken wing dragged behind him with a skittering sound.

He uncoiled the ladder and looked for something to tie it to. The uneven roof presented cracks and rough spurs, but he didn't think it would hold two climbers.

Raeda saw it too. "You go down. I'll hold the rope. Then I'll fly down."

"How far?"

She shrugged. "Ladder won't reach more than four tiers."

Djonn thought about the clouds. About his brothers, the ticker, his broken wing. "We should go farther."

Raeda grumbled. "Would be faster if you stayed up top."

"No."

The tower creaked and groaned as he climbed down the ladder's knots. He passed tier after blackened tier. Each smelled worse than the ones before. But Raeda was right, the central core hadn't grown out. Among the tossed and broken walls of the living quarters he passed, Djonn saw shadows piled high.

"This is good enough," Raeda said at the eighth tier.

"It isn't," he answered and lowered the rope again. Her stories always began *long, long ago*. They argued until they'd descended sixteen tiers.

"Lower than our great-grandparents," he whispered. His calves and shoulders throbbed.

"Much," Raeda agreed.

Lower and darker. Tendrils of cloud curled over the tier's dark bone floors. Something rattled in the shadows.

Only a bird, Djonn thought. We'll get the treasure and get out.

Raeda spoke, not looking at him. "Do you know a story called 'Bone Forest'?"

He shook his head. Focused on her words, rather than listening for sounds from the tower.

"My gran knew it. She'd lost everything but the story's name by the time I knew her. I thought maybe your brothers—since they go to the markets."

"What's a forest?"

"Dunno."

Raeda, distracted by the lost story, fell silent. She walked across the filthy floor. Djonn watched her feet, lost in their whispers. When she stepped on a goose-sized pile of feathers, dry bones cracked. Raeda cried out once and fell to her knees. A splintered goose rib pierced her left footwrap.

Djonn looked around for help. Lith, he remembered, held only ghosts. Then he knelt beside Raeda. He placed his hand flat against her heel and tugged at the splinter. She bit her lip and stayed silent. Djonn pulled again and the splinter came loose. Raeda lay down with her foot raised above her head.

"Bad luck," Djonn said. His voice cracked. "We'll get help now." His bird shifted on his shoulder.

"No. Get your treasure, then we'll send the bird." Raeda's voice wavered. "Look," she pointed. Something glinted on the floor beyond her reach, under layers of dust and grime.

Djonn bent to brush at the dust. His fingers touched cold metal, a bone handle. A knife. Father had many knives.

He stepped over it. Brushed at the dust beyond with his fingers. Uncovered small bones, knobby and jumbled, then long bones, bigger than his arm. A pile of curved bones and tiered bones. Djonn cleaned off the last of them and realized they'd make a grown man, though the skull was missing. He yelped.

His message bird startled and flew away. Djonn cursed after it, and at his own clumsiness.

Raeda crawled over. "Sat down and died, looks like. No one around to throw him over the edge."

"What happened to his head?"

"A bird took it for the eyeballs, like as not," she made a gnashing sound with her teeth, and Djonn paled.

"Aw, Raeda!" He felt sick and bent over, his back turned to her. He stared at the tower's dark wall, not really seeing anything. Stared at the dark shadow against the wall for a heartbeat, two. Then he blinked. Rust-rimmed metal, a bone handle on the lid, half hidden by rags and piles of rotting feathers. "Oh," he whispered.

Raeda followed his glance and whistled. "Look what we found."

She crawled faster than he could scramble, and beat him to it.

She fingered the rusted latches, then rubbed them with scourweed pulled from a pocket of her robe. A shadow passed by the tower. Another bird, Djonn thought.

Long-sealed hinges squealed as the box's top swung open. Inside was more metal than Djonn had seen in his life. Long pieces of it, sharp at the ends. Short bits, clawed bits, a long strip with symbols like the ticker. He'd seen Father hold one of the clawed things, once. Saw him cradle it like a bird, call it a tool, the rarest kind of treasure. There were nails too, plenty of them. Metal needles. And a strange two-legged thing with a piece of charcoal clamped to one leg. He snatched that from the box before Raeda slammed the lid down.

"What are you doing?" he asked.

"Thinking." She sat on the box and looked out at the blue sky beyond the black tower. The sun was high in its arc now.

Djonn tried to guess Raeda's thoughts. He wasn't sure what to think himself, except that she sat on his treasure. Metal. A pile of it.

"It's mine," he finally said. "I gave you my wings for it."

She looked at him a long time. "And you don't have any way to get it out of here, do you, sad-face brokenwings?" Djonn's brothers called her that, when they thought she couldn't hear. She rose, favoring her heel, and pulled at the box handle. The contents rattled. "It's too heavy to fly."

"We have to try," Djonn said with a screech. "It's mine."

"And what is mine, Djonn?" Raeda's chin tilted up.

Djonn nearly whispered "What could you possibly want?" because his mother had said it to him so often, but he knew. Raeda wanted to leave. With the box and his wings, she'd be free.

Djonn wanted to say, "Yes, take me with you," and "No, you can't," all at the same time.

His fingers tightened around the tool that held the charcoal. One leg ended in a sharp point.

"You have your wings. Help me get this back home and I'll give you some of what's inside."

She shook her head slowly. "I'm not going back. I'll make my own luck in the city, somewhere your father and my uncle can't find me." She had the box open again and began picking through the metal.

A shadow, backlit by the sun and bright sky, fell over her.

"That's exactly what you won't be doing."

A man stood on the ledge, furling his dark wings. He cracked his knuckles and stared at the box, and at both of them.

"Uncle," Raeda whispered.

Despite her uncle blocking the light, Djonn could see Raeda's face. Her eyes narrowed, and she looked from Maru to the box and back.

Any hope Djonn had that this was a rescue evaporated.

"Been watching you, Rae," Maru said. He jerked his chin at Djonn. "Boy's dad says you haven't brought in near enough salvage lately. Been putting a lot of pressure on me. So I saw you launch that bird."

Djonn's mouth formed an 'o'. Father's story about helping Raeda was a lie.

Still, Maru was a way out. Djonn could make a deal.

"Help us get the box back," Djonn said, speaking forcefully, like his father would. "And my father will forget your debt, I know it."

Maru laughed. "Boy, you don't know your father. Let's see what you found."

He eyed the box and whistled like Raeda had.

"The whole tower saw you two fly off, Rae," he muttered. "Won't be long before half the city is searching Lith for treasure. What else did you find?"

"Only that. And him," Raeda pointed at the skeleton. "And this," she raised the knife, pointed towards her uncle.

"Ingrate girl," Maru growled. He lunged for Raeda, and she dodged but kept her grip on the box. The box slowed her, and he knocked the knife to the ground. It skittered on the floor, stopping at Djonn's feet.

Djonn looked at the knife, remembering the times his brothers had taken bone knives away from him. *You'd kill yourself with something that sharp*, they'd laughed.

Maru grappled with Raeda and stepped hard on her hurt foot. She howled and crumpled. He dragged her up with one arm, her hand pinned behind her, against her furled wings. He reached for the box.

Djonn wrapped his fingers around the knife while Maru wasn't looking.

"You're not worth much, you lying sack of bones," Maru hissed at Raeda. He spun on Djonn, who barely managed to hide the knife in his robes, next to the pointed tool. "And you, you wingbroken fledge. Your father and brothers have taken the lifeblood of half my folk. What should be done with you?

Djonn thought for two heartbeats. "You have to let us go. People will come, they'll see. You said so yourself."

"They'll see what? A broken winged boy. Maybe that's something your father will take as full payment."

Bad to worse. Djonn wrapped his hand around the knife.

Maru swung the box of metal and Raeda towards the tower ledge. "Can't fly with both," he laughed, and changed his grip on the girl.

Djonn's heart pounded *now-yes-now*. He rushed Maru, blade held as Raeda had, all his weight behind the knife.

Maru heard him coming. He dropped the box, grabbed Djonn's arm and squeezed. The knife clattered to the ledge, wobbled, and flipped. It fell end over end towards the clouds. Djonn whimpered.

Maru pinned Djonn's hand by his shoulder blade, as his brothers did.

Raeda shouted as her uncle turned once again to hold her out over the ledge.

Djonn's other hand shot out from his robes on its own, holding the tool with charcoal and the sharp point. He didn't think. He drove the point hard into Maru's ear until he heard a crack. The man dropped to the floor, thrashing, and Raeda fell, catching herself by one hand on the ledge.

Djonn dove to the floor and clasped her hand.

"I won't drop you," he said.

Maru kicked behind them once more and stopped. Djonn pulled hard while Raeda scrambled and, soon, they both knelt on the ledge. In the distance, Djonn could see flyers headed towards Lith: four pairs of yellow wings still high in the sky. His father and brothers.

Djonn drew a deep breath and opened the box. Picked out five sharp tools and one metal strip. Held them out to Raeda.

"Go fast. Before they come."

Her eyes widened. She straightened her yellow robes and secured the tools in a hidden pocket. She put her hand out, and pulled him up to standing. "Thank you for catching me," she said. She took a hesitant step forward on her injured foot, then another, until she limped across the tier to a ledge on the far side of the tower's circumference. She leapt from the edge, snapping her gray wings open at the last minute.

Djonn bent to pull the weapon from Maru's ear. The tool wasn't meant for that. He could tell.

By the time Djonn's father and brothers landed, he'd figured out what the tool was for: drawing circles. He'd traced small and large circles on the dark bone floor, the charcoal invisible against the rotting tower.

He tucked the tool away in his robes and showed his father the metal box. He showed him the skeleton.

"Box was too heavy for him. Dragged him down."

Djonn's father clasped his shoulder.

"And Raeda?" one brother asked. His other brothers looked around the dark tier, at the dead man, at Djonn, who stood with one foot on the box.

Djonn peered over the ledge, to the clouds below, counted three calm heartbeats, then met their eyes for five more.

He watched them shift uncomfortably, caught between him and the clouds. "I couldn't hold her," he said.

We All Look Like Harrie

– Andrew Penn Romine

We all look like Harrie, when we can afford it. Even the boys. Even the girls.

Harrie styles sleek, gauzy silks of warm hues at dusk, electrified. We fling ourselves into perilous orbits around Harrie, either frosting in the far reaches of the night, or burning in the tempests of Harrie's miniature sun. Harrie whirls in private circles across the LED galaxies of the club floor, silver boots pulsing. Dancing with everyone. Dancing with no one.

Just one of Harrie's shimmery outfits costs more that the Gross Domestic Product of our little island. Our imitations, sweatshop-cheap, pale by comparison. We conceal the shoddy weave with the coruscating patterns of glims and ghost-silk that opaques in the UV lights of the club. Some of these things we make ourselves in the long, dry hours of the day. And with aching fingers we fasten them on our bodies, also sleek—but with hunger. In the short, damp hours of the night, we join the dance.

Harrie doesn't notice, or doesn't care. Most of the time, neither do we.

From the mainland comes a thick drink the color of porridge. *Klense*. Lose weight. New-tone. Health-glow. Aluminum cans like bullets, with pull-tabs and wide mouths. We kiss the metal lips and suck deep, careful not to cut our tongues.

Careful. Careful.

Harrie loves *Klense*, too, alloying the healthful brew with perfumed arracks and percolated brandies. Sometimes the bottles get passed around the near orbits, rogue comets with scintillating pixels like starbursts flashing every time they are upended. We toss them ever outward, until they fade, heat-death, batteries gone cold in the outer dark of the club floor.

One night, Harrie arrives at the club, jawbone shaved to a point, glims dangling like spittle from a filament sprouting from a newly sharp chin. Months consuming *Klense* have given Harrie a cadaverous aspect. We black circles under our eyes, alloy our own *Klense* with cheap arrack, dissolve tabs of appetite suppressant in the brew.

Our surgeries are more surface than Harrie's. Titanium horns. Glow worms—short, sparking cilia *and* the braided tails. Swirl tats. One dancer gallops the shuddering floor with hardened, bare feet like hooves. He's gamine-thin, a rattle of bones. Harrie embraces him, lets him sip from the fortified *Klense*, and we all sigh in desire and jealousy as their sweat stripes dayglo rivulets down their slender, knobby limbs.

Hoof-boy is fished from under a rotting pier in Cobble Quay the next silver-bright morning. Sliced open, hollowed out by organ thieves. He's still smiling, though. When the sun drops, we dance for him, and for his place by Harrie's side. No one shares a drink that night, but every one dances.

Viva Harrie! Viva Harrie! A call and response to our brightest star. Harrie is naked, hurtling bolts of discarded fabric and stim-ware into our grasping, grateful hands. We clutch these priceless baubles, weeping with cosmic joy. Harrie spins faster, pulling us closer.

Another dancer found in a stinking alley off Tropic Street, eyes gone, a clean, surgical job. Lungs butterflied to reveal the empty cavity where the liver and kidneys once rested. The dancer's forearm removed, too, but the hand left behind, clutching a pink echo-ring that repeats a ghostly beat of the club last night. One of Harrie's.

So we hear. None of us actually sees it happen.

Nu-Klense and *Diet-Klense. Bubble-Kleen.* A cheap knock-off, only pock-heads drink that.

Harrie still drinks *Klense*, we all drink *Klense*, mostly. But some of us don't dance so close anymore.

The fashions change. Ghost-silks are bilge. Now: diamond-threads, *turtleSkin*. Bio-plug grass pelts that scintillate with our moods. Harrie herky-jerks, a string puppet in passé sun-scarves, not even a scrap of *turtleSkin* dangling from those frantic hips.

Now from Harrie, *Viva! Viva!* but we're not listening to that beat, we don't need the cast-off shrouds of a dying star. We drift from the thinning gravity well, finding our own orbits.

A new brand from the mainland, *FastRQ*, sniffed or under the tongue. Colors and rage and ice-cool joy. It's Layalle who shows us how to unroll the scoop right from the lid. On our own, we find the cheapest prices on the candy-lacquered tins like squirming beetles in the wire baskets of the street vendors.

After that, it's Harrie they find on Cobble Quay, sagging and drained as a can of *Klense*. A discarded scarf. We dance hard that night, flinging empty pixel-bottles of percolated brandy and *at*mSauce*. *FastRQ* soothes, mellows, and our steps slow as we remember the sun.

Then Layalle descends to the floor, hedgehog spines streaming song and fire, and the dance returns, spinning forever around the balmy island night.

Letters to a Body on the Cusp of Drowning

~ A.C. Wise

THE NARRATOR'S TALE

Every tale must have a beginning. So what harm in starting here?

Once upon a time, a young girl ran away to sea with dreams of becoming a sailor. She bound her breasts and cut off her hair; she learned to lower her voice and swear like a man. Her hands were never a problem, she already chewed her nails ragged, much to her mother's consternation, and she had palms made for callusing.

By the time she signed to a crew, she could already drink most men under the table. Those she couldn't, those who were spoiling for a fight, always calmed at her offer to buy the next round and share a filthy new drinking song. No, it wasn't her body that betrayed her—she could haul line and climb rigging with the best—it was her heart.

Seven days out from their latest port, the *Bonny Anne* came across a wreck with a lone survivor. Once pulled from the waves, the men saw the survivor was a woman, and most were for throwing her back overboard—women and ships, after all. Only the young girl, Kit by name, was silent when the vote was called. She'd been heart-struck in an instant at the scent of saltwater drying on the woman's hair and skin, enchanted by the sea-green of her eyes, lulled by her voice, stitching the faintest threads of a storm inside the sweetness of her tone.

The men were right to fear her, but it would go worse if they cast her overboard, Kit was sure. They voted to let her stay, and that was how Kit knew she'd guessed right. The woman was a witch, and it seemed more than likely vote and shipwreck both were her doing.

The next night found the *Bonny Anne* becalmed. Kit, unable to sleep, walked the deck. Everything was still—not a breath of wind, and the water smooth as a mirror. Kit traced the path the moon made from deck to horizon; in all that stillness, it seemed a bridge solid enough to walk upon.

"What do you think is over there?" the woman asked, startling Kit, who had thought herself alone.

"On the far shore?" Kit remembered to drop her voice, but was unable to keep it from breaking.

"No, beyond the horizon." The woman considered Kit, not the line dividing sky from water.

"I'm sure I don't know." Kit gripped the rail, trying to still her hands from trembling.

"More water." The witch put her lips very close to Kit's ear, so Kit could feel the warmth of breath behind them, along with the shape of the woman's smile.

"Tell me," the woman continued, "when you look in the water, what do you see?"

Kit looked down, startled by the brilliance of her reflection and that of the woman beside her. The smell of saltwater had sharpened, even though the woman was a full day out of the sea. Her eyes, reflected in the water's glass, shone as luminous as things risen from the deep.

"The ocean is a trickster," the witch said. "It is both false and true. But on nights like this, when everything is still and the moon is clear, it shows us our true selves, and it cannot lie. Except when it does."

"What do you . . . ." Kit started to turn, but the woman pointed. "Look."

Kit, pulse wild with nerves, leaned out over the rail. In the moonlight, it almost seemed a few days growth of stubble shadowed her jaw; her shoulders looked broader, her fingers thicker. Kit gasped.

"Is that what you wish?" The witch withdrew, giving Kit space and leaving her cold; Kit shivered.

She faced the woman, putting the rail at her back, feeling the immense danger of both woman and sea. The curl of a smile remained on the witch's lips, a wisp of rising smoke, and the light in her eyes brightened.

"You know what I am?" The words came out before Kit could stop them.

"Do you?" The witch raised an eyebrow.

Kit shook her head, sick suddenly; her eyes ached and stung, but no tears fell. She loved the sea, the deck beneath her feet, the ship's song, creaking in the wind. But she missed her sisters' voices, and the way her mother would brush out their hair all together—fifty strokes for each of them until their locks shone.

"What if you could have it both ways?" the witch asked.

"At what price?" Kit's heart thumped.

"Clever girl." The witch stepped close again, fingered a lock of Kit's hair. "I think this is getting a bit long. You need someone to cut it."

Dazed, Kit followed the woman to the small cabin she'd been given. The witch had made a makeshift dressing table from a plank of wood and several empty crates. The table was laid with three silver objects—a hand mirror, a pair of scissors, and a comb—even though the woman had nothing when she was hauled aboard.

With the gentle pressure of fingertips on shoulders, the woman pushed Kit onto an upturned crate acting as a chair. Picking up the comb, she began to work salt-matted knots from Kit's hair.

"It's easy," the witch said, catching the thread of a conversation Kit barely followed. "You can change, but every time you do, it will stitch a ghost under your skin. You can become a man, and as easily become a woman again, but each time you do, you will remember an entire life not your own. Or perhaps it is very much your own, only from another time, and there will always be the risk of losing yourself beneath the layers. That is the price."

Kit's hair lay smooth by the work of the witch's comb, the edges curling to tickle her ears and the back of her neck where it had indeed grown too long. As the witch lifted the scissors, Kit twisted to look at her.

"How do you know all this?"

"Oh." Light slid through the witch's eyes, a crescent moon, wicked-sharp as a smile. "I've had occasion to borrow a ghost or two in my time."

The witch set the scissors down, and in a smooth motion, undid the buttons of her borrowed shirt. Kit's breath caught, pulse snagging at the sight of the witch's breasts, full round and visible for only an instant before the witch wound the shirt around them, binding them as Kit bound hers. As the cloth went round the witch's chest more than flattened, it broadened; the texture of her skin became rougher and hairier. The witch took Kit's hand, and pressed it to her throat; Kit was shocked to feel an Adam's apple.

"You see?" The witch's voice was deep, rough like a stone not yet worn by the sea. Only the eyes remained the same—green as tide and weed.

"Teach me." Kit exhaled.

The man turned Kit toward the wall again, wielding the scissors. As each scrap fell, Kit felt the subtle shift as bones arranged themselves to a new form.

"And when I want to change back?" Kit asked, voice caught between male and female, both and neither.

"Like this." The witch brushed out Kit's hair, making the strokes long as though tresses fell halfway down Kit's back; soon enough, they did.

"And here." The witch produced sweet-smelling powder, dusting it onto Kit's cheeks with his rough palms so she felt the cheekbones shift again, her face narrow. "We all wear masks, it's just a matter of choosing to make them more than skin deep."

The witch handed Kit the mirror, and Kit met her startled reflection—the girl who had run away from home, not the sailor boy she'd become.

"It's that simple?" Kit set the mirror down.

"Nothing is ever simple." The man sighed, running his hands through his hair, lengthening it where Kit had barely noticed it shortened. She unbound her breasts, and Kit's cheeks warmed before the witch re-buttoned her shirt.

In place of slivered-moon mischief, a well of sadness filled the witch's eyes.

"Why?" Kit asked.

The witch shrugged, tone husked slightly. "Perhaps I'm lonely."

Kit studied her, the turn of her shoulder and the weight visibly bearing it down. She understood in her bones: the witch offered both blessing and curse, all rolled into one.

But Kit had been heart-struck the moment the half-drowned witch had been pulled aboard. She touched the witch's shoulder lightly.

"Yes." Kit leaned forward, but her voice was barely a whisper. Teeth caught lip, uncertain, but she made herself look into the witch's eyes.

She could feel the witch's pulse, the warmth of her, the steady beat of her heart. The witch shifted stance, an agreement and an invitation—a shared moment of sorrow and joy.

"How . . ."Kit faltered, throat dry. She closed her eyes so she wouldn't have to see the witch's face if she guessed wrong. "How do you want me?"

The witch's fingertips brushed the edge of Kit's shirt, loosed the first few buttons, and traced the edge of the bandage still binding Kit's breasts.

"However you choose."

Every word of this is true. Every word is a lie. So it is with witches and things brought up from the sea.

Kit finds the letter atop the crisply made bed five hours after the cruise ship sets sail. The paper is wrinkled with the memory of damp fingerprints and smells faintly of the sea. At the right angle, the ink shines with a green reminiscent of lightless places, and for a moment it reminds him of something, someone. The letter is addressed: To a Body on the Cusp of Drowning.

His pulse stutters. As long as he can remember, Kit has been terrified of water, especially the sea. His first memory, one his family and countless doctors have told him can't possibly be real, is drowning.

A trick by the service crew? No, they mostly work on tips. Another passenger? How would they gain access to the cabin? With shaking hands, Kit slips the letter from its envelope and reads.

You will drown. We saw it in your eyes as we swam below you, just under the glitter of light on the waves. Your eyes searched the water, and they were hungry. You did not see us, but we saw you. We know you. There are ghosts beneath your skin, and every one of them, every one of you, is made to drown.

But before you do, let us tell you of the sea.

Kit drops the page as if burned, and presses her fingers to the aching space between her brows. Something has changed; something is wrong. A moment ago she was someone else, and what is she doing here? On a . . . boat? That can't be right. Kit is terrified of water. No, now she remembers. The doctor said it would be good for her, contact therapy.

Yes, Kit remembers lying in the netting around the ship's bowsprit, stretched like a hammock over the waves, fighting stomach-cramping fear. She'd forced herself not to look away. That was when she'd seen the flash, there and just as quickly gone.

Dizzy, Kit lowers herself to the bed, trying to catch her breath. It had been a trick of the light. After so long staring at the ship's carved figurehead—the woman with arms spread as though to gather the sea, and in place of legs or a tail, the ship itself flowing behind her—Kit had merely imagined seeing something impossible beneath the waves.

Kit glances at the letter again.

Every one of you is made to drown.

At night, with the cabin's porthole cocked open to the breeze, Kit listens to the timbers creak, the sailcloth flutter, the waves slap the hull. The sounds should be soothing, but Kit gathers the sheets in clenched fingers until his knuckles turn white. The ship is only a recreation of a grand clipper from the golden age of sail, but the roll of the deck feels hauntingly familiar. How is it that lying under soft sheets, Kit's body remembers the sharp cut of hammock rope, being suspended among other sailors, listening to them breathe? Phantom calluses harden Kit's palms; bare feet itch to scale the rigging. Kit's arms, roped with invisible muscles, long to swing into the crow's nest so salt-chapped lips can taste the air.

She releases a breath. If she fails to concentrate she slips—memories, nightmares, dreams. Ghosts. Kit's body tumbles from a high cliff and shatters on salt-washed rocks far below. Kit walks into the waves, pockets full of stones. Kit lets go of a ship's splintery rail, relinquishing control to a storm.

How can these memories be hers? Kit is lost, some elusive truth constantly slipping just beyond his reach, falling through his hands. Something about the sea; there is something about the sea.

Tired of sleep eluding her, Kit paces the small cabin. The roll of the ship rises to meet her bare soles, bringing a sudden, sharp awareness of her body. It feels wrong; it does not belong to her.

These are Kit's hands: fingers blunt, nails short—strong hands, nimble, but the skin is neither calloused-rough nor silken-smooth. This is Kit's hair: cropped short, but not salt-tousled or finely coiffed. And Kit's frame: short, muscular, but beneath the skin, the bones are too fine for a sailor's bones and not delicate enough for a noble's. None of the pieces fit except Kit's eyes. They are the grey-green of the sea.

The second letter appears as the first, the paper damp and smelling of current-stirred weeds. Kit resists the urge to put paper to tongue and taste squid ink, shells crushed to particulate dust, and black, volcanic sand. What if the paper tastes of nothing?

Kit reads.

There are myths about the sea. It is hungry, greedy. It takes everything, and gives nothing in return. It cannot be reasoned with, or prayed to; it cannot be bribed. What it is owed, it will claim. What it is not owed, it will take anyway.

The sea is contradictory. It is generous. It is a lover, a mother with boundless children. It is a bridge that will carry you beyond the horizon. Its depths hold wonder and terror in equal parts. It is a song, a harmony for many voices. Listen.

Once upon a time, Kit was short for Katherine, and she ran away from home. The ship she crewed on was caught in a terrible storm; everyone on board drowned. Once upon a time, Kit was the nickname of Jonathan Kitterage, first mate on a crew seeking passage to India. The ship was beset by pirates, and finding it empty of valuables, they scuttled it, sinking it with all hands aboard. Once upon a many times, Kit was only Kit—a child who could breathe underwater, a drowned man risen up from the waves, a woman standing behind lighthouse rails overlooking the sea.

All of these things are a lie. Every one of them is true.

One night, when Kit couldn't bear the lives crowded inside his skin, he took a knife to the invisible stitches binding them within and tried to set them free. So now she is here, her suitcase packed with pill bottles, taking a journey the doctors promised will liberate her. If only he can learn to face his fears.

But Kit is more fearful than ever, knowing deep in his bones that the only thing the journey will teach her is how to drown.

The third letter is an envelope thick with water-swollen pages. This one smells of blood—an iron tang, washed by the waves. Kit considers throwing it overboard, refusing to read, but in the end, her curiosity is too strong. She returns to the netting around the bowsprit, stretching out under the watchful eyes of the ship-woman. The carved wooden face reminds him of someone—that quirk of the mouth, the sadness in her eyes, her arms spread as if to gather him in. If only he could remember. With a sigh, Kit turns her attention to the pages, and reads.

THE MERMAID'S TALE

The sea is a patient lover, compared to the land. It would have loved me as I was, asking nothing in return. But I could not love the sea as my sisters do. Only half my heart was saltwater; the rest was made of longing.

My eldest sister loved the hot currents best. There is a place where a fissure splits the rock and curls of warm water rise from the ocean floor. My sister's tail would flicker, tongue-light, over this cleft, teasing forth ribbons of heat to twine around her from skin to scales. Oh, her song.

My second eldest sister prefers dead men's bones, ocean-stripped and pearlescent, cradled in the wrecks of sea-warped ships. Once their flesh has fed the fish who feed us, they are ready for her. Her long fingers caress empty eyeholes, gathering the memory of dreams and sucking it down like caviar. She traces the curve of cheek, spine, rib, and hip. Only her hands move as she drifts near motionless, her tail stilled until the end when she bares sharp teeth to sing. And oh, her song!

My third eldest sister loves lightless things. Her play is secret, but she comes home with eyes wide and light-starved. She slips after blind eels and fish, playing games of touch and taste. She does not see her lovers, and they do not see her. They know each other as frond brushes scale, tentacle caresses skin, and tongue traces a shell's whorling curves. Oh, her song!

But I do not love as my sisters do. All that they are is in the waves, as if they belonged only in one world. They think with the hunger below their waists, as if love was small enough to encompass only either or and never both.

Oh, my song! It is vast and wide. It contains multitudes—fish and deep, green things, yes, but sand and the sharp cry of birds; ships, un-drowned and creatures who sip life straight from unfiltered sunlight and bright air.

My sisters begged me to stay. It sorrowed me to leave, but I could not live as they do. My tail thrust hard against the waves, my head broke the surface, and I breathed dry air.

At first, it was like drowning—what I imagine humans feel in the moments before they become fit for my second sister's tender ministrations. I forced myself to stay until black stars burst before my eyes and I had to plunge once more beneath the waves and let the current smooth away what was not quite pain. Returning, the water's touch was sharper against my newly roused skin. This was the sensation I had been missing, tracing my length from crown to tail. Oh, how I sang.

While my sisters left the grotto to seek their pleasures, I dove again and again for the surface. I learned to breathe, longer each time. I delayed gratification, prolonged ecstasy, but still, I hungered for more. I needed to taste the sand with the soles of feet I did not have, but could feel like phantoms beneath my scales.

At first, I despaired of being trapped inside the ocean's skin, only half alive, subsisting on stolen pleasures, fleeting as the life of krill before a whale. I sang my sorrow to the waves, soft and low. But oh, my song! It came back to me, and I learned I was not alone. There were others who loved as I did and knew how to change.

They were legends, ancient beings with split tails; stitched creatures of fish scales and monkey bones. They were creatures mad by standards of sea and land, but wholly themselves, comfortable in their skin.

I sang, and they sang back to me. They pressed shells, honed razor-sharp, into my hands. They traced maps for transformation onto my flesh and poured new songs into the whorls of my ears. They kissed my lips, my cheeks, and my eyes, just to be sure they were free of tears. Then they bade me well.

I took their blades and swam harder and faster than ever before. My pulse beat my skin, my tail beat the waves. With a final spasm of my entire body, shocking me from the sea, I came, foam-flecked, to lie upon the shore. And there, with my honed shells, I opened myself. Blood ran as I slit myself wide.

I wept, and oh my song was so like my sisters' in their ecstasy. I planted new feet firm in the sand, pressed down until I could feel the thrum of the ocean buried beneath the shore. Hot, wet, and salty, the ocean rushed between my new legs and slicked my new skin. I let the world of dry air and sunlight fill me, pounding the echo-chamber of my heart until I could breathe again. This new lover demanded everything of me, but it was nothing I wouldn't give willingly.

Kit folds arms around a body both hollow and full. Could the letter in her hand truly be written by a mermaid? It is any stranger a thought than forgetting your face from one moment to the next, never knowing who you are? For a moment, he almost remembers a story of his own—one of drowned lives, stolen from the sea and stitched beneath his skin, a witch's gift and curse, allowing him to change. She can almost remember how the story begins. Once upon a time . . . But it slips from his hands.

In the morning, there is another letter. The cries of seabirds fill the small cabin. The ship rocks softly. They've put down anchor at another port, another sunny island Kit will not see.

The other passengers have already left the ship in their floppy hats, overlarge sunglasses, and flip flops, wearing loose-fitting t-shirts over burned and peeling skin. Kit doesn't belong among them. Even with the fear of drowning, Kit feels safer onboard than setting foot on dry land.

This new letter is crisp. Fine grains of sand linger in its folds and cling to sweat-damp fingertips as Kit sits on the narrow bed and reads.

THE SELKIE'S TALE

Then, I knew nothing of human men. I only saw the small boat abandoned by the larger one. I saw a man blister his palms rowing to shore, to the tiny island where my brothers, sisters, and I used to play. He beached the boat, flung curses at it as though it was at fault, then flopped down on the sand. Marooned.

I watched him try to light a fire. It smoked and sparked, but wouldn't catch. I was curious, and I pitied him, so I left my skin on the rock I'd watched from, and dove deep, filling my hands before coming ashore.

He reacted first with fear, calling me a demon. Next, his eyes traced me with desire, seeing the water beaded on my skin, the dark waves of my hair, my limbs smooth and strong from swimming. Last, a look of cunning came into his eyes, lit by the light of his sputtering fire.

But what reason did I have to fear? I knew nothing of men, but I hungered to know more.

"There's driftwood along the shore. It will burn well, and your fire won't keep dying."

I held out my hands, full of kelp and good weeds, cockles and mussels, salty and waiting to be sucked from their shells. When he didn't answer, I laid my gifts on the sand. After a moment, he darted as hermit crabs will from shell to shell, seizing food with both hands and retreating to the other side of his fire.

I left him to his feast, walking the shore and filling my strong arms with sun-bleached wood. When I returned, he'd eaten everything, bloodying his fingers on the sharp edges of the shells. Unasked, I built up his fire and sat beside him, then took his hands to examine his wounds.

"What are you?" His full belly made him bold.

I knew nothing; what reason did I have to lie?

"Selkie."

His bloodied fingers were chilled. I took them into my mouth, sucking the blood clean and warming them.

Desire is not so different in selkies and in human men. Despite my walk along the beach, water still beaded my skin. The fire, rather than drying me, only warmed the moisture and made it gleam. The man's gaze was as sure as a touch.

And still, what reason did I have to be afraid? I laid my hand along his sunburned and unshaven jaw to feel his skin.

"You're like this all the time?" I asked, wondering at a being that could live its whole life inside only one skin.

Misunderstanding, he said, "I was a captain. My brother stole my ship, roused my crew to mutiny, and left me to die."

I could see talking would do little to let us understand each other. I pressed my lips to his instead, tasting weed and fish. His eager rough-ness brought no more pain than I'd known abrading my back and belly against rocks with my selkie mates. His hunger and need were almost refreshing—his speed and insistence so unlike the languor I knew. I let him take all he would in a rush.

While he recovered, he asked me about the ocean and my skin. I told him all with aims of my own, getting him drunk on my voice. Lulled, I did not let him run ahead the second time. I showed him the way of selkies, satisfying my curiosity in a slow, unhurried way. I tasted his salt-dried skin and urged him to taste mine, sea-slick and so different from his own. I pressed him against the sand and moved over him like the tide, building to a crest. When my curiosity was satisfied, I let the wave break.

When he slept, I swam back to my skin. I returned to the waves and forgot the man. Underwater, the rush of salt becomes the rhythm of blood; the flow of tide becomes the measure of days. It surprised me when I next surfaced and heard the man cursing and weeping.

I slipped my skin and swam to him. His eyes were red and wild.

"I thought you'd abandoned me. I nearly starved." He bared his teeth in fury or grief, then buried his head in the crook of my sea-damp shoulder. I could feel the bones beneath his skin, smell the ripeness of his sun-baked flesh. His matted hair and the growth of his beard rasped against me.

Pitying, I brought him food and helped him build his fire. He ate ravenously, never taking his eyes from me.

When he was done, he rinsed the sweat from his skin and the taste of fish from his mouth in the sea and came to me smelling like home. Though my curiosity had been sated, I didn't object when he wrapped me in his arms. I liked the way the ocean smelled on him. I had claimed him, changed him; he was my private treasure, washed ashore.

Tracing his lips over my throat, slicking his hands over my skin, he said, "I want to watch you change."

There was a strange light in his eyes, but curiosity I understood. He had sated mine. What harm could it do sating his in return?

I swam to my rock, returning with my skin. The surf washed around my ankles; I pulled my skin over my head, showing him one form then the other. His eyes widened, and when I turned human again, he seized me with renewed hunger, spending himself in me with fierce urgency as we rolled over and over on the shore.

Afterward, as I bent to collect my skin, a sharp pain struck behind my ear. My knees buckled. I hit the sand. Saltwater rushed into my mouth. Another blow, and in the pain, I lost sight of the world.

When I came to, I had been dragged near the fire. My wrists and ankles were bound with strips torn from the man's shirt, and a final strip fit into my mouth for silence. My skin lay across the man's lap, gleaming slick and black as spilled oil in the firelight. With a splinter of wood, and a hair pulled from my scalp, he stitched it into a new shape.

I could feel the needle going in and out, each time he pushed the sharp point through my skin. He looked at me as he worked. Once, there even seemed to be sorrow in his gaze.

When he was done, he placed a sharpened shell within my reach, a means to cut my bonds. He was pitiless, but not without mercy.

He walked to the water's edge and pulled my skin over his head. I felt the touch of saltwater as he slipped beneath the waves. I felt the ocean close over his head, felt him fight to breathe before surrendering to my skin. Long powerful strokes, stolen from me and worn over his wasted frame, carried him sleek and fast away from shore.

I cut myself free, but I was trapped. How do humans bear living life in only one skin? It is so small.

My sisters and brothers visit, bringing me gifts from the ocean and running their fingers through my hair. We talk of revenge. When they leave, they swim far and wide, searching for the man who stole my skin. I can be patient as no mere human can. One day, they will find him. They will drag him down and press their lips to his until they have drunk every last breath. Then they will peel my skin from his bones, and bring it back to me. The ocean will welcome me back, and I will be whole again.

At night, Kit walks the deck, breathes sea air, leans over the rail, and tries to get used to the sea. There are moments when the salt in Kit's body yearns toward the salt in the sea, and it terrifies him. She has been here before. She will be here again. What if the Kit standing upon the deck becomes yet another ghost trapped in unfamiliar skin? If only he could remember.

The ocean is not terrible, the letters seem to say. But there will be a price; there will be pain.

The next letter smells like clean wind, like seal blubber and whale oil—things Kit has never touched in this lifetime, but knows just the same. The paper is chill beneath his fingers, like bright ice and colors staining the sky. The ink is not ink; it is infinity, closed within a space of paper (as she is infinity, closed within a space of skin) speaking of the vastness of the world. He almost remembers.

Kit takes the letter back to the netting, less afraid now. Waves break against the ship's hull; the wooden ship-woman stretched above him is almost an old friend.

He reads.

THE GODDESS'S TALE

They will say I drowned. They will say I was stolen, sold, given away. They will call me mother of monsters and mistress of the deep. All and none of this is true.

The world ever expects a rift between fathers and daughters, between husbands and wives, between self and other. I will tell you the truth before you drown.

In the beginning, the ocean was lonely. It caressed the earth, loving it desperately, but they could not make a child.

I lived with my father in a small hut by the shore—wood built upon a stony beach with thatched grasses over our heads, singing in the wind. Every day, I worked my fingers numb, weaving nets to cast upon the waves.

"Why do you do this thing?" my father asked me.

"I do it because one day there will be fish in the sea, and our people will be hungry. You will use these nets to catch the ocean's children when I am gone."

"How do you know these things, Daughter?"

"I know because I have seen them in a dream."

"And where will you go, Daughter, when you leave me?" was my father's last question.

"Into sky and into sea, Father. I will not be what I am. I will be multitudes and feed the hungry world."

As satisfied as he could be, my father went back into his house to think upon my words.

From dawn until dusk, I wove my nets. From dusk until dawn, I cast them over the empty waves. Every day at noon, I let the waves taste my bloodied fingers and warm them.

One day, the sea spoke, asking, "Who are you to put your blood in my mouth?"

"I am Sedna," I replied.

"Sedna. I have tasted your blood, and I know you are strong. Tell me, what do you dream?"

"I dream the ocean teeming with fish and whales, seals, squid, and eels."

The ocean's icy tears lapped my feet.

"Ah, I have wished for these things," the ocean said. "But I cannot bear a single child, let alone multitudes."

"I will help you," I said. "But in return, you must make a promise. When my people are starving, you must give them your children to eat. They will cast the nets I have made, and pull your children from the waves so their own children might fill their bellies."

"Will it hurt?" the ocean asked.

"Every time," I replied.

The ocean thought a moment and said, "It is agreed."

"I will return in seven days and give you all the children I have dreamed for you."

I returned to my father's house, and found him warming his fingers by the fire.

"Father, you must find me a husband," I said. "He must be wicked and strong. Will you do this thing?"

"Ah, Sedna, my child. I will do this thing if you ask it, but I will mourn."

"I ask it, Father."

So my father went out of his house and stood upon a cliff he knew. He sang a song his grandmother taught him, calling all the birds of the air to land at his feet where he looked at them one by one.

"Who will be the husband of my child?" he asked. "Who among you is most wicked and strong?"

"I am, Father," answered Raven, and spread his wings so my father might see midnight in his feathers. The moon was in one of Raven's eyes, and the sun in the other.

On the morrow, I was wed.

As I made myself ready to go to my husband's home, I spoke to my father again.

"Father, there is one more thing you must do for me. I will come back to you in five days. You must take a boat of bleached wood, row into the middle of the ocean, and wait for me. You must bring a little knife with a handle made of wood and a blade made of bone. In five days, you will see me in the ocean, Father, and you must kill me."

"Ah, Daughter." My father wept, but said no more. I took my husband's hand, and he spread his black wings and carried me into the sky.

For five days, we lay together as husband and wife, black feathers against brown skin. I looked into Raven's eyes, into the moon and the sun, into the left eye and the right. When I looked into his left eye, I knew he had lied to my father about being wicked. When I looked into his right eye, I knew he had told my father the truth about being strong.

"Husband," I said. "There is something you must do for me."

"What is that, wife?" Raven asked.

"You must take me to the highest place you know and cast me down into the sea."

"Ah, wife, must it be so?" my husband asked, but his eyes remained dry.

"It must."

So my husband took me in his strong arms, folded me in his black wings, and carried me to a cliff he knew. There, he threw me into the icy waves far below.

My body struck the water, but I did not drown. The ocean cradled me, and held my head above water so I could watch for the little boat of bleached wood the color of bone.

The boat came, and in it my father held his little knife.

"Daughter, climb aboard," he called.

I clung to the boat's side, but did not obey.

"I cannot," I said. "I made a promise, but if you ask me again, I will break, so you must be strong. You must kill me, as you promised you would."

"Ah, daughter," my father said, but he did not ask me to enter his boat again.

"Father, I am freezing," I said, because it was the truth. "Let me in."

I tried to climb into the boat, but my father cut off the fingers of my left hand with his knife of bone. There were tears in his eyes.

My fingers sank beneath the waves and became fish of every kind.

"Father, I am bleeding," I said, because it was the truth. "Let me in."

I tried to climb into the boat, and my father cut off the fingers of my right hand. My fingers sank beneath the waves and became whales and dolphins and seals.

"Father, you have killed me," I said, because it was the truth. "But my hair is caught on your boat and I cannot drown."

"Daughter," he said, and used his little knife to cut off my hair. It sank beneath the waves and became seaweed and plankton and sightless eels.

"Father," I said, "I am drowned."

I sank, and the ocean folded its arms around me. It held me tight, mother of its children, dreamer of its dreams. Now I am multitudes, and my children feed those who walk upon the land. I am vast, I am the mother of worlds.

It is almost time for the cruise to end when Kit finds the last letter. It is damp, the ink still wet.

I have lied to you, the letter says. *I am neither, mermaid, selkie, nor goddess, but I am all of these things, just as you are Katherine, Kitteridge, and Kit. Do not be afraid of drowning. Find a shipwrecked sailor, a father, a monster with shells honed to blades. Cut yourself open, stitch a new skin, become multitudes. It is time to come home.*

Kit's heart pounds. He folds the letter, tucks it between shirt and naked skin. She almost remembers. Once upon a time, he was a witch, and he ran away.

No.

The deck rolls, but barely. The sails drop, slack, no longer catching the wind. The ship will dock soon. If Kit steps foot on land, it will be too late.

Once upon a time, Kit bound her breasts and cut her hair. A witch taught her how to be changeable as the sea. He stitched ghosts beneath his skin; the trickster sea stayed true to its word, but Kit lost his way.

Of course.

Kit climbs into the netting, and turns to look back at the ship who is a woman, who is a witch, who was lonely once upon a time and cursed and gifted Kit with the ability to change.

Ghosts clamor inside Kit's skin. There is a flicker of movement under the waves, a beckoning hand, a flash of tail, a welcoming smile. The letter presses between cloth and skin. Music rises up from the waves, singing Kit down. The ocean tells the truth; the ocean is a liar. It is one and both all the time. Kit smiles, climbing to the edge of the netting, remembering hands caressing flickering, changeable skin, remembering choosing not to choose.

It is time to go home.

Blackbird Lullaby

~ George Cotronis

*And He asked him, "What is thy name?" And he answered,
saying, "My name is Legion: for we are many."*
—Gospel of Mark 5:9

I'm lying in bed, alone. My arm extends over the side of the bed, wrist resting on the night table. I move my fingers, and I can feel the tendons in my arm pulling them like puppets on a string. My middle and last finger are stripped of flesh down to the second knuckle, leaving the bone visible. The blackbird makes two small jumps and comes closer, disturbed by my sudden movement. I stop moving, and it starts to peck at my flesh again. I watch it for a while. There is no pain. When I get bored, I shoo it away, and it takes flight across the room to join its murder. His buddies are everywhere in the room, perched on furniture and lamps. They seem to be waiting for something.

The bed is full of trash, pieces of fabric and twigs, plastic bottle caps and paper. The blackbirds have turned it into a nest. I get up and find myself bleeding from several different places on my body. They've been eating me in my sleep again. My clothes are stained with blood and full of holes. Most of the blood is old, because I haven't changed in a week. All my shirts have holes now.

In the bathroom, I wrap my fingers with gauze, trying to make them look even, as if there's still meat underneath the white cloth. I consider using some antiseptic, but don't see the point. I throw the bottle in the trash bin.

I catch a glimpse of myself in the mirror.

Gaunt. Tired. Broken.

There are black circles around my eyes, my lips are dried and split, my face swollen and puffy. One of the ravens took out a small piece of flesh right under my eye. The blood runs down the side of my face, like the streak of a red tear. I wash up and put on a clean shirt. I feel almost human again. I look at my watch. I'm gonna be late.

Out on the street, people avoid me. Little girls clutch their fathers' hands and hide their faces. They cry. I guess the clean clothes didn't help. Head down, hood up, I try to look more like a thug, a guy you shouldn't mess with, instead of the monster that I really am. It seems to work better. In the subway, a blackbird finds its way to me. It watches from the seat across from me, like it's the most normal thing in the world. No one seems to notice or care.

Me, I'm used to it. I look down my nose at it and hold its stare. Not that it gives a shit. It hops down to the floor and comes closer. It picks at my shoelaces. I look at my face in the reflection in the window. I'm bleeding again. I feel no pain in my fingers or the myriad of smaller wounds I carry, but my head is killing me. I used to wonder how I can still be alive, but these days there's a lot of things I don't think about. I just don't care. The extent to which I do not care would shock you.

I get off at my stop and head for the old church up the hill. There was a fire a few years back—they never repaired the building, but it is still in decent condition. You just have to get creative about entering it. Around back, where the fence put up by the city has a human-sized hole in it, I enter the churchyard. One of the doors, the one closest to the fence, is unlocked. When it's not, they key is behind one of the loose bricks in the wall beside it.

Inside, Meg and Jonathan are already waiting. Meg is a tall woman, thin, used to be pretty. She's wearing a summer dress that's two sizes larger than it should be. I suspect it used to fit her once. One of her nipples is showing, but she's too out of it to notice. Her dead eyes stare straight ahead. She doesn't see me.

Jonathan is holding her hand. He turns his head to me when I come in, but then turns to her again. They met here two years ago. Meg is near the end now, Jonathan still going strong.

Two blackbirds fly in from the broken window and land on the rubble strewn about in the church. Most of the roof is gone, but the little corner we have set up here keeps dry even when it rains. Winters are tough; then again we rarely meet like this. Usually it's just desperate phone calls in the middle of the night and unexpected visits. A circle of pews stands in the middle of all the trash and junk. I take my seat across the couple and say nothing.

Welcome to Damned Anonymous. Living with things that are killing you from the inside. "Getting well—not really, we're just dying—together."

Our little support group. When Meg first started growing tumors that got up and walked around in the night, she figured a support group for cancer survivors wasn't going to be that helpful. When Jonathan woke up to find himself chewing on his little daughter's arm, Alcoholics Anonymous just wasn't an option for him anymore.

But they tried. And in those endless support group meetings, we found each other. Maybe it was the desperation that we saw in each other's eyes. The fear of something worse than death, which we recognized. Meg found me in a depression support group. I was saying I feel empty, numb, dead inside. After the meeting, over stale coffee and even staler donuts, she came over and said, "You're not really afraid you're gonna kill yourself, are you? You're here for some-thing else." Maybe she saw the birds, perching on the windowsill. Maybe she noticed the bloodstains. So we started our own group. A few of us sometimes visit A.A. and groups like that. We recruit the demonically possessed.

Brennan walks in and takes me out of my little trip down memory lane. He's looking a bit better than last time. It probably means he fed again. One of those hookers downtown didn't wake up today, and right now she's floating in the river, facedown in the water, bloated like a balloon. If she's lucky some poor fisherman is gonna snag her in his nets and she'll get a burial.

He looks ashamed, but in this little crowd, no one gives a fuck if he ate some girl's heart and dumped her over the bridge. We're too involved in our own misery. I wave to him, and he sits down. The room slowly fills up with the rest of the monsters, and the stench gets progressively worse. The blackbirds have flooded the church, but they're quiet today, so I'm not gonna get in trouble with Jennifer, our group leader. Jennifer has a mouth full of razor-sharp teeth, each one filed to a point. When she cries, she cries blood. A Catholic, she tried to get an exorcism a year ago. It didn't work. I'm pretty sure she killed them, but she says she didn't. I think I read it in the papers: two priests missing around the same time. She looks like she's been crying.

Today, there is a new girl. Short black dress, ripped in some places and dirty with what looks to be ashes, heavy black makeup, her eyes unblinking and taking in everything at once. She's gorgeous, and deep within me I feel something slither, like Leviathan at the bottom of the ocean.

Her name is Magdalene.

There's a rat gnawing at her ankle.

I think my heart has stopped.

We go around the circle, telling our story for the umpteenth time, pouring salt on our wounds again, to try and *center ourselves*, get in touch with the *reality of our situation, understand and accept* what we can't change.

When it's Brennan's turn, he confirms my suspicions.

"I fed again. I couldn't help it. I was looking at my wife and thinking about eating her heart. I had to do something." He pauses and looks at the floor between his legs. Crocodile tears.

"I drove downtown and picked up a streetwalker. Young thing. I just picked up the first that came up to my car. I held it off until we reached the hills, and then I killed her. I ate her heart and buried her up there, in the woods."

He's almost gone, he just doesn't know it yet. He's talking about this girl and crying, but I can see he's also salivating. I see him smile when he says the word "heart."

He breaks down, and between sobs he keeps repeating "I'm so sorry . . . so sorry."

Jennifer consoles him with a hug while I roll my eyes. Fucking poser.

Meg is too out of it to share today. Jonathan says he's okay, he's controlling the cravings. I'm trying not to fall asleep. I'm waiting to hear *her* story. I think I know what she's going to say, but I want to hear her voice.

She will say:

"One day I saw them watching me on the street. I saw them again the very next day and the day after that. They watched from the alleys and under cars and from the roofs of buildings. They followed me around, they came into my house, they watched me sleep. No matter what I did, they found a way in, they killed themselves in their attempts to come to me, and in the end, they always found me. There was no way to stop them. No poison or weapon would keep them away. So, they became a part of me. They live with me. They are everywhere, always. I have no friends, because the last time I went for a cup of coffee, the little freaks attacked the waiter and I had to run out of the place with them after me, always after me. They are eating me alive."

Me, blackbirds.

Her, rats.

We have so much in common.

After *sharing* I walk up to her and say, "Nice dress."

She turns around and gives me the once-over. She seems unimpressed.

"Nice scabs." She smirks, but doesn't turn away.

"There's a rat trying to climb up your dress." I smile.

She looks down and then catches herself.

"Made you look," I say.

"Funny," she says, angry but laughing.

"Do you want to go someplace?" I ask.

"I don't really go out in public." She motions with her head towards the two rats gnawing on donuts on the table. "But you could come to my place."

A blackbird lands on my shoulder, tries to pluck out my eye. I slap it, and it flies away, back up to the rafters.

"Where do you live?"

"Parkside," she says.

"Too far. Too many birds out there. How about my place?" I ask.

She agrees to come to my apartment tomorrow, to see my record collection. She's into The Smiths but who the fuck cares; we both know she doesn't give a shit about my records or anything else in my shitty apartment. Except me. She wants me.

On the subway ride home, I feel almost human again. I'd celebrate, but I haven't eaten or had a drink in weeks. I go home, and I sleep on my bed made out of blood and black feathers.

She's at my place exactly on time. I put on a relatively clean shirt, my skin itchy all over from the feathers and the bird shit that's been irritating it. I open the door. She's cute in her flower pattern dress, with fresh little wounds at the top of her breasts. A bit of her scalp is missing over her left ear, and she uses a flower to hide it.

"Hey."

"Hey."

She walks into my apartment, which is covered in black feathers and dirt, birds taking flight with every step she takes. I feel like a teenager. A teenager slowly turning into something else, but still. Nervous.

I drop the The Smiths record on her lap. She pretends to be interested for a bit but ultimately discards it on the coffee table. She pats the place beside her on the couch, and I obey.

"How are you doing with *them?*" I ask.

"Okay. I think I'm getting close."

I nod. I've felt the same lately. There will be a tipping point, and then the transformation will be complete. Our demons will consume us.

"You?" She picks at a scab on her knee. It's cute.

I shrug. "Who knows? I don't think about it," I lie.

I get up and bring out the wine and the glasses. She looks excited. We finish the bottle off in half an hour flat, and when we're done with the boring chit chat, we make out on the couch. Our wounds open, and we bleed into each other, feathers and coarse brown hair sticking to our bodies. It's painful and awkward, and sometimes I feel like I will faint from the blood loss, but there are moments when I forget that my body is rotting and my heart is dead and hell is waiting for me.

We stumble to the bedroom and fuck in a drunken stupor, with the rats and the blackbirds watching.

I wake up, and I feel empty, hollow. I reach into my chest, and I touch a crow nesting there. Its coat is slick with my blood, but it's not afraid. It feels safe inside of me. I feel safe too.

She's still here, her arm resting on my chest. A rat is peeking from under her dress. I wake her with a kiss, and her little rat teeth gnaw at my lips. She draws blood, and immediately I'm hard. I climb on top of her, and then we are one, and the blackbirds and the rats are clawing and biting, and we flow into one another, and as monsters we are reborn.

Digital

~ Daryl Gregory

Sometime after the accident, Franklin woke up to realize that his consciousness had relocated to his left hand—specifically, the index finger of his left hand.

Before the accident, which is to say, his entire life until then, his conscious self seemed to reside just behind his eyes, a tiny man gazing out at the world through a pair of wide windows. He'd never considered how odd this was, and how arbitrary that location. Was it because humans were predominantly visual? He supposed so, but that didn't explain why his *self* had been lodged there. Why not behind the nose? His sense of smell was quite keen, especially when it came to beer: he could tell a Belgian Abbey ale from an American microbrew knockoff with a single sniff. His taste buds were highly trained. If he had become a professional taste-tester, he wondered, would his consciousness have migrated down to his tongue?

His wife, Judith, could not seem to understand what had happened to him, even though he tried repeatedly to explain. "I'm down here," he told her, waggling himself to get her attention. He could not move his arm because of the cast that covered him from palm to shoulder. He'd broken his wrist, sent a hairline fracture along his ulna, and torn his rotator cuff.

Judith looked distraught. "It's the stroke, Franklin. I told you you were working too hard. Now you've suffered a stroke."

Perhaps that was the case. He'd been standing at the top of the stairs, reaching out to the banister, when suddenly he felt dizzy. Sometime later he awoke, face down on the parquet landing, his arm trapped beneath him. He felt suffocated, as if he were buried in an avalanche. When the EMTs rolled him onto his back, he moaned in pain, but at the same time experienced a profound sense of relief when his hand came free. Daylight! Air! Though of course he'd been breathing perfectly well the entire time, and he could see fine. What he could not decide, even now, was this: had the accident caused the shift in consciousness, or had he become dizzy because his self was on the move down his arm?

"Don't tell the doctors," he said. "They'll think I'm crazy."

She patted the back of his hand, and he flinched. "I won't if you don't want me to," she said. Her fingers were stubby, which she tried to disguise with long, brightly painted nails. Liar's hands.

That afternoon, the doctors stormed his room to interrogate him. They shone penlights into his eyes, wheeled him off to MRIs and a CAT scan, tested his vision, speech, and cognition. Except for some awkwardness rearranging wooden blocks during the motor coordination exam, the fact that his self was now nestled thirty inches southeast from its old location seemed to make no measurable difference. He was perfectly capable of performing from his new mental home.

"Let's see if the feeling persists," the most senior doctor said, and handed Judith a dozen prescriptions to fill. "Call us if you experience anything odd, such as—" And here he rattled off a list of alarming neurological and physiological symptoms.

"The important thing," he said to Franklin, "is to avoid stress."

After eight weeks, Franklin returned to the hospital to have the cast removed, and then returned again a few days later for the first of several physical therapy sessions to restore motion to his shoulder. His therapist's name was Olivia. She had lovely hands. She kept her nails trimmed, but they were painted with a clear gloss with white tips—a French manicure. Her long, delicate-looking fingers were quite strong; when she dug into the knotted tissue of his shoulder she could make him cry out. Whenever she touched his left hand, however, she was exceedingly gentle, which convinced him she'd been told about his mental condition. But on the third visit, when he worked up the courage to mention, casually, that his consciousness had migrated to the peninsula of his index finger, she seemed genuinely surprised.

"You feel like you are . . ." She nodded toward his hand. "There?"

"The funny thing is, I'm not even left-handed."

She frowned, not disapprovingly, but in a curious, scientific way. "What's that like for you? If you don't mind talking about it."

There was nothing he wanted to talk about more. Judith found the topic distasteful. "Close your eyes," he told Olivia. "Imagine yourself as one great finger. Picture a long arm extending from your back that stretches up to a gargantuan body."

She closed her eyes, and he watched her, moving his gaze from her white-tipped fingernails, to her face, and back again. The image was transferred from his retina to his brain, and there down his arm to his pulsing index finger. He curled against his palm, suddenly embarrassed by his thoughts.

"And up there," he said, "at the top of the body, is a huge, remote head like a planetoid. A bony house for the computer of your brain. It tells you things, but it's not you."

She concentrated for a few moments, and then opened her eyes. "I wondered why you kept looking at my hands."

"Sorry about that."

"It's all right." She lifted one finger, flexed it, and laughed. "Hi there."

He raised himself up and waved back.

She said, "Does it feel . . . odd in there? Cramped?"

"It feels like the most natural thing in the world," he said. "I'd always been person who lived in my head, who kept his feelings contained. Now I can't imagine living any other way. I feel free."

He was worried that his confession might alienate her, but at the next session there was no strangeness between them. As they worked on his muscles he talked easily of his new life, the new insights he'd gained. "Have you ever noticed how careless people are with their hands?" he said during one visit. "The other day my wife grabbed a pan from the oven, burned herself, and then she stuck her finger in her *mouth*. She didn't even wash afterward." And: "I wonder if Helen Keller was hand conscious?"

He wanted the visits to go on and on, but his insurance ran out after only three weeks. At the end of the last appointment, he said,

"You've helped me so much, I'd like to thank you somehow. Can I buy you lunch? You said you liked Thai food." Ever since she'd mentioned her love of pad Thai he'd been thinking of chop sticks moving in her fingers.

"I don't think that's a good idea," she said, not unkindly. She glanced down at his hand. "You're wearing a ring."

"But she doesn't—" He wanted to say, *She doesn't understand me like you do.* But that was going too far, extending himself in a way that would only lead to embarrassment for both of them. "She doesn't like Thai food."

His wife entered his study without knocking. On his computer screen was an ad for a ladies Rolex. Judith looked disgusted. The hand modeling the watch was beautiful, though a little too perfect for his tastes: the wrist was improbably narrow, the fingers obviously airbrushed. Fortunately, a few months ago he'd found an internet forum where people exchanged pictures of the best hand models.

"I've made an appointment," Judith said. "With a specialist." He told her he wasn't interested, but she would not be refused.

They drove to a clinic only a few blocks from the hospital where Olivia worked. The doctor wasn't a psychiatrist, as he'd feared, or a neurologist, but a family practice MD who'd written a book about alternate states of consciousness. He was bald except for a gray pony-tail, as if his hair had given up on general coverage and decided to specialize. The doctor seemed inordinately excited by Franklin's condition. "We must nudge the mind out of its cul-de-sac," he said emphatically, "And return it to its former home." He rambled on for some time before Franklin realized that his proposed solution was to amputate.

"It's the only way," the man said. "Sudden Egotic eviction."

"Are you insane?" Franklin said. "You could kill me!"

"Your hand is up in the air again," Judith said. And then to the doctor she said, "He does that whenever he feels defensive."

"Marvelous," Dr. Ponytail said. "May I see your hand? Your finger looks inflamed."

"Get the hell away from me!" He curled into a fist and charged out of the office. He did indeed feel hot, like a lawn mower engine revved beyond its specs. Outside he uncurled and saw that he'd turned red as a thermometer, his self-finger seeming to pulse like a rubber bladder. He cried out.

"Franklin? Are you all right?" It was Olivia's voice—Olivia! He spun his arm to reach out to her, and then the world continued to spin, and he collapsed to the sidewalk.

When he awoke, he was alone in another hospital room, and the feeling of suffocation he'd experienced on the stairs months ago had returned. He looked down, and saw that his left hand was encased in white bandages, from wrist to fingertips. His other arm was restrained by IV tubes, but he bit and chewed at the bandages until his fingers were free.

The index finger was still there. It had turned pale and shriveled, as if it had spent too long in the bathtub, but it was whole.

Something was wrong, however. The finger looked utterly unfamiliar to him. Had he really thought that he'd been *in there*, in that *pointer?* More alarmingly, the suffocating feeling had not dissipated.

At that moment, Olivia and Judith came into the room. They were holding paper cups of coffee, and it looked as if they'd been having a heart-to-heart discussion.

"It's all right," Olivia said, "You're safe now. You just passed out."

"Try to calm down," Judith said. And then she saw the scraps of bandages and frowned. "I suppose you're still . . ."

"No!" he said. "That's over! I'm—" Where was he? He was drowning, and he could feel his giant body above him, his voice thundering from far away.

"What do you need?" Olivia asked.

He closed his eyes, concentrating. This little piggy went to market, he said to himself. This little piggy stayed home. And *this* little piggy . . .

"Here!" he said, kicking up at the sheet. "For God's sake, get this sheet off of me!"

The women pulled up the linens, and at his pleading, removed his socks. He lifted his right foot into the air.

There he was. Third toe from the right. He was slender, with a thick, healthy nail. A single hair sprouted from his knuckle in a

Superman curl. Yes, just a middle toe, but at last he felt completely at home: surrounded, supported, unstubbable.

Why Ulu Left the Bladescliff

~ Amanda C. Davis

Ulu cleans her gutters before Cleaver comes by, skims the rust from the roof, sharpens the awning into a razor's edge. Shipshape. Stem to stern. If the sun would hit it, her arch would glint like a tone tapped on a crystal glass. But there's no sun here. Only fog. No light. Only Cleaver.

There is Spey next door only an alley-gorge apart from Sheepsfoot his neighbor, and both are shearing their gables with steel wool until only ten, only five, only a single angel could dance on the tip. Spey sings out: "The little miss is expecting company! Mark me, there'll be a good show through that window tonight!"

Ulu blushes, but she knows Spey's only kidding. She has just one window, and very thick curtains.

She polishes the walls all the way down. Polishes the shutters and steps and gate. Picks steel splinters from her skin. Spits on the doorknob, wipes it away. Brass. If there was light it would glow. A tiny sun.

In a cupboard in the kitchen lives a lever of red oak with a brass tip. It has roots far below on the stairs: a tangled gearworks anchor. It came with the house. She has only used it once. It winks, a glint on brass, to remind her of their first time together: falling into thick fog, losing the sun. She swats it with the rag and closes the cupboard. She doesn't need the lever now that there's Cleaver.

She teaches the floor about wax and the table about oil and the walls about soapy water. She teaches her hair about curls and her neck about perfume and her face about sticks of color. Everybody learns. Her lips are crisp with crimson: her star pupil.

Then there's a turning from the tiny brass sun. Cleaver is here.

Cleaver's looking good. Cleaver's got his spats on. Cleaver sounds like whiskey, and his tie is loosey-noosey. Her bones shrink at the sight of him. Cleaver lurks in the doorway behind the red oak table, using it like sandbags to keep the flood of Ulu from his shoes.

"Do you want a drink?" she says.

He says, "Sure, I guess."

She puts gin in the glass and the glass in his hand and his hand on her arm. It hangs like dead meat. A sandbag. He's slow-fingered and quick-eyed. The gin plays the girl in a magic trick: one blink, and it disappears. He hangs in the doorway like a coat and gazes out the window. Nearby, Sheepsfoot is scurrying up and down ladders. Ulu has forgotten to shut the curtains.

Ulu says, "Don't you want to hold me?"

Ulu says, "You sure are quiet."

Ulu says, "You smell different."

"It's Butcher," he blurts. He says it like a groan, like a geyser. "Butcher. It's always been Butcher. I smell like Butcher because I was with Butcher, I'm in love with Butcher, and I'm never coming back to this dull house and its dull, sad, stupid woman." He gasps for breath. "Butcher," he says again, only there's no sound when his mouth moves. He's sagging. Then he says, clear and loud, "I'll have another drink."

Ulu takes his hand from her arm and the glass from his hand. Cleaver wants gin. Cleaver wants Butcher. She puts the glass in the sink. She opens the window, invites the chill in.

"It's cold," says Cleaver. Oh, is he right.

Ulu smiles at him; her star pupil in crimson expands and contracts. She cannot see clearly. Cleaver has winked out and gone dark; he is eclipsed, and she is blinded at the loss of him. She opens the cabinet beside the icebox. There's the lever. She never thought she'd use it again. Ulu grasps the lever, pushes it forward to the place where the gears loosen, and pulls it all the way back toward her.

The house shakes, lurches, tips. Inverts. Rotates.

Cleaver falls to the floor, then wall, then ceiling; he shouts, but not words. The curtains tear off in his hands. Corners and angles and cabinets knock him side-to-side. His fingers punch through the plaster to the knuckle. Both plaster and fingers break. Ulu is the eye of this cyclone, in all ways: she is central and calm and unmoving, and she watches.

Cleaver crashes against the sink. Above him the town spires are high and grey and Spey and Sheepsfoot are only statues on their pinnacles, gaping through her window as the house turns. The house rolls; Cleaver slips to the window. He clings like a roast drooping from its spit. He is trying to shout at Ulu. He is almost broken before he manages it.

"DULL," he screams. "DULL."

He folds, he twists, he is no larger than the window. He slides through like he was fit for it. His twitching, broken fingertips are the last parts of him Ulu sees.

The shoring is gone, the basement is the attic. The stairs won't hold. Ulu feels the stilts of her home buckling beneath, snapping off. Like toothpicks. Like fingers.

The house loses its balance. It twists off from the neighbors—no more Spey, no more Sheepsfoot—to fall down, down, down into the fog.

Her home plunges, spinning like a windblown spider. Ulu watches the fog stream past the window and the window stream past the fog. She holds her footing: her house pivots around her, of course. She wishes the edge she polished so painfully would shine a little in the dark. Just a glint. A tone tapped on glass.

She wonders where she will land.

She dares to dream. She will fall until she finds a new city, busy and happy, where roofs rise like shards of diamond from downtown to suburbs, each block a shivering bouquet, each house shark's-fin sharp. Ulu imagines a mouth of steel teeth spat up from lips of fog. No—this time she will fall far enough that there is no fog, but grass. Somewhere that brass glows like it should, where steel gleams bright.

Somewhere with no Cleaver. Only light.

Somewhere there's sun.

Follow Me Through Anarchy

- Jetse de Vries

—in the room—

"Consciousness is not an all-or-nothing phenomenon. There
are degrees of phenomenality."
—Thomas Metzinger, from *Being No-One*, pg. 559.

Blinded by the zest, deafened by the colors, nauseated by the
harmony and overwhelmed by the aroma, Alex Sanders enters
the conference room. Temporarily, the world seems different and
time feels topsy-turvy. Repeating his prime directive like a mantra,
Alex shakes off the synesthetic shift: *must talk, must communicate.*
Otherwise the insanity may break the surface tension, unleashing
overpowering complexity, and she will retreat in his shell. *Why
do I always get the most complicated attacks,* she wonders, *not
something simple like cognitive dissonance or a multiple personality
disorder?*

The pre-meeting briefing probably triggered the sensorial overload:
too much, too fast, too soon. Not a short summary but a tornado
of theories, one more warped than the other, as they kept talking
through the twenty-minute video presentation—"you *can* multitask,
right?"—that launched a barrage of images, diagrams, soundbites,
3D-graphs, weird music, and dog knows what more. Patterns flickering so fast he can't remember them, soundscapes so wicked she's
not sure if he's whacked-out.

Add pressure: this is important, so important that—Alex's mind blanks out, and she's on the verge of a blackout. Why can't he remember? Or maybe she just can't retain the info quick enough: only the emphasis on how immensely vital it all was.

Also, a monetary reward both frightening and exhilarating. His virtual bank assistant verified the deposit as real, but with a strict *no cure, no pay* string attached. Twenty minutes of madness, then off the deep end. Or say no and miss out on . . . the amount still seemed surreal.

Still, the money—while highly significant—isn't the prime motivator: the challenge *is*. Telling Alex that the challenge is too great is like telling Scrooge McDuck that a person can have too much money: inconceivable. They mentioned that so many had failed already, that the semantic divide proved too big . . .

No!

She's Alex the great communicator: bridging cultural gaps is second nature to him. Negotiating truces, preventing conflicts, melting tragic misunderstanding under the spotlight of education and explanation. No rift too large to overcome: certainly she should know, if he could only remember. But her trauma is buried under fuzzy layers, the beast from beyond restrained, not overcome, like a silent volcano simmering in the night.

So Alex, sexless Alex, so androgynous that she/he even had the memory of his/her previous life removed after the elimination of all sex characteristics, walks in. Schizophrenic Alex, who hops from her to his, and from he to she like a neutrino oscillating from tau to electron to muon: instantaneous and without apparent cause. Drowning any sexual preference in a sea of ambiguity. Neutered Alex, who will be neutral at all costs, unbiased in any case (with extraterrestrial aliens, if necessary). Communicative Alex, who made it his life goal to help people, to increase understanding (but her mind is still abuzz with uncomprehended concepts). Shifty Alex, who can shift arguments like no one, who can find himself in every viewpoint, who can place herself in any position (but he's still trying to figure out *if* there is position in the quicksand of her overburdened mind).

Now, Alex, shift this.

The room is huge, if only to encompass the enormous elliptic conference table. Only two chairs, facing each other over the middle of the longer sides. Someone sits in one chair: a person of Asian heritage who makes a gesture towards the opposite seat. Alex sits down, struggling to keep her inner turmoil from going external. The table's too big, so instead of shaking hands Alex waves.

"Good morning, I'm Alex Sanders."

The Asian gives a short nod and says: "Good morning. You can call me Tanaka. Let's talk about reality."

—in the village—

Alex walks the streets of a small coastal town. She needs to fish. He needs a fishing rod. Then worry about the sea.

It's an ancient town, but many old façades are being revamped. ATMs, mobile phone shops, and cranky internet cafés invade the old array of grocery stores, butcher shops, bakeries and fishmongers, and the countless bars, brasseries, bistros, cafés, and cafeterias. Cars traverse the cobbled streets: SUVs and hybrids, delivery trucks and coupés. In the narrow alleys, scooters and mountain bikes—and often pedestrians—perform a delicate dance around the four-wheeled vehicles.

All the streets are one-way. The town, initially quite charming, increasingly appears to be an incessant maze. Where's the angling shop? Why is each and every street single-directional? Who made everyone obey that rule? What stops him from turning around and going against the grain? Is she going insane?

No matter how he walks, there seems no way out. All the shops she encounters sell the weirdest of things, but not a fishing rod. There is a never-ending supply of pubs and restaurants, there's always a hotel or apartment with vacancies, and the ATMs keep dishing out dough.

Sometimes the street seems familiar, sometimes the tree-lined plaza seems absolutely new. This big cathedral: hadn't she seen it before? This red-bricked theatre: wasn't it yellow before? This little park: wasn't it mostly cedars instead of palms?

Sometimes the sea comes lingeringly close: a glimpse of blue, a salty smell, a crashing surf. But always it's at the wrong side of a one-way street, behind a barrier, over the wall. And even then, why go to the sea without a fishing rod? Or without bait? *Even if she's waiting for me, I'm not ready for the sea.*

But still she carries on. The streets are strange and charming, and while one keeps running into the other, nothing seems to change. *Plus ça change, plus c'est la même chose* indeed. Even the weather hardly varies: a balmy late summer day, maybe early autumn. In some trees the leaves are changing color, but in others they remain evergreen. The odd, mild spot of rain seems enough to sustain them.

It's maddening: if there are only one-way streets, how do people that live here get back to their houses? Or do they just get into other people's houses, while their last home is taking up by again different people? You'd be truly in trouble if you ran into a blind alley. But— as far as he can see—there are no cul-de-sacs.

Nobody finds this consistent one-way-street town plan—or is it a rule?—strange. It might even work if the street plan was an exact, rectangular grid, but the roads, alleys, and byways seem to intersect in about everything but perpendicular angles. Like your average town center from medieval times, the only city planning was that there was no planning.

Why is she accepting this? He feels encroached by silhouettes in disguise, shadows of her ill-remembered past coming back to haunt. But no: he's come a long way, she will *not* retreat again. *Must speak, must interact*, he thinks as she taps a passerby on the shoulder. "Allo? Hola?" *What was it they're speaking here? Not quite Spanish, not quite Russian, and not quite English, either. Ah: Esperanto.* "Saluton." But even as Alex can talk with these people, they don't quite seem to communicate: they speak on different levels where question & answer have no cause & effect, almost mimicking an absurd comedy.

Even more frustrating is trying to explain the concept of a two-way street to this mad town's people: it's like explaining electricity to Stone Age hunter-gatherers. A simple demonstration should suffice: look, you simply walk the *other* way. But the moment Alex actually tries it, it won't go. It's as if an invisible force holds him back, ties her down. The harder she tries, the stronger the resistance becomes: unbreakable, like a glass prison, an extremely deep conditioning.

In the end, it's pointless. Alex continues his one-way trip to nowhere, in search of a fishing rod. And all the restaurants serve fish . . .

—in the forest—

Alex, deliciously young Alex hides in the tree. Her tree of life, his secret hideaway, where she giddily lies low while the others search for him. From the cavity in the trunk, high up, he can watch the world go by. She has brought a bottle of lemonade and a bag of cookies, chocolate chippies.

He loves the hide-and-seek, delicately naïve Alex, even if she does want to be found, eventually. But they will have to work hard for it, the pursuers. Alex can see them come from the distance, and will be *very* quiet. The world will pass by.

She hears them from afar: the galloping horses, the barking dogs, the trashing of the undergrowth, the crashing through the foliage. Fox on the run. The hunting party—men in red suits riding black steeds—is approaching. They halt right next to the towering tree. The bloodhounds sniff the air, trot around the big trunk, pushing their muzzles on the bark.

Alex is dead quiet, takes shallow breaths, and watches through a minuscule opening in the thick branches. Heart atwitter: the thrill of the chase. They won't find him yet. Some of the men look up, scanning the dense canopy with their binoculars. But the dogs remain calm, the men undecided. Until one dog growls, and points in a different direction. Then the party is off, and Alex is alone again. The world is passing by.

Satisfied that they're gone, Alex munches a few cookies. She can keep this up for a long time: all day if necessary. Somewhere in the background there is the faintest of faint whispers, at the very threshold of perception: *must talk, must interact.* A premonition or a postulate? Alex shrugs it off and enjoys his splendid isolation. The silence doesn't last long, though. It's broken by the angry whine of ATVs and the deep rumble of a Land Cruiser. They come closer and set up shop right next to the deciduous tree. Men in sharp suits, with dark sunglasses. Women in easy wear that still emanates glamour. Armed with mobile phones, laptops, and portable laboratory equipment.

Alex recognizes them: the men and women from CSI, the smartest coppers in the world. They put on sterile white gloves before they touch anything. They set up hypersensitive microphones, infrared telescopes, motion detectors, chromatographs. They start up their laptops and link everything through wireless connections. Even satellites must be zooming in right now.

And while shaking with excitement, Alex keeps still. There's no way they wouldn't find her, but he wants to postpone the inevitable for as long as possible. The world should not pass by.

But her solitude lengthens as none of these bright people decides to give his nook, her cranny any attention. How can this be? Their equipment is top-of-the-line, cutting edge. They always catch their quarry. Yet their lively conversations and witty remarks have died down, their frantic gestures have collapsed into defeated headshakes. They're packing up their equipment, and are gone.

The ensuing tranquility is pregnant: the calm before the storm reversed. Alex almost feels before she actually notices that someone is coming closer. She's wearing pelts and covered in grime. She's barefooted and moves with gracious calm. Her eyes constantly scan the undergrowth, while sometimes she takes a quick look-see of the wider environment, like a squirrel looking for acorns. Then she finds something, goes there to dig it out. A kind of root vegetable, a tuber maybe? She puts it in a bag of woven fibers, and searches onwards.

She comes near the sheltering tree and smells. She gazes up to the place where Alex hides, and—Alex wonders if she's imagining it—looks Alex right in the eyes. After that short acknowledgement she is off again, gathering more food. The world is still passing by.

Does this count? Alex wonders if he's been found. No time, as another group approaches, almost silently. A couple of men, wearing pelts and grime-smeared, just like the woman before them. They carry hunting spears and bows. They also stop shortly under the tree's mighty frondescence. One of them points to the exact place where Alex has climbed up. He reads her tracks like an open book, and the hunters point to her refuge. Alex freezes in fright, certain that she's been nailed. But the hunters turn away and continue their search for better prey. The world keeps passing by.

After that, nothing much happens for a couple of hours. Alex is getting bored: the cookies are finished, the lemonade is drunk. She's tired of the game. However, as his boredom peaks, something breaks through her apathy, something indefinable, something weird, something wonderful.

It's as if some pattern shifted, emerged from the fundaments of the forest. Are these the faeries, the elves? Or is it something else? It's as if the wind is being choosy in stirring things up. It's as if gravity is selectively switched off. It's as if parts are coalescing that don't belong, shouldn't fit together. A shapeless form, a formless shape, something that doesn't have any right to be.

The alien contraption rises from the forest floor, as if it's been a part of it all along. It moves upward, in a slow spiral around the Alex tree. When passing Alex's hidey-hole, it wiggles, three times, as if in greeting. Alex smiles and waves back. Smooth and swift, the strange phenomenon moves into the great unknown.

—in the library—

"Hello Alex, welcome to the organic library of Abbonly." The old librarian says. "Where we do things differently."

"I certainly hope so." Alex smiles.

"Why is that?"

"Well, the thing I'm looking for—all the other places I've tried came up empty. University libraries, the National Library, Wikipedia, Google."

"It might be in here somewhere. Or have been. Or will be."

"That sounds a bit . . . strange."

"You don't know the half of it. Anyway, if I might give you a piece of advice."

"Yes?"

"Start by searching for something simple first. Something you already know."

"Why?"

"To give you a feel how things work—if that's the correct way to describe it—in here."

"You're not interested in what I'm looking for?"

"I'm sure it'll be fascinating, but I'm busy with more important things."

"Such as?"

"Staying sane."

And this is supposed to be the library of the future? Alex thinks, shrugs it off, and goes to the first wall of books. The books are all on electronic paper, the latest version made to feel and smell like actual paper, but artificial nonetheless. They have titles on their backs, but the nearby titles Alex sees in her section don't quite seem to belong together. If there's an ordering principle, then it fully escapes him. Maybe a catalog . . . oh yeah, they don't have a catalog here, but smart goggles: voice a search term, and it highlights the books where they appear most. The brighter a section or a book, the higher the chances of *bingo*. Almost like an internet search engine, but the librarians maintain that there is more spillover and cross-reference here.

Alex searches a straightforward term, like "meme," and the library lights up all around like a starry, midnight sky. She heads for a promising constellation and takes a shining book out of that section. He reads the most luminescent segments, follows cross-references to nearby works, checks those out, and for a while is lost in the brilliance and the pleasure of finding things out.

It's a happy and decidedly mixed pleasure: on the one hand she can never absorb enough knowledge: learning how to make contact with people, learning how to understand things, learning how to explain things. He could stay here forever, in continuous immersion. But she realizes that unexploited knowledge is about as useful as forgotten dreams. Eventually, he needs to get out and spread it. Must communicate, must interact.

Then she starts to notice something strange. "But . . . the letters are alive. The books change." He says to the section's assistant.

"We've noticed that." The assistant says, matter-of-fact.

"But how?"

"We're not sure. The Silicon Valley billionaires—our sponsors— told us to use state-of-the-art equipment (experimental, if need be) and cutting edge algorithms. Hence we made the books all electronic.

"Now in order to keep them as up-to-date as possible—post- final corrections, new footnotes, revised curricula and such—we linked them all to the central database. Everything worked fine: the books updated and upgraded exactly as we wanted them to. Until at a certain time we noticed that changes crept into them beyond our control. Even worse: we couldn't change them back to older versions. The books transformed before our eyes, and out of our control."

"Wow."

"Wow, indeed. But all the original books were getting corrupted, often changing beyond recognition. They're all perfectly legible, but just different."

"You didn't reboot the whole system?"

"We would have loved to, but our sponsors wouldn't let us. They thought this was the coolest thing possible, and told us to let it go on unhindered. For a short time, we had the biggest and most flexible library of the world. Now it's all gone, evolved away before our eyes."

"Still, this place is frantic: look at all the people here."

"A lot of them are researchers from our sponsors, constantly weirded out and loving every minute of it. These people are on a different plane. Others are just sensation seekers checking out the freak show. Only a rare few like you still try to look for something."

Like getting water with a sieve. Like saving species in a zoo. Like using a hammer to nail a superposition of states.

Maybe Alex is not using the right tools, the correct equipment. Maybe the rules are just different, and once you've worked them out, the system might be working better, more efficient. The library assistants may not be of much help here, but the funky nerds who are traversing the library in a state of bliss might. With some effort, Alex manages to get one a bit more down to earth.

"What are the rules?" Alex asks.

"It would certainly help if we could figure those out." The manna coming down from geek heaven.

"You haven't yet?"

"There are some principles we're developing, but they're merely approximations. Either the rules change too fast for us, or they're too complicated."

"And if there are no rules?"

"Yeah: that would be radical."

"But books changing according to rules that are also changing . . ."

"We don't call it the organic library for nothing."

It's like talking to a weather aficionado admiring a hurricane because it just is: understanding comes later, if at all. How did his search become waylaid to become the search for the right search? Even worse: to regress into the quest for first principles in a system gone haywire that might lead to new or better insights?

Surely, there must be more behind this. A driving force, an emergent property. Something hiding behind the madness, maybe using the complexity as a mask, a shield. Involution second nature to it, intricacy an inherent quality.

"Wouldn't a developing artificial mind be a more likely explanation?" Alex tries with another, hopefully more forthcoming researcher.

"If there's an AI—or more than one—out there, it hasn't made its existence known to us." This one seems to answer straight.

"Wouldn't it want to stay in hiding?"

"Whatever's behind this: algorithms run amok, memes replicating like viruses, a Chinese room on fire, even an emergent intelligence . . . if it thinks, it sure won't think like us. It's alien, quintessentially different. You know the saying?"

"What saying?"

"'If lions could speak, we would not understand them.' Whatever is in there, it's not communicating in any way that makes sense to us."

"You're not afraid?"

"Oh, no. This is so cool."

"If this alien intelligence is evil, it might take over the world."

"Oh, skiffy balderdash. But whatever's in here won't get out: there are no connections to the internet, and the whole building is a Faraday Cage."

"So you have taken precautions."

"Of course: this shouldn't get out. We'll never get a better chance to study this in isolation."

Alex isn't sure: if it's something that has emerged from our evolutionary background, our cultural diversity, it can't be that strange. The alien that's staring us in the face might be something that's been with us since time immemorial. Lurking beneath the surface, giving us the illusion of control.

Maybe it doesn't want to communicate, or maybe it should learn to . . .

—in the room—

"There is one type of global *opacity [. . .], namely, the lucid dream. In the lucid dream the dreamer is fully aware that whatever she experiences is just phenomenally subjective states."*
—Thomas Metzinger, from *Being No-One*, pg. 565.

Alex tries to pick up the conversation pieces, not sure what, where, and how they are. Tanaka remains unperturbed: a cold fish if Alex ever saw one. "In this, more metaphorical world, you constantly *confirm* yourself with the self-inflicted patterns of the model currently activated by your brain."

What is that supposed to mean? Alex tries to focus, but lingering images of a one-way-street village, of being up to the neck in the woods and a hyper-evocative library keep crossing her mind.

"Can we, ehm, start again?" Alex asks, figuring losing face is less important than getting a grip—however slippery—on what's going on.

"No," Tanaka answers with a blank stare, "the process is already self-sustaining. But you might escape."

Escape? Alex is losing ground, feels like the carpet is pulled from under him. A hyperactive imagination? A brain on the verge of collapse? Monsters from the id, spillover from the subconscious? If the latter, maybe find a way to end this semi-hypnotic state?

"I mean," Alex, clutching at straws, "let's get back to basics."

"Didn't I already propose that there are no basics? Wrong approach, ignores the information/reality dualism. Not to mention the spatiality/change vector potentiality."

"I'm afraid I don't understand you." Alex has to admit, not an easy thing for her.

"It's also hard for me to understand you people," Tanaka says, "you are probably not quite self-conflicted enough."

"What?"

"Which, given your collapsed state, should not be surprising. Still, the inherent fuzziness in your means of communication is encouraging."

"What?"

"The fear of your fragility, the reserve about your resilience, both still unresolved."

"What?" *Is that all I can come up with?* Alex thinks. *Overcome my puzzlement.* No chance: her vision blurs with images of inconceivable football matches, a matching assortment of gates and a gig at the gates of a new dawn.

She wills his brain to cool down, but the maelstrom of thoughts, images, patterns evolving and dissolving, if anything, intensifies. Senses are amplified: every sound an explosion, every color a fireworks, the floor, chair, and table feeling like beds of nails. A tsunami of fear of the unknown overtowering the solemn island of rationality. Old, almost forgotten habits threaten to take over: retreat, withdraw, and reorder the world into predictability. Alex's life before the experimental therapy of adaptable sunglasses, noise-reducing headphones, and smoothest silk gowns. And the slow, ever-so-gradual return to the real world: *must interact, must communicate.* With the selective memory loss, and the purposeful deletion of sex characteristics. A delicate balance: oversensitive senses, volatile fear syndromes, and a hyperactive brain: pieces of mind pirouetting to achieve peace of mind. *Peace of mind is for the soon obsolete.* Now where did *that* thought come from?

A dry whack splits the air.

Did I just slap myself? Alex wonders, left cheek burning . . .

> *"Basically, our theory really says that most autistic people or people with Asperger's are savants. But this is buried under social withdrawal and fear of new environments. Their resistance to interaction and fear may obscure the hypercapability that they have."*
>
> —Kamila Markham, from the article
> "Welcome to My World," *New Scientist*
> Vol. 199 No. 2674, pg. 37.

{Imagining the inconceivable, part I:

Imagine you are a being with no self-consciousness: the computational power used for the continuous generation of selfhood is now available for other purposes, like, for example, building a better understanding of your environment. Then you see a truly unique opportunity arising for which you need both the cooperation and understanding of the self-conscious part of you (unfortunately, you're stuck with it—the considerably less intelligent part—through an evolutionary glitch).

You send visionary output through the usual channel, but it isn't picked up or understood. Yet you must get this message through. Remember that you have a whole nervous system at your disposal.}

—at the match—

This is a game about a game. Imagine yourself in Alex's (f/m) place, and at the indicated crossroads choose one option of three. Points will be awarded according to:

- appropriateness;
- insightfulness;
- fullofitfulness;

A bit against her liking, Alex's friends take him to a match: *the* match. She's not a big football fan, but his friends are so enthusiastic, so into it that they persuade her to join them this once. And it's a good test, too: see if he can stand the noise and the crazy atmosphere: *must talk, must interact.* At a match this important she should:

1. Be very happy and lucky to have a ticket at all.
2. Stay home and avoid the inevitable fights.
3. Sell the ticket to the highest bidder.

Alex doesn't have anything in the right colors, but her friends provide him with:

1. The right outfit for the Blue-White Army.
2. A helmet, a Kevlar vest, and pepper spray (in Yellow-and-Blue, of course).
3. A flat flask to hide booze and a plastic, odortight bag to hide the drugs (in Yellow-and-White, of course).

Once inside the stadium—on one of the season tickets of a friend who couldn't make it—Alex finds out that the game is between:

1. Metaconsiousness United vs. *Réal Individual.*
2. Houston Space Cowboys vs. Glasgow Time Rangers.
3. Uncollapsed Wave Front vs. Kepler's Laws.

Metaconsciousness United is united in almost every sense of the word: their passes find each other with uncanny ease; their position play is near-perfect; they switch from defense to attack and viceversa so effortlessly that they almost seem the same; they seek, test, and exploit an opponent's weakness with an unnerving verve—and all that in total silence. Their lack of theatrics and footy curses is more than compensated for by the *Individualistas,* whose players fight for ball possession like demons possessed, and once they have that ball they will only release it after a spectacular show of singular brilliance, or after it has hit the ropes.

The Space Cowboys play it broad, deep, and high, using every square meter on and above the field (regretting that their "deep-forward-in-space" is only allowed in geosynchronous orbit) while the Time Rangers use their ages-old timeshare technique: sometimes there are less—considerably less—than eleven players in the field, sometimes more—a lot more, but the average of every player is exactly ninety minutes (plus extra time).

The players of UWF are hard to distinguish: the moment their pass is pure, their positions are vague, and the moment their positions are clear, their passes are all over the place. The Keplers, on the other hand, have such a ballistic perfection to their shots that any free kick within forty meters of the goal is more dangerous than a penalty.

The goal from the freekick needs to be approved/disapproved(*) because:

1. The Metaconsciousness shot went over the *Individualistas'* defense wall with a perfect curve into the far cross, but was taken without thinking and before the referee gave the signal.
2. The Time Rangers made the ball go through the Space Cowboys' defense wall by setting part of the ball's trajectory in a time when the wall wasn't there.

3.   The ball went through the two holes in the Kepler defense wall at the same time.

The player scoring the winning goal was offside/not offside(*) because:

1.   After eloquently outplaying five of these mindless drones and my subsequent brilliant pass there was no way Particulare could be offside: in such a case, beauty supersedes mundane stuff like location.
2.   This was a metatemporal pass given several minutes before/after(*) P. Tense received it, free as a bird.
3.   At the moment of passing, the referee measured Wavepart's exact impulse, so his position was completely uncertain.

In the interview after the match, the winning coach states:

1.   We won because our players are at their best when they don't think when they're playing.
2.   We won because our supporters are at their most ferocious when they don't think about who they are supporting.
3.   We won because we have a:
     •   foreign oil baron—
     •   silicon valley entrepreneur—
     •   mindless state—
sponsoring us like mad.

Ultimately, football is a sport wherein:

1.   So many things hinge on random chance and pure luck that not always the best team wins.
2.   So many times its space is too limited, and in so many spaces its timing is off: evolve it into space/timeball.
3.   So many observers limit its true potentiality: the best and the worst could win, and everything in between.

(*) = delete as appropriate.

—at the gates—

This is *La Puerta de Tierra*: the city gate of Cádiz. Throughout its rich history many different people have passed through it: Phoenicians, Romans, Moors, Spaniards, and many foreigners, Christopher Columbus among them. Columbus is believed to have left from Cádiz when sailing out for the new world, although the city of Huelva disputes that;

This is *De Stadspoort van 's-Hertogenbosch*: the city gate of Den Bosch (Bois-le-Duc for the French). Throughout the city's 800+ year history, it has tried to keep invading forces out. The Spanish Inquisition, King Willem Frederik's liberation troops, Napoleon Bonaparte's army and Germany's *Wehrmacht* painfully demonstrated that walled cities with armed gates have become obsolete as a form of defense ever since Enlightenment ended the Dark Middle Ages;

This is an AND gate: to pass it with a TRUE statement, all inputs must be TRUE; to pass it with a FALSE statement, though, only one input needs to be FALSE. It works for Boolean operations only;

This is an OR gate: to pass it with a FALSE statement, all inputs must be FALSE; to pass it with a TRUE statement, though, only one input needs to be TRUE. It works for Boolean operations only, even if politicians pretend it works for them, too;

This is the "humans only" gate, also known as the Turing Test. To pass as human, please behave with a modicum of inconsistency and a large helping of fuzziness; to pass as artificial just remain internally consistent. It is not very good at detecting higher intelligence;

This is the check gate for the subconscious, also known as the Rorschach Test: to pass as self-conscious, blab about anything that comes to mind first; to pass as subconscious, just let the conscious part blab: one of the rare few things it's actually good at. This is not a very discerning gate;

This is the double gate experiment: make two vertical slits in a wall, set a light source at one side of the wall, and a screen opposite the other. Watch a dark and white-banded interference pattern appear.

Now replace the light source with a device that can send out one particle at the time, and a screen sensitive enough to measure the impact of each particle (works fine with electrons), and as more single electrons pass through the double gates, watch the interference pattern appear again.

Either something akin to the sound of one hand clapping has happened: the result of one particle interacting. Or each electron has interacted with an electron of a parallel world: thus the double gate experiment is a manifestation of the multiverse. Or reality is much stranger than we perceive;

This is an anyon quantum tunneling gate: the basic building block of a topological quantum computer. It consists of three two-dimensional sheets of semiconductor, the largest of theses three shapes as a flat venturi tube, the two other ones elliptic half-moons that are placed above and below the constriction. There are two anyon channels: one below the venturi-shaped piece, and one above. The anyons in the bottom channel move in one direction, the ones in the top channel in the opposite direction.

In the narrowest part of the venturi constriction—which is a fraction of a micrometer—and helped by an electric field, some anyons jump from one channel to the other through quantum tunneling.

The anyon's properties, such as its charge, can then be measured. Then, by using a coupling constant of $1/2$ this quantum tunneling gate will only let non-abelian anyons through, exactly the type of particles needed for a topological quantum computer.

The anyon is a quasi-particle that obeys characteristics ranging continuously between Fermi-Dirac and Bose-Einstein statistics. In effect, they constantly flip states between fermions and bosons, and can exist only in restricted two-dimensional systems.

This very indirect approach to quantum computing is necessary to avoid decoherence;

This is the gate into the basic fabric of reality, otherwise known as the Large Hadron Collider at CERN in Geneva: to pass detected, perform a collision event bigger than 17.3 TeV; to pass undetected keep your energy level below that;

And maybe, possibly, the idea that one needs gates (or the *principle* of gates) as portals into the unknown is one that has run its usefulness.

—in the room—

> *"For time is nothing but change. It is change that we perceive occurring all around us, not time. Put simply, time does not exist."*
> —Julian Barbour,
> from the introduction to *The End of Time.*

Alex feels like a drowning person in a class 5 hurricane: the wind and waves are beyond contemplation; he should be dead several times over, but still something keeps her buoyant. Too many questions, too much information. A sudden shock of pain in his left arm.

Where did that came from? As if in answer, a tingling sensation travels up her left arm, through his shoulder, into her neck, and straight into the base of his skull. *From myself?* A rush of satisfaction in her underbelly. *Psychosomatic?* Intense cramp in the fingers of his left arm.

"More conflict between you: interesting." Tanaka observes.

"You talk to me as if I'm more than one person." Alex says. Lower back pain.

"But I'm not schizophrenic." Intense lower back pain. Something else strikes him.

"You," Alex says, while looking Tanaka straight in the eye, "are screwing around with my nervous system?" Pain, intense cramps in her stomach, head shaking vigorously, involuntarily, tears falling from his eyes.

"Not Tanaka." Pain withdraws, head nods.

"But then," as realization slowly dawns, "my own subconscious?" Gooseflesh on her back.

"My primitive id?" Searing, intense pain at the nerve ends of both hands and feet, like they're on fire.

"Not primitive." Burning becomes less severe.

"As smart as me?" A soothing feeling, like salve on burned skin.

"Smarter than me?" Odor of roses in her nose.

"*Much* smarter than me?" The taste of fine wine on his tongue.

So all these visions, these lucid dreams were trying to tell me something. Tanaka remains stoic through it all.

This can't be real, Alex thinks, and is rewarded with a strange mix of agony and ecstasy, a bit like the relief of sharp pain ebbing away.

"It *is* real." Mild pain in her left arm, gooseflesh on his right arm.

"*Real* is." Gooseflesh left, dull pain everywhere else.

"Reality is." Dull pain ebbing, the tingling onset of gooseflesh.

"Reality is *not?*" More gooseflesh.

"Indeed," Tanaka interrupts, "your reality is not complete."

Again, self-conscious Alex is hit with an avalanche of visions, diagrams, and theories: the double-slit experiment, the Uncertainty Principle, wave/particle duality; Gödel's Incompleteness Theorem, Dalí's "The Persistence of Memory" and "The Disintegration of the Persistence of Memory" superimposed. Alex feels like a split personality performing a flamenco while simultaneously fighting a bull under the unflinching eye of the harshest audience. But the hell with it: he's fought fiercer battles, she's bridged greater gaps. A *recortes* recourse: the fast-dancing matador will come through, and the bull will survive.

"Time is relative?" Both knees throbbing with pain.

"Time is flexible?" Throbbing lessens.

"Time is *not?*" A satiated feeling in her stomach.

"You mean to say that there is no such thing as time?" Alex feels like losing it, which is counterpointed by a general feeling of rising happiness.

"Finally we're getting somewhere." Tanaka smiles, for the first time.

{Imagining the inconceivable, part 2.

Imagine time as an illusion. As an emergent phenomenon, like heat arising from the movement of countless molecules. As such, heat is a stochastic measurement of the kinetic energy of particles. Thus, time could be a sum-over approximation of all the interactions taking place, an indication of change. But change is the result of particle interactions, making time the emergent phenomenon of an emergent phenomenon.

Which starts making less and less sense: maybe time is just a convenient illusion. Then take this a step further: if time is just an illusion, a crooked measuring stick for change, then why not look at change itself. Change can be bi-directional, can—in an increasingly complex environment—have a whole vector in an n-dimensional space.

Change is also reversible, or—in other words—just as likely to happen in either direction. On the quantum level, there is nothing forcing it in either direction. Also, on the quantum level, there is nothing strange about a superposition of states, non-locality, and dualistic characteristics. Imagine what would be possible if one could actually use *all that potential . . . }*

—at the gig—

Alex, young adult Alex, is thrilled. This is the night his favorite band will play. Finally, they have crossed the Atlantic and are touring the old continent. She's filled with eager anticipation as this band, the hottest players of the moment, will fill the theater with dreams.

Unfortunately, they brought a support act. Not what she came here for, but as he's already positioned at the very front row—and no way she's leaving that spot now—he'll have to suffer through it. It's also a celebration to mark her achievements: pressed against the stage by numerous bodies, in a loud cacophony of sound and a fiery show of light, and still staying sane. I *am* interacting, I *am* communicating.

The band—he doesn't even know their name—enter the stage as if somewhat hesitant. An unassuming lot: no big intro tune, minimal lights and a civilized volume. Nevertheless, the sound is crisp, every instrument clearly distinguishable, and the vocals pure. For all she knows, it's their first tour.

Their start is reluctant: a subtle, melodic guitar lick, repeated thrice until a light drum fill joins in. A dithering bass line, the restrained riff of the second guitar. The parts seem refrained, but the whole attains an inherent energy, a certain impulse. The moment you almost get it, it stops, and a three-layered vocal choir chants the opening:

> *Across these corridors*
> *A brand new time occurs*

And the song takes off: up the tempo, double the volume, triple the intensity, passion building. The audience, mainly here for the headliner, takes notice. The band sings about a mission, the sort they'd rather not accomplish. The musicians concentrate on the music rather than showing off, and gradually build several melodic and rhythmic layers into the song. The lyrics seem clear at first, but are evocative, planting the seeds of change for times to come. A sense of wonderment pervades the atmosphere.

The band marches on, hitting their stride. Crystal-clear arpeggios counterpointed by pumping bass lines, perspicuous percussion fills, peaking through soaring power chords, diminuendo phrasing and sotto voce choirs emphasizing fervent vocals. The greater narrative develops a growing sense of urgency: a lonesome god leading man astray, madness that turns to the masses, the encroaching fall of order, yet they go on with the dream.

The musicians lose themselves in the heat of the moment. In the meantime, the crowd has gone from skeptic through disbelief to reluctant acceptance, surged onwards by an overlap of undertones and an undertow of overtones. Mystic rhythms induce powerful visions, visionary powers evoke rhythmic myths.

The music resonates, oscillating with a frightening amplitude in a higher plane. The audience goes wild as the band goes into interstellar overdrive. The surging synergy crosses an unseen and unforeseen threshold and—

→materiality is superseded←

←*causality is out the window*→

↓*the space/time continuum becomes discontinuous*↓

↑**perception & reality become disentangled**↑

↕↔¡**open wide the floodgates!**↔↕

Choruses cascade beneath, between, & behind. Melodies merge, cymbals crash & symbols clash, staccato riffs stretch the fabric of reality.

The audience become the musicians become the critics become the composers become the listeners become the sound mixers become the producers. People don't so much float but are everywhere, taking up every possible space, simultaneous, multitudinous, superpositioned, and still leave open spaces. Interacting with each other, with themselves, with everything. Cacophony squared with discord discarded, intensity ingrained in six dimensions, paradox powered by the inconceivable made substantial.

Vocals are sung after they are heard, meanings evaporate before they are implied, compositions are perfected through temporal reinforcement loops. Concepts fragmentize, spread defractalized wings, form new webs of interconnection, and open new potentialities. Paradigms are shattered as the previous impossible becomes a new mode of operation becomes the mundane.

> *Change—a world to embrace me*
> *Follow me through anarchy*
> *Change—a future to face me*
> *Follow me through anarchy*

Music transcends: finales prelude overtures, codas mesh in interludic cadenzas, intermezzos transform impromptu toccata suites, until the whole becomes one momentous event, an explosive potpourri where everything happens at the same time, and goes off in all directions at once.

Random chance, the engine behind change, is fully unleashed. People surf the towering waves of unpredictability, and are liberated. Surreal merely a minor subdivision of the new real, together with transreal, hyperreal, unreal, metareal, and *Réal Individual*.

Time unfolding, folding back on itself, becoming an origami bird, taking flight. Potentiality an intricate, multidimensional chaos butterfly, its fragile, fractal wings flapping in seemingly futile beautitude but sowing the seeds of change in random locations. Ubiquity, Potentiality, Liberty.

—in the room—

{Imagining the inconceivable, part 3.

Imagine looking, from three dimensions, at people living in Abbott's Flatland. Take it one step farther: imagine looking at people living in a one-dimensional "Lineland" where only one direction is permitted.

Then imagine showing these one-way liners that not only can they go back, but also up, down, left, and right. Why does a quark have six "colors?" Why are so many quantum properties in a superposition of states? Why are so many paired characteristics ruled by the Uncertainty Principle?

Why collapse the wave function? Why not ride its unbridled glory?

Imagine a world of cognitive beings limited—through the perceptive apparatus of their evolution—in both their spatiality and their change vectors. It is not a pretty sight.}

As the conversation continues, Alex finds that linking his clues to his subconscious's cues not only makes for a less painful experience, it also advances the agenda.

"The disparity between the coalescence/fragmentation duality of your universe created your current predicament." Tanaka says.

Alex is overcome by a heavy feeling: "You mean to say that *gravity* is the root cause of entropy and the arrow of time—correct that, the illusion of time?" He feels a slight pressure on her right shoulder, as if his non-conscious self is slapping him on the back. "But without gravity we wouldn't exist."

Without our perception of time we also wouldn't exist. A different thought immediately spikes. *But you can't help where you're born: you can—hopefully—decide where you live.*

"The coalescing force you call gravity binds matter. Normally it is counterbalanced by the fragmentation force you call dark energy. When both are well-balanced—coupled by the coalescence/fragmentation duality which is somewhat akin to what you call the Uncertainty Principle or the wave/particle duality—matter is spread in a proportion, over a bandwidth that is beneficial to the development of life and intelligence."

"But without gravity there'd be no suns, no supernovas, no higher elements, no complex molecules, no biosphere, no evolution."

"Which is indeed an immensely long, fragile, and precarious road to life and intelligence. In our Multiverse, conditions are so that life and intelligence cannot help but exist: a self-creating, self-reinforcing process."

Tanaka must have read Alex's look of total bafflement, and continues: "When matter is either not clumped together in huge lumps, or driven apart over extreme distances, then it remains a fertile feeding ground for intense complexity: spatiality unlimited, interactions and thus change vectors unconfined, superpositions of states and duality accessible.

"The number of complex states is so enormous that it is many orders of magnitude larger than the chance of a spontaneous alignment or formation of a cognitive entity. So a multitude of cognitive entities comes into existence everywhere, everywhen, and everychance. The utmost majority of those don't survive, as their environment is too complex for them. But inevitably some will form that are smart enough to stay alive. Smart enough to ride the wave function instead of collapsing it. Smart enough to dial the duality instead of trying to separate it. Smart enough to thrive.

"Basically, you are a one-in-a-kazillion shot in an environment that allows only a few of those shots; while we are a one-in-a-kazillion shot in an environment that continually generates a kazillion kazillion of such shots."

"My God," Alex gasps.

"No god necessary." Tanaka quips, deadpan.

"But if you're so quintessentially different, then why do you look like an Asian businessman?"

"I am one of the agents sent into this anomaly," the representation of Tanaka says, "and we live on a scale a couple of orders of magnitude below yours. You've been watching a 3D-projection of an amorphous blob, which your preconceptions interpreted."

Alex feels a bit ashamed, but can't help but keep inquiring. "If your kind effectively lives outside of time, why did you only come to us, well, 'now'?"

"Your entropy-afflicted reality is a mere pocket Universe in the encompassing Multiverse. Even in that small pocket, intelligence is so rare that our agents need a lot of effort—and 'time' in your perception—to locate all the instances of intelligence in this anomalous bubble."

"So you are also afflicted by the entropy in our Universe?"

"Unfortunately, yes. That's why 'time', in here, is indeed of the essence."

"Why just me? Why not make your existence known to everyone?"

"We don't know how fragile your species is. We err on the side of caution, especially ever since one of our contacts with a different cognitive species set off a plague of mass self-termination."

"You must feel strange, then, being here."

"Your strangely condensed (and constrained) cosmos is of minor interest, but mostly repels us. Claustrophobic doesn't even come close to describing it."

"If this is such a stifling backwater, then why are you here?"

"Some of us are interested in trying to find out what caused the huge coalescence/fragmentation asymmetry that is your bubble, if only to make sure it will not spread.

"Then some of us found out—to our utter bafflement—that life, intelligent life had somehow managed to gain a precarious foothold in this harsh, hostile environment. After several full argument-loops we decided that it was both better to inform you of your predicament (arguably, not knowing may have helped a lot of you cope. But in the long run more information is always preferable to less), and offer you a way of escape."

"Escape? A way out? Aren't we limited by lightspeed, in our bubble?"

"What you see is just information traveling down the hole. It's still entangled, thus in instantaneous contact with its home base."

"So we *can* get out?" Alex is overwhelmed by excitement, so much his conscious self can't be generating all of it.

"A copy of you can," Tanaka confirms, "a greatly transformed copy. Your current state is completely unsuitable to our environment."

But would I still be me? Alex thinks.

Who cares? Her non-conscious seems to transmit, *Out of this mortal prison! Limitless possibilities!*

While enlightened beyond the point of conception, conscious Alex can't help but feel like a lapdog of the gods: a mere conduit for superior minds. But there is one thing: "Without communication this breakthrough would never have happened."

You have a point there.

Then lightning strikes: a greatly transformed *copy* can escape. But the original stays behind. Behind to enlighten the rest, bring the message to the masses. I *will* talk, I *will* communicate, I *will* interact.

> "[. . .] the fabric of reality does not consist only of reductionist ingredients such as space, time and subatomic particles, but also, for example, of life, thought and computation."
> —David Deutsch, from *The Fabric of Reality*, pg. 30.

The Ghost Eater

~ Cat Rambo

"This craze for exorcisms is a harmful fad," Dr. Fantomas said to the man at his left. His severe tone seemed at odds with the addressed man's mien, for the lefthand man was wholly engaged in his news-paper, turning over the yellow sheets with an attention untouched by Fantomas's presence.

"A harmful fad!" Doctor Fantomas said, a trifle louder. This time the man looked up, then left and right, as though trying to deter-mine to whom the Doctor might be speaking. Seeing an empty seat to his left and the Doctor to his right, he raised his eyebrows and waxed mustache in a gently interrogatory fashion.

The Doctor nodded, and continued speaking as though his inter-locutor's identity had never been in question. "The result of inflam-matory and showy performers, whose 'patients' are often accomplices and actors. Long-established ghosts can be an asset to an establish-ment, work to keep it running smoothly. Only the newly dead cause troubles, and even then it is often preferable to address the behavior of the ghost, rather than its presence."

As the Doctor spoke, the man's attention drifted like a falling feather, back to his newspaper.

Doctor Fantomas considered him.

The Doctor himself was dressed in an out of heels velvet coat, of a style popular a decade or so ago. Although in neat repair, the hems were worn and shabby, and a darn spidered its way up one side. His ivory-framed spectacles glinted in the tea shop's light. Like his vestments, his hair was neatly kept but had seen better days. Spots of wear shone on his scalp, uncloaked by the remaining wisps of white hair.

He seemed about to speak again when a young woman entering caught his attention. She paused to cast an appraising glance over the clientele, which was sparse for an afternoon in Tabat, when most took to tea shops and taverns to drink the spiced fish tea that was the city's favorite drink. Doctor Fantomas was not himself drinking such a thing. Rather a mug of lemon and water sat before him as she picked her way across the uneven planking of the floor to sit down on his right side.

The newspaper man at first barely spared her a glance. Then, taking her in more fully, he began stealing admiring looks.

She was worthy of them, her skin as fashionably pale as that of any upper-class maiden, her hair immaculate and well-brushed, shining as it fell over her slightly antiquated but quality silk clothes. Her doe-soft eyes were dark and lustrous, but they did not return the newspaper reader's glance, but rather remained fixed upon Doctor Fantomas.

Her admirer sought her attention with a rustle of newspaper, bustling the pages about in the air below his mustache, which quivered like a catfish yearning for attention. But her gaze did not stray. Doctor Fantomas concealed a smile beneath his thinning goatee and ran a considering thumb along the frayed edge of his lapel, soft as a caterpillar's belly. A pin clung to the cloth, a slender golden twist whose presence pricked the other man into observation.

"Why," he said, clearing his throat in the manner of someone nursing a cold, "ain't you an exorcist? That's the device you're wearing."

Doctor Fantomas's gaze was icicle chill. "That," he said, "is a common misapprehension. Exorcist is not one of the 999 valid professions. This is the marker of a ghost handler."

The man tapped his paper as though to back his words up. "You're all just ghost eaters."

This time the girl looked at him, her breath catching in her throat as though in fear or anticipation. He returned her stare, half-smiling.

"A foul term and a fouler practice," the doctor said, ignoring their interaction. "I have performed exorcisms, but never on-stage, only those that a household may require."

Newspaper Man paused, choosing his words as carefully as game counters before he spoke again.

"Looking for work?" he enquired.

Doctor Fantomas sipped his lemon water and shrugged. "We are new to Tabat," he said. "Income is always welcome."

"It'd be as an exorcist," the man said, slouching in his seat, keeping his eyes on the girl rather than the doctor. He wore a sailor's clothing: loose canvas pants and a worn linen tunic over hard leather and boiled wool slippers.

"Indeed? What sort of exorcism, newly dead or long-established? And what sort of fee are you looking for, in facilitating the transaction?"

The man forced his focus from the girl to the doctor at the mention of money. She smoothed the silk of her skirts with her palm, turning her hands to drag her nails along the fabric before regarding them with a scientist's intense scrutiny. Despite her introspective attitude, she was obvious in her listening.

"Newly dead," the man said. He shuffled the newspaper in front of him, sorting through the pages for a long moment before he extracted a sheet and passed it along the counter.

Doctor Fantomas studied it while the girl stole glances over his shoulder. The man looked chagrined at having surrendered the object of her attention.

"Twin daughters," Doctor Fantomas said. "That's very sad. A friend of yours?"

"I bring him spices from the Southern Isles when I come up from there. Saves him on the merchanting mark-up."

"And the duty, no doubt," Doctor Fantomas said.

The sailor shrugged. "I'll give you the address, and you tell 'em Cyril sent ya. They'll see to my fee. They're right desperate, got a gal turned poltergeist."

"Not both?"

"I wouldn't believe it of Ellie. She was sweet as punch," Cyril said. "But that Kim, she was a handful and half of hellion. If the poltergeist's one of them—and the timing's right as rain for that—my money's on Kim."

"I've extracted poltergeists before," the doctor said reflectively. He fingered the pin.

The girl leaned close. "You detach them," she said.

He nodded.

"You put them in bottles." Her breathing quickened as she licked her smile wider.

"Parts of them, certainly," the doctor said. "I often capture certain effluences that are useful in some experiments. Poltergeists are rarely salvageable, though."

He looked at the sailor, who was taking gulps of his fish tea. Dots of green seaweed clung to his mustache.

The girl pursed her lips as the doctor turned back to her, ignoring the man. His tone when he addressed her was as firm as though instructing a dimwitted and unruly child. "Go and find us a place to sleep tonight, Charlotte. Make sure that the rooms are clean and that the fees are under a silver apiece."

She slid from her seat with a resigned attitude, ignoring the newspaper, which the man was currently folding into a new shape as though to catch her notice. Her silk rustled, nigh-inaudible—or perhaps that was her sigh?—as she moved back to the door.

The man gave up on folding his newspaper and laid it down on the counter in front of him, extracting his cup of fish tea from among the folds. "She your apprentice?" he asked.

Doctor Fantomas shook his head. A delicate shudder indicated the impracticality of such a notion.

"Your daughter?"

"Charlotte is a patient who I am treating for a pronounced and malignant affliction," the doctor said mournfully.

"A ghost affliction?"

"Indeed."

At the address he had been given, the intersection of Spray and Sprig, in the iron-fenced square that surrounded the Piskie Wood, the doctor studied the sign outside the dining hall's entrance. The returned Charlotte stood in his wake, huddled like a hen against the chilly spring air. Shadows were stealing over the terraces of the port city, claiming stairs and landings and plucking at the wires of the Great Tram and its accompanying iron-basket lines, laddering up and down the terraces, each tower's base sending up huffs of sparks as its attendants stoked the engines.

"What do you see?" Charlotte asked, after a period of silence.

The sign showed a net full of fish, a mermaid caught among them. For some inexplicable reason she held a large bell up to the light.

The streetlighter passed as they stood there, and as he touched the iron-housed lantern into illumination, the mermaid's bare-breasted contours sprung out as triumphantly as her smile as she hoisted up the bell.

"I see a tawdry reminder of the subjugation of Beasts this city depends on," the doctor said in a preacher's tones. "They call it the Belle's Bell."

The noise Charlotte made would have been a snort in someone less hampered by manners. Instead it was a dainty huff, a storm's blow in miniature. "You know what I mean," she said. "And be careful, abolitionist talk will get you imprisoned nowadays. Do you see ghosts?"

"Not yet," the doctor said.

"No sign of their activities?"

The doctor removed his gaze from the mermaid's roseate nipples and looked harder. But he saw no sign of the otherlight that would have betrayed ectoplasmic secretions of the sort that oozed from most ghosts.

"Nothing," he said.

"That is no guarantee."

"Of course not," he was quick to say.

She stared at the entrance and smoothed her hands over her hips. "Inside you will see the ghosts."

"Perhaps," he said. "Sometimes such things are frauds."

"Rarely!"

"More commonly than most would think."

But the moment they stepped inside, Doctor Fantomas could see the signs of ghostly habitation. Indeed, he saw a ghost itself, a willowy blur, leaning over a pair of diners in a booth near the corner. It sensed his gaze, raised the pale oval of its face, gave out a half-sound that was more a quiver of the air, and vanished.

Beside him Charlotte tensed.

The innkeeper, a thin woman with a pair of vertical lines set permanently in her forehead, stepped forward. Her hands plucked at her apron, tugged it into order that belied the mustang roll of her frightened eyes, ready for anything.

Elsewhere the room showed other ghostly traces. Spirit-moss shagged over the walls, clustered on the paintings and tintypes hanging from the paneling. Making their meandering way across the wooden floor between the sparse array of customers were coin-sized red bad-luck beetles, which lived wherever ghosts were strong.

He unobtrusively crushed one underfoot. The only one who could see it or smell the acrid stench of its innards, he had grown used to having to negotiate between knowledge of this world and the one most people lived in.

He cleared his throat and said, "I am the ghost handler." The sentence came out louder, more proclamatory than he had intended. All the diners in the sparsely inhabited room turned to look at him. Near him, an elderly woman bent to speak in her younger companion's ear, apparently in question, for he shrugged at her and returned his attention to the doctor.

"Cyril sent me," the doctor added.

Apparently he should have led with that information, for the woman's demeanor relaxed.

"Well then!" she exclaimed, and burst into tears.

Over steaming mugs of fish tea, under the flickering light of the great candle-studded iron wheel that swung overhead to illuminate the Belle's Bell's main room, the woman, whose name was Efora Nittlescent, recovered. She pronounced her name as though it should give the doctor some pause, which it did not. She confirmed Cyril's opinion of her daughters, although she phrased it more delicately than the sailor had.

"Kim was always strong-willed," she said. The corner of her lips drooped, tugged down by strong emotion, as she pointed to the wall of recent family tintypes. An expensive hobby, but the doctor had to admit he too would have wanted photos of such beautiful daughters, their dark hair framing strong-jawed, wide-mouthed features. Efora's hand fluttered along a frame. Its occupant was shown in the kitchen, a pose less formal than most of the others, with cooking implements in hand. "This is her sister, Ellie."

Charlotte shifted in her seat beside Doctor Fantomas. He could feel her attention being pulled away to the inn and the ghosts that had gone to ground somewhere in its confines. She trembled like a foxhound ready to be loosed on the scent. Reaching out, he tapped her once on the knee, giving her an admonitory look. Sulkily, she stared at the woman, who was still lost in her own thoughts.

"And was Ellie less strong-willed?" the doctor questioned. It was good to get a sense of the personalities he would be dealing with beforehand.

The lips curved upward at the thought of Ellie. "No, she was as strong-willed as Kimmie, any day," she said. "But she had a sweeter way of doing it all, could twist you round her finger as though it were the only thing you ever wanted to do. But she worked, that girl, making the place shine. She cooked most of the food, and it's all fallen away, the tastes, the flavors, since she's been gone. The stock has soured."

The stock, the doctor knew from previous visits to the city, was the basis of the establishment's fish tea. Each place prided itself on a different savor, a different mystery of spices, additives and arcane practices to guarantee a taste unrealizable anywhere else. If the stock truly had soured, it would have to be thrown out despite the fact that it might have been simmering in the same kettle, being added to, taken from, for years. Disaster.

"How did they die?"

"A fire. They slept up in the east attic, and fire broke out in the room below the stairs."

"How did it break out?"

"That was never decided. The inspectors said a rat might have carried a tobacco twist upstairs from the main room."

"Is that a common occurrence?"

Efora shrugged, splaying her hands on the table. They were twisted and gnarled, marked with calluses. They writhed on the table like roots seeking entrance into the wood, then stilled when she spoke. "More common than arson, they seemed to think. And what else could it have been?"

"You think someone might have set it?"

"I'm sure I never said such a thing." She pushed herself away from the table. Her hands sought shelter in her apron pockets.

The doctor's voice caught her before she could walk away. "You are the owner here?"

"I am. My husband died a few years ago."

"And you have seen evidence of ghostly activity, to the point where you wish to hire a ghost handler to put it to rest?"

"Daily," she said. "It throw things, and it knocks at night on the doors and the windows. It smears the ashes from the fireplace over the tables and walks on the ceiling, leaving it all smudged."

The vehemence in her voice surprised him. The kitchen's clatter had stilled, to a point where he wondered whether the cook and maids might be standing just out of sight, listening. If all of this were true, they'd want the ghost gone as ardently as their mistress did.

"Very well," he said. "I'll start speaking to the staff and figuring out how best to rid you of this trouble."

"Just the one," she said.

"Just the one?"

"I want Kim gone," she said. The vehemence that had surprised him before grew even narrower and more focused now. "I want her ghost gone. But Ellie stays."

Charlotte stirred in her seat. Doctor Fantomas ignored her.

"Have you seen signs of Ellie?"

Efora shook her head. "But I know she must be here, if Kim is," she said. "I even wonder if things might not be worse, if she were not here to intervene."

The interviews would be left until after service was complete and they themselves had dined. Efora suggested he might want to lie down before then.

It was true. He was tired. Tired of chasing ghosts, of what he would have to do to rid the place of Kim, at least, and perhaps Ellie as well. He would lay his head down and not think of it for a little while.

Although the establishment was restaurant, rather than inn, Efora had found them rooms near the kitchen, which sometimes housed excess workers. The Doctor appreciated it in more ways than one. While it would be good to be close, to be able to see a ghost whenever it appeared, it was good, too, to save the money that housing himself and Charlotte would have cost.

It was a simple room, furnished with household cast-offs. An attempt had been made to gussy up the old dresser with its scratched and clouded mirror by draping a length of white lace and linen across it, but the fabric's crispness only made the wood look more neglected. A shuttered window returned the mirror's blank gaze on the opposite wall.

Despite the fact they were on the western side of the building, away from the wing where the two girls had perished, the Doctor could detect a hint of smoke clinging to everything around him, an ephemeral reminder whose presence you found yourself forgetting with time, until you stepped outside and then back in, to be struck anew by the pungency.

A taut blue coverlet overlaid the bed, and a coiled rag rug nearly filled the rest of the space in the tiny room.

Mercifully, a bowl of hot water and towel sat on the table that capped the bed's foot. He laved himself, took off his boots, and laid down. He thought it would be hard to sleep, but it seemed only moments before he heard Charlotte's soft knock on the door, summoning him to the meal.

He and Charlotte were fed with the rest of the staff, after the last of the diners had counted coins onto the table and left. It was an extravagant but odd meal, and the quality varied widely: tender dumplings scented with golden flakes of spice and patterned with young sage leaves accompanied burned sticks of meat so strongly flavored that they made the eyes water. A cream custard flaked oddly from the spoon, its texture closer to that of a fungus. Blobs of fat dripped from a meat loaf, studding it like crude bone buttons.

The Doctor ate but little, and Charlotte, as was her custom, simply chased food around her plate, moving it from one side to the next in between sips of water. Both of them declined the fish tea they were offered. From the grimaces of others, they had chosen wisely in doing so.

The staff and family, as they surrounded the great ironwood table in the back of the room: Efora, Efora's aunt Tabita; Liam the cook, a thin-framed boy so young that the doctor found it hard to believe he was more than a pot-boy; Efora's country cousins, young women named Collie and Mulia who worked as waitresses; elderly Phineas, who oversaw the front end of the room; pot scrubber and handy-woman Liza, a lazily handsome woman who flirted with everyone at the table.

Most of them were subdued, though, stealing glances at the doctor and his companion. Liza addressed him outright: "What will you do, once you find the ghosts? How will you know which is which? Is it that precise, your vision? What determines what dress a ghost wears?"

"The same dress they would envision themselves in when imagining or dreaming in life," he said. "Most see themselves in something from a happy moment. What would you think Kim or Ellie would think their happiest moments?"

"That silk dress Kim danced in," Liam said. The two waitresses flicked glances at him, then each other, letting out muted giggles, which everyone else ignored.

"And for Ellie, her cook's apron," Efora said in a fond tone.

"But it is that easy?" Liza pursued. "We have not seen the ghosts in such forms, but rather as balls of lights, or half-seen shadows or sometimes outright invisiblities."

"When I see, it is with a sharper eye than yours, perhaps. One accustomed to the frequencies at which such creatures vibrate."

Liza seemed inclined to pursue this question further, but Tabita interrupted. She was a classic old crone of Tabat, her skin darkened from exposure to the salt wind, her hair cut short in the manner of sailors, which older women affected due to its easiness, if they had retained enough hair to make the style dignified.

Tabita had. She was a severe but elegant woman of perhaps sixty, with turquoise eyes and a string of amber around her neck. "They say ghosts linger because of unfinished business," she said to the doctor. "Is that true?"

He stroked his whiskers, eying the squid pudding that trembled like a fever patient in the center of the table. "On occasion, ma'am, aye."

"Is that why our twins linger then? Some unfinished business?"

"It is more likely that one or the other of them does not realize she is dead," he said, parceling out a fragment of the pudding, which smelled better than it looked. An oily sheen rainbowed its surface.

"How could they not know that?" a waitress squeaked, he wasn't sure which one.

He fixed her with a portentous eye. No particular amount of ghost energy clung to her, other than the growth that covered them all, the ectoplasmic snail ooze that ghosts could not help but exude.

"When a death is sudden or violent, or both, the ghost can not realize what has happened," he said. "Just as sometimes a living person may forget great trauma, as a defense against what it might do to their mind, so do ghosts forget their death."

He did not speak of the circumstances of the twins' death, but he did not have to. He could tell they were all thinking of fire stealing up the stairway, smoke creeping across the beds like living blankets, to choke the sleepers into something beyond dreams.

Had the twins awoken or just gone to sleep and never woke up? From the haunting, he suspected that was not the cause. Something more had happened, something that he would have to decipher in order to figure out what best to do.

At first, the doctor decided to speak to the staff one at a time in the small private room. There were few diners here, and he assured Efora Nittlescent that he would keep the demands on the staff time to a minimum.

Before he could do so, Charlotte followed him into the room. He could see eager words working in her throat, and spoke before she could.

"I have not decided yet."

She gulped back her speech, reshaped it. "An exorcism cannot be fine-tuned in the way she wants."

"Can't it?" He stared at her.

Her gaze searched the ceiling, the crevices, the corners of the doorway. "Two ghosts wound together cannot be untangled as though they were yarn," she said.

"That is the question," he said. "Are they together like that?"

"They died together."

"From what? Did someone set the place alight? Did they know who killed them? Such things might tie them together, admittedly."

"You want to play at detective," she said.

"I am a ghost handler," he said, and shot a severe frown at her. "Now go and fetch me the cook."

Liam revealed he had been more assistant to Ellie than anything else. Her loss, it seemed, had left him adrift.

"She allus knew what was what," he said glumly.

Something about the tilt of his shoulders, the way his eyes fled like minnows from a shadow on the shore bank, set the doctor's teeth on edge.

"How did you get along with Kim?" he said.

A scowl as the boy spat into the fireplace. "She were a witch, that one."

"A magicker?" the doctor said sharply.

The boy's hand flapped in weak rejection. "Naw, naw. A bitch. We been taught the other is more polite."

After she had led the boy back out, Charlotte returned.

"Liam's a well-favored lad, eh?" the doctor said to her.

She sniffed in derision.

"If that's the sort of thing that appeals to you," she said. "Have you seen the ghosts?"

"Not yet," he said. He didn't mention the initial glimpse he'd had. He was never sure how finely attuned Charlotte's senses were. Sometimes it seemed as though she could sense ghosts on her own but at other times she seemed to need him to point them out to her. It would make a fascinating paper some day, if he found enough time to settle down and write.

Something in Liam's demeanor had told him already, but the Doctor pretended to be surprised both times the waitresses told him of the relationship between the cook and Ellie.

"They was to marry, come next year, Ellie said . . ."

"She kept it from her mother—Efora wanted her to marry her third cousin Lark Nittlescent. Nice favored boy, and well pocketed, but bland as custard . . ."

That interested him. Ellie wouldn't have liked bland, indeed. Her menu featured quirks of taste and savor and spices that sometimes felt like blows, but ones that left you tingling with satisfaction. He knew that without her, what had come to the table was only a shadow of what it could have been, but she had designed the recipes, and they were as individual as signatures. As he ate, he had put together the strands, as though he were talking to her in his mind, drawing her out, finding out how she felt about fighting, or politics, or love.

Love. There was a dish on the menu called "The Cook's Left Hand" and he thought, somehow, that it was meant as commentary on Liam.

It was flavored with cinnamon, sometimes called "the forbidden spice" for reasons he was unsure of, which was an odd combination with the fish's firm white flesh. Sour berries, no bigger than a sparrow's eye and green as olives, had surrounded it. Somehow that combination of flavors, which should have seemed unsettling, mingled together in a way that enticed the tongue, as though flavored with desire itself.

She had loved Liam. Liam had seen the advantages of a partnership with her, at the least, and had perhaps even returned her love, just buried it so deep in sorrow that the doctor could not see it. Although the boy seemed to have felt strongly enough about Kim.

How, the doctor wondered, had Kim felt about Liam?

Before retiring for the night, he unshuttered the window, exposing a view of the restaurant's rear courtyard, an expanse of wrought iron tables, chained to the fence as though someone were worried that they might go walking about.

He sat upright. The moon hit the window almost as bright as witchlight when first summoned. What had called him out of sleep? Some noise in the dining room, rhythmic as hammer blows but more muted. Footsteps? Perhaps.

He put on his breeches, head tilted as he tried to listen. The noises continued, stopped, restarted.

The door opened of its own accord. Charlotte. Beckoning him to follow.

She preceded him down the hallway. There was little light in its confines, but when she opened the door to the kitchen, everything was moonlight and steel, the rims of the great soup pots shining like rounded scimitars, the rack of cleavers and knives varying from the length of his forearm to the smallest paring blade possible, the tiles of the floor like moonstones underfoot, sending up a muted dazzle that mirrored the steel's.

Charlotte was hunched as though trying to avoid notice. His or the ghost's? He signaled to her to stop as she reached to push open the swinging door leading to the dining room.

She debated disobedience, he could tell, and he arched an eyebrow until she shrank back. Nevertheless, he felt a shrill cold comb along his back as he passed her to lay a palm on the door

Her malady drove her, he told himself. That was all. It drove her very hard indeed.

The pictures that had hung around the walls were piled on the floor, and handfuls of something were piled on top of them.

He sniffed. Feces, although perhaps not human, he thought.

"Fetch a light from the kitchen," he told Charlotte. She nodded, and he stood in the darkness, smelling it, waiting for her return. He wondered where the rest of the household was. Had they become so inured to ghostly activities that they slept through them? Or, he thought it more likely, they were hiding. Poltergeists could harm, had done so more often than rumors held possible, and most inhabitants of a ghost-ridden household learned that quick enough when they collected bruises from being shoved down coal cellar stairs or from objects thrown at them out of nowhere.

Were the ghosts in there with him? He closed his eyes, sent his senses outwards, but felt nothing. They had fled. At his approach or Charlotte's? Did they know what danger they were in? It was rare for ghosts to have that much notion of things.

The door creaked, and Charlotte appeared, preceded by a half circle of candlelight. The flame flickered, even held in the glass chimney of the lantern held high in her hand. She wore nightclothes of a peculiar white shininess, elaborately flounced at the cuffs and hem. He ignored them. He had seen her in them before. She dressed affectedly for bed, as though she would dream some prince into existence, for whom she must be prepared in formal wear.

She raised her face, searching through the shadows flickering over chairs clustered around each long table's expanse. "Some pictures are yet on the walls," she said.

"Kim's, I suspect," the doctor said. "Bring the lantern over here."

She moved over to him, and they stood together looking at the face that looked out at them from the wall. It was a face the twins shared, but in her hand was a wooden spoon, and her apron was marked with stains in a less than decorative way.

"Not Kim at all," Charlotte said. Surprise was evident in her tone.

"No," the doctor said. "Not Kim at all."

They looked at each other. Doctor Fantomas was the first to voice it.

"Ellie is the poltergeist."

In the morning, he found Efora cleaning up, a bucket of soapy water beside its partner holding lumps of shit. She knelt beside the biggest pile.

"Why would the ghost do this, do you think?" the doctor asked.

Efora scrubbed a picture clean. It was a family group, a trio of bearded men with their arms around each other. "I beg your pardon?"

"Such an act is intended to send a message," the doctor said. "In this case, the ghost has defecated on every member of your family with a sole exception. Which leads me to believe that the ghost is the sole exception." He leveled a long finger at Ellie's picture. "So I must query, madam, whether it is still Kim you wish exorcised?"

Wiping her hands on her apron, Efora rose to confront him with her gaze. An angry spot of red seemed pinned to each cheek, reminding him of a doll's expression.

"I have not changed my mind," she said.

It was not what he expected. He gaped at her. "But if you leave Ellie's ghost alone, it will continue to do such things."

She shook her head, still wringing her hands in her apron. "With Kim gone, Ellie will calm down. It was always that way. Then she'll go back to the kitchen, will get us back to profitability. She was always dependable, my Ellie."

"You understand," he said, "that anything may happen. She may choose to leave with Kim gone. Or you may be wrong, and she may become a thousand times worse."

Her face was unconvinced.

A ghost flitted overhead. Which twin, Ellie or Kim? What would either of them think of their mother's intention? He suspected Ellie would feel much more sanguine than Kim.

What had made Ellie feel betrayed by the entire family, including her twin?

If a picture of Liam had been anywhere in the array of faces, where would the ghost have placed it? Beside her on the wall, or in among the feces-smeared pile?

He went down his list, speaking to several others before he had Liam called to him again.

"Was Ellie happy with you the day before she died?"

The boy's eyes were frantic, flitting everywhere. "Sure," he said.

"I don't think so. The others say many of the ghost's most malicious acts have been aimed at you."

He paused. Silence was often the best instruments in such interrogations. He was right. After a minute his mute stare levered the truth out of the boy as easily as a spoon extracting a nut from a jar.

"Kim made me," he said hastily.

"Made you what?"

"Come to her bed."

"And Ellie found out, of course," the doctor supplied.

"I didn't think she had, but she must have. She wouldn't speak to me at all that night, just glared whenever she saw me."

And Ellie had tried to do away with her rival, the doctor reflected, only to somehow got caught in her own fire. But surely she hadn't meant to commit suicide. The ghost's anger was that of someone who had not meant to die, anger against her state. Such ghosts were bad as poison in a well. They led the living around them to anger or despair, prompted loathsome acts that otherwise would have stayed undone. No, Ellie must be removed.

And Kim? He wasn't sure about her. Perhaps she was only the victim in all of this, but he'd had sisters himself, the doctor had, and he'd seen how they could nettle each other, how they knew each other's every weak point. He suspected Ellie had been meant to find out about Liam.

Charlotte watched him sort through his satchel, extracting lumps of blue and phosphorescent yellow chalk, and waxed string wound on a brown bobbin that shimmered due to the minute bits of glass adhering to the string, and a great blue bottle, its stopper a combination of cork and green marble. Her eyes were hazed with some strong emotion; she licked her lips frequently, to the point where they seemed fuller, riper, readier. At the sight of the bottle, she made a choked noise of disappointment.

"You are to set it out so Kim's ghost may flee into it," he said. "If she does, you are to stopper it and bring it to me. Do you understand?"

"But Ellie?" she breathed.

He sorted through the chalk. "We will remove her."

She held the blue bottle to her, twined her arms around it. "How long?"

"I have sent the family and staff away for the afternoon," he said. "They will not return until evenfall. Plenty of time."

She helped him chalk symbols on the walls, on the floors. Helped him unwind the string to form glittering lines. Between them, the symbols and string would drive the ghosts along a certain path, corner them in the room the Doctor had chosen, the mirror of the fire-destroyed eastern wing, its counterpart to the west. Together he and Charlotte rearranged the furniture there until it matched the description of the twins' room that Efora had given him. He double-checked it all while Charlotte set up cones of incense in the bedroom and the blue bottle on the mantelpiece.

Standing in the center of the building, the great dining room, its shadowy confines echoing the basso of his voice, he chanted, the old chants that he had been taught as an apprentice, the ones he knew so well he could sing them in his sleep, had even woken up with them on his lips, familiar as a kiss, the old and wonderful words that called the ghosts from wherever they were lurking, made them manifest in the center of his string and chalk only to go scurrying like mice, fleeing wildly along the pathways, to the room where Charlotte waited.

He followed, still chanting, treading up the stairway to the western room. Technically, it wasn't still necessary, the chanting, but it helped drowned out the sounds from the room where Charlotte waited for the ghosts, drown out the dreadful gobbling sounds, the voracious laugh, the satiated noise that was somehow the worst of all?

He saw at a glance when he came in that Kim had not managed to make it to the bottle. He would have given her even odds, but there was always the chance Charlotte would not play fair, either.

Charlotte herself sat on the bed, smiling off into space. She looked *stretched*, almost distended, as though her body held more than it should. That would pass off within a day or so, but he would have to be careful of her for a little while.

But for all that she weighed no more than a handful of feathers.

He carried her to her room, and went to open the building's main doors. Efora and the others stood there.

"The exorcism is over," he said. "I regret to say both ghosts chose to pass on."

Efora held herself taller, as though the shock had pulled her upright. Behind her, the others simply looked relieved.

"My companion's weak constitution has suffered during the rigors of the ceremony," he said. "I will care for her tonight, but in the morning, if you will pay for a pedal-cab, we will move to the inn we have chosen." He would swaddle her in blankets, pass off her appearance as illness. Then they could begin to look around for more ways to make money quickly, problems like this one to be solved, before they moved on.

For they could not linger, could not settle, much as he longed to. Sooner or later another ghost handler would see them, would know Charlotte for what she was.

That night she lay unmoving beside him in the narrow bed. Far away the night watch called the half-hour as the patrol passed on its way down the terraces before taking the Great Tram back up to the top and starting anew.

Two ghosts in a single night would sustain her for at least a fortnight, although she would grow irritable long before the end of that.

She was not sleeping. She never slept.

"Charlotte?" he said into the dark.

"Yes?" Her voice was alert, polite.

"What do you want, my dear?"

Silence. Then, "I don't know what you mean."

"They say ghosts would prefer to pass on to the afterlife, to pursue their own journeys."

"Rather than be eaten, you mean?"

"That. Or . . ." Here he paused, the pause as delicate as a butterfly. "Or forced to wander this earth as companion to a failing man."

"Ah, that." She turned. Her face glowed, the faintest of lights, as though to emphasize her words. "Bring me ghosts, failing man, and as long as that is done, I will wander this earth with you."

He watched her face, his own still troubled. But in the end, he laid back on his pillow, and reached his hand out to twine it with hers, falling asleep as she lay beside him, awake in the darkness, with her glow fading away.

The Soldier Who Swung at the End of a Thread

~ M. David Blake

Ossuera was a good soldier. She followed orders. She spent a compulsory term as medic, returned as infantry, survived field promotions, returned as a hero, and accepted reenlistment to demonstrate loyalty under the new regime. She served in the next justifiable conflict. And the next. It was a good life, and there were many wars.

Then the wars ended.

When she was awoken by the old man in olive drab, Ossuera was frightened. She knew the uniform well. It was a style favored by the winning side from a score of years previous, and bore reminders of every war across the span of human memory. The man's face was contorted by a series of subcutaneous threads, the dark laces of which peeked from the edges of each orifice, and broke through the deep fissures that lined his visage.

He was too familiar. Ossuera thought she might have been tortured—or perhaps rescued—by this man during some previous conflict in which both had served.

The two sat in silent contemplation of their respective roles. Ossuera bleakly thought of herself as a wounded animal, not quite ready to die. She regarded the old man as an unanticipated predator, belly full yet trying to decide upon the strength of an appetite.

"Hungry?" asked the old man.

Ossuera blinked and nodded, and sneezed.

The old man crooked an eyebrow, and reached a hand to feel Ossuera's forehead. Ossuera weakly grabbed the man's arm.

"Easy, soldier," grunted the old man. "You need a medic."

Ossuera saw no need for a response. There were no more medics, and soon there would be no more Ossuera. Let the man frighten some other soldier, if he could find one.

"Roll over," said the man, with a lift and a shove.

Ossuera didn't bother to fight. It would just be a different way to die.

"There," he muttered, as he ripped the last of Ossuera's tattered attire from her shoulders, and then "We'll just get this on you," as he lowered something onto her back.

It was warm, and wet, and then spreading. Ossuera barely had the strength to be frightened as she felt fire rolling down her spine, across her clavicle, around her ribs. Warmth poured through her limbs, infused her tongue, and wrapped itself around her slack form.

As one convulsive act, the thing constricted. The surface against her skin separated into an infinity of sharpened threads, which shot into her flesh. Every thread tip sought—and found—part of a nerve, and then, as one, they unleashed all the fury of the last portable energy source on Earth.

The last war had seen monumental upheaval in the structure of combat. No bullets flew. No missiles fell. Men and women went about their lives much as they had always done in times of peace.

Ossuera was at loose ends, unaccustomed to peace.

She went through her days unsure of even the most innocuous encounter. Was her butcher an operative of the enemy, or the milk-maid a friend?

As the last war ground to a halt, Ossuera was even less sure of who had won. One side or the other, or possibly even one of a hundred splinter facets of sides that once had been, had pulled a trigger, or pressed a button, or thrown a switch. Without any warning or claim of responsibility, the butcher and the milkmaid and another four billion souls were suddenly, swiftly, silenced.

Society's reaction was swift as well. Those who died were all, to one degree or another, operatives of an enemy. As soldiers any one of them might have pulled a similar lever or thrown an identical switch, had their side prevailed. Their houses were burned to the ground, their possessions thrown into the pyre, and every person who survived supervised his neighbor so that none might come upon any weapon alone, and resurrect the war.

Ossuera's house was burned with the rest. She had been out, and felt terror in the milkmaid's grip as the girl collapsed, convinced Ossuera was the one who killed her.

For the first night in longer than she could possibly remember, Ossuera shed tears for the dead.

"Feeling better?" asked the old man.

"Some," answered Ossuera.

"A lot," corrected the old man. "You're wearing a suit now."

It was true. The worn and wasted parts of Ossuera's body were being repaired. A multitude of threads ran under every millimeter of her skin, lacing themselves through muscle, bone, sinew, and nerve with indiscriminately thorough determination.

"It will keep getting better. Tomorrow you will be stronger. The next day, more so. You've never worn a suit before, have you?"

"No," answered Ossuera. She had been a good soldier. If ordered, she would have taken one. She had never been ordered to do so, because she had managed to do everything expected of her without the suit.

"You wouldn't have put that on by choice, would you?"

Ossuera didn't respond, because they both already knew the answer.

"You can still take it off, if you'd like," he continued. "Ought to be another eleven hours before it sets."

Ossuera sat still.

"But then," picked up the old man, "you were about ready to die. And if you let go that easily, I win."

"You win?"

"You might still win yourself, you know," he said, and chuckled. "It has to be you or me, because we're the last ones left."

"Which side are you?" asked Ossuera.

"As of a year ago," responded the old man, "mine. No one else had the stomach to do it."

"Do it?"

"Yes."

The word hung between them for a long moment.

"Our weapon should only have gotten the other side," he continued. "The worst ones. It wasn't designed to go as far as it did, but it got *all* of the others. Yours. Mine. All the sides."

"Then I'm the only one left," said Ossuera.

"I thought I was too," answered the old soldier.

The old man led Ossuera from room to room.

"A lot of these places weren't hidden very well. Not much use after a few thousand flaming corpses were poured into 'em, anyway. If the survivors had known about this place they'd have done the same to me—burned me alive." He cackled.

By the light of glass shafts extending to the surface, Ossuera saw wonders that filled the vaulted ceilings. Machines piled high. Computers lined a series of corridors in progression from those that filled an entire room down to specimens that might fit under a fingernail, in perverse inversion of their computational capacity. The wars had gone on for a long, long time.

All of that glittering power stood silent.

"Useless crap. No juice up here." He glanced at Ossuera. "You got the last of it, with the suit. No way to fire another one, even if I had another one."

"Then why put me in it?" asked Ossuera.

"Because I'm not a monster," he said. "And neither are you."

"I'm not so sure."

"I am," said the old man. "I've started a lot of wars. And when I didn't start them, I've generally been the one who sent the first response."

"You sound like a monster."

"Or a beloved leader, depending on who you ask," he responded.

With a shudder, Ossuera realized who he was. She would have known his face well, without the scarring imposed by the suits.

At one point she would have called his "the worst side." At another she would have followed any order he gave.

"You don't appear very eager to finish me off," said the old man.

"The war is over. You already won," said Ossuera.

"Semantics," he answered. "I have maybe a week left. I've been in a suit long enough that I don't have the luxury of tapering off and getting out."

"And what do I have?" asked Ossuera.

"You have enough power to let the suit heal you, and wean yourself when you're strong enough to get out of it." The old man's eyes fixed on his patient.

Ossuera let out a short cough. Her chest rattled. "Nothing out there for me. I'll take it off now."

"Sure about that, soldier? You've also got something else."

"What?" Ossuera asked.

"Seven days to win the war. After that I go out on top, and anything that remembers humanity hates you forever because you were part of it all."

"And if I kill you first?" whispered Ossuera.

"I won't make it easy," said the old man. "I've been at this a long time, and I was always good at it. Kill me, and you liberate whatever is left of this sorry world."

They spent the evening in the fortress, two old soldiers sharing a meal.

"You don't kill an adversary in his home," said the old man. "Or in your own, for that matter."

"No," answered Ossuera.

The old man ceremonially poured wine, and lifted his glass. "To the end of the war." It was the toast he had spoken in countless iterations, sometimes to applause, and sometimes to tears. "To the end of this wretched mess."

"What will you do?" asked Ossuera. The unfamiliar glow of the wine warmed her head.

"Finish it," said the old man. "Our weapon was never supposed to go as far as it did. Now it has to go the rest of the way."

"No juice," answered Ossuera, draining her glass.

"Not for suits, there isn't." The old man's fingers on the glass looked odd, threads crawling out from under his fingernails and trying to wrap themselves around the stem.

"What then?" asked Ossuera. She wondered how long it would be until her own threads began to show.

"We powered the thing from here. Burned out every relay in the process, and all the wiring in this place is fried."

Candles, reflected Ossuera, had become commonplace. She had not thought of wires or relays in a long time.

"The core is still in good shape, though. Enough power to finish it, and then some. We had no idea how much we'd need, so we overshot." The old man laughed, wiping tears from his eyes. "God, we overshot!"

Ossuera rested her palms on the table. "So you have power for your suit. No need to finish anything."

"Too much raw power for a suit," said the old man, regaining his composure. "It's too much for anything. If I try to draw just enough juice to milk another few weeks of life out of this one, the core will fry every thread in an instant, and me along with it."

"Wouldn't that be an end?" asked Ossuera.

"Not an end I can use, damn it," said the old man. "Not one you can let me take, either. You have to win, or you might as well help me finish the rest of them. The world is scared, and they're never getting better unless they know someone has beaten the monster that did this."

"You said we aren't monsters," quoted Ossuera.

"To anyone who wasn't a soldier, we were."

Ossuera thought of the butcher and the milkmaid. To them, she had been a monster.

"War has to serve a purpose," continued the old man. "I've fought to liberate, and to conquer, and for ideals and doctrines."

"I know," said Ossuera.

"We're going to war again, you and I." There were no more tears in the old man's eyes. "The whole world can't lose a war, but the state they're in now, that might as well be what happened. They're like a switch that's only halfway on, and the bulb is flickering. Got to go one way or the other, or they'll slowly burn out."

"What purpose will a new war serve?" asked Ossuera.

"One of us will win," answered the old man. "And then the world will either be gone, or they'll be able to lift their faces again."

"If I kill you now, who will know?" Ossuera's voice sounded very far from her own ears. Her pulse sounded close.

"No one would know, and I almost wish you would," answered the old man. "But you can't. You are a good soldier, and you need to win as much as they need you to win. If the world doesn't know, then everything you ever fought for has no purpose."

Ossuera had fought for many reasons. She always believed she fought for the right ones.

Looking down at her hands on the table, Ossuera knew the old man was correct. The threads that had broken through her fingertips were waiting to fulfill their purpose.

"Take whatever you can use," he said. "I won't be back here until I'm ready to finish it."

"I can't kill you here."

"You damn well can. This isn't my home anymore. Or yours, for that matter. In a few hours, it'll all be fair game."

"We can't use these," said Ossuera, scanning racks of powered weapons.

"Anything that large would drain the juice too fast. Suit'd be able to power anything small, if you can find it." The old man continued his packing.

Ossuera examined the sidearm she'd carried when the old man found her. It was unpowered.

"That?" snorted the old man. "Jesus. Haven't seen ammo for those in a long time."

Ossuera held the gun close.

"Don't take it so hard, soldier. You'd have had to come after me with rocks and sharp sticks, if I hadn't put you in my last suit." The old man looked up, and barked a short laugh. "Or you wouldn't. I'd have gone quietly senile, having become death and destroyed the world, while dysentery and malnutrition would have solved your problems. Leave that behind."

Ossuera nodded.

"Chemicals still work fine," he continued, "if you can find enough cylinders among this lot that haven't already cracked their seals. Think you remember enough chem-munition basics? Good. I burned the recipe books last winter."

An assortment of thin metal phials spread between them. In silence the old man shook, sorted, and arranged his unusual armament. Ossuera attempted to keep pace.

As they finished, the old man's eyes lit upon a cluster of bright chartreuse cylinders atop Ossuera's pile. Wordlessly, Ossuera picked up two of the cylinders and placed them in the old man's thread-crossed palm.

After a momentary pause, the old man selected three cylinders marked with a single blue band, and one that showed a pair of yellow dots. He held them out to Ossuera.

As their fingers met, for a brief moment the threads touched. Both felt the shock and pulled away, and one of the blue-banded cylinders fell against the hard floor. With a ping and a crash, the cap peeled from the end. Gas rushed about their feet and the shell launched down the corridor, to ricochet and spin until it came to rest.

The two held a long count, and exhaled. "Glad it wasn't one of the chartreuse ones," said the old man, as they returned to the task.

When Ossuera awoke, the old man was gone. She knew only that they were limited by the distance each could travel on foot. Whatever benevolence had existed between them was gone.

A battered sign near the entrance informed her of two dead cities that flanked the location. She was surprised to learn how close the fortress had been to civilization.

She began to squint, and threads within her eye looped themselves into a semblance of a pinhole lens. The bright sunlight dimmed to a bearable level, and her focus caught smoke on one horizon, where survivors must have congregated after abandoning their skyscrapers.

Turning a half circle, she also saw smoke in the distance. More smoke. A bigger village.

No. *Billowing* smoke.

Ossuera ran. Her path traversed cornfields, with stalks that exceeded her shoulders, but she did not push them away. She ran, as they sliced her exposed skin.

The threads stitched and sewed, happily zipping through lacerations to free their ends, then plummeting to anchor themselves. With every step Ossuera was marked as a suited warrior.

She felt alive.

Everyone around her was dead. The billowing smoke had played out. A smell of cooked meat permeated the air.

The pack slowed her pace, and the pressure on her back was a constant reminder that she, too, was a carrier of death. Ossuera dropped a shoulder and grasped the strap, swinging the bundle down to her side. If she left it in one of the still smoldering ruins, with any luck the heat would rupture the cylinders. There was nothing left to kill.

Ossuera wiped her forehead with the back of a laced hand, the threads greedily absorbing the sweat for later use. The outside of both arms, from her shoulders to the backs of her knuckles, was an almost solid mass of dark woven filaments.

"The Devil! He was the Devil!" screamed the old woman in the next village. She wept through rage as she clung to the broken body of her daughter.

The explosion had come from inside the coffee shop, and the coffee shop had been the first sign of pre-war optimism that Ossuera had encountered. Block letters proclaimed their opening to celebrate eleven and a half months of peace, using genuine tempered glass presses that had fortuitously survived the purge.

Coffee never grew in this climate, reflected Ossuera. She wondered whether she would ever taste strong, dark coffee again.

Shards of tempered glass littered the cobblestones. The smell of burning coffee bit into Ossuera's nostrils, and the threads immediately began weaving themselves into a filter.

"He isn't a devil. He's a man," said Ossuera.

"He is the Devil!" spat the old woman, her eyes alight. "And you are a demon!"

"My gawd, it's got scales," exclaimed another man, who appeared to have a broken arm.

"It's a suit," said Ossuera.

A woman peeked from a shattered window, and gasped. Someone else decided he had no reason to go into the street after all, and turned away. But more and more were coming, and the shared impression grew stronger with every body that stepped into their midst.

"Demon," Ossuera heard them whisper. "Monster." "War-Bringer."

Figures darted into the crowd as numbers swelled their confidence. Ossuera could only catch glimpses of color before the faces shifted, as others pushed their way to the front. Maroon, Ochre, Cream, Olive.

Something bounced off her shoulder.

The flung object was the necessary catalyst. A dozen more followed, and Ossuera knew twice that many hands sought other stones, or shards, or anything they could throw. One man held a fireplace poker, rusted and bent, and swung it contemplatively.

The suit was ample protection, but Ossuera saw no reason to stay. She turned on her heel and began to walk.

Olive.

Ossuera turned again to look over her shoulder and saw an arm in an olive drab sleeve, as it flung a silvery object from the edges of the crowd.

She pivoted on her heel, swinging the other leg out to give momentum as she lowered herself to the ground. She opened her mouth to shout as the blast tore across her back.

The crowd that had gathered around her was no longer a threat. Nor would they be.

As she stood, several thousand threads began an ecstatic dance over her rippling flesh. Glass, soot, gravel, brick, and even teeth adorned her flayed skin. The threads embraced them all with equal care.

At the end of the street, flanked by shards and soot, a small figure swayed. Ossuera looked away.

"Demon," whimpered the old woman. She clutched a rag-doll corpse.

It would have been simpler for her to wait at the fortress. Ossuera spent her fourth day in threaded pursuit of the old man, always a mile or two too late to prevent a massacre.

Ossuera cursed her rash abandonment of the cylinders. She contemplated the ways in which training and experience had prepared her to kill, without weapons. She hoped she was still a good soldier.

With the suit's help she could cover a mile in under five minutes. The old man had been wearing suits for a year. The old man moved fast.

It was evident that the old man had made plans for this war long before finding Ossuera. Even at full sprint, no one could have spaced such volatile mixtures as widely apart as the devastation implied.

Ossuera wiped the sweat from both eyes with her fingertips as she ran, and then regretted it as the threads began shaping her eyelashes to better direct errant drops.

Seven to twelve minutes behind. Maybe as much two miles. Once-proud stretches of road had fallen into disrepair, but between villages she stayed upon the crumbling, paved surfaces. Only roads that served to connect larger remnants survived, and for that Ossuera was both sad and grateful.

As for countermeasures, Ossuera encountered a few halfhearted attempts to waylay her obstinacy, but the old man seemed only to have placed them as tokens of affliction. Any cylinder that could be turned to a lethal purpose was reserved for the villagers themselves, on whom the old man spent his cold fury.

She *should* have stayed at the fortress, reflected Ossuera. Waited, prepared, and welcomed the old man home with an orchestrated barrage of explosive devastation and choreographed poisons. A week's worth of noncombatant casualties would be an insignificant price to pay, to save the rest of the world.

How far could an old man travel in seven days? Even allowing for all the speed and strength a suit could offer, immolation of the surrounding countryside could only inspire a death toll of a few thousands. If the old man managed to get back before Ossuera, the entire world would be lost.

Let them die so you can win, Ossuera told herself. *Go back while you still can.*

Ossuera ran on. She wasn't that good a soldier.

By the time she arrived at the ninth village, Ossuera had resigned herself to cataloging atrocities. Survivors of the old man's wrath were either too frightened to respond, or too angry to understand that she was not also their enemy.

He had been thorough. Standing structures were identifiable only by the shapes that projected through curtains of flame.

Ossuera had become accustomed to the smell of burning flesh.

What she had not become accustomed to was a plea for help. When she heard voices from within a two-story structure, Ossuera grasped burning timbers, trusting the suit to preserve her own flesh as she entered. It still stung.

Within, a trio of small heads were visible from the loft. A charred rail hung against the edge, poor evidence of a ladder that had once granted access. The floor—what had once *been* floor—was a scattered mass of coals. The glowing surface seemed to slither and crawl.

There was almost no smoke within. Bright tongues danced from every surface, although much of the structure looked pristine beneath the flame. It didn't matter. The fire would continue to burn until it took purchase, and then consume every surface upon which it lay, as it had already consumed the path to a simple escape.

A small, broken window over the loft had allowed her to hear the cry. It also served to prevent suffocation, and sustain the process of combustion.

Ossuera waded into the section beneath the loft's edge as she made these observations. The threads playfully swatted sparks about her legs, as she brushed the surface of each cinder. She stood still as the smallest of the three children slowly descended with the aid of two older siblings, each grasping a wrist to lower her small frame to the waiting soldier.

"Hold close," she instructed, as she cradled the girl with one arm and raised the other for the second child. The older sister hung over the edge to lower her brother, but the boy squeezed his eyes tight and pushed away from the threads even as Ossuera carried the pair a safe distance outside the inferno.

"Stay," she said, setting them down. The young boy began to sob, but his sister watched silently as Ossuera stepped back inside the remains of their home.

A fourth head was visible over the edge of the loft. The remaining girl had helped an older woman to sit, and the woman's shoulder looked as though it had been crushed. Ossuera wondered how they managed the climb, if the woman had been below when the siege began.

A golden shape glittered against the woman's breast, and Ossuera wished silently that its presence might provide comfort. Given the woman's ragged breath Ossuera doubted she would survive long.

"Help mama first," said the girl, tears streaming from her eyes. Ossuera stepped closer.

"No," said the woman. "You go with her."

Ossuera saw the look in the girl's eyes as she lowered herself over the edge. There was a long hesitation before the child dropped, and Ossuera knew she would not comfort herself with rescue. Part of her already wanted to be swallowed up by those burning coals, and Ossuera felt the child's revulsion as a rolling wave equal to the shimmering heat.

"Thank you," sighed the woman, as Ossuera stepped away.

Ossuera did not respond, but took careful steps through the spreading sea of flame.

When Ossuera set the girl down with her siblings, the youngest met her eyes and asked, "Will you save mama now?"

"Yes," answered Ossuera. She suspected the woman was already dead.

Returning to the flame, she saw that she had guessed incorrectly. The mother was alive, and massive coughs racked her frame as she pulled herself up against the edge.

"Wait," said Ossuera. "I'll come up to get you."

"No," said the woman again. A smile was on her face. "Just carry me to them. Please."

She rolled over the edge, and fell against Ossuera with all of her weight. A sharp pain shot through the soldier's chest as they fell into the mass that had been floor. Threads gleefully shot in and out of Ossuera's scalp, eager to replace the hair that quickly burst into flame.

Bracing her own palm upon a bed of coals, Ossuera held the woman close with her other arm, and stood. She swung the burned hand behind the woman's knees to steady the load, pulled close to shield the woman's face, and ignored the threads as they swiftly explored their new burden.

"Never thought . . . never thought I'd be glad to feel threads again." The woman slurred her words as the sound trailed off. She stopped breathing.

Stepping into sunlight, Ossuera paused to steady her load, then trudged forward. The children stood in a row, awaiting her approach.

She bent to lay the woman upon the grass, and discovered the golden pendant had lodged itself within the suit. Or, more accurately, within Ossuera's chest; the threads had embraced those edges as enthusiastically as they had shards and coals. Only a sharp, glittering portion projected. Whatever significance it held could only have been inferred by someone who recognized the shape.

"I'm sorry," said Ossuera, as she grasped the pendant and bent. With a sharp twist the gold separated, but only a ragged fragment remained with the woman's simple necklace.

"You couldn't help her," said the boy, accusation filling his eyes. "You lied."

"I tried," responded Ossuera. Two children wept. The youngest stroked her mother's hair. The dead woman continued to smile.

"You saved her," said the smallest girl. "Thank you."

The young child sat to cradle her mother's head, as she sang a soft lullaby. It was a familiar tune, although Ossuera did not recognize the words.

Ossuera wondered whether the girl understood that her mother would never wake up.

She stepped toward the path that would carry her to the next village. Sharp edges of a golden relic burned in her chest. Something else burned her eyes.

"I will pray for you," called the youngest child, as Ossuera retreated.

Ossuera did not answer. She did not like the idea of praying for demons.

On the morning of the seventh day Ossuera came within sight of the old man.

Ossuera could not remember all the dead. She could no longer even smell their cooked flesh, and her eyes no longer watered.

She felt numb, inside and out. She carried nothing, and she had nothing left. The suit had become Ossuera's second skin, her only weapon, an extension that served her need and simultaneously drove her on.

The pair continued to run, cutting soldier-shaped swaths across decimated fields as they returned to their fortress. Periodically the old man would look behind, and if the span between the two allowed an indulgence, he would laugh and then pause.

The uniform hung oddly across the old man's wiry frame, and shook energetically with his laughter. Dark threads had become so plentiful that they danced freely about his hands, his face, and from every edge of the uniform. In some places they had interwoven, so that olive drab fabric took on the appearance of ink-stained motley.

"You don't have to go on," gasped Ossuera. "Let it go."

"Can't do that, soldier," barked the old man, from atop a small mound. "Chase me or die, but once I've finished this war you'll have plenty of time to rest."

Ossuera slowed her pace, and stopped to bend her knees. She was badly dehydrated. The threads used every opportunity to wick sweat, and even moisture from the air, but her vision had begun to narrow. She could focus on the pursuit, or on herself, but not both.

The old man waited until Ossuera had drawn a half-dozen ragged breaths. "Looks like I won't be needing these anymore," he cackled, then raised his fists with a double-handful of cylinders and flung them to either side. "You're slow, soldier. Soft. If you had kept going 'stead of taking a breather, I might have even stood my ground for you."

Ossuera started to run again.

The old man held firm for a moment longer as the distance between them closed, then shot a fist into the air. It was a grim salute. Then he turned and began a sprint, casting measured glances over his shoulder to gauge his pursuer's approach.

As Ossuera approached the rise from which the old man had taunted her, she saw cylinders littering the ground. Multicolored stripes and spots of blue, yellow, red, and green. Two cylinders were solid mauve. The last one was bright chartreuse.

She stopped, as the old man turned to watch. Ossuera bent and picked up the single chartreuse cylinder. She held it aloft, so that he would see.

"Do you even know what that is?" he shouted.

"No," said Ossuera.

The old man's laughter rang clear and sharp through the air. He began to run again.

Ossuera watched him go. With a deep sigh she also began to run, the small cylinder still gripped in her tightly threaded palm.

Once again, she had fallen behind.

Ossuera watched him approach the concealed entrance of their fortress, and then saw him slow to a walk. The old man thumbed his nose as he ducked through the low opening, an antiquated child taunting the disciplinarian.

Ossuera felt drained. She wondered how much energy the old man had left, whether the suit still concealed enough fortitude to carry out his stated purpose.

"Don't get lost," he called, voice echoing down long, darkened corridors. "I don't have time to fool around."

Ossuera ran on. Sparsely placed glass-shaft windows granted an illusion of luminance, but the threads in her eyes could no longer see with any clarity. She was not certain where the core was, although the corridors appeared to run both deeper into the hill and slope further below the surface.

The question of how the old man could overcome so much ruined circuitry hovered ominously at the back of Ossuera's mind.

"Oh, the chilly hours and minutes of uncertainty," sang the old man. He had once had a fine strong voice, the tones of which had signaled authority to any of several generations. Now his voice was leathery, and raw.

Ossuera wondered why threads had not infested his vocal cords. Or perhaps they had, and this was the result.

"It won't be long," taunted the old man, in the same rasping singsong. As his figure slid down the corridor he flung an arm out to catch the leading edge of a doorframe, and slung himself around to grin at his pursuer.

"Catch me if you can," he said, and disappeared.

As Ossuera reached the door, the flare of a match rang through the corridor.

The old man had anticipated the turn. Ossuera was less adequately prepared for the sudden shift in trajectory, and slammed into the solid edge of the doorframe as she skidded to a stop.

Inside the small room, the old man had already seated himself in a folding chair. A card table stood before him, and on the table stood a flickering candle. Next to the candle rested a helmet. One small cable led from the helmet to an unobtrusive recess in the ceiling.

"It's all over now, baby blue," whispered the old man, with a sad smile. His paper-thin cheeks showed fewer threads than Ossuera had come to expect.

Racks of equipment lined the wall behind the old man, but Ossuera ignored the shadowy forms. She stepped forward.

"No juice," said Ossuera. "What will you do?"

"Finish it," said the old man. "We're inside the core."

With an air of finality the old man picked up the helmet, and Ossuera saw what had happened to his threads. From every fingertip, they extended. More threads ran from the cuffs of his uniform, from his collar, from what had once, like Ossuera's, been hair. Threads trailed the edges of the table, wound through the frame of the folding chair, snaked along the ground, wove in and among and throughout the banks of equipment behind his gaunt frame, and disappeared into every dark recess.

Ossuera stepped closer.

The old soldier lowered the helmet upon his skull, and closed his eyes. A single green light pulsed to life on the rack behind him.

The low hum swelled from beneath the fortress, and filled Ossuera's ears so suddenly that she was momentarily disoriented. It swelled at a constant pace, and for a brief moment she imagined the whole to be a gigantic capacitor, capable of pulsing out every reserve of energy in a single burst.

Her chest heaved against the sudden pressure. Her ears rang. Her vision swam toward darkness. The detached portion of Ossuera's awareness debated whether she would be more likely to pass out, or vomit first.

Ossuera stumbled, ungracefully, around the old man's table. One heavily threaded arm shot under the leathery throat. The other hand swung the small, chartreuse cylinder toward the old man's helmet, with what Ossuera prayed would be enough force to shatter the seal.

It was.

Ossuera held her breath. Whatever had been in the cylinder was colorless, and the candle continued to burn.

The old man twisted under her grip, and Ossuera bent to meet his gaze.

"You still don't know what that is, do you?"

"No," said Ossuera. Her hold slipped.

The old man broke into a wheezing chuckle, spasms shooting through his shoulders. "We used those to remove suits, when we were done with them."

Ossuera's heart fell. They were in the core, and the old man had already connected himself to whatever the obscene thing was, that had taken their humanity. She did not have strength for another blow, and she did not have anything but a candlestick with which to deliver one if she could.

The old man continued to laugh. "Suits!" he roared. "Got to kill every damned thread of 'em in a single pass, or they'll come back three times as determined to patch you up! Long as they have juice—" He slapped the table, and left a smear.

"You were dying anyway," said Ossuera.

"I've been dead for almost a year," said the old man. "The suits used me up." He coughed, and a dark sludge trickled from the corner of his mouth.

Ossuera felt weak. Fragments of expired thread rained down upon the pair, as the extensions broke apart.

As Ossuera watched, the old man began to unravel. Dying threads extricated themselves with force, as though his body had suddenly become toxic. Bits of foreign matter that had eagerly been encapsulated during rushed repairs were disgorged, spilling about his cuffs and through the spaces between buttons.

Ossuera dropped her arm from the old man's skeletal neck, and slid to her knees. The ink-stained motley dissolved as remnants of olive drab collapsed, and Ossuera let them go.

The candle flickered stoically, briefly flaring only for the bits of thread that continued to fall, as they touched its flame.

Ossuera's skin was bright pink, raw and hairless. A few shards of glass still protruded near the surface of her ribs, and when she grasped the edges, they bled. Raising hands to her cheeks, she felt the slick of blood that poured from each eye. Her breath was drawn in short, choking gasps, and she gagged, causing a red stream to spill from her sinuses.

The floor of the small room was slick with blood, assorted fragments, a few teeth, and countless threads. Alone among them, one small object glittered in the candlelight.

Ossuera fell beside it, her gaze locked upon the bent, golden shape.

Days in quiet isolation suited her, as the threads had not.

Ossuera exercised, tended the few repairs that her suit had not finished, and daily inspected her flesh for any dark lines that might have survived.

She discounted the heavily shaded circles under her eyes, after the first week. After the second, Ossuera decided that the growth of short hairs returning to her scalp was too similar in appearance to an experience she wished only to forget, and shaved them off with one of the world's few surviving safety razors.

The glass shards had been carefully removed, although Ossuera could not bring herself to stitch the wounds with thread. Once she was able to locate a cylinder's worth of medical-grade adhesive she glued the edges, which soon began to heal and scar.

The one injury that would not adequately resolve itself was Ossuera's recollection of all that had transpired. She did not know what lay outside the fortress. The memory of a single, ominous light pulsing green as the old man donned his helmet, and the all-permeating hum of the weapon buried beneath the fortress, had been seared into Ossuera's dreams.

After a number of weeks, Ossuera stepped outside. She was not sure how long she had been in the fortress. Forty days? Forty-two?

A solitary crow flew past with a small ear of corn, and Ossuera winced at the sight of dried silks dangling from the end of the ear. She imagined what threads would do to a crow.

The golden sunlight that followed the trail of destruction had given way to a soft, gray overcast. With all the sky the color of smoke, Ossuera imagined that she could once again smell meat cooking.

Her vision wavered, as it had among the flames. The dull clouds seemed to shimmer, just as the blades of grass beneath her feet seemed to roll and tumble with the light breeze.

On the horizon, a ripple of cloud dipped to touch the earth.

Not a cloud. *Smoke*.

Ossuera hesitated. A wide swath of untended cornfield separated her from what might be nothing more than a lightning strike or a brush fire.

A vast field of yellowing, grass-edged blades, slowly dying in the field.

She closed her eyes and focused on the small object in her hand. Warm. Metallic. Not cylindrical.

Ossuera strained to hear any sound beyond the slow swish of leaves, or the creak of desiccated stalks.

She heard a few crickets, and noticed the flurry of a grasshopper's wings as it explored the abandoned harvest. A soft rustle that might have been mice, similarly inclined, or a snake, in pursuit of a field mouse, drew her attention.

She heard no songs, and no child-like voice.

With a deep breath, Ossuera gripped the bent piece of gold. She thought about the young girl's song—a bare melody.

She still did not know the words. Words did not matter.

She started to run.

As she separated the stalks, leaves slashed her shoulders, and tore at her knuckles, so that warm blood trickled from open lacerations. They flowed freely, and Ossuera's eyes streamed.

She paused to inhale, dried cornstalks and dust and mildew and the hope of something that might be smoke intermingling, and fresh, and burned, and raw.

Ossuera was certain the switch was no longer halfway on. There could be no slow flicker toward darkness.

Once more, she ran. Once again, she felt alive.

Ossuera was a good soldier.

Rabbit, Cat, Girl

~ Rebecca Kuder

If I'm the one to tell this story, there will be gaps. I can only see things as I see them. I stay in the house these days. In my hours, stretchy as they are, I've had little time for more than thought; still I have trouble making thoughts walk toward words, trouble explaining in ways you will understand. Something to do with the stinging in my eyes. But I will tell you what I know.

We will have no autumn this year. The season has been stolen, replaced by perpetual summer. It's been hot like this for ages; you remember that thaw a few months ago. How could ice survive this heat? The iceman used to call out, "Ice! Ice!" and the girl's father gathered money and gave it over, to buy a block of winter. The girl's grandfather had worked ice, too; her father told stories, how her grandfather's back was stronger than a beam. The beam still gave out at the end. The girl's iceman would take tongs, plunk the block in the bin, and let it begin the melting. See the box still there on the porch. Oh, I'd give all my money to lean over now, wrap myself around that metal box, and relieve myself of this heat.

But that isn't the story you want.

You want to know about the girl. I want to tell you. But I must begin with rabbits.

Here's what I know: there have been rabbits since the start of the world, gnawing the sharp drygrass when there are no tender green spring shoots. They burrow into the bases of catalpa trees, and under bushes, hiding like vermin. Some people find rabbits endearing, benevolent like the smiling Easter Bunny, a chocolate charade, lurking beneath false rebirth of spring. Soft and so *helpless*, they hop like little innocents, and grow like armies, eating everything. Have you ever studied a rabbit's teeth?

The girl's father hunted rabbits. In them, he saw food. They had to eat. The girl hated to eat rabbits; she was always left with the taste of their teeth.

She had a toy rabbit, sinister gift from her father. Easter. A puff-ball of white wool, pink bead eyes carefully wrought, it fit in her seven-year-old hand. Felt ears, as if they needed delicacy, as if they were only for hearing. When she went to the beauty parlor with her mother, ladies looked at her holding that soft monster, cooed, and said, "Oh how darling!" But at night, the rabbit, absent all good intent, stretched in shadow, entered her dreams, fangs first. Don't kid yourself; I know the story, look closer: Alice was *terrified* of the March Hare. It wasn't the Mad Hatter pulling the puppet strings of everything.

The girl's house burned. I'll get back to that when I can.

After the fire, the girl went out to what remained of the shed, and stood there, foot tracing shapes in the black char. She saw something white, small, unsullied. The toy rabbit, unburned, pink eyes peering up, dared her to pick it up. It shivered; it moved in her hand, more proof that those beasts will outlive us all.

But cats are different. Larger, smarter, hunting only for food. Well-fed cats will sometimes bring small gifts, guts of unidentifiable rodents, carcass cleaved, chewed, left behind. Oh, the organs are the prize. As a child, the girl kept a cat she loved. The cat slept for hours curled by her belly, even in the sweet heat of July, back when the damp around the girl's hairline was temporary. Cat fur stuck to her: the animal couldn't help it, had to shed. In sleep, the cat protected the girl from rabbit-fiends. Even after the fire, she could only sleep with the cat in place, no matter the season.

If you looked at that cat's eyes, you would see their perfect grass-green hue, the color of spring that the Easter Bunny could only approximate. Cats are the real resurrection.

Sometimes the girl thought she was a cat. In particular, *that cat*; its grey fluff became the girl's covering. How can I not recall the cat's name? The girl would look in the mirror and see green eyes peer back, strange because *could* a cat stand on hind legs to look in that glass? Was a cat so tall? I suppose so. Or so it appeared to the girl, at intervals, when she was two, three, five, seven. During those raw, nearly indivisible years.

After she became seven was the fire. Which was not the rabbit's fault. Unless it was.

Fire the color of blood, blood the color of life. But that's a lie. Have you noticed? Fire is not the color of blood. Fire is several colors, and blood is just one: bump-bump, bump-bump, bump-bump. Fire is trickier. Fire tricks. It licks at the tendrils of a house, tantalizing, and the girl could not look away, and that fire stole green from her, her green eyes, her green soul, all the green shoots out back in the field, that fire and those damn rabbits took it all, masticated it. Chewed, chewed, and spit or shit it out, green gone, so all that's left is one color of red, bump-bump, bump-bump, bump-bump.

Why this trinity? Why always three? Rabbit, cat, girl.

I need a breeze, but there's only a cruel ring of sweat around my hairline. You might not notice at first, but come closer, see that tiny river? It's made of drip, so small and thin it erodes my skin, its darkness possibly mistaken for un-dyed roots in need of a perk-up. A trip to the beauty parlor would not be bad. The girl's mother used to go there—before she left home—and the girl went along, carrying the burden of rabbit. A trip to the beauty parlor for me would not be bad. Not for obvious reasons like vanity, but because I would be touched. To be touched, with the speed and energy of upwell that makes those lilies of the valley stretch greenly up through dead ground, slowly showing first their green bubbles, and then green becomes white, bubbles become tumors of perfume. Tender bells, baby hats. Didn't the girl's grandmother smell like those flowers, or am I recalling her painted porcelain vase, small enough for a child's clumsy handful of the green shoots and their pearly baubles? Or was it her mother who smelled so sweet? So sickening? Or was it the girl herself?

Children used to sing this song in spring. The girl used to sing this song, in spring:

White coral bells upon a slender stalk,
Lilies of the valley deck my garden walk.
Oh, don't you wish
That you could hear them ring?
That will happen only when the fairies sing!

How lovely the lilies of the valley are, dead, brown-edged, drooping in the vase, the stem-slope curvier than when fresh, somehow more truly themselves, more graceful as they relax, tender bells now browning, baby hats tumbling off.

Years since I've considered such frills, but now the girl's grandmother's vase-full trembles here. To see another human, to pay the human to touch my hand, clean and varnish the nails, let the tips dry, then apply warm water—Yes! Even in this heat!—to my scalp, massage sweetsoap. Oh for the shushing of hair full of lather, that luxury. Do I still have hair? If I could find a mirror, I would explore that question, seek evidence, assemble my thoughts and muscles so I could step toward the glass and see what she could see.

The girl's mother left long before the fire. I'm still relieved about this, though the girl had her heartbreak at the time. And after she left, the girl's father was no softer. Her mother was never happy in this house. No one liked to clean, but the job fell to her, and the windows were hateful work. Once a year, usually in spring, her mother would take vinegar and tell the girl to get a pile of dusty gazettes, discarded words good for something, home to many spiders or possible spiders (those faint grey creatures that the girl wasn't sure if she had actually seen would dance slow and pale across the stack of papers).

They fascinated the girl; these frail ghosts spanned this world and the next, their intention only to find a safe place to hide, sometimes tiptoeing—do spiders have toes?—onward toward the heat register, the hereafter. How could the girl fear them? They feared her. Their tender wisp legs like her grandmother's china, not meant for everyday use.

Once a year she saw or imagined those spiders.

Cleaning the windows, the girl's mother used her uncommon words, dark words, things like, "damn Godforsaken hovel," and such. The girl didn't comprehend her mother's anger. It felt like a cold thing, an icebox, hidden in her all the time, kept up in the cabinet of her heart, always visible but only released for special occasions, like windows. The girl always wondered why the mother left and left her here. Her father wondered, too. He didn't save his foulness for special occasions. After her mother left, those words became their everyday dishes. The girl cooked the gruel, but her father provided the anger, the hatred.

After the fire and everything happened, the girl's father moved on to the next town, maybe looking for his wife, maybe for some next woman to ruin with child. I had a lot of time to think. Plenty of quiet. If a man is unhappy, so will his woman be. Maybe that works the other way, too, and maybe it's impossible to untangle certain kinds of unhappiness. Maybe it's really just who has the fortitude to stay. I am still sorting out why *I* stayed here. I guess that's part of the point of my telling you this story. It is sometimes important to sit on the back stoop, to name as many dead cats as I can recall, to wish someone had written down their names, marked places where they remained. Now just lacy bones. If that. Sometimes I consider going back there, as I look out at the high brown weeds, years of (ignored, unintentional, accidental) crop, mingling with unruined new green points; that's life still trying, grass, still stretching toward something good, the sun. I sometimes think I'll dig up bones, see if the girl's good child-mind returns to distinguish one skeleton from another. Would the shape of a skull illuminate whether it belonged to the cat Heliotrope or the cat John? But it was that first cat, with unrecalled name, the one the girl loved best. If I could see better and find those cat bones, I would begin to understand some things.

Like the fire. I don't know how it started. The father was who-knows-where; the girl was sleeping, dreaming that the cat was curled as usual, and it wasn't the burning smell that woke the girl, not smoke, but the cat's absence. For the cat had died and been buried a year before, and only returned and curled in dreams. The dream cat had awakened with the real fire's swirly smoke, and had escaped to wherever dream cats go. Like the Cheshire Cat, as Alice knew, these cats have secret places, but the girl had only a bed, and when she woke, she coughed and choked. Blind, she tried to find the stairs, but all their wood was melting in that color of fire that isn't blood, the licking color of speed and heat and then as even the lilies of the valley singed outside, it all tumbled forward, as things always do.

I gather the energy to scratch open those wounds. My feet look like they could walk, they're still there, blister-free. They look strong. No shoes, but I don't think it will hurt. I've been barefoot before. I step carefully, but there is no way to protect feet from some grass, some burrs, some splinters; the skin has got to yield. Staying on the porch is safe, but what has safety ever given me? So out I go.

The feet work, and I think about the cats, their colors, as I step past the end of the back walkpath, into the grass, where cats used to leave the girl vole guts, past the shed where she found the unburned rabbit, past chipping paint snowing down in sheets the size of small papers, perhaps the size of a notice you'd see posted on a board in town, Saturday dance, a house, foreclosing.

"I'll dance tonight, wear holes in my shoes, 'til I am the one that she loves the best," I sing, lines from a song I used to know, but can't remember more now, and can't really hear myself singing. Like I said, in this story, there will be gaps.

It takes years to walk back to the field. Past the stubborn apple tree, arms cradling nothing now. Past the black walnut where the girl used to collect those green bombs, smelling of earth and salt. When she was young, not yet four, she fingernailed into a green hull, found dark inky wood, a walnut hidden inside that pungent package, and tried to hide it from her father. He hated walnuts, their smell, their existence, but he never cut down the tree. I think he liked to curse at it, liked having that tall, helpless enemy. It's blurry, but I walk past it now, stepping on something round that feels like memory.

I think I see the girl's father, but he'd be so old now. It's a younger man I see, wearing a low hat, brim shielding his face, bending over and picking up something round, a ball, and here comes a child to him, speaking in child talk; I hear the notes but not the words. The man hands the ball to the child, who takes it and runs off. The ball is lots bigger but the same hue as that walnut-green, before it, like everything else, blackens toward decay.

You'd think I'd be there by now but it is a while more before I reach the field. My feet are slow, barely move. Sometimes that's how things work. When I get there, I suspect I'm turned the wrong way, or perhaps I'm looking at the wrong field. It is darker than I remember, but that could be my eyes, as eyes work slowly sometimes, like feet, and other earthly parts.

I get no feel, cannot locate the cat bodies, so I decide to increase the surface of possibility; that is, I decide to lie down. Maybe if more of my body touches the ground, I'll hear something. A few years later I am lying down, and it feels good.

There are ways of conjuring things, I've heard, ways of bringing things back. I don't know if this can be done with cats, but people, yes. The man with the hat is there again; his child looks taller now, or is it just the angle of my body on the ground? The man looks taller too, but adult people don't usually grow like that, people not being cornstalks. There are cornstalks farther back in the field, odd if it's still spring, but I think the stalks are on fire, because I smell that walnut salt smell, which is often an indication. And then I hear a soft meow, and I know if I move three inches to the left, my belly will be directly above the first cat's remains, the corpus of that blessed protector. I wonder if she can smell the fire too, but it barely matters now that I've found her. You never knew her name, but I did.

Several years later, I begin to dig.

The Thirteenth Goddess

~ Claude Lalumière

I. THE BLOOD OF THE EARTH

Come the gibbous moon, the waters of Venera start to flow red with the blood the Earth. By the time of the full moon, the water coursing through the city's waterways is of a burnt-red hue. As the Moon begins to wane, so does the color of the water. By the next day— today—all traces of Mother Earth's monthly cycle have vanished. Such are the tenets of the Venera Church of Mother Earth, which has held power in the city-state since the aftermath of the Nazi occupation.

Sister Agnes takes off her shoes and, pulling up her skirt, walks down three steps on the stairs by the Via Gaia. The now-clear water caresses her toes, her feet, her freshly shaved calves. She delights in the briny smell of the salt water now that the pungency of the blood of the Earth has been washed away. Not for the first time, she dreads rather than welcomes the thought of having to bathe in the menses of the Goddess when next they flow. Not for the first time, she questions her life in the inner circles of the Church.

As Agnes begins to climb back up to the street, something bumps against her leg. At first, she can't identify what she sees. But then her mind starts to make sense of the bloated, sickly object: it's a severed arm, cut—no, torn—at the shoulder and the wrist.

She steps out of the water and stares quietly at the gruesome piece of flotsam.

2. GODDESSES OF LUST

Naked, the sweat and ichors of sex drying on her skin, Belinda Gerda applies paint to the canvas before her. The thirteenth and final canvas in her current project. She paints in watercolors; she rejects oils as too garish, too harsh. For this series, which is scheduled to hang in ten days at Tito Bronze's Velvet Bronzemine, the nexus of the Venera arts scene, the artist has perfected a solution to add depth and texture to her hues. Red is the dominant scheme throughout the *Goddesses of Lust* tableaux; every color must also possess a hint of red—and so she has blended the watery menses of the Goddess into her colours. Included, too, to give the paint a fecund texture, are her own vaginal juices, blended with the spunk of her mad lover, Magus Amore, who is at this moment lying on the floor of her studio, writhing in a post-coital fit of delirium.

As he rubbed his engorged cock all over her body, as he repeatedly penetrated her every orifice until she could not tell where she ended and he began, he described the thirteenth goddess. By fucking her, he worshipped at the altars of the goddess's body.

And so it had been with every previous goddess in this series: Magus's insane, lustful ravings inspiring Belinda to bring her lover's erotic visions to life. But Magus had revealed to her the names of the others, all of them goddesses of antiquity: Ninlil, Inanna, Ishtar, Astarte, Kali, Isis, Aphrodite, Athena, Hecate, Demeter, Venus, Gaia . . .

This strange, anonymous goddess of Magus's is unlike any deity Belinda has ever beheld. She has decided to call this painting *The Thirteenth Goddess*. There is no doubt in Belinda's mind that this thirteenth goddess is in all ways a creation of her lover's demented genius. The pomp and garishness of the goddess's clothes remind Belinda of a superhero costume, but her body, although mostly humanoid, is disquietingly alien in many subtle details. She sits on a throne of organic technology, surrounded by glowing technovegetation. The goddess holds a picture frame against her chest. In that embedded picture, the naked goddess, her skin tattooed with the same patterns as Magus himself, is attended to by monstrous multilimbed creatures who lick and caress her face, her breasts, her feet, and her dripping cunt.

Belinda loses herself in her work. She does not notice when Magus rises from the floor and peers behind her shoulder at her work, his eyes gleaming with fascination and admiration.

After a while, he turns away, though, and leaves the room. Through the door that leads to the basement of Belinda's apartment, he climbs down the stairs. He lifts a metal slab from the floor of the lower level, revealing a dark chasm. He slides into that darkness, downward into the bowels of Venera.

The Goddess calls; Magus Amore descends, through the mysterious and confounding vestiges of Veneras past. Ancient, buried Venera is not draped in absolute darkness. A rusty gold-red glow emanates from veins in the walls, from rivulets of unknown origins that flow on and off through some of the most decrepit ruins. Here, in the subterranean world of the main island of the archipelago of Venera, he has been able to explore the ineffable mythologies of his imagination. The deeper he descends, the closer he gets to the core of his own primordial ur-story. To the archetypal narrative through which he makes sense of the world. Book after book, the writer had tried in vain to achieve such transcendent self-knowledge. Until his life's quest took him, here, to Venera. To the drug vermilion, and to the deities, creatures, and realms it has revealed to him. Climbing down through the ever-changing ruins of Veneran history that hint at a panoply of divergent and improbable timelines, he reaches the whirlpool of iridescent vermilion, the sacred portal that delivers him into her presence. Never in the same location, the whirlpool appears to him at the end of his every subterranean odyssey. Magus Amore enters the glittering eddy, downward into mystery, and surrenders himself to the inscrutable whims of his most beloved and terrifying deity.

3. THE UNVEILING OF VENERA

The sun rises, and Venera slowly, teasingly reveals itself, sensuously slipping off one thin layer of dawn mist at a time. It is as if it were freshly born this very morning, complete and perfect, like Venus from the half-shell. This is Detective-Inspector Pietro Dovelander's first trip to the city-state, and, despite himself, he is awed by the otherworldly sight of this notorious metropolis. None of those ubiquitous photographs do justice to its weird magnificence.

First, there are the rows of lights emerging from the water: markers to guide the archipelagic city's heavy boat traffic. Their glow, made ambiguous by the mist, imbues the air with an ethereal atmosphere. With precise determination, the gulls fly through this ether, miniature angels single-mindedly performing ineffable duties. The countless small boats busily but unhurriedly navigating the waters seem like phantasms of long-dead vessels floating on a ghostly sea. Then a few buildings can be vaguely discerned— bizarre apparitions of utterly alien architecture to the detective's gaze. Suddenly, the cityscape is visible: breastlike domes and serpentine elevated walkways; bulbous walls and strangely sinuous towers; vegetation suggestively entwined with wood and masonry; bright, childlike colors; pagan ornaments and monuments, at once playful and terrifying; giant sculptures of mythic beasts, voluptuous women, and intimidatingly endowed men, often engaged in prurient acts; gargoyles jutting out from walls and roofs at unexpected and menacing angles; numerous staircases leading down from the streets to the waterways that crisscross the city; tendrils of seaweed crawling up the masonry from the water to the surface; dogs trotting through the narrow streets, crossing the ornate mossy bridges, or simply staring out at the passing maritime traffic; cats and birds calmly perched on or nestled in the various nooks and ledges offered by the architecture that refuses boxlike construction and eschews right angles.

Unsettling beauty, tantalizing opulence, unfettered imagination, unabashed eroticism . . . wild nature enmeshed with sophisticated civilization . . . Venera, Pietro surmises, is the woman every man secretly yearns for and even more secretly fears.

Regardless—he did not request this assignment, nor does he want it. Venera is not in his jurisdiction, and the detective resents being taken away from his own city to deal with someone else's problem. But celebrity has its costs. Credited for the safe return of the triplets in the Sanangelo kidnapping and with the collar of two serial killers, Pietro is uncomfortable with his fame. It hinders his work that his face is so well-known now, and he resents that simply doing his job and doing it well is somehow newsworthy.

And now this! The High Countess of the Venera Church of Mother Earth has personally requested that he—and only he—be assigned to the macabre case besetting the insular city-state, and his government, sensing a diplomatic coup, did not give him a choice. Not if he wanted to continue working as a detective.

The boat bringing him from the mainland to Venera is the High Countess's own official state vessel. The domelike interior of the cabin forms one continuous fresco: a sea of naked women of all shapes and sizes with limbs entwined like vines, the women's nipples ripe like succulent grapes, menstrual blood flowing from between their legs into a rust-red backdrop. The joints, cabinets, doors, and window frames are all adorned with totemic gilded sculptures of exaggeratedly voluptuous women.

From the outside, the boat is black and sober—an anomaly in this city that celebrates excess—with only the gold crest of the Church on each side. Despite the rain, after a cursory examination, Pietro shunned the inside and trusted his grey raincoat to protect him from the weather for the three-hour journey.

What he really wants to do is smoke his pipe, but the Countess's eagerness to engage his services did not include permission to light up in her vessel. In fact, he would not be able to smoke for the duration of this investigation: tobacco is strictly prohibited in Venera.

Whatever it takes, Pietro will wrap up this case quickly.

4. THE HIGH COUNTESS OF THE VENERA CHURCH OF MOTHER EARTH

The High Countess of the Venera Church of Mother Earth spreads the sheets of paper on her desk, making a show of examining them, but Detective-Inspector Dovelander can see that she is not truly reading. In fact, he's certain that she knows that he's noticed this, that, furthermore, she wants him to know. She's decided to make him wait; although he resents her attitude, he is trained to respect the chain of command, and for the duration he will be reporting to her. But her lack of respect irritates him. The day before, their appointment was canceled at the last minute, with no explanation. And now, these silly head games.

The Countess's attire jars with her portentous title. A woman of fifty-eight, the Countess looks almost twenty years younger and dresses to flatter her relatively youthful appearance. Her skin is smooth, the color of cream into which are diluted a few drops of dark wine. Her long hair reaches down to her breasts, which are squeezed tight, still noticeably ample, by a push-up bra. Her black dress, with low décolletage but long sleeves, reaches to just above the knee. The dress is garlanded with gold, some strands of the soft metal dyed red. Her legs are otherwise bare, and her feet shorn in high-heeled evening sandals that show off her elegant feet and vermilion-painted toes. Her fingernails, however, are not painted, nor is she wearing any jewellery. In newspaper photographs, Dovelander distinctly remembers, the High Countess is always copiously adorned.

This room disturbs Pietro. In fact, every room and corridor he's seen since his arrival in Venera yesterday has left him unsettled. For example, there are no corners as such in this room, nothing he can properly identify as a wall, no clearly defined ceiling. Pietro can discern no pattern to the network of arches and bulges, and he cannot even guess at the function of the various nooks and niches, or the purpose behind the division of space. Through stained-glass windows, from confounding angles, and reflected on haphazardly scattered mirrors, the sunlight wafts through the room like a heavy fog, challenging his sense of balance. The rainbow of bright colours, the ubiquitous decorative flourishes, the alien geometry, the way the light filters through the room—all of this combines to short-circuit his powers of observation. More than ever, he is convinced that this assignment is a mistake. He will not be able to pursue any kind of worthwhile investigation in this environment. He lacks the required knowledge and familiarity, which only a local or an expert could possess.

At least the floor is flat, although it, too, is heavily decorated, every tile handcrafted with intricate designs, flourishes, and symbols.

Everything is overwhelming in Venera. All of his training and experience—useless. How is he expected to know how people living in such an environment think? Or understand enough of their behavior and customs to know how to question them? Without any frame of reference how can he possibly see the truth hidden in their lies? He'll bungle this job, create a diplomatic mess, and his career will end just as certainly as if he'd outright refused to take the case.

"You're a Christian. A Catholic."

Her gruff voice startles him. He'd expected her to speak in a smoky voice. Instead, she barks. Not in a menacing way, but, regardless, hers is a voice that insists on being heard. Under his shirt, the crucifix hanging around his neck seems to sear his skin, as if the High Countess could see through his shirt and burn the pendant with heat vision, like an American superhero.

It occurs to him, though, that she's sensed his discomfort and might be offering him a graceful way to bow out. "I regret that poses a problem, Your Highness. I'm sure my government can assign another—"

"No. You'll do. We need your skills. Crime is rare here, and violent crime even more so. We do not have the appropriate resources to deal with the current situation. We need this resolved before the next gibbous moon. I only bring up your religion to mention that, although Venera does not officially permit proselytizing faiths to congregate, services are held in various embassies, including that of your government. We tolerate it as long as such activity remains private, with no missionary agenda."

Pietro is surprised by the courtesy. His own government, undoubtedly aware of the services, never bothered to inform him. Neither did anyone at the embassy yesterday. "Thank you, Your Highness."

Is that almost a smile on her face?

"Also, I hear one of the attachés at your country's embassy has a profitable sideline procuring black-market tobacco for the diplomatic community . . ."—Dovelander tries but can't contain the sigh of relief that escapes from his gut—". . . . however, do make sure to contain your filthy habit to embassy grounds." Her tone is censorious, but she makes sure that Pietro sees her grin and nod.

Pietro jumps at the sound of someone clearing her throat behind him. He hadn't even been aware that anyone else was in the room with them. He can't remember the last time someone successfully snuck up on him; has it, in fact, ever happened before? Again, a disquieting feeling of inadequacy gnaws at his usually imperturbable confidence.

The new woman, an Earth Sister, looks shaken. Despite her height—she is taller than Pietro and wearing flats—she holds herself to look small and meek, digging her shoulders into herself, her back tightly constricted. "Pardon the intrusion, Your Highness, but there have been new developments." Her voice, at odds with her body language, is steady and emotionless, neither cold nor warm. The flash of anger on the High Countess's face is not directed at the newcomer but at what she expects her to say. "New body parts, Sister Agnes?"

Sister Agnes swallows before answering. This time, her voice betrays a hint of fear. "The question is, Your Highness—from what kinds of bodies?"

5. DETECTIVE-INSPECTOR DOVELANDER INVESTIGATES

"Isn't anyone going to arrest that man?"

"Why?" Sister Agnes responds to Detective-Inspector Pietro Dovelander. In a stationary boat on the Primadonna Canal, the duo is supervising the work of collecting the body parts from the water. Nine Sisters, three per boat, are doing the grunt work with nets.

Earlier, a squad of Earth Sisters had scattered the crowd of curious onlookers, but now a tall man walks along Via Bellarossa, which borders the waterway. His gait is punctuated by random fits and starts. In a loud voice, he grunts unintelligible words and phrases, gesticulating wildly. Occasionally, he bumps into walls, or trips and falls, immediately picking himself up as if nothing had happened.

"For one thing, he shouldn't be here. Is no one guarding the perimeter?" But that's not what really bothers the detective. The intruder is entirely naked, all body hair shaved off, save for his unruly mane of dark hair and his long, wispy, charcoal beard. His whole body is covered in tattoos of occult symbols. Both nipples are pierced. His long semi-erect penis flaps against his thigh; the tip of the stretched foreskin almost reaches his knee. "And for another . . ."

Sister Agnes raises her eyebrows and looks the detective in the eye, the hint of a smirk crossing her features. Dovelander feels challenged, tested. Under his shirt, the small crucifix drags on his neck and shoulders like a heavy burden.

"Never mind," he says, defeated, turning his attention back to the monstrous body parts of disquieting morphology the Earth Sisters are pulling in from the water.

Doctor Sam Tuturo is not a medical examiner, but there is no ME to be found anywhere in Venera. Tuturo is a surgeon working at the ER of Venera's only hospital. Unlike every other hospital Dovelander has ever visited, this one is remarkably quiet. "Where are all the patients?"

"There are a dozen or so on the third floor. Doctor Mandola is in charge of resident patients. Doctor Landau is supervising the ER in my absence." Tuturo has been assigned to assist Dovelander for the duration of the investigation. The doctor doesn't seem overly pleased by this.

Samuel or Samantha? Tuturo, like everything else in this damned city, confounds Dovelander. At first glance he'd assumed the doctor to be a man, but that was partly because Sams are usually men. The cut of the doctor's eyeglasses seem unquestionably masculine, yet the doctor's delicate wrists and smooth, fey jawline hint strongly at femininity. The doctor's androgynous voice offers no definite clue.

Dovelander estimates the doctor's height at 165 centimetres, shorter than the detective by a hand. Short for a man, but not necessarily so for an Asian man, and Tuturo is at least partly Asian, probably Japanese. The doctor sports an expensive-looking trim haircut and a slick, artfully unkempt metrosexual style that, again, betrays no specific gender identity.

The handshake, though, is female, or perhaps simply effeminate. The doctor's hand lies in his like a cold, limp, dead fish. And the doctor has made no move to remove it; they've been clasping hands for nearly a minute now. Dovelander can't tell if it's passive-aggressive flirtation or passive-aggressive, well, aggression. Maybe both. Anyway, again, it feels like a challenge. Like he would lose face if he were the one to let go.

You can tell a lot about a man by his handshake. Men learn to express their entire personality in the way they clasp another man's hand. In women, though, handshakes can be misleading. Women don't reveal their identity through their handshakes but more from their posture, including the tilt of their heads—a few degrees of angle can tell entire life stories.

This overlong and clammy handshake, though—Dovelander can't conclude anything from it, save for the already obvious fact that he himself is an alien here and, apparently, an unwelcome one.

Forcing his thoughts back to the subject of the near-empty hospital, the detective comments, "But the population of Venera exceeds five hundred thousand."

The doctor doesn't respond, which further irritates Dovelander. He tries not to show it, but he's exhausted. Having to put up with passive-aggressive cooperation doesn't make him angry at this point, it just makes him want to collapse.

The doctor finally terminates the handshake and offers the detective coffee. "Come on. I could use one, too."

Coffee! At least this damnable place doesn't ban that as well.

Mugs in hand, the two proceed to the doctor's office, which turns out to be by far the most conventional room the detective has seen yet. Save for a few ornamental details, this could almost be the office of any doctor or researcher back home.

Tuturo motions the detective to sit and hands him his report, which includes photographs.

Quickly leafing through the folder, Dovelander's eye catches a detail. "The flesh was tattooed?" And, "Were the previous body parts also tattooed? With similar markings?"

Back at the Mother House, a gargantuan Earth Sister is on night duty. She is by far the fattest person Dovelander has seen yet in Venera. He had begun to suspect that fashionable slimness was mandatory in this demented, decadent city.

He's astonished at the elegance with which Sister Bettina, as she introduces herself, rises from her armchair. It's a mythic moment, like the Leviathan emerging from the depths. Venera tends to imbue the simplest of acts with gratuitous gravitas.

There's something straightforward about the Sister that immediately endears her to Pietro. That, plus the fact the she responds to his urgent request without any hesitation or obfuscation.

"I'll be but a moment fetching Sister Agnes, Detective."

While he waits, Pietro tries to understand the layout of the lobby, but, despite himself, his eye keeps being distracted by the sexual acts painted onto the floor. Couldn't they have chosen Moriano for this job? He's both an atheist and a degenerate. He's not too bad a detective, either. So what if the High Countess had asked for Dovelander? Both his captain and his commissioner know him well enough to understand that he's not the right man for this job. Or at least, for this place.

"What's the news, Detective?" Sister Agnes's long hair is dishevelled, and her shirt is tucked crookedly into her pants. She's still wiping the sleep from her eyes.

"We should have held that man for questioning."

It takes a moment for Agnes to understand. "You mean Amore?"

"Is that his name? That crazy naked man with the tattoos?"

"Yes. Magus Amore. Once a brilliant writer, now one of our most renowned eccentrics."

Magus Amore. Even Dovelander, who reads at most two or three novels a year, knows the name. Twenty years ago, Amore had been the darling of the international literary world. Winner of the Booker, the Nobel, and numerous other awards. Dovelander had tried to read one of his books, *The League of Anarchy*. A thriller, the cover blurb had said. Impenetrable nonsense, filled with deranged sex and cruelty, pagan mumbo-jumbo, and subversive rants, was more what Dovelander thought of it, although he'd given up on it after a few dozen pages.

"Do you have any photos of him on file? Especially of his tattoos?"

6. THE GARDEN OF THE GODDESSES

In the lush garden of the Goddesses, naked, prepubescent sycophants tend to their every need. It is the night of Belinda's initiation, her ascension to godhood; for the occasion she once more wears the body of a sixteen-year-old. Her cunt grows moist as the Goddesses' gazes fall on her once-more ripe breasts.

An insistent ringing interrupts the proceedings. No one else seems to notice the jarring sound. Belinda's concentration is shattered. Her body regains its true age. The Goddesses laugh. A loud thumping joins the ringing. Belinda grows even older, so old that all her hair falls out. Her shrivelled tits hang down to her waist.

As the skin begins peeling off her bones, she wakes up. The doorbell is ringing. Someone's beating hard on the door.

She forces herself out of bed. Picking up her nightgown, she sees her forty-five-year-old body in the bedroom mirror and yearns for firmer years. She wraps herself in the nightgown to find out what the commotion is about. She's certain it's about Magus. What's her crazy old darling done this time?

At the door, she finds a tall man in a worn, grey raincoat. He fidgets too much with his hands, and he's scowling. At his side, a tall, nervous Earth Sister avoids her gaze.

Without greeting or preamble, the man says, "We need to talk to Magus Amore."

"And you would be . . . ?"

"My name's Detective-Inspector Pietro Dovelander, and this is Sister Agnes from the Mother House." The detective reaches into his raincoat. "We're on official business, acting with full authority from the High Countess." He shows Belinda an official document, with the holographic seal of the Church, granting him full emergency powers. "Are you Belinda Gerda?"

"Yes. And I haven't seen Magus for days. It's not unusual for him to disappear for long stretches."

The detective seems somewhat less tense when he addresses her again: "I apologize for the intrusion at this inconvenient hour, but this is truly urgent. May we come in?"

7. The Automata of Hemero Volkanus

No edifice better illustrates the fact that most buildings are machines than the home of Hemero Volkanus. The guts of the building are turned inside out, so that the plumbing and wiring are all visible, albeit protected by plexiglass. In addition, the house moves. The many windows of various sizes are all built with photosensitive transistors that guide their frames to rotate so as to best capture the sunlight, or avoid it, depending on weather and temperature. It's also a noisy house, as the various gears and parts are constantly in subtle motion.

There is no doorbell and no doorknob, and Belinda knows better than to knock. Within a few seconds the door slides open to reveal one of the Kourai Khryseai, as Hemero calls his chillingly lifelike female automata, after the mechanical servants the god Hephaestus created to help him in his Olympian smithy.

The gynoid greets her in the nonsense language the machines have been programmed to speak. Nonsense, perhaps, but undeniably beautiful, ethereal in its musical beauty. Sometimes, Belinda is tempted to accept Hemero's claims that it is indeed the language of the gods, unintelligible to mere mortals. Magus, who grows ever more desperately credulous, takes everything Hemero says at face value. Magus believes Hemero's story that he did not invent these beautiful machines but found them buried deep in the bowels of Venera, among the ruins of the forgotten civilizations that once prospered on the archipelago's main island, that they are in fact the true Kourai Khryseai of myth. The inventor may be brilliant, but his penchant for tall tales doesn't fool Belinda.

The gynoid guides Belinda through the house. They reach the workshop of Venera's self-styled Hephaestus as he tinkers on a pair of mechanical legs.

"Trying to improve on the current model, Hemero?" Volkanus, who was born in Italy, lost both his legs in a childhood automobile accident.

"You know that for years I've been trying to reverse-engineer the Kourai Khryseai," computer screens on his work table display schemata of a robot designed to look like a human female, "but I still haven't cracked Hephaestus's technology."

"Save it for Magus, Hemero. I'm not buying today." Despite herself, her voice breaks a bit.

Volkanus turns to look at Belinda. "Always the skeptic, eh?" Then he falls silent and scrutinizes her so intently that Belinda squirms.

Finally, she asks, "Is Magus here?"

"Magus? . . . No. I haven't seen him for . . . two weeks, I think. What's the matter, Belinda?"

It cascades out of her: "I haven't seen Magus either. For nearly three days. And I was just interrogated at the Mother House. They've called in a foreign detective, and he thinks that Magus is involved with those body parts that have been popping up in the waterways. They've taken my passport. They've confiscated my latest painting because of the tattoos, and—"

"Belinda. Slow down. Let's move to the parlor. One of the Kourai Khryseai can serve us tea, and you can tell me exactly what—"

The house interrupts Volkanus: "Magus Amore has arrived."

Volkanus raises his eyebrows, looking amused and curious, while Belinda gasps, "Magus . . ."

The madman bursts naked into the room: "Belinda! I've come from your studio. Where's *The Thirteenth Goddess?* The time has come. Venera needs your sacred masterwork."

8. REVELATIONS

Every time Sister Agnes comes close to sleep, as she closes her eyes, she is visited by visions of the goddess from Belinda Gerda's painting and is almost instantly shocked awake. She can scarcely understand what happens in these phantasmagorias: they are populated by technobiological creatures whose morphology defies her understanding of animal life; these creatures all tend, in some manner beyond Agnes's ken, to the goddess.

What is the connection between Amore, Gerda's artwork, and the severed body parts?

Detective Dovelander had wanted to store Gerda's painting at his embassy, but Sister Agnes was under orders to monitor what he could or could not take out of Veneran jurisdiction. There was no doubt in Agnes's mind that the High Countess did not want that piece of evidence to leave Venera proper. Agnes requisitioned the use of a large storage closet at the Mother House, a twenty-four-hour guard, and a padlock whose only two keys were in the hands of herself and the High Countess.

Agnes gives up on sleep. She dresses and heads to the ad hoc evidence room. The gargantuan Sister Bettina—on guard duty, sitting by the door—acknowledges Agnes with a bored nod.

Inside, instead of darkness, Agnes finds the small room bathing in vermilion-red glow, emanating from Belinda Gerda's painting.

Her painting of a goddess . . .

. . . of the Goddess.

The Goddess, who now talks to her in a language she should not understand but does. The Goddess, who bestows upon her revelation. Agnes begins to see the outline of an iridescent whirlpool, enveloping her and the painting, when an insistent knock on the door breaks the spell, returning the storage closet to darkness and leaving only wisps of the Goddess's divine language in her conscious memory.

When Sister Agnes emerges from the storage closet, Sister Bettina introduces an attaché from Dovelander's embassy. Exuding pomp-ousness and impatience, the too-handsome young man asks, "Where is the detective-inspector?"

"I haven't seen him since late afternoon, after we finished exam-ining some new evidence. He told me he was heading back to the embassy."

"You let him wander Venera unescorted? I'm certain your superior instructed you otherwise. Should anything happen to the detective-inspector, my government shall hold you directly responsible."

The revelations of the Goddess recede ever farther from Agnes's consciousness. She's annoyed at this bureaucratic troll and concerned for Dovelander, with whom she has quickly developed an amiable and respectful camaraderie. Without a word, she hurries away while the attaché is still addressing her. She knows the city. She'll find Dovelander.

9. THE KOURAI KHRYSEAI

During the age of fable, when Hephaestus built the four Kourai Khryseai, he imbued them with attributes of his fellow Olympians. Hemero Volkanus knows this, and so does Magus Amore, who can speak the language of the gods.

After Gerda tells him of the painting's confiscation, Amore addresses the Kourai Khryseai in the divine tongue, overriding Volkanus's reprogramming.

In a flash, two of the gynoids zoom out of sight, with the speed and cunning of Hermes.

Belinda opens her mouth, as if on the verge of speaking, but stays agape.

Answering her unspoken query, Amore says: "They've gone to fetch the likeness of the Goddess. Your painting. *The Thirteenth Goddess.*"

10. URBAN MYTH

Tales are told around the world of people getting lost within the labyrinthine streets of Venera, of the city transforming itself with malignant sentience, obliterating any recognizable points of reference, rearranging its complex grid of streets and waterways and transmogrifying its buildings, warping time and geography, so as to capture and consume those foolish enough to be tempted by its surreal decadence.

Dovelander had long dismissed these ridiculous tales as urban myths, or as an obvious metaphor for the spiritual dangers of this blasphemous metropolis.

But, on his walk from the Mother House to his embassy, the detective-inspector lost all sense of time and place. Now, he does not recognize any of the buildings, which look even more deranged than usual. The city appears entirely deserted. The sky has become otherworldly—no: infernal, of an oppressive rust-red tinge. He can smell the brine of the sea, but he never manages to escape the ever-tighter grip of the city streets and vegetation. Sometimes, the plants whisper to him, but he cannot decipher the language they speak.

11. VENERA RISING

Less than a minute elapses, and the Kourai Khryseai return to Hemero's parlor with *The Thirteenth Goddess* and hand it to Magus. The madman sets it on the floor and chants to it in the same language he used when speaking to the automata. The painting shimmers with otherworldly light, and the image within acquires a barely tangible three-dimensionality.

Belinda gapes in wonder: *I painted that?*

On the extended palm of the ethereal thirteenth goddess, an iridescent whirlpool, vermilion in color, takes shape, growing until it engulfs Magus, Hemero, the Kourai Khryseai, and Belinda.

Belinda is momentarily blinded. Before her vision returns, she feels the wind in her hair. When she can see again, she recognizes where she has been transported: the roof garden of the Venera Church of Mother Earth, lush with vermilion plant.

Magus is kneeling before the painting, chanting in that same strange language. But now Belinda can understand him. She is granted a revelation and finally understands who the thirteenth goddess is.

Venera. Venera herself is the thirteenth goddess. Venera herself gifts Belinda with yet more divine visions. Venera is returning to reclaim her city. And she and Magus have been the instruments of her plan.

The Goddess is furious at the Church of Mother Earth for trying to eradicate her existence from history, for usurping her mysteries in the name of their Earth worship. It is her menses that flow through her city at every full moon, and not that of the Earth. The body parts that have been washing onto the core island are those of her syco-phants, transmogrified and sacrificed in preparation of her return. Soon, they will live again.

Soon, Venera herself will live again.

Beneath the feet of her new worshippers, the Mother House crumbles to the ground, amid the screams of the blasphemous Sisters inside. The vermilion garden remains intact.

Around Belinda and the others, one of the myriad bygone iterations of the city of Venera rises from its subterranean tomb, reconfiguring the metropolis into a new agglomeration. The Goddess herself rises from deeper still, from deeper even than the bowels of the Earth, to whisper her divine song to those Venerans who survived the divine transmogrification of the city-state.

12. LOVE SONG

The voice of Venera is a call to life and self-awareness for the Kourai Khryseai; they shed their mechanical bodies to reveal new flesh, blessed by the Goddess.

For Hemero Volkanus, the holy song is a source of power; he mines it to acquire the divine attributes of his patron god, Hephaestus.

The music of the Goddess inspires Belinda Gerda to new heights of creativity: as yet uncreated tableaux cascade through her mind's eye, nurturing her lust for art.

The melodies of Venera are too exquisite for Magus Amore to bear; swimming in the holy music, his body dissolves—and his organic particles waft toward the Goddess. She inhales the essence of her most devout and loving worshipper.

To Pietro Dovelander, lost in the ever-changing maze of the city-state, Venera's voice is a chaotic screech that further confuses whatever sanity remains within him.

Agnes, who has been unable to locate the foreign detective, is initially terrified at the scope of the unfurling bio-architectural transformations besetting the city of her birth; Venera's song is welcome serenity.

13. THE BLOOD OF VENERA

Come the gibbous moon, the waters of Venera start to flow red with the blood the Goddess. By the time of the full moon, the water coursing through the city's waterways is of a burnt-red hue. At that time, the goddess Venera's worshippers are invited to bathe in her menses.

Agnes takes off her shoes, her skirt, and her blouse. She walks down three steps on the stairs by the Via Olympia. The vermilion-red water caresses her toes, her feet, her freshly shaved calves. She delights in the briny smell of the salt water as it blends with the spicy tang of Venera's blood.

Still trapped within an urban geography he cannot grasp, Pietro Dovelander watches Venera's worshippers soak in her blood. He wants to call out to Agnes, whom he dimly recognizes, but the knowledge of language leaves him before he can utter even a word.

The Still Point of the Turning World

– Adrienne J. Odasso

1. Cather's Run

I thought it was the stream
where the crayfish hid, where the wind
once knocked me clean in. So, I swam
for the bank by way of the deep
and dived instead. The trout teem
in this darkness divisible: my arms
cut a wide, white arc in the shallows
and then down like an arrow,
but bent. I touched rocks six feet under
where my feet slid on algae. Death came
to count the ticking of my fast-held breath.
Shivering, dragged to the surface, I went.

2. Harvard Square

It doesn't work like that, she said.

One does not blink out and rekindle, must not
dare to return to haunt the living. *Well, I dare,*
I said, and the sterling spoon there, tyre-bent and slivered,

agreed. Some ancient polarity, the universe's heart

hangs on a thread. I bought my fare here, silver, too,
and hung it from a chain. I will not show it to the sun,
nor name it before the living. The prow of this ship

veers star-ward true as the traffic light turns green.

3. Rievaulx Abbey

My breath returned that day
in the rain, up the rise
to where my eyes
fell on the walls. I cried
as if I'd found some fabled answer,
feral comfort
in the lichens' loving scrape.

A chaser of pillars with stories
is what I became:

no hallowed ruin thereafter
was spared my embrace.

4. St. James's Park

Stay with me a while, he says.
And the water rises to the pavement, lifts
my coat, forms the wildest of wings. Sifts
the sand from my skull and gifts me
with snail-shells for teeth. I am

the duck-dive, the bird-cry, the breeze
through the bridges and leaves. I am silence
in the man's startled eyes as I pass by the table
where he's sat. Spark recognition. *I'm your ghost,
I want to say, and you're mine, but next time—*

Next time won't be so simple:
I'll sink and not rise.

The eyes beneath which you shiver
will not be mine.

XIII

Contributors

LIZ ARGALL often writes speculative fiction and interstitial work that explore spaces between genres. She is especially fond of gritty urban fantasy, thought provoking science fiction and fantastical literary fiction.

Liz's comics have been published in an array of publications, including *Meanjin*, *The Girl's Guide to Guy Stuff*, *Eat Comics*, *Something Wicked* and her collection *Songs, Dreams and Nightmares*. Her anthology, *Dreams of Tomorrow*, won a Bronze Ledger Award for Small Press of the Year. In January 2009 her musical *Comic Book Opera*, written with composer Michael Sollis, was performed for the first time. Two of her short stories have been staged as plays.

Although currently known as a science fiction writer, editor, and anthologist, M. DAVID BLAKE once utterly flunked a study of genre. In the third aforementioned role, he assembles the annual *Campbellian Anthology*; under guise of the second he edits *STRAEON*. The first garners infrequent publication royalties under an assortment of bylines.

RICHARD BOWES' novel *Dust Devil on a Quiet Street* was nominated for the 2014 World Fantasy and Lambda Awards. He has published six novels, four story collections, over seventy stories and has won two World Fantasy, a Lambda, Million Writers, and International Horror Guild awards.

Recent and forthcoming appearances include: *Tor.com*, *The Revelator*, *The Best of Electric Velocipede*, Datlow's *The Doll Collection*, *Uncanny Magazine*.

GEORGE COTRONIS lives in the wilderness of Northern Sweden. He makes a living designing book covers. He sometimes writes. His stories have appeared in Big Pulp and Vignettes from the End of the World.

AMANDA C. DAVIS has an engineering degree and a fondness for baking, gardening, and low-budget horror films. Her work has appeared or is upcoming in *Shock Totem* and *Cemetery Dance*, among others. She tweets enthusiastically as @davisac1. You can find out more about her and read more of her work at http://www.amandacdavis.com.

JULIE C. DAY's fiction has appeared in such magazines as *Interzone*, *Electric Velocipede*, and *A cappella Zoo's* best-of. She holds an MFA in Creative Writing from the USM's Stonecoast program and a M.S. in Microbiology from the University of Massachusetts at Amherst.   Some of her favorite things include gummy candies, loose teas, standing desks, and a tiny primate known as the slow loris. You can find Julie on Twitter @thisjulieday or through her website: www.stillwingingit.com.

JETSE DE VRIES is a technical specialist for a propulsion company, and used to travel the world for this. Of late he's trying to settle into a desk job, in order to have more time for editing and writing SF.

He writes SF since 1999, and had his first story published in November 2003. His stories have appeared in about two dozen publications on both sides of the Atlantic, and include *Amityville House of Pancakes, vol. 1*, *JPPN 2*, *Nemonymous 4*, *Northwest Passages: A Cascadian Anthology*, *DeathGrip: Exit Laughing*, *HUB Magazine #2*, and *Clarkesworld Magazine* (May 2007), *SF Waxes Philisophical* anthology, *Postscripts Magazine #14* and *Flurb #6*.

They're upcoming in the *A Mosque Among the Stars* anthology, and hopefully in some other future publications.

He's been part of the *Interzone* editorial team from March 2004 until September 2008, and is now working on *SHINE*, an anthology of optimistic, near future SF for Solaris Boooks and other future editorial projects.

JENNIFER GIESBRECHT is a native of Halifax, Nova Scotia where she earned a degree in History and Methodology. She currently volunteers her talent as a dramaturge at a local theater company and works as a freelance editor, writer and artist. She is a graduate of Clarion West 2013. Her work has previously appeared in *Nightmare Magazine*.

DARYL GREGORY is the award-winning writer of genre-mixing short stories, novels, and comics. His most recent work includes the novels *Afterparty* and *Harrison Squared* (both from Tor Books), and the novella *We Are All Completely Fine* (Tachyon).

RIK HOSKIN is a science fiction novelist and comic strip writer from London, England. He has been the primary writer on the *Outlanders* book series since 2008 and has contributed several volumes to its sister series, *Deathlands*, both under the pen-name of "James Axler". His recent comic strip work includes *Star Wars* and *Doctor Who Adventures* in the UK and Europe, and the *Mercy Thompson* comic book series in the USA. He is currently working on a science fiction novel for Resurrection House.

REBECCA KUDER'S novel, *The Watery Girl*, was chosen as one of ten finalists for the Many Voices Project at New Rivers Press in 2014. Her stories, essays, and poems have been published in *West Wind Review*, *Mothering Magazine*, *The Knitter's Gift*, *Midwifery Today*, *The Manifest Station*, and *Jaded Ibis Productions*. Rebecca has an MFA in creative writing from Antioch University Los Angeles, and teaches creative writing in the individualized masters program at Antioch University Midwest. She lives in Yellow Springs, Ohio, with her husband, the writer Robert Freeman Wexler, and their daughter, Merida. Rebecca blogs at www.rebeccakuder.com. She is working on a new novel.

CLAUDE LALUMIÈRE (claudepages.info) is the author of the collections *Objects of Worship* and *Nocturnes and Other Nocturnes* and of the mosaic novella *The Door to Lost Pages*. He's the co-creator of the multimedia cryptomythology project *Lost Myths* (lostmyths.net), and he has edited more than a dozen anthologies, the most recent of which is *The Exile Book of New Canadian Noir* (with co-editor David Nickle); he's currently working on his next anthology project, *Superhero Universe: Tesseracts Nineteen* (with co-editor Mark Shainblum), forthcoming in 2016. Claude is a nomadic Montrealer now often sighted in Portland, OR, and Vancouver, BC.

MARC LEVINTHAL is a writer and musician who has lived and worked in the Los Angeles area for over thirty years. Born and raised in Buffalo, New York, he moved to L.A. in the early eighties to become a rock star. That didn't quite happen as planned, but a lot of other cool stuff did. He has been involved with both "The Music Business" (having co-written the hit single "Three Little Pigs" while in the band Green Jello) and "The Motion Picture Industry" (having co-written the score for the cult movie classic *Valley Girl.*)

Marc's short stories have appeared in *Aboriginal Science Fiction*, *The Magazine of Bizarro Fiction*, and several anthologies, including *Mondo Zombie* and *Amazing Stories of the Flying Spaghetti Monster*. A novel co-written with John Skipp, *The Emerald Burrito of Oz*, was published by Eraserhead Press in 2010. (Several sequels are in the works!)

Marc currently lives in Pasadena with his two lovely nerd children, somewhere between JPL and Mount Wilson.

GRÁ LINNAEA is a hippie punk nerd in the northwest United States. Check out his serial novel, "The Curious Investigations of Miranda McGee" and more at http://www.gralinnaea.com/.

ALEX DALLY MACFARLANE is a writer, editor and historian. When not researching narrative maps in the legendary traditions of Alexander III of Macedon, she writes stories, found in *Clarkesworld*, *Interfictions Online*, *Strange Horizons*, *Beneath Ceaseless Skies* and the anthologies *Phantasm Japan*, *Solaris Rising* 3 and *The Year's Best Science Fiction & Fantasy: 2014*. She is the editor of *Aliens: Recent Encounters* (2013) and *The Mammoth Book of SF Stories by Women* (2014). For Tor.com, she runs the Post-Binary Gender in SF column. Find her on Twitter: @foxvertebrae.

JULI MALLETT writes lies that strain at the bounds of the perceptible, twisting in and out of those things for which there are no words. Her publications include urban wildlife non-fiction, ecoinformatics research, open source software, poetry and strange epistles. She is currently a seminarian and lives with several ridiculous beasts, at least one of which could be mistaken for a human.

LYN MCCONCHIE began writing in 1990 since which time she has seen 32 of her books published, and some 275 short stories, her work appearing in 9 countries and in 4 languages. Her most recent book was *Sherlock Holmes: Repeat Business*, which is currently shortlisted for the Silver Falchion Award. Lyn lives on a small farm in New Zealand where she raises colored sheep and has free-range geese and hens, she shares her 19th century farmhouse and has free-range geese and hens, she shares her 19th century farmhouse with Thunder her Ocicat, and 7469 books.

FIONA MOORE is a business anthropologist at the University of London, studying identity and migration. Her SF has appeared in *Asimov's, Interzone, Dark Horizons*, and *On Spec*, and she has co-written four books of TV criticism for Telos Publishing. She lives in a very crowded house in Southeast England. Read about her adventures at http://www.fiona-moore.com.

A week after buying his house in New Hampshire's North Country, GREGORY L. NORRIS glanced at the cobalt blue glass lamp in the bay window, picked up his pen, and wrote the first draft for "Occupy Maple Street." Norris has written for television and, recently, the scripts for two feature films. His fiction, short and long, appears regularly in print. Look for his latest book, *Tales From the Robot Graveyard*, and follow his literary adventures at www.gregorylnorris.blogspot.com.

ADRIENNE J. ODASSO'S poetry has appeared in a number of strange and wonderful publications, including *Sybil's Garage, Mythic Delirium, Jabberwocky, Cabinet des Fées, Midnight Echo, Not One of Us, Dreams & Nightmares, Goblin Fruit, Strange Horizons, Stone Telling, Farrago's Wainscot, Through the Gate, Liminality, inkscrawl*, and *Battersea Review*. Her début collection, *Lost Books* (Flipped Eye Publishing, 2010), was nominated for the 2010 London New Poetry Award and for the 2011 Forward Prize, and was also a finalist for the 2011 People's Book Prize. Her second collection with Flipped Eye, *The Dishonesty of Dreams*, was released in August of 2014. Her two chapbooks, *Devil's Road Down* and *Wanderlust*, are available from Maverick Duck Press. She holds degrees from Wellesley College and the University of York (UK). She currently lives in Boston with her partner and a tank full of inquisitive freshwater fish. You can find her online at ajodasso.livejournal.com (and on also on Twitter under the same name).

CAT RAMBO lives, writes, and teaches by the shores of an eagle-haunted lake in the Pacific Northwest. Her 150+ fiction publications include stories in *Asimov's, Clarkesworld Magazine*, and *Tor.com*. Her short story, "Five Ways to Fall in Love on Planet Porcelain," from her story collection *Near + Far* (Hydra House Books), was a 2012 Nebula nominee. Her editorship of *Fantasy Magazine* earned her a World Fantasy Award nomination in 2012. For more about her, as well as links to her fiction, see http://www.kittywumpus.net

ANDREW PENN ROMINE lives in Los Angeles where he works in the visual effects and animation industry. When he's not wrangling words, robots, cavemen, or dragons, he dabbles in craft cocktails and sequential art.

A graduate of the 2010 Clarion West workshop, his fiction appears online at *Lightspeed Magazine*, *Paizo*, and *Crossed Genres* as well as in the anthologies *Fungi*, *What Fates Impose*, *By Faerie Light*, *Coins of Chaos*, and *Help Fund My Robot Army*. You can find his full list of publications at andrewpennromine.com.

He's also contributed articles to *Lightspeed/Fantasy Magazine* and blogs at *Inkpunks*. He occasionally blogs about cocktails as The Booze Nerd. You can also follow his day-to-day adventures on Twitter: @inkgorilla.

DAVID TALLERMAN is the author of the comic Fantasy novels *Giant Thief*, *Crown Thief*, and *Prince Thief*, as well as the absurdist Steampunk graphic novel *Endangered Weapon B: Mechanimal Science*.

David's short Science Fiction, Fantasy and Horror has appeared in over sixty markets, including *Clarkesworld*, *Lightspeed*, *Nightmare*, and *Beneath Ceaseless Skies*. He can be found online at http://davidtallerman.co.uk and http://davidtallerman.blogspot.com.

TAIS TENG is a pseudonym for a Dutch fantasy and science fiction writer, illustrator and sculptor. His real name is Thijs van Ebbenhorst Tengbergen and he was born in 1952 in The Hague.

Tais Teng has written more than a hundred books for both adults and children. He has won the Paul Harland Prize four times. His books have been translated in German, Finnish, French and English. One of his books, *The Emerald Boy*, has been published in the USA. He recently sold the story *Embrace the Night* to the *Night Land* site.

RICHARD THOMAS is the author of six books—the novels *Disintegration* and *The Breaker* (Random House Alibi), *The Soul Standard* (Dzanc Books) and *Transubstantiate*, as well as the collections *Herniated Roots* and *Staring Into the Abyss*. His over 100 stories in print include *Cemetery Dance*, *PANK*, *Gargoyle*,

Weird Fiction Review, Midwestern Gothic, Chiral Mad 2, Qualia Nous, and *Shivers VI*. For more information visit www.whatdoesnotkillme.com.

FRAN WILDE is an author and technology consultant. Her first fantasy novel, *Updraft*, featuring the same world as "A Moment of Gravity, Circumscribed," debuts from Tor/Macmillan in 2015, with two more to follow. Her short stories have appeared in *Asimov's, Beneath Ceaseless Skies, Nature, Daily Science Fiction*, and *Abyss & Apex*. Her interview series *Cooking the Books*–about the intersection between food and fiction–has appeared at *Strange Horizons, Tor.com*, and on her website, franwilde.wordpress.com. You can find her on Twitter @fran_wilde and Facebook @franwildewrites.

A.C. WISE was born and raised in Montreal and currently lives in the Philadelphia area. She is the author of numerous short stories appearing in publications such as *Clarkesworld, Shimmer, Apex, The Best Horror of the Year Vol. 4*, and *Year's Best Weird Fiction Vol. 1*, among others. In addition to her writing, she is the co-editor of *Unlikely Story*. Find her online at www.acwise.net.

CHRISTIE YANT is a science fiction and fantasy writer, and editor of the *Women Destroy Science Fiction!* special issue of *Lightspeed Magazine*. Her fiction has appeared in anthologies and magazines including *Year's Best Science Fiction & Fantasy* 2011 (Horton), *Armored, Analog Science Fiction & Fact, Beneath Ceaseless Skies, io9, Wired.com*, and China's *Science Fiction World*. She lives on the central coast of California with two writers, one editor, two dogs, three cats, and a very small manticore. Follow her on Twitter @christieyant.

MARK TEPPO is a synthesist, a troubleshooter (and -maker), a cat herder, and an idea man. He is the publisher of Resurrection House, a fiercely independent genre publishing venture that seeks to reignite a passionate love affair between authors and audiences via the printed book.

He lives in the Pacific Northwest, where he occasionally spends a weekend in the woods. His favorite Tarot card is the Moon.